A Storm Came Up

By Doug Segrest

authorHOUSE

AuthorHouse™
1663 Liberty Drive
Bloomington, IN 47403
www.authorhouse.com
Phone: 833-262-8899

2021 Second Printing

Published by AuthorHouse 01/25/2022

ISBN: 978-1-4634-1397-2 (sc)
ISBN: 978-1-4634-1398-9 (hc)
ISBN: 978-1-4634-1396-5 (e)

Library of Congress Control Number: 2011909123

Print information available on the last page.

This book is printed on acid-free paper.

CHAPTER 1 /
Outside Takasaw, Alabama / September 1958

DEAD LEAVES CRACKLED as the three boys hurried along the haphazard trail, a hoped-for shortcut home, before the dying sunlight filtering through the canopy of trees disappeared for good.

"Shee-it," said the oldest boy, coming to a stop. He spit a thick loogie on a clump of bushes while straddling the seat of his bike. "This is *his* problem," he said, eyeing the smallest of the younger boys. "Why can't you get a bike that's worth a shit? It's not my fault we got lost in the woods."

"There's nothing wrong with Moses' bike," said the third boy calmly. "He can't help a tire gone flat. Besides, it was your idea to take the shortcut."

Actually, Braxton knew Moses' bike was a reprieve from a junk heap. Andy, the complainer, was the eldest of the three and a tag-along at that. The two 12-year-olds, Brax and Moses, had been biking down Main Street when they'd come across Andy. It was Andy's suggestion to ride out on the Shorter Highway, a decision that was about to get them all into hot water.

Brax and Moses had strict orders to be home for supper, which meant seven. Brax's Timex showed a couple of minutes until then and the sun was setting. Realizing it was late, they followed the shortcut Andy had recommended through the maze of woods. They were lost, Moses' tire had gone flat and they were facing serious trouble at home.

Without another word, Andy stepped off the bike and began pushing it ahead. The other two followed silently, trying to keep up with his longer strides.

Fifteen minutes later, darkness made it hard to see more than a few feet ahead. The pace slowed. Andy had been certain they'd eventually run back into Main Street, no more than a mile or so from downtown.

Yet the thick, piney Alabama woods seemed endless. Now the shadows were gone altogether.

Brax's legs burned and his back ached from pushing the bike over rough terrain. His anxiety increased as he checked his watch more frequently. He looked at Andy, who was sweating profusely. Moses showed no sign of wear, but his eyes darted nervously.

"Here. Over here. C'mon," said Andy. He left the trail, cutting through waist-high weeds. He pointed toward his left, where two faint lights cut through the maze. "Some car lights, see? Maybe a clearing. C'mon," Andy said, and the boys trailed.

A hundred yards down the lights pierced through the trees. Brax felt a sense of relief. They could be in Montgomery for all he cared, but as long as they were near a road – or a house with a phone – the ordeal would end. He liked the idea of a phone. If they were going to get into trouble, they might as well get a ride home.

"I knew ..."

Andy's words were cut short by a *thump!* And a groan.

"Uhhhhh," came the raspy voice, which gave way to a sickening sound. Someone was simultaneously gasping for air and spitting up.

"God damned nigger!" yelled another voice.

The boys froze. Brax could only see Andy's silhouette a few feet ahead, but he saw the image as the older youth delicately lowered his bike to the ground, shush-ing with an index finger. He waved the two boys to do the same.

Brax lowered his bike nervously and turned to Moses, who hadn't moved at all. He pulled Moses' bike away, leaned it against a tree and grabbed Moses by the hand. With a finger to his lips, he beckoned him to follow silently.

The steps came slowly. The underbrush crackled as they moved, but the noise was easily drowned by the ruckus going on a short distance away.

Andy found the edge of the woods first. Brax and Moses joined him, kneeling to peer through the foliage. Head beams from a single car in the middle of a pasture illuminated three men. Two were standing. One was struggling to get to his knees. His head was brushing the ground as his hands tightly clutched his stomach.

"Ughh, ohhhhh," spit the hunched figure as a foot kicked him in the forehead. His body jerked on the ground spasmodically once, twice, and then went still. The moaning ceased.

"Think he's dead?"

"Hell no. Not yet. Just playin' possum."

"I thought we were gonna scare him. Rough him up. You're gonna kill him!"

"Shut up, dumb ass. Let me think."

In the beam of the headlights, one figure began walking in a fast semi-circle. The other peered down to get a closer glimpse at the wounded figure, blocking the light as he leered. When the accomplice arose, the beaten man's condition became more obvious.

He was black, like Moses, but darker. His hair was matted and darkened with what had to be blood. A cheek was swollen the size of a grapefruit half and shiny. A white T-shirt, soiled with dirt, had spots of maroon trailing toward the waist from the top.

"Keith? Keith?" asked the one who'd checked on the colored man. "What do we do now?"

"Shut up," said the other. He'd stopped his pacing. Slowly, he reached behind his back, pulling out an angular shape with his right hand. A long knife blade flashed in the beam of light.

"Keith!?!"

"Shut up!" The man with the knife bent over the bleeding colored man. He punched him savagely in the face with the butt of the knife, but the colored man didn't react. He lay motionless.

The attacker placed the knife to the man's throat. Still nothing.

Suddenly, the colored man's eyes opened wildly. He grasped for the knife, rolling over as he made the attempt. The man atop thrust a knee into the belly and pulled the knife away – slicing tendons in the palm of the colored man's hand. He then plunged the knife into the man's chest again and again.

And again.

Andy had Brax by the arm, making sure he didn't move and give the hiding place away. Brax's free hand clutched the hand of Moses even tighter.

"Keith!" screamed the other man, who stood a few feet away, not knowing what to do.

Keith pulled the knife out of the colored man's chest one last time and nonchalantly wiped the excess on the T-shirt of the dead man.

"Keith? Keith?! Jesus Christ, Keith!" The other man was shaking. "You killed him!"

Keith ignored him. He looked over the dead body, the way a hunter would kneel over a dead buck. He brought the knife down again, and began sawing at the dead man's head.

"Jesus, Keith. Jesus! What are you doing?"

Keith said nothing. He sawed another two strokes, and then pulled something away, lifting the bounty to the light for the other man to see clearly his bounty.

The dead man's ear.

"Let's get out of here," Keith said, running toward the car. "We got proof."

He stopped momentarily, scanned the surroundings. Damned if he didn't stare directly at the line of brush covering the boys. Brax sucked in his breath so hard he thought he'd die. He could feel Moses tugging at his leg, urging him to get away.

Satisfied no one was around to witness the crime; Keith hopped in the car, racing the engine ferociously. He backed up, spinning wheels in hard earth to face a distant dirt road. That was enough to prompt his accomplice to run toward the passenger's side and hop in.

Minutes later, even with the car long gone, the youngsters remained paralyzed by fear. Brax realized his own numbness fading when he noticed his jeans were sticky. The humidity had soaked his shirt through, but the dampness in his pants? Rubbing absent-mindedly, Brax got a whiff of evidence. He'd peed in his Levi's.

Minutes passed before Andy peered out of the foliage and took a step into the clearing, pushing his bike.

"I'm getting out of here," he said as he pushed his bike out of the woods and toward the dirt road.

"Andy!" Brax said. "Wait for us."

Andy pivoted and paused. "I ain't waiting for *him*," he said, glaring at Moses. "We just saw one nigger killed. I ain't getting caught with another one. What if they come back lookin' for seconds?"

Andy leaped onto his bike. Pedaling over the uneven pasture toward the dirt road, he disappeared into the darkness.

"Brax?" Moses said in a whisper. "What are we gonna do?"

"We're going to find a house, a fillin' station – whatever we can. And we'll call for help."

"No, Brax, no." Moses said, pulling his hand away from Brax's. "I'll stay here. I'll stay till morning."

"No you won't." Braxton unwrapped the light jacket tied around his waist and gave it to Moses. "Put my jacket on."

Moses slid it on while Brax took off his baseball cap and placed it on Moses' head. A size too big, it sank to the top of Moses' ears, pushing them out awkwardly.

"Leave your bike here. We'll come back for it later," Brax said, pushing his Schwinn into the clearing. "Stay behind me. When we get to the dirt road, we'll ride double. Just keep the jacket zipped up and your hat as low as it'll go."

Moses nodded, following.

The dirt road was uneven, full of shallow potholes and covered with stray rocks. It would have been hard enough riding the bike alone, but with Moses sitting on the handlebars in front, Brax' legs were painfully straining to keep the bike moving and upright.

It became more difficult as the skies opened, with one of those out-of-nowhere late summer rains. They had nowhere to go for cover and needed to find a way home, so they continued even as the rain pelted away.

They were long out of sight of the clearing, around two bends and up and down a hill when they saw a farmhouse to the left with a mailbox marking the beginning of a driveway.

Brax brought the bike to a stop then stumbled to get it steady before he and Moses tumbled.

Moses pulled the cap down again, leaving his ears sticking out sideways. Brax dropped the bike on the edge of the road.

"You stay here. I'm gonna see if they'll let me use the phone," Brax said.

Moses nodded, and slumped down against the mailbox post, hiding his face.

Brax had taken only a few steps when Moses called him, the voice still barely more than a whisper.

"What is it?"

"What are you goin' to tell those people, Brax?" Moses asked.

"That my bike broke down and I need to call my Daddy," Brax said.

"You ain't goin' to say nuthin' about what happened, are you?"

"Not to them, no."

Moses remained quiet. Brax walked the rest of the way, tracing a grassless path that led to the front porch. He knocked loudly a couple of times. A porch light came on. An old man in overalls answered the pounding, listened to Braxton's request and opened the screen door, allowing him in.

Moses remained doubled over, peering at the house. He heard a car in the distance, and lay flat so no one would spot him. But the car never came down the road.

A few minutes later, the front door opened. Brax was waving at the old man.

"No, sir," Moses could hear him saying. "I'll be fine. He said he'd be here in ten, fifteen minutes, tops."

Brax rejoined Moses. Neither said a word. The Indian summer afternoon and unexpected rain left them both shivering, and the temperature was falling fast. Brax didn't know if he was shaking out of fear or due to the cold. The clammy Levi's made it even more uncomfortable. He wished now he'd kept the jacket Moses was wearing.

A car came up over the next hill. Brax quickly realized it wasn't his dad's Ford. Instead, a pickup lumbered toward them. He picked up the bike and straddled it as if he had a purpose, signaling Moses to lie flat. Moses did so, and rolled a few feet away toward the house into thicker grass.

The pickup roared by, spitting mud, pebbles and remnants of a puddle.

Moses didn't move. But he broke the silence.

"Who are you goin' to tell, Brax?"

Brax could see a halo of lights in the distance. Maybe, it was his father.

"Daddy," Brax said. "I'll tell him. He'll know what to do."

There was an uncharacteristic sternness in Moses voice as he replied. "Don't tell him, Brax. Don't tell anyone. Ever. You gotta promise me that."

This time, it was a car. Maybe the Ford.

"Moses, we've got to tell somebody. We saw a murder."

Moses voice faded again. "We saw a colored man murdered, Brax. A nigger."

A Nigger... Moses was using the word Brax wasn't even allowed to use. The inference was clear: *A nigger killed by two white men in some pasture in McMahon County. Who would do anything about it?*

"OK, Moses, OK," Brax said. "I won't tell nobody."

"Promise me, Brax. Promise me. They won't do nothing to you but they'll come after me."

It was Harold Freeman's Ford. Brax waved him down, and the car pulled up beside the mailbox. Expecting an instant lecture or a cussing, Brax got neither. His dad emerged from the driver's side with a big grin.

"Thank goodness, son. We were worried about you," he said, embracing his son. "Where's Moses? Adele said he was with you."

Moses stood up behind the mailbox. "Here, Mr. Freeman."

"Good, good. Let's get your bikes in the trunk and let's get home before it rains again."

Brax wheeled his bike to the back of the car and lifted it into the trunk. His father helped him push it to the front, leaving enough room for another bike. Then the adult looked for Moses, but the youngster had already slid into the backseat.

"Where's Moses' bike?"

"It broke down," Brax said. "We had to leave it. That's why we're so late."

"Let's go get it, then."

Brax froze. *We can't go back. But ... maybe Daddy could do something about it.*

Moses had rolled down the window. "I left it with somebody to fix, Mr. Freeman," Moses said. "I'll get it in a couple days."

Brax's father nodded, then escorted his son to the front of the car. Brax slid in first, still battling with the decision to tell or not. His father pulled in behind the steering wheel. The car came to life with the radio blaring a melancholy Hank Williams song.

"How in the world did you get stuck out here like this?" Mr. Freeman asked.

"A storm came up," Braxton Freeman replied.

CHAPTER 2 /
July 1963

SQUINTING TO FOCUS while using the back of his hand to block out the sun, Braxton Freeman zeroed in on the Coca-Cola thermometer hanging on the wall to the men's locker room.

Ninety-eight degrees.

Brax had had enough of the never-ending, steamy heat. He stood in the lifeguard chair and stretched toward the sun, ironing out the wrinkles in his swim trunks before taking a cooling dive into the Takasaw Country Club pool.

"B-Bear, we've got a problem!" yelled Kyle Anderson, who stood below Brax on the lip of the pool. "Two bobcats at nine o'clock."

Nine o'clock? Needing better directions than Kyle's military heading, Freeman glanced toward his friend to follow his gaze across the pool. Entering through the gate leading into the shallow end was a golden-skinned girl with blonde hair held in a ponytail.

The legs were toned. The bobcats were incredible. The blonde was threatening to bust out of the top of her red-and-white, one-piece bathing suit.

"Good God almighty," Freeman muttered as he tried not to leer too obviously. "Who is it, Kyle? I've never seen her before."

"Gotta be Miz Seaver's niece. Look!" He pointed to the girl, who clutched the hand of one of the Seaver twins as Mrs. Seaver dragged the other child a pace behind.

"Can't be. Katie Sullivan? Geez, did she ever grow up."

Katie Sullivan lived in Birmingham, where her dad practiced law. But she spent most of her summers in Takasaw with her aunt and uncle.

Daily stops at the club were routine in the past, but she hadn't been around this year.

That was another Katie Sullivan – at least she had never looked like this. A year younger than Brax, she'd been, well, a kid just the year before – flat-chested with a non-descript baby face.

Mrs. Seaver stopped a few feet from the kiddie pool and began spreading a towel over a tanning chair while one of the twins tugged at the seat of her bathing suit. Katie didn't bother with the towel, picking up the other twin and flopping her on the next chair. A bag came over her shoulder. After digging in a few seconds, Katie pulled out a bottle of sun lotion and began applying it on the toddler's shoulders.

"B-Bear, she used to be sweet on you. Think she'll like you now that she's all grown up?"

Brax wasn't paying much attention. "Huh?"

"Never mind," Anderson replied. Then he began laughing. "Brax, you might think about getting in the pool. Or at least sitting down. You're causing a scene."

"What?" Brax turned away from Katie and back toward Anderson. "What?"

"You're standing at attention."

Brax didn't immediately understand. Then he realized as the delayed reaction carried blood from one head to the other. The summer debut of not-so-little Katie Sullivan had become obvious to anyone looking at him.

"Queer!" he muttered at Anderson as he dived into the pool. Under the water he cursed himself for not wearing a jock strap.

Anderson was still laughing when Brax climbed out of the pool. The water wasn't *that* cold, but Brax had been able to reposition himself on the swim up from the bottom of the pool.

"What were you doing looking?" Freeman grumbled with a shake of his head.

"Looking? Shit. You almost poked my eye out with it," Anderson guffawed.

"Shut up," Freeman said under his breath, emphasizing the words with an elbow to Anderson's exposed back – exposed because he was now doubled over – as the lifeguard headed toward the tower's ladder.

Three minutes later, Anderson was still giggling.

Back in the lifeguard's chair, Freeman realized how much he needed sunglasses now. No such luck. The pool director had banned them, reasoning that it made the lifeguards complacent.

But if Brax had sunglasses on, he could give Katie Sullivan a better once-over. Instead, he looked until he realized how obvious he was, then desperately began searching the pool for an infraction.

Rough play. A drowning. Anything to distract.

Ah, little Robert Muehler walking fast on the concrete edge. Good enough. Freeman blew his shrill whistle, getting the attention of everyone at the pool.

"Slow down, Muehler!"

The tow-headed boy looked at him dumbfounded, and shrugged his shoulders.

"Slow down!"

In search of a distraction, Freeman had instead created one. While the youngest kids played unheeded, everyone else craned in the lifeguard's direction wondering what had happened.

Everyone included Mrs. Seaver and her niece. When Brax returned his gaze back toward his new obsession, Katie Sullivan was smiling at him. She punctuated the smile with a wave.

"I guess that answers that," Anderson said. "She's still sweet on you."

"Go jump."

Freeman had 90 minutes until his next break -- if he got one. It was July 4th, and the part-time help, lifeguards included, were notorious for not showing up on the holiday. But that gave him 90 minutes, if he was lucky, to figure a reason to go over and talk to Katie Sullivan.

"Dang, Kyle. She's beautiful. Kyle? ... Kyle?!"

Anderson wasn't answering. Freeman leaned over, but his friend was gone. He scanned the pool. No luck. He turned to his left, then his right. Where was he?

"Freeman!" The familiar voice came from behind.

Freeman twisted toward the back fence. Anderson had wandered over to talk to Coach Halliday through the chain links.

Freeman gave the coach a wave before returning his gaze to the pool, where an elderly lady was trying to swim laps with little success amid splashing children.

Minutes later, Anderson returned with a message.

"Coach wants to see you at the break."

The temperature had crept to 99 degrees and the time to break was down to 25 minutes when Freeman lost sight of Katie Sullivan.

In the pool? The old lady was still there, churning away. Mrs. Seaver had gone into the shallow end and was taking turns catching the twins, who alternately jumped into her arms with a splash from the ledge. But Katie Sullivan, who had been tanning facedown was nowhere to be seen.

"Braxton? Braxton Freeman? Do you remember me?"

It was the recognizable voice with the unrecognizable chest. Katie Sullivan now stood below the tower, just where Kyle Anderson had been when she'd first inadvertently elicited a half-mast salute from Brax.

"Katie Sullivan? How are ya? How's Birmingham?"

"Hot as Hades. Just like here."

"Oh, yeah. Guess so."

Conversation came easy with the guys. It *used* to come easy when Katie Sullivan spent half the day at the pool underneath the tower talking to the young lifeguard.

But it was easy to talk to a 15-year-old built like a 10-year-old.

Now she was 16 going on Marilyn Monroe. So he struggled to think of something to say: Anything to say, anything at all.

"Can you believe how hot it is?"

Katie giggled. "Yeah, I can. It's called summer, I think."

Brax nodded, then began searching the pool for a good mugging. *You are so dumb, dumb, dumb.*

"You playing football again?" she asked.

"Yeah. Well, not now. Football doesn't start for another month. But, yeah. We ought to have a pretty good team. You?"

She giggled again.

"No, I'm not playing football."

"I didn't mean that. I ..."

"I'm a varsity cheerleader. That's where I've been this summer. We had cheerleading camp for two weeks in June, and the rest of the time we were on vacation down in Florida."

"Cheerleader, huh? Congrats."

"Thanks. I should be the captain by the time I'm a senior."

"That's great, Katie. Great."

The conversation grinded to a halt. Luckily, two kids were playing chicken too close to the deep end. The one underneath was struggling to keep his head above the water.

The whistle shrieked. "Hey, you!" Brax shouted at the boy on top of the drowner's shoulders. "Get off, now!"

The youth complied with a forward dive and the other one came up gasping for air before following his partner to shallower water.

Scanning the pool provided the perfect excuse. It wasn't that Brax Freeman couldn't think of something to say. He merely had a job to do. That was the impression he wanted to make.

It was a relief, because he was now too nervous to look at Katie Sullivan. The top of the one-piece suit showed little cleavage. But from his vantage point, what it did show was almost too much to bear.

"I'm going to be here the entire month, Braxton."

"Really? That's great. We gonna see you out here a lot? I'm working four days a week. Just don't drown on my watch, will ya?"

She giggled again. This time, maybe – hopefully – because he'd said something halfway funny.

"Yeah. I'll be out here with Aunt Susan and the twins a lot. But ..."

But? Brax would have dared to stare in the sun rather than let his gaze drift below. The bobcats were still there. But Katie Sullivan's eyes weren't there to meet him. She was staring at the cement.

"Something wrong?"

The eyes reverted to him, accompanied by a grin.

"Well, Aunt Susan doesn't want me to spend *all* my time with her and the twins. She wants me to make some new friends."

"Heck, you've been coming here since you were a kid. I'd think you've got a lot of friends here."

"I do. But that's not what she means. She doesn't want me stuck at the house or babysitting all the time. Maybe find someone to go to a movie with, or something like that."

A movie? Opportunity was knocking. Now only if Brax Freeman could find the doorknob.

"Sounds like a great idea. I mean, you're a junior now. Gotta act the part, right?"

"You're so silly." She giggled again. "Braxton Freeman, I'm asking you to a movie."

Silence. Dead, agonizing silence.

The Coca-Cola thermometer was still stuck at 99 degrees. Surely, Brax Freeman knew, the mercury had boiled over. It had to be 120 degrees, at least.

"Don't make this so hard." Her voice was softer now, almost too soft to be heard above the racket in and around the pool.

"What?"

"Braxton," she said, dropping her voice another notch. "I'm asking you to a movie."

It was the kind of nervousness you felt just before a game, when you didn't know whether to return to the locker room and heave or tap dance to midfield. Half end-of-the-world terror, half giddiness.

Brax felt it in the pit of his belly, followed by another sensation. He felt cocksure, the feeling that came after the first good hit.

"A movie?"

She was blushing now. When Brax looked down again, Katie looked away back to the cement deck. Now he was embarrassing her.

"A movie? That would be great!"

She returned her gaze to him with a blush.

"One problem. The closest movie house is in Auburn. Or Montgomery," he said, a little uncertain of where he was headed.

"Aunt Susan says that's not a problem. Provided they approve of my date. I just have to get back before curfew."

"Never missed a curfew yet," he said. *Never had one. Never needed one.*

"We could go see one Saturday night. I don't know what's playing, but we'll figure something out. I'm fixin' to get paid Friday."

"Saturday. It's a date," she said. The budding smile was now in full bloom. "Come by at five. Aunt Susan wants to have you over for dinner before."

"FREEMAN!!!" Halliday was yelling from behind the fence.

Brax turned around where the stoutly built coach stood against the fence.

"You on break yet?"

Brax pulled his Timex from underneath the chair. Five minutes to go.

"Not just yet, Coach. I got another five. That's if someone shows up. Cassidy ain't here yet.'

"ANDERSON!" Halliday bellowed. Kyle was across the pool, sunning. He bolted toward the fence at the invitation, stumbling in his haste and nearly ending up with a mouthful of pavement. "Fill in for Freeman until the next lifeguard gets there. I need him for something."

Brax stood up, slipped the Timex on his wrist and grabbed his T-shirt, which he put on wet. Katie stood beneath him, next to Anderson, who was waiting to climb the ladder.

"Saturday at five, Katie. If I don't see you before then," Braxton Freeman said as he made his way down. "We'll figure out something good."

She gave him half a wave before returning to her aunt and the twins.

"You get a date with the bobcats?" Anderson whispered as he replaced Brax on the ladder, drawing another elbow to the back.

Halliday was waiting outside the fence. Brax had to go through the men's locker room to get out to the golf course. Halliday saw him coming and pointed toward a golf cart. The football coach took the wheel and began driving almost before Freeman had settled in the other seat.

Ralph Halliday was built like a fireplug, muscular but losing the battle around his middle to the occasional beer. Everyone was wearing flattops, but Halliday's hair was cut into such stubble he might as well shave it all.

He taught history and P.E. at Takasaw High School, where Brax was about to begin his senior year. During the autumn, Halliday coached the football team. During the spring, the baseball team. Freeman played both sports for the coach.

"Following your workout, are you?" Halliday asked as he motored slowly down the cart path leading from the opening tee to the first green.

"Yessir. Running ten 50s and a half mile and jumping rope thirty minutes every other day. Swimming twenty-five laps every day I lifeguard, before the pool opens."

"Good, good. I'm counting on you this fall. You're my number one halfback."

"Yes sir."

Too small to make the team as an eighth grader, Brax wasn't much bigger a year later, yet he'd backed up Gary Brokur at halfback for two years and started on defense, in place of the quarterback. In the one-platoon system, only the quarterback could come out when the team went on defense.

But the summer before eleventh grade he grew rapidly, so much that his legs constantly hurt from the growing pains. It was meant to be his breakout year, the halfback job finally his. But it ended a week into preseason practice, when he broke his collarbone doing the Oklahoma drill. He'd be on the mend the rest of the fall as Takasaw struggled with the uncommon losing season.

"You ought to be one of our best players this year," Halliday said. Compliments were rare, indeed. Halliday spent most of his time yelling and criticizing, pointing out everything the player had done wrong.

Yet the gruff old coach was well liked by everyone who played football. And despised by those who didn't, who only got to know Halliday through P.E. classes that resembled boot camp.

"Ever since that growth spurt, you've started to become a football player. Guess the body had to catch up. Shee-it! I grew into my body at age twelve. Never got any bigger or better."

Brax nodded. You didn't talk to Halliday as much as you listened. And listened.

"If we can beat Opelika and Lanier, we're going undefeated. All we need is a quarterback."

Freeman nodded as Halliday steered toward the second green.

"That new kid, the one whose family moved from Georgia. He any good?" Brax offered, figuring Halliday's silence meant he wanted dialogue instead of a soliloquy.

"Not good enough for us to go undefeated. I've worked him out a few times. Too slow. So-so arm. We ain't passing much, not if you turn out as good as I think you'll be with a lot of work. If you don't turn out to be worth a crap, we're in trouble."

Was Freeman supposed to say anything?

"Get the God-damned cart off the green!" Halliday screamed, jerking his cart to a halt. A foursome was approaching the pin on number two. One of the carts was pulled too close to the burnt out grass.

A golfer nodded and headed for the cart to comply. Halliday spent his summers as the country club's assistant golf pro. Few wanted him for lessons – he may have been the worst golfer in all of Takasaw.

The high school boosters had arranged the job to supplement Halliday's income and provide him with daily rounds of golf. He often played by himself, working nine or 18 holes at a brisk pace for the exercise.

With the offensive cart pulled back toward the path, Halliday began his meandering toward the next hole.

Couldn't they have had this conversation by the pool? Brax wondered. The heat and humidity had already done more damage to the greens than any errant golf cart could manage.

"I was in Tuscaloosa last week," Halliday began. This one definitely seemed like a monologue. "Talked to The Bear over a Jack and Seven. He loves the stuff."

Brax nodded affirmatively then waited for the sequel he'd heard a few hundred times before..

"You know I played with The Bear and Hutson back at Alabama?"

"Yes sir."

Halliday was a popular coach because he won a good bit more than he lost. He was more popular because 30 years or so ago he had been a seldom-used reserve on an early Rose Bowl team at the University of Alabama.

Bear Bryant, the Crimson Tide's head coach, had been the *other* end – a good player, but not the best. That honor belonged to Don Hutson, a player with deer-like moves who'd gone on to a Hall of Fame career with the NFL's Green Bay Packers.

But the fact that Halliday had been on one of Alabama's great teams *and* knew Bryant, a state legend, made Halliday a bona fide local personality.

He'd even managed to lure Bryant to speak to the Takasaw High football banquet a couple of years earlier. Bryant arrived late, but he'd quickly endeared the crowd to Halliday even more when he regaled everyone with a couple of anecdotes about how Halliday had pushed the Bear and Huston to greatness, so fearful were they of losing their starting jobs to the young upstart.

Of course, Brax, like most everyone, knew Halliday had been a third-string tackle. Not that it mattered. This was the gospel according to Bear Bryant.

"Bear asked me if we had anybody who could play for him. I told him a couple, if they improve a helluva lot. Course we haven't had a big college player since Myers went to Auburn a few years ago. But I told him we got a couple."

Who? Brax thought.

"Wanna know who?" Halliday asked. He paused, to see if it got a reaction from Freeman. It did, of course: A wondering up-and-down of the shoulders.

"I told him Lomar had a chance to play college ball if he got his pansy ass in gear. And I told him we had a rising senior who could be our best halfback in the last decade."

Halliday saw the perplexed look on the youngster's face. "You, ya dumb sumbitch. If you work your ass off. You got a long way to go, but you can get there."

Damn, Brax thought. *Me?* He started to bask in the compliment then stopped. *If I'm so good now how come I wasn't good enough to play in front of Brokur?*

What to say? Brax had thought talking to Katie Sullivan had been hard. But how was he supposed to act when Hardass Halliday was paying a compliment?

"Really?" Freeman asked. It was all the response he could muster.

"Yep. You've cut your time down by three-tenths of a second. I bet there ain't a faster player on the team. Hell, in three counties."

"I've been working at it, Coach."

"I know, boy, I know. Got good genes, too. Your dad ran track or something in college didn't he?"

"Yessir. Well, he played basketball. At Howard."

"Well, that's the genes. He jumped. You can run."

"Yes sir."

They were passing the seventh green now. While the pool was packed with housewives and children, the golf course was mostly barren due to the heat and the holiday. They'd passed just two foursomes. Halliday let the second quartet play on without a warning.

Between the ninth and tenth holes, Halliday pulled the cart to a stop. Getting out, he reached into the bag. Where the clubs normally rested, Halliday had a Styrofoam cooler instead.

"Coke?" he asked, grabbing a cold bottle before Brax could answer and freeing it with a metal opener. Halliday handed it over, then grabbed a Pabst Blue Ribbon from the bottom, prying that cap off as well.

"Freeman, I need to ask you som'un, and I don't want it going no further than right here."

They had settled at a stone picnic table under an aluminum shed. A water cooler and cola machine stood at one end, a restroom at the other. Halliday leaned back against the table, facing the course.

"Your dad's on the bi-racial committee right?"

"The what Coach? I don't know."

"Rumor has it that some civic leaders, Negro and white, have formed a committee. Know who Judge Johnson is?"

"Yes sir, I've heard of him. The federal judge, right?"

"Yep. The one who said schools have to integrate. From what I hear, this bi-racial committee your dad is on is thinking about mixing the Negroes and the white kids together. At our school."

Brax shook his head. What Halliday was saying didn't sound right. Coloreds and whites didn't go to school together. Not in Alabama. Certainly not in Takasaw, where even the water fountains – "colored" and "white" – were segregated.

"I haven't heard that."

"Well, I have," Halliday continued. "And I've heard your dad's on this committee, pushing it through."

He lifted the bottle of beer and chugged it halfway down. Brax did the same with the coke.

"What I'm about to say to you, Freeman, remains between us. Got it? This is serious stuff, and I'll kick your ass every day to Sunday if I hear otherwise, got it?"

"Yes sir."

"This bi-racial committee I hear your dad's on is supposed to be trying to work out a compromise. They're going to try to handpick some Negro students. Don't know how many. Five? Fifteen? Fifty? Hell, I just don't know. But I'd like you to do some snooping and find out."

Brax nodded. He and his dad talked openly. If something were going on, Harold Freeman would tell him.

"What would you think, son, if Negroes went to school with you?"

"I don't know," Brax replied. "Nothing, I guess."

"Me either," Halliday said. "Me, either. 'Cept I would never say that publicly. I'd get run out of town."

Halliday finished the beer and headed to the cooler for another.

"I didn't grow up like you. I grew up in Takasaw, sure, but we were poor. My dad died before I was five," Halliday said. "Mama worked like a lot of coloreds did, as a cleaning woman. Six days a week. She had three mouths to feed and no husband."

Brax nodded. Where was he going?

"Negro families lived next door to me, on both sides. Hell, I grew up not knowing they were any different. Wasn't till I went to school that I realized there was. But I gotta be honest. There wasn't a helluva lot of difference 'cept skin color. The Negroes who wanted to make sum'in of their lives did, just like the white folks. The ones that didn't didn't."

Brax nodded. He'd never really understood why Negroes and whites lived such different lives, even if they lived houses apart on the same street. He'd grown up playing sandlot ball with whites and Negroes. No big deal. At least his parents never thought so.

Other white kids gradually faded away from the games as years passed, finding something else to do. But Freeman was one of a handful in the neighborhood, and the last white kid who gathered on the vacant lot next to the old Douglass house for Sunday afternoon games of football until, eventually, everyone quit showing up.

"I don't see much difference either, Coach."

Halliday belched, then slumped back against the table.

"Now, from what I hear, this committee is going to handpick some Negroes, like I told you, and put them in Takasaw High this year. They're working on a peaceful solution, but you can bet that some yahoo will call some colored a nigger. Just hope it doesn't get out of hand."

"Yes sir. I agree."

"The thing I've been wond'rin is, what if we get them to pick an athlete or two? Think you could play ball with a colored boy? Share the locker room, too?"

"Don't see why not, Coach."

"Good. Think the rest of the team would feel that way?"

Brax shrugged. "Don't know Coach. Most of 'em would, I'd guess. If they can play …"

Halliday gulped the last of the beer, the second in a matter of minutes. Freeman had never seen the coach do more than sip a beer, and then only after a big win, between puffs of a fat cigar.

"Ever hear of a colored kid named Moses Burks?"

Moses Burks was Braxton's oldest friend. He lived six doors down, albeit in a shotgun house half the size of the Freeman home. The two had been playing ball, cowboys and Indians (Moses was always the Indian) together since they were kids.

"Yes sir. Known Moses a long time."

"Heard he can throw the hell out of a football. He's a quarterback, right?"

"Yes sir. Better than any I've ever seen. Used to beat me in a sprint by two or three steps, but I bet I can match him now."

"That's what I've heard." For the first time since they'd started talking, Halliday's grimace disappeared. "We need a quarterback, don't we?"

The coach paused, rubbing his head as if to see if the sun had burned the last refuge of stubble away.

"That would be sum'in, wouldn't it? A Negro quarterback at Takasaw High? Hell, I could make it work. If that's who the committee sends us, I can make it work. Not many people can in this town, but I can."

Brax nodded. If anybody could, Halliday could.

"Find out from your dad what's going on. I want Moses on our team.

Geez, Braxton thought to himself. *Moses at Takasaw High? Man, we'd be good.*

"With you and that colored kid, if he's half as good as I hear he is," Halliday said, "we'll go undefeated."

* * * * * *

The madras cotton, short-sleeved shirt wasn't helping. Brax Freeman was dripping sweat, thanks to a combination of the unwavering heat and the smoke and fire from the grill.

Flame erupted from underneath one of the sirloins. Brax grabbed the cup of water and dipped his hand, then flicked the liquid onto the dancing flame. It died down, but not away. With tongs, Brax lifted the endangered steak and flipped it over.

Was it ready? *How the hell do I know?*

Grilling out was an area of pride for Brax's father, Harold. During the summer and early fall, the Freemans barbecued once a week.

This was the big Fourth of July barbecue, with 30 or more guests. But Harold Freeman was inside with a half-dozen other men – locked in what Brax had determined to be a pretty fierce discussion.

Thus Brax was stuck as chef, a task that on the discomfort scale ranked there with his afternoon conversation with Halliday but just below his stammering acceptance of the date.

"Mom! Mom?" Brax looked around for Peggy Freeman. Was that her coming across the backyard? It was hard to tell due to the smoke from the steak-eating flames.

It was. Dressed in a red-checked dress that reached the top of her calf, Peggy Freeman arrived with a tray of ice-filled plastic cups.

"What's wrong, hon?"

"Everything. Where's Dad? This is *his* job."

"He's inside. He'll be out in a few minutes."

21

Now there were two flames. *Hope everyone likes their steaks extra-well done.*

"Brax. Take the steaks off for a minute. Let it cool down."

"Yeah, OK."

Brax removed four steaks, laying them on a platter atop the brick façade of the grill. Next to it was another platter with uncooked hamburgers and hot dogs.

"Your father can finish in a minute. Relax."

"Thanks."

Peggy headed out into the mix of people again, some sitting at two picnic tables. Most of the adults were chatting on the brick patio. Most of the kids, none close to Brax's age, were playing tag in the yard. The majority of grownups were clients of Harold Freeman, an accountant, or members of the church.

Peggy returned in a few, the tray now empty.

"Hon, go into the garage and bring out more sodas."

He nodded, removed the steaks from the grill and headed off. Crates of individual Coca-Colas were stacked in groups of 12. He lifted the top two crates and took them into the yard, lowering the bottles one by one into a metal tub full of ice.

"When's your next ballgame?" Peggy asked, sidling up.

"Friday night at Notasulga," Brax grunted.

"Good. Daddy and I want you to go with us Saturday to Grandma's."

Brax shook his head. "Mom ..."

Peggy Freeman's parents lived in Fairhope, a small town on the east bank of the Mobile Bay. At best, it was a 5-hour drive. Brax loved the trip, but at age 16 visits to Grandma could wait.

Besides, he had plans – big plans.

Peggy started laughing. "Braxton Freeman, you don't want to see Grandmama Saturday?"

"It's not that. It's just ..."

The laughing picked up. She covered her mouth in vain, then reached out and grabbed his shoulder, pulling him in for a quick hug.

"I know all about it, hon."

Perplexed, Brax looked on at silence.

"You know what?"

"I know all about your date with Katie Sullivan. Susan Seaver told me all about your plans. You don't waste any time."

"Gee, word spreads fast."

"I knew before you got home from the club. She called me as soon as she got home. You were set up. Susan and I've been planning this since school let out," Peggy said, flashing her smile. "We knew Katie would go for it. We figured you'd go for it – once you saw Katie again."

"She's changed a lot. That's for sure."

"It sounds fun. Oh, to be a teenager again."

"Yeah, it is. It's sad when you get so old you can't remember, huh?"

She hugged him again, pulling away to get a last look. She grabbed his chin with her right hand. "Yes, hon. We old folks can't remember much. So we have to live vicariously through you."

To Brax, it was good to see Peggy upbeat more consistently. That's how he remembered her, as a child. But the last few years ... She masked things well with a smile that sometimes seemed plastic – fooling everyone, perhaps, except her son and husband.

But gradually, she was re-emerging from an emotional funk. When things were good, Peggy was vibrant with chatter and energy. Of the three Freemans, she could be the most social. Harold, by contrast, had the ability to listen and listen, doing it in such a way that one felt he was hanging on every word. Harold said little, but when he did it seemed to be thoughtful.

That's where Brax differed. Grades came easier in some aspects than athletics, yet when it came to transferring the whirring activity in his head to his mouth words got jangled. He tried Harold's silent approach with little success. When it came time to offer something to conversation, he stumbled and fumbled.

He didn't stutter. Nor did he stammer. He just struggled to verbalize, knowing what he wanted to say but not how to say it. More often than not, Brax Freeman's idea would be five seconds ahead of his mouth and he'd forget what had been left in the wake. Or, like at the pool with Katie, he wouldn't know what to say at all.

Physically, he took more after Peggy. In heels, she stood a good two inches taller than her husband, one reason the couple rarely dressed formally. She and Brax had the same eyes and nose. The difference was the hair. The light brown color was the same. But her hair was thick and she wore it longer than most women her age. Brax's was finer, so much that despite its short length it remained in a forever changing ebb and flow of motion. Not even a little dab of Brylcream could do him good.

Peggy had returned to her role of hostess, so Brax peered through the window into the den, to see if the meeting had broken up. The men were still in an animated discussion.

Brax turned around, planning to return to the grill. But his path was blocked. An older boy stood in front of him, also peering in.

"Guess what everybody's saying is true," offered the intruder. Andy Laduke was straining to see what the fuss was about.

Laduke was Brax's first cousin. Laduke's mother, long deceased, was the older sister to Harold Freeman. The two youths had grown up in proximity, but had never been close. Andy was two-and-a-half years older, so they'd rarely seen each other around in school.

Besides, Andy had dropped out after the tenth grade to work. Exactly what he did now, Brax hadn't figured out and neither Harold nor Peggy Freeman had volunteered to tell him.

But there had been plenty of rumors, mostly about things illegal or bordering on the sinister, such as running moonshine in dry McMahon County. You could buy a beer in Takasaw but nothing harder. Outside the city limits, it was totally dry. Unless you knew Laduke, you were out of luck, people said.

And what about playing the numbers? Brax had never seen any gambling, but it was an accepted reality throughout the county that gambling went on and Andy supplemented his income representing bookies.

Andy and Brax didn't look like they were related. Andy used to tower over Brax, but now they stood eye-to-eye. The older boy had coarse, dark hair buzzed to the nub. And he was heavier. Stocky didn't suit him, he was husky. Braxton always thought he could be an athlete if he'd ever get off his lazy ass.

"What's everybody saying?" Brax asked.

"They're going to bring niggers into our school. Jesus F. Christ. Niggers."

"Who?"

"Your Dad and those other dumbasses inside," Andy said sarcastically. "They're giving in, and letting the niggers in. Might as well kiss Kennedy's ass one more time."

Halliday … Andy Laduke … how come everyone knows what's going on but me?

"Haven't heard anything like that," Brax said. "But best I remember, you ain't been in school in a long time."

"Don't matter," Laduke replied. "Our schools are white for a reason."

"Yeah," Brax replied, not in agreement but in an effort to bring the discussion to a close.

It didn't work. Laduke kept talking, muttering, venting. Brax ignored him, focused on trying to determine what was going on.

Harold Freeman sat at the head of the family dining room table. Carlton Armstrong, the town's mayor, sat opposite. Rev. John Ed Mullens, minister at First Presbyterian, and First Takasaw Bank president Guff Martin were on Harold Freeman's left. The high school's principal, Winford Atchley, and a man Brax hadn't seen before were on the right.

Armstrong was doing the talking, and he looked none too happy. His face was red, a vein bulging at the forehead, he pounded the table with a flat palm once, twice.

Only muffled sounds came through. Two rooms of distance, the picture window and the noise outside eliminated any chance to snoop.

Laduke said something and was heading for the sliding glass door. But before he could open it completely, Peggy Freeman intercepted him.

"Andy, hon, where are you going?"

"Got some talking to do, Aunt Peg. Got to say my piece."

She gently grabbed his arm, tugging him around and away.

"Aunt Peg!" he said urgently. "I gotta say something to them."

"I don't think so, Andy. Let them finish their meeting. And when they're finished, you don't say a thing. Not here."

He stopped, yanked his arm away and glared. "Don't tell me you're a nigger lover, too!"

The commotion silenced the small gathering on the patio. Elsewhere, the play and conversations continued unabated. Peggy Freeman flashed a smile at Andy, but the warmth had drained.

"We don't allow talk like that in this house, Andy."

"Damnit, Aunt Peg, I can say anything I damn well want!"

"Not in this house. Not in my house, Andy." She crossed her arms. The teeth disappeared as she tightened her lips and reclaimed her grip on his forearm. "Andy, I'd suggest you go home."

He didn't say anything. Laduke looked at his aunt, toward the men through the window, then back to Peggy. Pulling away, he whirled and walked briskly through the iron gate that led from the backyard to the driveway. Moments later, the engine of Laduke's old pickup truck could be heard gunning out of the gravel driveway. The final sound was a screech of rubber as it backed out onto the street and squealed away.

Peggy Freeman tried to compose herself. Brax could sense the discomfort even if he couldn't see it. He understood.

"Some people are filled with hatred and fear, hon," Peggy said, almost in a whisper, as she joined Brax back at the grill. "I'm afraid your cousin's got enough for ten people. He just doesn't know better."

Brax could only shake his head, stunned at the exchange.

Racism had been rampant as long as he could remember. It was a way of life. Old-timers -- anyone out of school -- talked about the days when Negroes and white co-existed peacefully, at least in Takasaw and in Alabama. Negroes knew their place, then. So they said.

It began to change a decade earlier. Brown vs. the Board of Education, the landmark ruling that forced the integration of Central High in Little Rock, Arkansas.

Then the civil rights battle moved to the frontline, Alabama, turning a middle-aged seamstress named Rosa Parks and a youthful Montgomery minister, the Rev. Martin Luther King Jr., into national figures. It also ignited a rebirth of the Ku Klux Klan.

From the Black Belt, the stretch of south and central Alabama that earned its name because of the fertile land as well as the large concentration of blacks, to booming Birmingham the civil rights war had an epicenter.

Just a month before, an attempt to integrate the University of Alabama had drawn national attention after Governor George Wallace vowed to stop the move. Wallace eventually gave in, but not before becoming a political icon for state's rights.

The movement hit home in Takasaw. For two years, Negroes boycotted local white businesses in the city to protest the lack of voting rights. Civic leaders publicly ignored the effort, yet even Harold Freeman had ruefully admitted a few times that the boycott was impacting most everyone.

Even a decade after Brown vs. the Board of Education, the idea of blacks and whites going to school together wasn't considered a possibility in Alabama.

Yet that was all about to change in Takasaw.

And Harold Freeman, if what everyone but Brax seemed to know was true, was part of the process.

The term "nigger" wasn't allowed at the Freeman house, or in most polite gatherings in Takasaw. Now, "colored," though meant politely, was becoming an old-fashioned term. "Negro" was preferable.

The unspoken rules were confusing. Brax had known Moses Burks as long as he could remember. They'd played together in the same playpen, while Moses' grandmother used to do housework for the Freemans.

Yet they never socialized. They played ball together out in the yard. They'd ridden bikes together before they'd become acquainted with automobiles. But go together to a movie or a high school game or a double date?

Brax had never asked why not. It had never occurred to him.

Had he been daydreaming? A tap on the sliding glass door got his attention. Peggy signaled toward the dining room, where the meeting was apparently over. The men were all standing around the table, smiling, laughing. Harold Freeman was beckoning.

Braxton wiped his hands off on the front of his jeans and slid the door open, heading through the den into the living room. The tension had disappeared.

Harold Freeman wrapped his right arm around Brax. "You know everyone here, don't you son?"

Brax nodded, going down the line. He stopped at the man he didn't recognize. The stranger was closer to Brax's age than the rest of the men, and dressed in a starched white, short-sleeve button-down shirt and pressed khaki pants.

"I'm sorry. I should've introduced you earlier. Son, this is Mark Rosenberg of the federal government. Mr. Rosenberg, my son, Brax."

The man stood a couple of inches shorter. Lean, he had the hint of tight biceps, and a narrower waist than anyone else in the room. His black hair was thick and matched dark eyes.

Rosenberg extended his hand, then grasped Brax's offering, shaking it firmly.

"Nice to meet you, sir," Brax said, wondering if someone would tell him what was going on. Certainly his father would, if not now, later.

"Who's hungry?" Harold Freeman asked.

The other five men replied affirmatively, eliciting a chuckle from the elder Freeman.

"Let's go get something to eat, then," Harold said. "Everything ready?"

"Uh, no, sir," Brax replied. "The steaks were on the verge of getting a little too well done. Mama told me to hold off until you got back out."

Harold chuckled again. "Right, right. What would a barbecue be without Harold Freeman's cooking?"

Back outside, Harold turned his attention toward the steaks, finishing the ones Braxton had already cremated before adding the next quartet to the grill. Hamburgers and hot dogs followed.

While flipping burgers, Harold Freeman talked about everything: Brax's upcoming baseball season, the impending date with Katie Sullivan (Susan Seaver didn't limit her circle of co-conspirators, did she?) and the prospects for the Takasaw High football team.

But nary a word about the mysterious meeting.

* * * *

The barbecue concluded at dark, when the last stragglers left the Freeman house. Brax had helped set off the fireworks, climbing onto the roof to make certain 12-year-old Denny Davis didn't fall off as he and his father fired roman candles and Dixie Devils into the air.

Harold Freeman picked up paper plates scattered throughout the backyard while Peggy cleaned off the picnic tables and ordered Brax from one task to the next. Finally convinced everything that could be done had been done, she piled the leftover meat on a clean plate.

"Hon, why don't you run this over to Adele's house. Maybe they've eaten, but it doesn't matter. This'll make for good leftovers."

With the plate wrapped in tin foil, he headed out the driveway and turned right on the sidewalk toward Adele's house, a few hundred yards away. There weren't any streetlights. The only illumination came from the light within the homes.

Adele Wright had worked off and on for the Freemans for years, as a babysitter, housecleaner and cook. Six months ago, they'd let her go. Harold explained business was falling off, something Brax didn't understand. He was an accountant. His clients were nearly all white. What few black clients boycotted him couldn't have had much impact.

But, in truth, the boycott had crippled other businesses so much that they could no longer afford the services of an accountant.

Adele had remained a friend, as had the family that remained with her. At times, Adele's house swelled, but now there were but three since her youngest girl, Ruth, had remarried and resettled with her children near Atlanta.

There was Josiah, who had Down Syndrome and was almost 30, who had played with the younger kids as long as Brax could remember. Now he was slowing down.

And there was Moses Burks, whose birth followed Brax's by weeks. Brax spent the first 10 years of his life thinking Moses was Adele's son before realizing the age difference meant something else. Adele was his grandmother, but had raised him since birth.

"You fellas must be twins," she'd say. "I can't separate you with a stick."

Moses' younger brother and a cousin grew up wearing Brax's hand-me-downs, which Peggy passed on before they were too worn. Another cousin once wore baby and toddler clothes passed down from Brax's sister, Candace.

He could still remember Candace. He was seven when she was born, and he had to wait a month for her to get out of the hospital due to Candace's premature birth. The first part of her life remained fuzzy. Brax couldn't remember much -- except her laboring to breathe in the incubator at the hospital, and the tiny, tiny hands and feet when she first arrived home.

From the time Candace could walk, she followed Brax – and Moses – everywhere. If they set up the train set in the living room, Candace wanted to join them, helping them operate the Lionel set and making the artificial "woo-woo" noises, before Moses yelled, "All aboard!"

Cowboys and Indians outside? They had to play around Candace, with strict orders from Peggy and Adele not to leave the yard because Candace would follow. Sometimes the boys would get lucky. Peggy would already have the playpen set up outside, and Brax would lift Candace and place her in the mesh confinement. Bloody screams followed, but it meant a few minutes of uninterrupted play.

Then she started kindergarten. After the first day, Peggy let Brax walk Candace up Gautier Street to the kindergarten, where he'd drop her off before heading a few blocks to the grammar school.

She had given him his nickname. B-Bear. For Christmas, the year before, he had given her a stuffed brown teddy bear, and she'd lug it with her to his room before going to bed. Leaning back in his arms, staring at the toy animal, she'd make the introductions. "B," she'd say, looking at her brother. Then she'd turn to the furry creature and say, "Bear." Then she'd repeat it. "B. Bear. B-Bear." Most nights, she fell asleep clutching the teddy bear. Brax would rest his chin on her soft, golden hair until Harold or Peggy would come in and move Candace to her own room.

Kyle Anderson spent the night the summer before fifth grade and had watched the ritual. Forever after, he'd tease Brax in front of their peers. "Hey, B-Bear. *B-Bear*." The name stuck.

She could be a pest or an unwanted appendage at times, but the moment she lost interest in what he was doing stung. The nights she fell asleep before he finished his homework or his chores left a void. He'd find himself missing the visit, which helped him head off to his own dreams so quickly …

Now Brax found himself standing at the walkway leading to Adele's front door. He walked up the steps of the splintered wooden front porch and knocked on the door.

Adele flung the door open. "B-Bear!" she said warmly.

B-Bear. He barely noticed anymore when Kyle Anderson said it. But now, after thinking of Candace …

He lowered his head so she wouldn't see his eyes welling, thrusting the covered plate out. "We thought ya'll might want something from the barbecue," he mumbled.

She took it without a word as Brax turned and began to sprint toward home.

* * * *

The three Freemans were gathered at the breakfast table the next morning, Harold reading the morning *Montgomery Advertiser* he picked up during his early-morning walk past the corner store. Peggy had grits and biscuits on the table already.

His father pored over the front page as Brax scooped a generous portion of the white meal onto his plate. He took a biscuit, cut it open with a butter knife and spread jam over both portions.

If he were going to find out what the meeting was about, he would have to ask.

"Dad?"

The paper rustled. Harold folded it accordion style to look at it his son.

"Yes, Brax?"

"Maybe it's none of my business, but ... but I was wondering what y'all were meeting about last night."

Harold closed the paper and placed the front section on the table next to his coffee. He shifted in his chair and looked his son in the eye.

"We're putting a plan together to integrate Takasaw High School."

"Integrate. Mix Negroes and whites together?"

"Yes."

Harold took a sip of coffee. "What would you think of that?"

"I'd think it makes sense."

"You would, maybe," Harold said. "I'm not sure that opinion will be universal."

"Then why are y'all discussing it?"

Coach Halliday had been right. Harold explained how Judge Johnson had ordered Alabama schools to desegregate so that black children were afforded the opportunity of an equal education. To Brax, it seemed sensible. But common sense couldn't match emotions across the state that were raw when it came to change.

"We've put together a group – we're calling it the bi-racial council," Harold said. "Twelve members, six blacks and six white. You saw all the white members, except, I guess, one, last night. What we're working toward is a peaceful solution."

Brax nodded, wanting and waiting for more information.

"Brax, the feeling of most of us is that this is something that's going to happen eventually with or without our input. Truth is, not everyone on the council is for it – not even all the Negro leaders. But we're afraid that if we don't act now, it's going to be forced down our throats. No one – no one – wants that. Now, to be honest, it's the moral thing to do."

Brax bit off a portion of biscuit, waiting for his father to continue.

"If we don't do something, it might get dangerous. Fights, maybe shootings and lynchings, and the Klan will get in the middle. There are some people in this town with strong opinions about mixing. What we're trying to do is get a plan worked out, one we can then sell to leaders on both sides, Negro and white."

That made sense. One thing didn't.

"Why was the man from the government here?"

"That was my idea. As well as Mr. Douglass, who wasn't here."

Brax knew whom Harold had alluded to. Scott Douglass was the county prosecutor.

"The man, Mr. Rosenberg, is with the FBI. Like I said, Brax. There are people with strong opinions who will oppose this. But there's also a concern that the Klan will get involved. They're not a huge presence here, but outside Takasaw, in other parts of McMahon County, they're pretty strong. Mr. Douglass had worked with Mr. Rosenberg in the past and felt we needed him here to guide us through some potential problems."

Brax nodded, trying to urge his father. Before Harold could continue, Peggy exited the kitchen and joined them at the table.

"What are you two talking about? You seem so serious."

"The bi-racial council," Harold said.

"Oh. Well, that is serious," Peggy said, turning toward Brax. "What do you think of it all?"

"I don't know what I'm supposed to think. Mixing ... um, integrating Takasaw High, doesn't sound like that bad an idea, I guess. But ... I don't know, really. Some people ain't ..."

"Some people *aren't*," Peggy interjected.

"Some people *aren't* going to be happy. Andy for one."

"Your cousin Andy?" Harold asked, looking from Brax to Peggy and back.

"Yeah. He was asking questions about it last night. He seemed to know what you were doing, and he wasn't too happy."

"Harold," Peggy intervened, "I sent him home. Andy got a little out of line while you were meeting."

"Sheez," Harold said in frustration. "If Andy knows about this, no telling how many people know. But I'm not worried about the Andy Ladukes of the world. Just the hotheads."

"Coach Halliday knows, too," Brax offered.

"Halliday? Well, I'm kind of surprised — though that explains at least one of the leaks. Actually, he probably should be one of the first to know. He'll have to teach in the environment we're about to hand him. If he bucks this, it may not work."

"He's not worried about teaching. But he is wondering about coaching them."

"What's that, Brax?"

"Dad, he wants to talk to you."

"I guess we should, at the right time. But he isn't going to be able to stop it, once we get everything going."

"I don't think he wants to stop it."

"What do you mean?"

"He kind of feels the way I do. It's not such a bad idea. And he wants a quarterback."

"You've lost me, son."

"He wants Moses Burks to be one of the Negroes y'all send to the high school."

Harold's head reared as he burst out laughing. "Hardass ...

"*Harold!*" Peggy said sternly.

" 'Scuse, me. *Coach* Halliday wants himself a quarterback. Now I've heard it all. Damn if he wouldn't have himself a helluva quarterback. I've seen you guys play. And the paper claims he's the best quarterback the Negro school has ever had."

Peggy laughed, forgetting to reprimand her husband.

"To be honest, we haven't even considered that," Harold continued. "All we're talking about is getting these kids in school. Nine of them, hand-picked. We want to find the best nine Negro high school students out there. We want them hand-picked so that no one can say they're not properly prepared for a white school. But no one has even brought up the idea that any of them might play ball. I don't know how that'll go over."

Brax let the words sink in. If the colored kids were coming, wouldn't it make sense to let them play ball, play in the band, do whatever everyone else did?

Especially if one of the new students was Moses.

"Will you talk to Coach Halliday about this?"

"Absolutely. When are you going to see him again?"

"Tomorrow."

"Good, then. Tell him to come see me in the next couple of days. Tell him he doesn't need to make an appointment."

* * * *

Two of the five light poles illuminating the baseball field at Lightfoot Park were out, leaving much of the left side of the diamond in murky shadows.

Maybe that had explained the error – a worm-burning ground ball that shot through Brax's legs at shortstop. Or maybe he didn't make the play because he had too much on his mind.

Halliday was in the stands and was watching Brax's every move.

Nothing new there, except Brax knew the reason this time had nothing to do with sports. And Katie Sullivan was two rows above, with Mr. and Mrs. Seaver and the twins. Freeman was accustomed to playing before small crowds, but outside of one school dance, when his mother had goaded him into asking Betty Sue Miller, he hadn't really had a date. Nor had he really wanted one that bad. Dancing and girlfriends would come later.

At least until Katie came back to town.

"Move in, Brax. Move in." Brax glanced to his left. Kyle Anderson, playing second, was motioning him to move up. In the dugout, Coach Crumpton was furiously waving Kyle and Brax in, to double-play depth. With runners now on the corners, he was willing to give a run for the chance at two outs.

Crumpton had been slurring his words a little before the game, a sure sign he'd had a nip or two before arrival. He always had a nip or two when Charlie Jr., his son, was scheduled to pitch. He had plenty of reason to drink: Junior had a mean fastball -- and no idea where it would go.

The stocky Notasulga catcher was up. First at-bat, he'd rifled one into the thicket bordering the outfield. There was no fence at Lightfoot Park. A ring of brush and weeds formed a perimeter, which measured a distant four-hundred feet from home plate in center field that hardly anyone reached. Even if you did, a home run wasn't automatic. Ground rules said you continued to play the ball. Outfielders would often go looking into the mess, which extended another fifteen feet. More often than not, the outfielder would return after a futile search, the ball nowhere to be found. Little kids would scurry out of the bleachers in search of the ball as play resumed, often finding it with an accompanied, "Here 'tis! Here 'tis!" and then trade the ball for a free snow cone at the concession stand.

His head drifting back to the game, Brax summed up the Takasaw dilemma. The Notasulga catcher moved fairly well, so the double play wasn't a given. Even then, Junior had to keep the ball low enough to induce a grounder.

Two balls, not even close. Then Junior came back with a change up that must have looked like a beach ball. Too eager, the Notasulga catcher swung from the heels before the ball arrived.

"Atta boy, Junior!" Brax yelled. *Geez, you got lucky.*

Junior's brother, Chip, signaled for a fastball. Junior nodded, checked the runner at first, then third, and threw low and inside.

The anxious hitter swung again, scorching a bouncer into the hole. The Takasaw third baseman didn't react initially, and the ball scooted out of reach. Brax moved with the contact, backhanded the ball and righted himself quickly to throw to where Kyle was supposed to be.

Anderson got there just in time, took the throw high and made the pivot cleanly.

"You're outta there!" The bases umpire signaled the second out. One run in, two men down.

"Good turn!" Brax grinned at Anderson.

The double play seemed to give Junior some confidence. He threw three fastballs to retire the next batter on strikes.

In the dugout, Brax took a seat at the far end. He was due up sixth in the inning, if it went that far. The kid out at the scoreboard had yet to post Notasulga's latest run, which made it 5-3 in the bottom of the fifth.

"Freeman," said Halliday, peering around the near corner.

Brax got up, then looked for Crumpton, who was talking to the first batter of the inning at the on-deck circle. Halliday seemed to sense Brax's delay.

"Charlie, I gotta talk to Freeman for a minute."

Crumpton glanced over, nodded, and returned to his task.

Brax followed Halliday, who'd already begun walking down the third-base line, where the small crowd had thinned.

They stood, watching the first batter work the count to 2-2. Halliday hadn't said a thing, but he'd spit twice, aiming the tobacco juice between webs of wire mesh on the fence. The splatter dripped messily.

The first batter drew a walk, bringing the number eight hitter, Chip Crumpton to the plate.

"Had a good talk with your daddy today," Halliday said, punctuating the conversation with another *pa-thump* of expelled tobacco juice.

And?

Halliday and Brax watched Chip crumple to the plate when a fastball nicked him on the left shoulder. He lingered for a minute. When neither the ump nor the catcher showed any concern, Chip slowly rose, dusted off red clay and glowered back at the pitcher, who smiled wickedly in return.

"It was a good talk," Halliday began. "They're doing what I'd heard they'd be doing. 'Cept they hadn't planned on the colored kids playing ball. Said we might make it work."

"With Moses?"

"Shit, yeah. Won't work without him."

Pa-thump.

Damn, Brax thought. *A clean shot, right through the fence and onto the grass. That's a first.*

"Got a couple of problems, but I think I can fix it," Halliday said. "The Negroes they're bringing gotta speak two languages. Think Moses can?"

"Damn, Coach. I don't know. Hell, I can't hardly. I've had just one year of Spanish."

"I can fix that, I can fix that," Halliday said. As the number nine hitter, Kyle, took a called third strike, Halliday turned to face Freeman for the first time.

"I've already started, in fact. I've talked to the Spanish teacher at the Institute, and she's willing to work with the boy the rest of this summer and try to get him ready. Now, I gotta talk to others on this committee and make damn sure he's included. Your dad says not to even mention that Burks might play football for us. We'll worry about that after we get the colored kids into school."

Here's the other problem: They're only bringing in seniors.

Junior hit a weak grounder to third. The Notasulga third baseman bobbled the ball once, twice, but recovered to beat the runner to third for the second out.

"Freeman? Freeman?" Crumpton was coaching third. He spotted Brax and Halliday. "You're on deck, son."

"Yes sir."

He took a step toward the dugout. Halliday grabbed the loose flannel jersey.

"One question, Freeman. Is Burks smart enough for all this? Or am I wasting my God-damn time?"

It seemed like a dumb question. True, Brax had never taken a class with Moses, nor had they ever talked much about school. But he seemed as smart as anyone else.

"Yeah, I don't see why not."

Halliday released his grip.

"Damn, that's good son," Halliday said with a chuckle that released a sliver of tobacco juice onto his lower lip. "We're going to have one helluva football team."

"Coach, he's as smart as anyone we've got," Brax said. He searched for his batting helmet and his favorite bat, a 34-ounce Louisville slugger – Stan the Man's model.

The Notasulga pitcher was well over 6-feet tall and skinny as a snake. A regular *Ichabod Crane,* thought Brax every time he faced him, finally pulling something useful out of that tenth grade American Lit class.

Ichabod had a so-so fastball. But he never showed it to Brax. Play summer ball against the same towns long enough and everyone knows your weaknesses. Brax's was the curve. He always struggled with the curve.

Digging his spikes in at the plate, Brax was determined not to see a curve. *Don't let him get ahead of the count. Make him throw a fastball.*

Leaning toward the plate, hands on his left knee, the pitcher peered in for the signal.

"Freeman!" Crumpton yelled from the third-base coaches' box. Brax threw his right hand up signaling for time, which the ump granted.

Brax had forgotten to get the signal from Crumpton. He looked over and got the sign he didn't want. A touch of the bill of his cap, a swipe across the letters meant Crumpton was telling him to take the first pitch.

He knows I can't hit a curve, yet he's forcing me to hit one.

The Notasulga pitcher went into his stretch and delivered a waist-high fastball, right down the middle.

"Stee-rike one!"

"You can do it, Braxton Freeman!" yelled a female from the stands. It had to be Katie Sullivan, but Brax was too embarrassed to look.

Brax stepped out of the box and fixed back in on Crumpton. Kyle Anderson was standing atop the dugout steps, mouthing "Bobcats" – proof it had, indeed, been Katie.

Again, Crumpton gave him the take sign.

Brax could hear Halliday in his head. "That Crumpton's weakness," the old football coach always said, "is that he thinks he knows the game. Let the kids play."

Brax couldn't agree more. Obviously, Crumpton thought Brax had a good chance to draw a walk. But in the process, he was digging himself too big a hole by taking fastballs he could hit.

The stretch. The pitch.

"Stee-rike two!" Another fat fastball.

At least I won't get another take sign.

Brax choked up on the bat a half-inch and opened his stance, bringing the left foot out a little. If the guy threw a curve on the inside of the plate, he had a chance to hit it squarely. If he came in with a fastball on the outside, Brax was done.

But he wouldn't throw a fastball.

The curve came, just as Brax expected. It began toward the middle of the plate, low. Brax lunged at the pitch as the ball began to make its sharp sweep to the outside.

"Clack!" the ball rolled weakly off his bat, foul.

"Nice swing," mocked the stocky catcher. "Real nice."

Brax grinned. He was right. It was a weak-ass swing.

Two strikes. The Notasulga pitcher still had room to flirt with a curve.

It came again. Again, Brax fouled it off. At least this time it sizzled a little, alas 10 feet foul of first base.

There wasn't any sense guessing. He knew what was coming. If the Notasulga pitcher had the balls to throw a fastball, he deserved the strikeout. But he didn't, and he wouldn't. Brax knew that.

He returned his grip to the base of the bat. He closed his stance, then took a lateral step toward the pitcher.

If he hangs it, I'll get it. Just drive it into the outfield.

The pitcher leaned in again and nodded at the first sign given. He went into his stretch, ignoring the runners, then kicked toward the plate.

The ball came on the inside of the plate. Brax jumped on it, driving with his legs and hips.

The sound of the sweet spot of the bat making contact resonated throughout the park. Brax drove it, the ball taking off in a fast-rising arc toward center field.

One run in. Brax looped around first. The ball continued to climb. As he took the first step toward second, the ball disappeared beyond the thicket. He'd be at third before the center fielder even got to edge of the grass. Brax hit second and dug in for third.

In the coaches' box, Crumpton was waving him home like a madman.

Two runs in. Three runs in. Brax hit the bag at third and glanced back. The center fielder was nowhere to be seen. Brax crossed the plate, past the catcher standing with his arms akimbo, before the outfielder picked up the ball.

"Grand slam! Grand slam! Way to go B-Bear!" Anderson was the first one to grab him as he turned toward the dugout. The rest of his teammates stood behind Kyle, thumping Brax on his helmet.

The two-run lead would be all Junior needed. He retired Notasulga in order in the sixth and worked a pair of strikeouts and a lazy pop up to right field around a walk in the seventh for the win.

The Takasaw players were still celebrating throughout Crumpton's postgame meeting. He didn't care.

With Kyle slapping him on the back, Brax got up from his kneeled stance and looked back toward the stands. His parents were still sitting, smiling. Peggy waved. He then began looking for Katie.

Where was she?

"Hi, Braxton," she said. She'd walked behind the dugout to greet him and met him with a quick, unexpected hug. "Congratulations."

"Thanks." He couldn't stop beaming. The grand slam was only half the reason. "Thanks."

The Seavers were walking up behind Katie. Mrs. Seaver was holding the hand of one of the twins. The other was asleep on Mr. Seaver's shoulder.

"Congratulations, son," said Mr. Seaver, extending a hand.

"Thank you, sir. Thank you. I got lucky."

"Lucky? No, that was a blast."

Brax's face ached as the grin expanded. How goofy must he look?

Mrs. Seaver spoke as Katie grinned back at Brax. "We're looking forward to having you over for dinner tomorrow night, Brax. Have you two figured out what you're going to see?"

"Uh, no ma'am," Brax replied. "Really, this is our first chance to talk."

"Tell you what," Mr. Seaver said, shifting the sleeping twin from one shoulder to the another. "You kids talk for a minute while we get the girls in the car."

Brax grinned his acquiescence. When the Seavers had turned toward the parking lot, Katie grabbed one of his hands.

"Aunt Susan got the Montgomery paper this morning. *To Kill a Mockingbird* is playing at the Paramount at seven-thirty."

"That would be great, great," Brax said. Would it? He'd heard of the book. *Who's the movie star? Bill Holden? Did it even matter?* "Yeah, great. Will we have time?"

"Sure. Dinner right at five sharp. We'll have plenty of time to get there."

"Great," Brax said, the words eclipsed by the grin. *What a heck of a fine day.*

CHAPTER 3

BRAXTON WAS STRUGGLING to cut the chicken with his fork, just the way Peggy Freeman had made him do at the dinner table. It was an unnatural act, made more unnatural by the nervousness of the situation: Saturday supper at the Seavers.

"Son," Heathcliff Seaver said, getting Brax's attention. Seaver didn't say anything, but a wink as he bit into a plump chicken breast held in his two hands delivered the message.

So intent on not embarrassing himself with bad manners, Brax had not dared more than a passing glance around the table. He finally took the gamble and realized everyone else -- even Mrs. Seaver and Katie -- was eating the fried chicken with their hands.

He hadn't been able to do much all day. He'd worked a four-hour shift at the country club in the morning, long enough to see Katie and the bobcats sunning again. That didn't help.

Then he'd headed home, spending most of the afternoon watching NBC's game of the week. Who else, but the Yankees and Tigers?

He watched all nine innings of the game -- Whitey Ford was pitching, so that was a plus. Normally, Brax couldn't stay indoors long enough to watch an entire game, except for the World Series, but he'd done it this day. And he'd done it alone. Sure, Peggy had traipsed in and out of the living room all afternoon, but Harold Freeman was off at a "meeting." No specifics were provided.

None were needed. All Brax had on his mind was not screwing up his big date.

He'd spent an hour trying to decide what to wear. Madras shirt and khakis? Jeans and a T-shirt. *Not for a date.*

Brax Freeman, who never gave fashion a thought couldn't make up his mind. Enter Peggy, who picked out the wardrobe: Carolina blue

41

cotton button-down shirt, half-wool/half-polyester tan slacks and his blue blazer.

"Too dressy?"

"No," Peggy said, giving him the final once over. "Very classy. Very good first impression."

With Brax free to attack the chicken with his hands, the dinner went surprisingly well. The Seavers kept the conversation simple, focusing on the school year ahead for their niece and her new beau. The twins piped in every once awhile, but were well behaved.

By six, Brax was at the wheel of the Freeman family sedan. Katie sat next to him at a comfortable distance. The Atlanta Highway, the only major road heading east into the capital city -- at least until the interstate was finally completed -- was a simple drive.

Best of all, you could pick up the Montgomery radio stations when you hit Shorter. Harold Freeman usually tuned it to a station in Auburn that played the lame stuff, like Sinatra and big band music. The only other choices in Takasaw were the country stations and black gospel.

"You like rock 'n roll?" Brax asked, fiddling with the dial.

"You bet."

He had the perfect answer. WHHY out of Montgomery. Carl Perkins singing *Blue Suede Shoes*. Drum accompaniment on the steering wheel by Brax Freeman.

"Do you like the Beatles?" Katie asked.

"The what?"

"The Beatles? They're new."

"I've never heard of them."

"I don't know how to describe them, really. It's rock 'n roll, but it's different. And they're adorable," she said. "They've got a hit song, *She Loves You*. Heard it?"

"Oh, yeah." Brax knew the song, not the group's name. Truth is, he had better things to do than listen to the radio.

At least he didn't have to do much of the talking. Katie talked enough for both of them. For 10 people, actually. She went on and on about her high school, Mountain Brook, about cheerleading, about living in a big city like Birmingham. And how good it was to get away for the summer, going back to Takasaw.

Brax's contribution: A nod of his head, a grunt of approval or a thrown in "Uh-huh." She was making him even more comfortable by not making him participate in the conversation.

The Atlanta Highway hit the outskirt of Montgomery through the eastern suburbs. New and old subdivisions quickly gave way to shopping centers, strip malls and brick business buildings before the highway merged with Madison Avenue.

Paterson Field, the ballpark home of the minor league baseball team, stood on the right, a cliff covered with ivy providing the backdrop in right field. To the left stood stately Cramton Bowl, easily, Brax figured, the grandest high school football stadium in all of Alabama. It served as the home of the annual Blue-Gray All-Star Game every December, but also hosted the two Montgomery public high schools on Friday nights. Takasaw had played Lanier there Brax's sophomore season. Lanier creamed Takasaw, but Brax couldn't get over the rows and rows of bleachers climbing into the heavens. The stadium must have seated 10,000 people – every man, woman and child and Takasaw, and then some.

Madison Avenue climbed a gentle hill that leveled off before beginning a steep descent. Downtown Montgomery lay ahead full of four- and five-story skyscrapers -- none more majestic than the old First Alabama Bank building.

The Paramount was a grand Hollywood movie house, standing two stories tall, with a brick face. There wasn't a single parking space available on the street, so Brax drove around a couple of blocks until he spotted one.

He hopped out of the car. Katie remained in the passenger's seat, taking in downtown Montgomery.

What's she waiting on? Brax wondered. Then it hit him. *Open the door, idiot.*

He did, bowing in a self-deprecating nod to his forgetfulness. She stepped out elegantly. Katie was wearing a yellow gingham dress with a white sash. She had yellow shoes on her feet and a white bow in her hair that framed short bangs and left the rest flowing in the back.

As good as she'd looked at the pool and the ballpark, she now looked better. She seemed older, more mature.

Totally out of his league.

Brax took her hand to cross the street, not to be forward but to make sure an oncoming car didn't end the date early with a splatter. Safely across, he checked his watch. They still had a good half hour to spare.

"Do you like to read?"

"Of course, silly," Katie said with her first giggle of the night.

"I know a great bookstore. C'mon."

Capitol Books stood diagonally across the street from the Paramount. It had a great selection of Sunday newspapers from across the country, including *The New York Times, The Chicago Tribune and The Atlanta Constitution,* as well as all the latest periodicals. When the Freemans headed to downtown Montgomery, Harold Freeman always made a stop at Capitol Books. He'd never leave without a couple of out-of-town newspapers under his arm and a magazine or two in tow.

What Brax liked best was the wide selection. Not just the current bestsellers, but aisles of specialty books: Sports periodicals, historical non-fiction, and one biography after another. When he was younger, Brax would always try to talk his dad into the latest Chip Hilton story, the fictional series by NYU basketball coach Claire Bee. He didn't read as much now. He didn't have the time for pleasure reading, what with the year-round reading list his English teacher provided. And every one of those books, dusty and yellowing, was available at the Takasaw Public Library.

He allowed Katie to lead, and she gravitated toward the back, where she found an entire row on dance. Boring stuff.

"Oh, my gosh," she said, leaning toward the bottom row to pull a thick book, full of photos, featuring a colored woman on the cover.

"Have you ever heard of her?" Katie asked, causing Brax to squint at the title.

Josephine Baker. Who?

"No. Who is she?"

"Who *was* she," Katie corrected. "Josephine Baker, an American colored woman who became the rage in Paris after the first World War."

Brax nodded with little interest.

Katie lowered her voice, then leaned toward Brax. "She was known for dancing naked in public."

She had his attention now.

"She was scandalous. She married a white man. But she was supposed to be a really great dancer and singer."

Katie put the novel down and moved up the aisle to the travel selection. A coffee table book featuring a photo of the Eiffel Tower -- even Brax recognized it -- got her attention.

"That's where I want to go, Paris, France," she said. "What about you?"

"I hadn't given it much thought," Brax replied. "Yeah, I think I would."

"I want to go there for my honeymoon some day," Katie continued. "I want to live there, on the West Bank, and paint for a living."

Brax nodded. He couldn't picture Katie in Paris, but he could picture some of the Parisian models he and Kyle had looked at time and time again. Kyle's father had an exotic magazine he had stashed at the bottom of the trunk in the cellar. Neither understood much of the wording, all in French. But they understood the pictures. Beautiful, naked women. With hair coming out of their armpits.

He and Kyle agreed. Except for the underarms, they were gorgeous. As good as anybody in *Playboy*, except when Jayne Mansfield posed.

But he'd never actually thought about going to Paris. New York, maybe. The only person in Takasaw he'd ever heard of going to Paris was Scott Douglass' father, Brantley Allen Douglass, at the end of WWI.

"Paris would be nice," he said.

"What do you want to do?" Katie asked.

"See the movie."

"No, silly," she laughed. "When you grow up, what do you want to do?"

Geez, Brax thought. *I just turned 17. How do I know?*

So he thought out loud.

"Play college ball, I guess. Coach says I've got a chance to play somewhere next year, but I don't know 'bout that. If I don't play football at a big school I'll probably play baseball at a smaller school. Ever heard of Presbyterian College?"

Katie shook her head affirmatively.

"It's in South Carolina. They've signed a couple of guys from Takasaw in the past, guys ahead of me in school. It's supposed to be a good school. Since I'm Presbyterian, it would be a good fit. And I could play ball to pay for the tuition and room and board."

Katie continued to listen, but Brax was done.

"But what about after college, Brax?"

She's thinking ahead. What is this? The inquisition?

"I don't know. Guess I'll become an accountant, like my dad, and come back to Takasaw. Maybe go into business with him. Freeman and Freeman, CPAs, I guess."

The answer apparently wasn't what Katie Sullivan was looking for.

"Brax, don't you want to get out of Takasaw? Out of Alabama?"

"Yeah, at some point, I guess. But I like it here. What about you?"

"No," she said strangely. Brax gave her a quizzical look. "There have got to be better places than Takasaw, than Birmingham, than Alabama. That's what my parents have always said to me."

"Well, I think Alabama's just fine."

"It is now," Katie said. "But ..."

Brax was getting impatient. He was being forced to carry too much of the conversation now. An absent-minded check of his watch showed it was a quarter past seven.

"Hey, Katie, we better get a move on and get our tickets."

She shrugged her shoulders and followed him out of the store and across the street.

* * * *

The bright lights flashed twice. Andy Laduke stubbed the last of his cigarette against the cinder block wall and jogged the 30 yards.

The pickup was full. Three men were in the cab, four more in the bed. Andy jumped in the open back and slid down to sit. The passenger's door opened, and a balding blond got out and joined Laduke and the others. Hooking his thumb at Laduke, he motioned toward the cab.

"Keith wants you up there with him."

Laduke jumped out, excited to have the invitation. Another man piled out of the passenger's side, holding the door open so Andy could squeeze in the middle.

He did, and the driver brought his right hand down fast, slapping Laduke hard on the lower thigh. Ashes from his own cigarette spilled onto Andy and the worn fabric of the truck.

"Hah! We goin' to have some fun tonight, boy!" Keith said. "You up for it?"

"Yes'm," Andy said. "Yes'm."

"Then put this on when we get there, boy," Keith said, handing Laduke a thick, folded white fabric.

Keith Lockett put the truck in gear and headed down the dark rural road away from the house as Laduke began slipping the robe over his clothes, not wanting to waste time.

Andy knew most of McMahon County, but he soon lost his bearings. A turn here, another there, from pavement to dirt road, back to pavement. At one point, Lockett cut through the yard of a farmer. The meandering trip continued for 30 minutes until Laduke could see a soft glow in the distance.

It was his first Klan rally. He was one of the boys now.

The truck pulled into a makeshift parking lot, a patch of grass-covered farmland somewhere out in the boonies. Dozens of white-robed and hooded men stood casually, while a fire to warm the night burned in a metal trashcan.

A 20-foot cross had been erected, but had not yet been lit.

Five men spilled out of the bed of Lockett's pickup, accentuating the arrival with whoops, pulling on hoods as they joined the others. Andy put his hood on in the truck and was surprised it fit so well. The holes were arranged perfectly. His peripheral field of vision was almost complete.

Only Keith Lockett remained in his civvies. He was reaching behind his seat, where he pulled out a fabric much like the one he had given Andy. Except it was dark red, with gold piping around the neck and arms.

Two things impressed Andy: The solid, muscular forearms Lockett displayed as he slipped the cardinal robe on and the hunting knife hooked to the back belt loop of his jeans.

The McMahon County Chapter of the Knights of the Ku Klux Klan had convened for a meeting. Now it could start. Keith Lockett, the imperial lieutenant, had arrived.

Without a word or command, the men milling around the fire began forming a perfect circle around the cross. Two men ran to the middle, carrying gallon cans, and began dousing the lower third with kerosene. A third man followed behind and ignited the cross with a torch.

Andy quickly fell in line, but Lockett grabbed him.

"Follow me, neophyte."

Laduke fell in line behind Lockett, who took a stand 10 feet in front of the now roaring fire. He was joined by a man in a maroon robe, the Grand Dragon. Even with the hood on, Laduke knew it was Albert Simmons, the county's public face to the KKK.

"Brothers, we have gathered here," Simmons began, using the rhythmic cadence of a tent evangelist, "to welcome a new member into our brotherhood! A new member, worthy of being a McMahon County Knight. A new member, who will help us in our eternal and righteous fight!"

A loud chant began. A frightening chant, unintelligible to Andy, yet thrilling. He could feel the pricks on his arms and the back of his neck as Goosebumps formed.

"Neophyte, come here!"

Andy, standing just behind Lockett, moved forward as he'd been directed to earlier. He kneeled before the grand dragon, head bowed, eyes closed.

"This neophyte has been brought before us on the recommendation of a worthy brethren, our imperial lieutenant! We are told he has the courage, that he has the blessings of the Lord Almighty God, that he has what is mandatory and necessary to help us fulfill our mission! We are told that he has the heart and desire to join us! This is what we are told!"

"Yeah, thee, Grand Dragon!" chanted the brotherhood.

"We ask now and forever more, are there any disbelievers? Is there a man among you who can dispute this neophyte's character? His commitment?"

"No, thee! Grand Dragon!"

"Arise, neophyte!"

Laduke rose slowly, as he'd been told, head still bowed.

"You, neophyte, have been asked to join the brotherhood. You have been deemed worthy of inclusion in our great mission! Are you indeed worthy?"

"Yes, sir," Andy said solemnly.

"Then I present you with this." Lockett extended a red patch Laduke would have to have sewn on later. He already knew where it went, over the heart. "Will you swear your allegiance now, to this brotherhood? To our mission?"

"Yes, sir!"

Simmons stepped away, then moved beside Laduke. He extended his arms, raising them skyward.

"Brothers, do you accept this neophyte into our brotherhood?"

"Yea, thee! Grand Dragon!"

"Then let us pray before the cross of Jesus Christ almighty!" Lockett dropped to one knee. As one, the brotherhood copied him. Andy, caught up in ceremony, paused momentarily before following suit. Only Simmons remained standing.

"Lord God Almighty, we ask you, before the cross that represents the sacrifice of your son, to bless our holy mission! And to bless each and every one of these God-fearing, all-American white men who kneel humbly before you! We ask for your constant oversight and your wisdom! In his name, amen."

"Amen!" echoed the brotherhood.

"Whoo-haw!" yelled one of the hooded brothers, and others followed. The meeting was officially adjourned.

Lockett slipped an arm around Laduke's shoulder, pulling him tight as the others broke the circle.

"Boy, we've got big plans for you. All I ask is your full commitment and trust. Can I count on you for that?"

"Yes, sir!" Laduke shouted. "Always, sir!"

"Good, good. Now, let's have some fun!"

Lockett pulled his hood off, folding it in two and stuffing it into the back pocket of his jeans, which he reached by pulling up the ankle-length robe. Like a puppy dog, Laduke did the same. Simmons, after glad-handing a few fellow Klansmen, had headed to his car and was leaving.

Though new to the Klan, Laduke knew enough about the history. The hoods were worn to ensure the privacy of the brotherhood from outsiders. But Alabama, like most states during the nationwide rise of the KKK in the 1920s, had passed anti-hood laws, banning them in public. More ceremonial than anything else, they were meant to disguise and intimidate. Thus, they were still worn on "missions" -- missions Laduke was certain he would be a part of soon.

"What are we gonna do now, Keith?" Laduke asked.

Lockett wheeled. His gray eyes had narrowed, as if they were looking through Andy's soul.

What did I do?

"Stupid shit," Lockett said harshly. "You can call me by my name anytime around civilians. But when you're wearing the uniform, or when you're doing Klan business, you show me the proper respect! You understand me, boy?"

The enthusiasm of the night was gone, replaced by fear. A kind of fear Laduke hadn't known for years. Since ... well, years ago.

He could only lower his head.

"Understand?"

Laduke looked up gently. "Yes, sir. I understand."

"Good, you dumb son of a bitch!" The harshness gone, Lockett popped him on the back. "Wanna know what we're goin' to do? We're goin' to get some beer and get some poontang!"

Lockett a drove a couple miles, toward the next county, pulling in front of a trailer with a wood front stoop. Two kegs of beer were tapped and ready in front of the steps leading to one of two doors. A deep crowd of Klansman sat out front at a weathered picnic table.

"Make room for the new brother!" Lockett said. The cluster separated, allowing Lockett and Laduke leg room while a balding guy handed the two overflowing steins of beer.

"Think you can handle some sweet 'tang, boy?" Lockett asked, leading Laduke out, arm back around him again.

"Yes, sir," Andy said, not believing his luck.

Andy Laduke had never been with a woman. He'd never had a girlfriend and only a couple of dates. Andy Laduke was a loner. He took pride in that. He had a life to lead and didn't need any distractions. Not that the Klan would be a distraction. The Klan would provide the kind of direction he'd never had at home. Not from that drunk old bastard …

Lockett guzzled about half his beer, grabbed Andy by the shoulder with a big paw and told him to follow. He went to the back of the trailer, where there was another door.

"Boy, you're in for a treat," Lockett said. "I'm letting you have a go at the best girl around here. Hope you're man enough."

Lockett was laughing. Did he know how inexperienced Laduke was? What'd he mean?

"Got big plans for you, boy. And this is the first of many rewards to come."

He opened the door. Inside, a young girl roughly Andy's age, with curly, red hair flowing past her shoulders, reclined on a small bed. She was buck naked. She had heavy breasts that swayed with her breathing and a dark mound of red hair below her belly, which was only partially covered by a sheet.

There was a flicker of recognition when the girl saw Andy. But he couldn't make the face out clearly in the dimness. Lockett walked in first.

"Boy, you wait your turn. I get first crack," he said before slamming the door shut.

Andy couldn't see much through the small window, but he could see enough. Lockett pulled the robe up. The girl said nothing, but got off the bed and moved toward him. Embarrassed, Andy turned away.

This was supposed to be an intimate act, but Lockett approached it with a ferociousness, the kind Andy had seen just minutes before when he'd mistakenly called the Klan's second-in-command by his first name.

Though he refused to look, the sounds were fierce. Lockett was mumbling under his breath, cursing, until he let out a long groan. A minute later, everything back in place, he exited with a last word to his conquest.

"Treat my boy good. He's new to this."

The girl nodded showing no emotion, just resignation as she climbed back on the bed.

"She's all yours."

He pushed Andy, who stumbled across the threshold and landed head first on the bed. The girl helped him up the rest of the way as Lockett left the room.

For the first time, Andy looked at the girl's face. Her lipstick was smeared. Her eyes were red and full as if she'd been crying. Who could blame her, considering Lockett's savageness? Half of Andy wanted to leave, but the stirring inside was overwhelming.

Then he recognized her. Donna … Donna what? He couldn't remember the name, but he definitely remembered the face. Donna … Donna … She'd been a year ahead of him at Takasaw High. He'd never talked to her, yet he spent two years, at least until he dropped out, imagining what it would be like if he had the courage to approach her and ask her out for a date.

Imagining, better still, that she'd accepted.

"I know you, don't I?" she said. The voice was delicate, but monotone.

"Yeah," Andy said nervously. "I think we went to school together."

"What's your name?"

Was he supposed to say? It was a Klan function, where some form of anonymity was expected.

He whispered, "Andy. We went to high school together."

"Oh, yeah, Andy," she said. Was the recognition real or merely polite? He couldn't tell.

She didn't say anything. She merely laid back, her head resting on a rolled up towel. What was he supposed to do?

Andy leaned toward her, and tried to kiss her on the lips. She pulled away, shaking her head and he was suddenly thankful when he realized why she stopped him. Instead, she grabbed the front of his jeans and began yanking them down. He caught on and helped and she reached out again and discovered he was ready.

It didn't last long. She pushed him on his back and slowly moved on top of him. He expected the first time to be filled with fireworks and passion, yet it was over before she lowered herself a third time.

"Baby, that was good," she said in a low moan. She fell forward on top of him, draping her hair over his chest and holding him tight. Despite his disappointment, the afterglow was better than the act itself.

He hoped the moment never ended.

* * * *

The sleep felt luxurious, and getting to bed so early had, indeed, been a luxury for Moses Burks. Saturday night was the lone night he had off and he'd fallen asleep before the sun had dropped over the horizon.

But now he woke up with a start, stirred by an acrid smell. Even in a groggy state, it just took him a second to realize the culprit.

Josiah, sharing the tight quarters of the small bed, had peed in his sleep yet again.

Shaking his head, Moses got out of bed and retrieved a dirty towel from the hamper, moving Josiah enough to slip it under him to absorb the mess.

Even though he wasn't wearing a shirt, Moses was covered in sweat. Adele couldn't afford an air conditioning unit, and the heat, combined with the proximity of Josiah, proved unbearable. Moses had to get out of the house.

As quiet as he could, he opened the squeaky screen door to his bedroom and headed out the back of the house and into the woods, about a quarter of a mile on the trail he and Brax had cut through years of adventures. In a small clearing he found his spot.

A large rock, covered with moss often proved to be his refuge on stifling nights and it did again as he laid down and felt the immediate coolness.

He gazed into the stars as he began plotting an exit. He had to get out of Takasaw somehow. He loved Adele and Josiah. He had plenty of friends. But he would be living the same way, in a cramped house, making next to nothing, if he didn't get away somehow.

College was the answer and football the ticket. Letters were trickling in expressing interest in him, from Alabama State, Morehouse, Tennessee State and Grambling. The latter was the most impressive, because he knew the name Eddie Robinson and was impressed by the embossed lettering that looked so stylish and expensive.

There were also letters from schools he'd never heard of, like Kent State and Miami of Ohio. White schools, he reckoned, not stuck in the segregated South.

The coaches at Takasaw Institute talked to him all the time, stopping by his practices and classes. He was welcomed there, he knew, and he couldn't get a better education. But to stay in town, to stay at home, meant he was giving up on getting out.

Moses gazed heavenward, until his eyes became heavy and he slipped into a dream.

* * * *

All through the courtroom scene, as Gregory Peck pleaded his client's innocence, Katie Sullivan held Brax's arm in a vise. It wasn't a scary movie, but the darkness of the Paramount added to the suspense. For that, Brax was thankful.

The movie had her transfixed, but Brax was bored – bored even with the great Peck's histrionics. By the time they'd arrived at the Paramount, most of the seats had been taken. They'd walked down both aisles in the lower section without finding side-by-side vacancies. Up in the balcony, as the previews began flickering on the screen, they'd found an empty row of four seats two rows from the top.

Trying not to be obvious, he kept sneaking glances to his right. In the back row, a couple no older than he and Katie had been making out the entire movie, stopping only for a few nibbles of popcorn before resuming their frantic kissing. If only he could see better without drawing attention to himself. The guy's left hand had disappeared into his date's blouse.

Katie drew him back to the movie by tugging his arm. Had she noticed? Or was she reacting to the climax of the scene?

It was the movie. Her gaze remained unabated, straight ahead at the handsome Peck.

He looked into her face, the oval eyes with the long lashes, the button nose, and a slight overbite. No, Brax knew instantly, he had never been this close to this pretty a girl before.

He followed the goody trail, the fine blonde hair, the longish neck and the bronzed shoulders to the magnificent bobcats, the tops peeking at him from the dress, with just a hint of cleavage showing.

Brax felt the stirring again and was thankful Kyle Anderson was nowhere to be seen.

The movie, the movie.

He was able to return his attention to the film as it reached a conclusion. The houselights lit the theater. Katie turned to Brax.

"Let's watch the credits," Freeman said.

They scrolled slowly as Brax tried to match the stars' names with the lineup of characters. Peck, he knew. Robert Duval? Never heard of him. What was the Negro's name? Had he missed it?

The theater had thinned, with the first wave of the audience for the late show trickling in, as Brax led Katie out the exit door and back to the car.

They had just passed the state office buildings that surround the Alabama capitol when Katie kick started conversation. Unlike the drive to Montgomery, she made it clear Brax would have to participate.

"What a wonderful movie. Didn't you think so, Braxton?"

"Sure. Great. That Gregory Peck sure can act."

"He's dreamy."

"I liked that Duval guy. The one who played Boo Radley. That was a strong performance," Brax said, as if he had a clue.

"Who played Boo Radley?"

"Robert Duval. New guy."

"Oh. He *was* good."

"Yep."

The silence lasted only a few seconds.

"I really liked it, Brax. Do you think it was true?"

"True? The story?"

"Not true, as in it happened. I know it was made up. But true, as in it could happen."

"Don't know."

"I mean it was set a long time ago, in Alabama. Small-town Alabama. Do you think a colored could be treated like that?"

"I don't know. I mean, I reckon."

"I don't know if it would happen like that. Not in Birmingham. Not that way, at least. I mean, any time some colored person gets in trouble now, they've got to march somewhere, protest something."

"Yeah, times have changed."

Katie grew quiet as Brax passed the Cramton Bowl again. It had looked majestic earlier, in the dying sunlight. Now, in the darkness, it loomed eerily. He could remember the game he played there, how bright the lights were, as if they were playing a day game.

He could see Katie stifling a yawn out of the corner of his eye. It was getting late.

She's tired. Or bored. Think of something to say.

It took him a few minutes. In his limited experience, he'd never had to talk much to a girl. They did the talking. And he always could pretend he was listening. Besides, Katie had done nearly all of the talking. But now, she wasn't saying a thing.

"There's talk that they're going to bring Negroes into our school this fall," Brax said.

"No, really? Colureds at Takasaw High?"

"Yep."

More silence.

"What do you think of that, Katie?"

"I'm glad it's not my school," she said seriously.

"I don't think it's such a bad idea."

She turned to him, her oval eyes looking at him differently.

"You don't? Gosh, I've got nothing against coloreds. But I wouldn't want to go to school with them."

If only he'd kept his mouth shut … His inexperience was showing. Should he change the subject? Or dive right in?

"It's not so much going to school with 'em that I like, it's just that we should have one of our best teams in years," Brax said. "And one of the Negroes, Moses Burks, a guy who lives down the street from me, is a pretty good ballplayer. He'd put us over the top."

"Well, it will not happen at my school. Honestly, I've never met a colored kid my age, except for the children of my maid. We don't have any coloreds in Mountain Brook, thank God."

More silence. Lesson learned

"I thought the movie was a little too long, to be honest," Brax said, grasping.

"That's what I'm talking about."

"Huh?"

"The problem with coloreds is they don't know their place anymore. You can't read the newspaper or watch TV in Birmingham any more without finding some kind of trouble they're causing, Brax. Daddy says they want to go to our schools, they want to live in our neighborhoods. They want to be just like us."

"Yeah, I guess," Brax said.

"I just don't think it's a good idea. They have their place. We have ours. Thank goodness we have Governor Wallace."

"Yeah, guess so," Brax said. *This ain't working.*

Mt. Meigs, a sign he'd seen often but a town he'd never visited, appeared on the highway marker. He was a half-hour from Takasaw, from freedom, from dropping Katie off and going home to his own world -- free of conversation, free of conflict.

"It's just not going to happen at my school," Katie said after a few minutes of silence. "There isn't a single colored person in the Mountain Brook city limits. And there never will be."

Brax remembered the time his dad had driven the family through Mountain Brook, to show him where the Sullivans lived, on the way through Birmingham for a conference in Nashville. It was a neighborhood of stately homes, manicured lawns, expensive cars on large lots nestled on sloping hills. Brax was so used to the flat terrain of Takasaw. But Birmingham had mountains -- small mountains, he guessed, but mountains nonetheless. And it looked like the costly homes in Mountain Brook had been built on the side of the biggest mountain he'd ever seen.

The silence continued even as Brax pulled off the highway onto the Shorter road, a shortcut back to town. He glanced at his Timex. It wasn't eleven. The Seavers had set curfew at midnight, so he'd get Katie home early, make a good impression.

The Seavers lived a good mile outside the city. As Brax turned onto her road, Katie grabbed his arm again. It was the first attention she'd shown him since their conversation ended abruptly.

"What time is it, Brax?"

"I don't know," he lied. "He looked at his watch and read the dial in the shadows. "Let's see. Not quite eleven."

"I've got to be home by midnight."

"I know. We got back quicker than I thought."

She was still clutching his arm. But now, it was soft, almost a caress.

"It's too early to go home. Let's go somewhere."

"Ok. Yeah, sure."

But where? This wasn't the big city, with soda shops open till all hours on a Saturday night. The only places open at this hour were dives where Brax Freeman and Katie Sullivan were not welcome.

He could drive on to Auburn, a half-hour away. It was a campus town, true, and something had to be open on a Saturday night with college kids around. But it would take a half-hour to get there, a half-hour to get back. They'd miss curfew and the good impression he intended to make would sour quickly.

"I doubt anything's open this late, not here," Katie said, the smile returning. "What do teen-agers do late on a Friday or Saturday night in Takasaw?"

You're asking me?

He and Kyle had gone cruising a couple of times. It was unorganized time killing, with teens driving up and down Main Street, whites on one end, blacks at the other. You waved at girls and you sipped a beer, if you were bold enough. You tried to be cool. Once, a couple of dumbasses had driven alongside Brax and Kyle in a station wagon, slowed, then mooned them.

Brax Freeman didn't care much for cruising.

"Well?" Katie asked.

"A lot of the kids go cruising," Brax said, trying to see how Katie reacted. She didn't. "I think that's kinda immature."

"I think it's kind of redneck," she said.

"Yeah."

"Is there a place we could go sit and talk?"

"Yeah, sure," Brax replied. But where? Did Takasaw even have a park?

When he and Kyle wanted to get away from everyone else, they drove over to the high school, parking in the back. They'd go out onto the darkened football field and play pantomime football. A long pass without the ball. A spectacular catch, followed by a stiff arm and a gallant dive into the end zone. Then, they'd collapse onto the turf and stair into the heavens, counting the stars.

But that was Kyle Anderson. Not Katie Sullivan. Brax didn't know any other options.

"It's real quiet over by the high school. We can sit and talk without anyone bothering us."

Katie looked at him gently before releasing his arm for the first time.

"That sounds nice."

He turned into the Takasaw High driveway, following it to the back, behind the cafeteria. There wasn't a soul in sight. The football field, with the rickety wooden stands, stood behind them in the vague blackness.

He turned off the car engine and pivoted toward Katie, who had shifted to face Brax.

"Wanna go out to the football field?" Brax asked.

Katie shook her head. "No. Let's just sit here and talk."

"OK."

Talk about what? Every time they'd talked that night – every time Brax had joined in the conversation -- the date had gone awry.

He made a quick mental note not to bring up the subjects of integration, Negroes or the damn movie. He was still searching for a topic when Katie spoke up. "I know what we could do. Braxton, have you ever played 20 questions?"

"Uh, no. I don't think so."

"We each ask 20 questions. The rules are simple. You take turns. And we have to answer each question honestly."

Brax nodded. "Sounds, uh, fun."

"Good," she said. "I'll start. Question number one: how many children do you want to have?"

Children? Geez. I'm 17 years old. Children?

"Two, I guess," said Brax with a hesitation. It sounded like a good number. Brax and Candace had been all the Freemans ever needed.

He waited for her response. But there was none.

"Uh, what do we do now?" he asked.

"Ask *me* a question, silly."

"OK. Um. How many children do you want to have?"

Katie held her right hand up, fingers extended. "Five. Three boys and two girls. And one dog, a sheepdog. And I want to live in New York -- after I get back from Paris."

That was more information than Brax needed. But Katie seemed to be having fun. She continued. Katie asked and Brax answered, then he parroted her question.

"Question number twelve," she said. She paused, bringing a hand up to cover her grin. "Have you ever kissed a girl?"

There was a light pole off the street in the distance. It gave just a little illumination, enough to cast shadows across Katie's face. But it was enough light that she had to be able to see him blush.

Boys weren't supposed to blush, but Brax Freeman was blushing.

"Geez, what a question," Brax said, bringing his hand to his chin. He hoped he looked like he was deep in thought and not embarrassed.

"Well, Braxton? Got to tell the truth. That's the rule."

"Well, I ... Sure. I've ... uh, kissed plenty of people. My mom, my aunts, my ..."

"No, Braxton Freeman. A girl your age. A romantic kiss. The truth."

"Well, no. Not really. ... I mean, I've had my chances, but ..."

She was laughing. Not laughing at him. Laughing with him. He laughed back. The discomfort was beginning to fade.

"OK. My question. Has Katie Sullivan ever kissed a boy?"

"You know the answer to that."

"Huh?"

"I kissed you last night."

She'd flustered him again. "That's not what I mean. Like you said, a romantic kiss."

"You didn't think that was romantic?" she teased.

"Well ..."

"I know what you mean. The answer is ... no. David Bowden tried to kiss me the school dance last year, but I wouldn't let him."

You're already going to school dances? Damn, Birmingham was a fast town. At Takasaw High, they only allowed the juniors and seniors go to the school dances.

Yet even as a junior, Brax hadn't gone to a dance. None of his friends had. It had seemed kind foolish, really, something for sissies.

"My turn," Katie said, regaining Brax's attention. "Next question, number thirteen."

Brax waited. Was Katie blushing now? The light wasn't good but, yes, she might be.

"Brax, would you like to kiss me?"

She was smiling broadly now. But she had shifted back against the door, creating more distance.

Kiss Katie? Brax had thought about it a lot of times since seeing her on the Fourth of July at the club. He'd thought of freeing the bobcats. He'd thought of flying to the moon, too. Didn't mean any of it would happen.

"Braxton Freeman? The truth."

Did she want the truth? The answer came much easier than the words. Was she playing him for a fool, setting him for humiliation? Or was she serious.

She brought it up, didn't she?

"The truth?" Brax stammered, trying to stall. "The truth ..."

"Yes, the truth, Braxton."

He looked at the squat, perfect nose, the soft lips.

"Yes, Katie. I do."

She giggled. He continued looking at her intently, staring as if she would fall into a trance and make the first move.

"Well, then, kiss me."

He leaned over closer. She remained stapled to the door. Closer, closer. Gently, nervously, he pressed his lips to hers. One second, two seconds, three ...

He broke it off, and returned to his side of the car.

He was flustered. She wasn't.

"Your turn Brax."

"My turn?"

"Your question."

Katie, would you like to make love?

He settled for a more gentle approach. Again, he remained totally unoriginal.

"Would you, Katie Sullivan, like to kiss me?"

"Braxton Freeman. Aren't you forward?"

A rebuff? No, the smile remained there.

"Well?" he asked. It was his question. It was his turn to grow impatient.

"Not like you kissed me."

What did I do wrong?

"You didn't like it, Katie?"

"I liked it. Only ... only, it was like kissing my grandmother."

She was still smiling. If she was trying to humiliate him, she was doing so expertly.

"I don't think I ever kissed my grandma like that," Brax said indignantly.

She ignored him. "Braxton, do you know what a French kiss is?"
Duh. He nodded.

"Would I like to kiss you? The answer is yes. But I want to give you a French kiss."

He wasn't blushing now. He was too excited to blush.

He leaned toward her again. This time, she met him halfway. She pressed her lips against his. They were closed. As were his. Then he felt the faint trace of her tongue, trying to part his lips.

* * * *

Lockett had dropped off the others, and Andy Laduke had expected him to take him directly home. It was nearing midnight, and he knew Lockett never missed church services. That's where they'd first made introductions.

But Lockett hadn't taken the road back to the house Andy shared with the old bastard. Instead, they were driving up Main Street -- cruising like the high school punks.

"Know what I like about this?" Lockett asked.

"No, sir."

"Not so formal now," Lockett advised him. "Know what I like about this so much? It's a Saturday night, the high school kids are looking for a little action. But here, the niggers know their place."

Andy acted as if he understood. They'd come up the south end of Main Street, where the colored kids congregated. The action lasted maybe a few blocks, centered on an AME Baptist Church – a colored church. There were no marked boundaries, but two blocks short of the Dairy Delite, the whites could be seen. The action was pretty much the same. The only difference was the model of cars.

The blacks drove in older models, many with body blemishes or rusting paint. The white kids had better cars. The preferred car? Not a car, really, but a Chevy pickup. Nice, but not like the new Ford pickup Keith Lockett was driving.

Main Street went four lanes throughout the heart of downtown Takasaw, eventually merging back into two lanes and taking on the name "Opelika Highway." The movement was continuous, except for a pair of stoplights just before the town center, where a statue of Chief Takasaw overlooked the square from the foot of the City Hall building.

Lockett was stopped at the first traffic light when a honk got his

DOUG SEGREST

attention. He quickly rolled down his window, shouting, "What's up, sonuvagun?" to the occupant in a car below him. It was a county sheriff's patrol car.

"How'd the ceremony go?" asked the voice. Andy leaned over toward the middle until he could see who'd gotten Laduke's attention.

The fat deputy, the one with the greasy mustache, glanced up at Laduke and nodded his head to the newest member of the Klan.

"How'd your boy do?"

"Great," Lockett said without hesitation. "Great. He's one of us now."

The fat man gave Laduke a glare. He knew Andy as well as Andy knew him because they'd had at least two run-ins while Andy was on a moonshine run to Tallassee. Andy had kept his head, but didn't like the way the fat ass had tried to intimidate him.

"Tell him to keep his nose clean, and he'll be OK," the fat man said.

Lockett turned to Laduke and winked. "He's one of us now, sheriff." The guy wasn't a sheriff. Andy knew that. Lockett knew better. He was just flattering the cop.

"Make him useful, then. If anyone can do that, you can Keith."

Lockett waved in reply and grinned at the deputy. The light had already changed, and the brown car slowly moved ahead.

Lockett put the truck back into gear and headed up Main Street again.

"He's one of us?" Andy asked.

"Nah," Lockett replied. "Used to be. The new sheriff put an end to that. He still helps us from time to time. Kind of like an associate. But he's about the only one you can trust to give you a heads up."

The old sheriff had been outspoken about his support of the Klan. City leaders complained about him for years, to no avail as he kept winning one re-election after another, carrying the countywide vote easily.

The sheriff had even cost old Brantley Allen Douglass his seat in the state senate. Ten years back or so, black leaders had gone to the state senator, complaining that the sheriff was regularly intimidating colored drivers on some of the solitary county backloads.

There'd been charges of verbal abuse and demanded bribes. There'd even been rumors that he'd killed a couple of Atlanta blacks who'd made the mistake of driving through McMahon County one night.

Only a handful of whites in town seemed to care. The only one who'd made a fuss was the old man, Brantley Allen Douglass.

He'd asked the state to investigate the sheriff on charges of misusing the office. How far the investigation probed depending on who was telling the story: Eventually, the sheriff had come up clean. Others said there'd been plenty of smoke, but only a couple of people were willing to testify against him. Even then, the word of a couple of small-town blacks wouldn't carry weight in an all-white court.

Either way, the sheriff continued to survive another eight, nine years until felled by a heart attack one Sunday afternoon coming home from church.

Douglass' political career proved to be short-lived. During his next re-election, fliers began appearing all over the county showing the state senator in the company of black leaders from the local university. There wasn't anything sordid about the pictures – Douglass in his suit, talking to suit-wearing colored men. But the wording above the picture said it all for too many people. "Do you think this man will represent white folks fairly?"

Douglass was crushed in the next election. Welcome to small-town Alabama politics.

Still, the sheriff's reputation had remained questionable. Thus, when he died, his successor – a former state trooper from Notasulga – had vowed to run an incorruptible office. His first task: Cut all ties with the Klan. He'd fired all but one deputy with ties to the group and had the audacity to hire a black to the position.

Ever since the new sheriff had been elected, Laduke felt he had been hassled more. He'd never been arrested, but he'd been followed and pulled over numerous times.

For nothing.

"Time, boy?"

Laduke lifted his left hand, catching the light of another car.

"Eleven-forty."

"That late? Time flies, huh?"

Lockett reached under his seat and pulled out a red light, like the ones policemen used. A wire attached to it reached back under the seat.

"Got to get home soon. Preacher's out of town, so I got to lay preach. You comin', ain't ya?"

"Yes, sir. Wouldn't miss it."

"Good, good." Lockett placed the light on the dash of the truck, sliding it to the inside edge of the windshield. "Before we go in, let's have just a little more fun, okay?"

"Yeah," Laduke said, wondering what he had in mind. "Where'd you get it?"

"Sheriff James," Lockett said, referring to the deceased McMahon County lawman. "He told me I could have it as long as I didn't cause any real trouble."

Lockett turned right on Orchard Street. Down the street no more than five blocks was the city ball field, where the little leaguers played every Friday and Saturday. But Lockett pulled into another parking light, turned off his lights and began driving toward a parked car. A couple of car lengths away from the passenger's side, Lockett turned his truck off. Reaching underneath the seat, he flipped a switch. The red light began rotating like a fast beacon, just like the one on a police car.

"Stay here, boy. I'm gonna have some fun."

Lockett opened the door. Standing on the running board, he reached into the bed of his pickup, opened a strapped-in metal trunk and pulled something out. With a little click, Lockett turned on a powerful light. A 10-inch searchlight, bigger than any flashlight Laduke had seen.

"Out of the car, kids!" Lockett said as he approached the parked auto, the search light cutting through the gloom. Before anyone had a chance to respond, he flung open the passenger's side door.

Laduke watched from the truck, not believing the Klansman's gall.

Lockett leaned in, running the search light over the front seat and into the back.

"Empty," Lockett said with a shrug. "What dumb ass would leave his car parked here overnight? Just askin' for trouble."

Lockett returned to the truck and turned the engine over again.

Where to now?

The answer came quickly. Lockett turned back on to Orchard, returning toward Main. But he took a right on Academic, the road leading to Takasaw High. He cut the lights off as he headed toward the back parking lot.

* * * *

Katie held Brax's head with one hand as they kissed. The tongues danced together, and Brax wanted more.

She was crushed against him now. Her thigh, her naked thigh, was pressed against him. Pressed against *it*.

Kyle Anderson always talked about it, the progression. First base, obvious -- though Brax had never gone there before this night. Second base, bobcats. Third base and a home run? As obvious as it sounds.

Kyle had even provided a replay about his double with Sally Beckham, who he'd claimed he'd felt up on a date last month. How he'd seduced her, gotten her bra off before she'd known what was happening. And how, once he did, she'd let him play with her budding youth for a good ten minutes. He'd tried to get into her panties, but she stopped him cold.

No problem, Kyle figured at the time. Save that for next time.

There would be no next time. A week later, she told Kyle she was in love with a freshman at Auburn.

Brax had wondered if there'd even been a first time. Kyle was famous for his tall tales. Frankly, Kyle was full of crap.

Brax's hands had taken a stronghold of her back from the minute she'd grabbed his head. Brax had been hesitant to let the hands wander, but he could feel the bra straps. Just an inch lower, and he'd know what he was up against. Did it unhook in the front or the back?

Maybe, like Sally Beckham in Kyle's story, she'd unhook it for him. Should he just ask? Or go for it?

He took a gamble, letting his left hand come back and rest on her shoulder. No resistance. He began rubbing her upper arm, gently, telling himself, "Slowly, slowly."

Still, no resistance. He ran his hand back up her arm. He opened one eye just a bit to get his bearings. The bobcats were within reach.

He rubbed her arm again, this time the inside. In one motion, he managed to brush the back of a breast with his bare hand. He waited for her to pull away and admonish him.

She didn't.

Every once in awhile, she'd pull away for a second, then begin nibbling on his upper lip before returning her tongue. The first couple of times, he hadn't bothered to look. The third time he did, just to see what was happening. Hard to tell. Her eyes remained shut.

It's now or never.

He turned his hand over, the left palm facing her, and, with only the slightest pressure, placed it on her right breast. Over the dress.

Her elbow moved his hand out of the way.

He returned to his focus on the kissing, settling for the occasional backhand brush. What had Kyle said? It took him three tries – and two solid "nos"-- before he'd succeeded with Sally. So he tried again with the same result. Katie again brushed him away with an elbow but didn't break the kiss.

One last time.

Except this time, the nervousness building, his reach wasn't as gentle. He placed his palm square on the breast. For a moment, he thought he'd reached heaven.

"Braxton Freeman!" Katie said after pulling away from the kiss. This time she grabbed his hand and moved it away, resetting it safely on the dash before she resumed kissing him.

* * * *

"There," Lockett said, pointing toward a solitary car. This time, the searchlight was beside him. He opened the door, reached underneath the seat again and clicked on the light.

"Out of the car, kids!"

Of course, he didn't give anyone a chance to react. He grabbed the passenger's side door of the sedan and opened it abruptly. Laduke heard the shriek before seeing the girl and boy breaking off a kiss through the light that now blinded them.

Startled, Katie leapt off the seat, an innocent knee hitting Brax in the groin. Nothing broke, but the pain caused him to clutch his privates while trying to shield his eyes with the other hand from the light.

"Out of the car!" Lockett yelled. He grabbed the girl by an arm and pulled her out forcefully. Shining the light in the boys' eyes, Lockett told the lover to follow.

Lockett placed the girl against the car, then pushed the boy next to them. Brax couldn't see a thing. The light was so bright, he had to shield his eyes. The figure was nothing more than a dark shadow.

"Boy! I know what you're trying to do to this flower of Alabama womanhood!" Lockett said in a menacing, but official, tone.

Laduke cackled inside the truck. This was a hoot.

Lockett ran the light up and down the girls' body, stopping at the impressive bustline. Then he swung the light back into the boy's eyes, forcing him to block the beam with both hands.

"Good thing your clothes are on!" Lockett said menacingly. "If I'd caught you without some, I'd have had to take you down to jail for the delinquency of a minor. Know what statutory rape is, don't you, boy?"

Brax shook his head, then lowered it when realizing it was the only way to block the light.

He thought he recognized the voice, sort of. It sounded like every redneck he knew. He'd met a deputy or two, but they seemed middle-aged. This guy was younger.

What's he goin' to do?

"This girl's jailbait, boy!" Lockett said.

Laduke cackled again. Lockett knew how to mess with people.

Lockett ran the light over the girl's body again, pausing for another good once over of her breasts.

"Good thing I didn't catch you doin' nothin'," Lockett said. "Good thing for you, boy!"

Brax nodded. He would've pleaded guilty to anything short of murder to bring this to an end.

Lockett turned the girl around with a twist of her arm. He did the same to the boy, then used the opportunity to shine the light on the girl's rear.

"You two get back in the car," Lockett said. "And I'd suggest you head straight home. If I catch you two anywhere else tonight, I'll take you in."

He opened the passenger's door. The girl scooted in. Lockett pushed Brax in the other direction, and the young boy complied without complaint, going around the car to get in on his side. As Freeman opened the driver's side, Lockett flashed the light on him again, to keep him from being able to see who was menacing him – not that Brax would dare look. He was too frightened.

That's when Laduke realized who it was.

Whoa, cousin. I got some tonight. Now you're trying to get you some.

Lockett kept the light shined on the car until Brax had pulled out of the parking lot. Then he flashed off the light and returned to the truck with a broad smile.

"God-damn, boy," Lockett said. "What a hot piece she was. You get a good glimpse?"

"Yeah," Andy said. "Never seen her before. But I know the boy."

"Do ya? Who was it?"

"My cousin, Braxton. Brax Freeman."

"The damn integration committee man's son?"

"One and the same."

"God damn. If I'd known it was your cousin, I might have laid off him. Course, if I'd known who his daddy was, I might've beaten the hell out of him just for principle."

Lockett said it casually, but it still sent a chill through Laduke.

Lockett hopped back in the cab and cut off the flashing red light.

"Should have sent him home by himself, and given the girl a ride home," Lockett said. "Make you walk the rest of the way. I could've had a good time with her."

"Yeah," said Andy, adding nothing more.

Lockett started the truck and kicked the lights back on and began driving Laduke home. Twenty minutes later, he pulled up in front of Andy's house and kept the truck running.

"I'll see you soon, boy. Better get goin'. Told Emma I'd be home before the crack of dawn. Don't want to go to church in the morning with her all pissed off."

Andy said nothing, just grabbed the handle to the door and opened it.

"Expect you there, boy," Lockett said, looking at Andy intently. "We all need to heed the Lord's word."

Andy looked at him blankly, then turned around and headed toward the door.

* * * *

Neither Brax nor Katie had said anything on the way home. Even with Brax going well over the speed limit, Katie hadn't complained.

He pulled into the Seaver driveway and turned off the car. He looked at Katie, struggled to say something that never came. He got out of the car, walked around and opened the door.

Finally, the words came.

"Katie, I'm sorry," he said, not knowing what he was really sorry for. Sorry for trying to feel her up? Sorry for getting caught by a policeman? Sorry for both?

She seemed a little out of sorts, but protested to the contrary. "Don't be, Brax. You didn't do anything wrong. *We* didn't do anything wrong. That policeman was a pervert."

Brax gave her a hand and helped her out.

"Yeah, he was," he said, relieved she hadn't brought up his incomplete – and ill-advised – pass.

Brax could see Mr. and Mrs. Seaver sitting inside on the living room couch through the window, waiting for their return. He didn't even know what time it was, but felt they were close. Considering the scare, they were lucky to be here at all.

"See me to the door, please," she said. He'd already planned on it. They walked quietly, until reaching it.

Katie turned to Brax.

A good-night kiss? Geez, I don't think I can handle that with all we've been through tonight.

That wasn't what she wanted. "Braxton, please don't say any of this to anyone, okay?"

"Course not," said Brax, the keeper of all secrets.

"I mean, how'd we explain what we were doing? It just wouldn't look right."

"I ..."

The door opened. The Seavers were there. Mr. Seaver was tapping his watch.

"Twelve-oh-five, young man," Seaver said in mock seriousness. "I guess we can live with that this one time."

"Sorry, sir," Brax said, forcing a goofy grin. "Promise it won't happen again."

"Did you two have a good time?" Mrs. Seaver asked.

"Yes," Katie said, the enthusiasm returning. "We had a wonderful time, didn't we, Braxton?"

"Yes, ma'am, we sure did," Brax replied, aiming the answer at Mrs. Seaver.

"Call me, Braxton, please?" Katie asked before laying a flat kiss on his cheek and heading inside.

"You bet," Brax said.

Mr. Seaver patted Brax on the shoulder before slipping his arm around his wife to lead her back inside, closing the door.

Brax turned around and faced the car wondering how much he'd just screwed up a good thing.

CHAPTER 4

THE **SERMON WAS** familiar, but Andy Laduke had never seen Rev. Brown, the church's usual preacher, deliver it as passionately as Keith Lockett.

His hands gestured wildly – one paw gripping the Bible opened to a verse from the book of Matthew – as the lay preacher's tone fluctuated from solemn to fiery brimstone. Lockett's eyes burned through the congregation. As Andy looked around, no one was fiddling with the mimeographed program or fighting off sleep. Lockett had everyone hooked; it came so naturally to him.

In the front row sat Lockett's petite, pretty wife, dressed in her Sunday best, with the three young children beside her without a fuss.

It was a perfect picture, yet it bothered Laduke. How could Lockett be so devout on Sunday, hours after violently taking Donna in the tent? Leading the Klan, well that was clear in the Bible itself. Had not the Lord turned sinners and nonbelievers into other lower races as punishment?

That part of Lockett he could reconcile. In fact, he had reconciled it long ago, since that darkening day in the woods when he'd seen Lockett kill the colored man and take the ear as a trophy. This was the good fight, and no one was truer or braver than Keith Lockett in the battle to protect what the white man had earned through his own blood and sweat.

Was it seeing Lockett with another woman that bothered Laduke so much? No, all men had desires. Even Andy Laduke had desires. He'd simply never had the chance to act on them before. Now he'd had it, and he couldn't get it off his mind, Donna's full body on his as they drifted off.

Yes, that was a man being a man. But Lockett's attack – that was what it had been, after all – wasn't the act of a righteous man. Donna wasn't a nigger nor was she white trash. She'd been a good student, from what Andy could remember of their high school days, a girl with a good reputation. She hadn't deserved what Lockett had savagely delivered.

Lockett concluded the sermon with a prayer, bowing his head. When he raised it, as "Amen" echoed throughout the church, the lay preacher's eyes were wet.

"Brothers and sisters," Lockett said, scanning the congregation. "As we tithe," he continued as ushers heading from the back of the church with collection plates, "let us share. Let us give our testimony."

Lockett crossed his hands and waited. An older man, balding with white sideburns and an ill-fitting suit, stood and shuffled toward the Klan leader.

"Brother Jackson, do you have testimony?"

"Yes, I do, Preacher, yes I do."

The man stood uncomfortably, stuffing his hands into the front pockets of the suit. He looked back in the direction from where he had come, then lowered his head.

"Preacher, I'm battling the demon whiskey again," he said. The congregation remained hush, save for the clinking of coins as the collection plates made their way down the rows of pews.

"Tell me more, Brother Jackson," Lockett said, placing a firm hand on the man's slumping shoulders.

"I haven't done any work in weeks, Preacher, cause of the demon whiskey. Today's the first day I've been sober in I don't know how long."

The man looked up at Lockett, who covered him with a hug. When Lockett pulled away, they were both tearing. The Good Lord had reached out and touched them both.

"Why are you sober today, on the Sabbath set by the Lord, good man?"

The man looked toward the back, then sobbed loudly and dropped his head in shame.

" 'Cause he beat the livin' hell out me last night!" shouted a woman, Brother Jackson's wife, as she rose from her pew. The congregation stirred, turning to face her. She wore a wide-brimmed hat, a fake flower tucked into the headband, with a light veil covering her face. She peeled the veil back and revealed a nasty black eye. The congregation gasped.

"Demon whiskey!" someone shouted.

Jackson's wife made her way through the pew until she was in the aisle headed toward the front. She took the hat off, allowing everyone to clearly see the blackened eye.

"You're a good man, Jeremiah," she said softly as she reached him, grasping his hand in hers. "You're a good man when you avoid the temptation. But when you're drinkin' ..."

The man heaved in a fit of heavy crying and sunk to his knees.

"He's never hurt the children, Preacher," she said, looking down at the humiliated man. "He's the best Paw Paw to the grandchildren. But when he goes on a drunk, he's an evil man. And I'm the one who pays the consequences. Me, Preacher, me."

Lockett grabbed the man by the collar of his suit and pulled him up. Roughly. "Is that true, Brother Jackson?"

The man didn't answer. Instead, he continued bawling, while shaking his head in agreement.

Lockett yanked him again, this time pulling the man to attention. With his other hand, Lockett roughly grasped the shoulder he'd held gently a few moments before.

"You know what I think of someone who lets whiskey rule him?" Lockett asked fiercely. "You know what the Lord thinks?"

The man wiped snot and tears away. He mouthed something, but no one could hear over the heaving and weeping.

"You've got one choice, Brother, if you're man enough ... if you're truly a man of the Lord," Lockett said, eliciting a tremor from Jackson. "You know what that is?"

Jackson looked Lockett in the eye and said, softly, "Yes, Preacher."

"You go home now and you pour every bottle of whiskey, every bottle of beer, every bottle of temptation in your home down the drain, you hear? You stop it, now, before you lose the best thing that ever happened to you. Before you lose your wife, your family and your relationship with the Lord. You understand?"

"Yes, I do," the man said, the crying resumed. His wife leaned forward and hugged him, the way a mother hugs a little child.

"And if you don't, you know what happens?" asked Lockett. The man continued crying into the bosom of his wife. Lockett grabbed his head so he could see the lay preacher. "You've confessed before these witnesses and before God. You touch the demon again, and you're going straight to hell the moment you take your last breath on this good earth, you understand?"

Lockett let the words sink in.

"And if you ever touch Sister Jackson with evil intentions again, well, there's not a man in this congregation who won't hesitate to give you an early taste of that Hell. Do you understand?" Louder, "Do you understand?"

"I do," the man said before returning his head to his wife's chest.

"And Sister," Lockett continued, turning toward the lady. "If he ever gives in to this temptation again, you get out of there and you come get me. But if you let it happen and do nothing, you're going straight to Hell with him, understand?"

She seemed taken aback by Lockett's ultimatum. Yet, after pausing to look at her weeping husband, she nodded affirmatively.

Lockett wrapped his arms around the couple and began praying for their salvation. Finally, he ended it and pushed the couple gently back toward their pew.

There would be no other testimonials. Not this week. Not a person wanted to risk the wrath of the lay preacher, even for the slightest indiscretion. Rev. Brown was much easier to deal with.

Lockett turned to the choir. "Brothers and sisters, let's sing our praises to the Lord."

As the service broke up, Laduke lingered in the back of the line for the ritualistic good-bye to the preacher. Lockett stood at the front door, next to his wife – the children were off playing somewhere – as one by one the members of the congregation congratulated him for the inspiring service.

The line passed quickly with quick greetings and congratulations. Andy was near the end when he reached Lockett, hand extended.

"Hey, there boy. Good to have you in the Lord's temple," Lockett said beaming, shaking Andy's hand like the pump on a well.

Andy blushed. Church wasn't his thing, especially since his mother's death. The old bastard never went and he certainly didn't push Andy to go.

"Hey, you know my wife Emma, doncha?"

Andy nodded, then awkwardly extended his hand, not knowing if he should. The pretty brunette clasped his hand in both of hers and greeted him warmly. "I've heard a lot about you, Brother Andrew. Keith thinks a lot of you."

"Thank, you, ma'am."

Lockett had already turned his attention to the next person, a blue-haired lady. Emma Lockett was still grasping his hand, but she, too, had turned her head toward the next in the receiving line. Andy pulled away.

"Hey, Brother," Lockett said. Andy turned back, where Lockett was looking at him. "Hang around a minute. I want to talk to you a little more."

Andy milled around the front steps. Others from the congregation were doing the same, exchanging pleasantries on the sultry, but cloudless July day. There were a couple of dozen people, but he felt as if he were watching from somewhere far off. He didn't know anyone.

A young girl in pigtails came up and pulled on his coat.

"Who are you, Brother?"

"Andy Laduke," he replied cautiously.

"Nice to meet you Brother Andy," said the young girl. She was school age, probably still in grammar school. She smiled at him, said, "I'm Sarah," and then took off.

"Nice to ..." Andy began. He didn't finish. Sarah had run to catch up with her parents.

Lockett announced his presence with the big forearm, slinging it around Laduke's shoulder.

"Good to have you here, boy. I mean that," Lockett said. "The Lord's given us a beautiful day. We need to rejoice in it."

"Yes sir, we sure do."

Lockett beckoned him inside the church, leading him to The Reverend's office. It was tiny and cramped, but had a certain regal bearing to it, with burgundy carpet and bookshelves on three of the four walls. Lockett sat behind The Reverend's desk, in the leather chair, and motioned for Andy to sit in a folding metal chair across the way.

"So, Andy, what'd you think of last night?"

"I enjoyed it very much sir. I'm proud to be a member of the ..."

Lockett cut him off. "We don't say it out loud, boy. Least not where the wrong people might hear." He grinned, the first time he'd delivered Laduke a gentle reprimand. "Hell, things sure have improved since I joined. I had to rough up a nigger just to get in. And we sure didn't get to enjoy female delights afterward! Jesus!"

Andy laughed. Yet he was uneasy that Laduke could talk about sex so openly in a church building.

"I've told you I've got big plans for you, right?" Lockett said. "Well, they start tomorrow."

Andy leaned in. *What, a cross burning? Roughing up a nigger or two?*

"I want to you to see Frank Carruthers at the textile mill in Tallassee. Be there at half-past seven in the morning."

Andy nodded. *What the hell for?*

Lockett could tell he was perplexed. "Boy, I gotta get you a real job. This moonshine shit ain't gonna cut it if you're gonna be one of us."

Andy nodded, but he was even more confused. Moonshining paid well. And the risks were minimal. At worse, a car chase might lead to a night in a jail. The locals weren't going to do more than fine him and send him on his way.

"Boy, you can still run your numbers. I figure you deal mostly with niggers anyway, so it's not like you're taking money away from some hard-workin' white man. You keep it low-key, and you're fine. But I want you workin' at the mill, where you can help us."

Andy nodded again. This is why he'd had so much trouble at school. Half the time he didn't know what the hell the teachers were talking about, but was too embarrassed to ask.

Lockett laid out his intentions. Andy would get a job at the mill, where they made fabrics from raw materials. Cotton and wool, mostly, but they had a new line putting out polyester. Laduke would start on the line, but if he did his job and did it punctually, he'd soon be promoted to an assistant foreman. That meant a good raise and good money and a chance to quickly climb the ladder. The mill owners weren't Klan people, but some of the leaders at the mill were. Andy could go far.

But that wasn't the goal. The mill had begun employing coloreds a few years ago. None had yet advanced past a line job. Andy needed to make sure it remained that way. And he needed to make sure the numbers of the coloreds didn't increase. If there was an opening, it was up to Andy and the other Klansmen to find a good white worker for the job.

"If you're gonna become something in our organization, you need to be respected. You need to be successful," Laduke said. "I'm opening the door for you. Are you man enough to make something out of it?"

"Yes sir, course I am," Andy said, the voice sounding far more confident than he felt.

* * * *

Braxton Freeman's team needed just one more touchdown to win. The only question: how quickly did they want it over with? Moses Burks provided the answer in the huddle.

"Brax, you run a post and I'll hit you," Moses said. "Everybody else, do your own thing. We won't need you. On one. Break!"

The five players broke the huddle. Brax lined up wide right while Moses settled five yards behind the center, who was prepared to snap the football sideways.

"Down," Moses barked. "Set ... hut!"

Braxton took off in a sprint. The guy covering Brax was a half-foot shorter, yet quick as a hiccup. But he had a bad habit. He covered Brax by looking into his eyes. Brax dug down 10 yards and faked a quick hitch. More important to the deception: Brax swiveled his head to look back at Moses.

That was enough. The defender broke in, expecting the pass. With only the brief hesitation, Brax broke diagonally. He was in the clear when he saw Moses launch the ball. There was little arc, just a rope shot. It was a touchdown – if Brax could catch up to it.

He did, catching the ball in stride and bounding past the goal-line marker he and Moses made each Sunday.

Touchdown!

"Aw, shit, man," said the cover guy with mock exasperation. "We gotta separate you two next time."

Moses was sprinting toward Brax in the end zone. "That's what you say every week, E.J. Except I'm the only one who ever picks the white boy."

E.J. laughed and said, "Dang you, Moses."

The Sunday afternoon football game, played every Sunday no matter the season, used to be a ritual in the neighborhood. When they began, Moses was one of only a couple of colored kids they let play. But the whites soon began dropping out, and the coloreds poured in. Kyle Anderson used to be a regular, but had bowed out before the ninth grade.

"I got to help Daddy on Sundays," Kyle had said in explanation and Brax never pressed him.

The field was a bumpy, unused lot behind the S&C Grocery, the neighborhood store that served both races. There was a protocol at the store, of course, if a white customer stood in line, the black customer had to wait his or her turn. It wasn't a posted rule, but it was one everyone seemed to understand without dissent. Takasaw, like most of the Deep South, was governed by unspoken rules.

It was just a few blocks to Moses house, where Adele would have Sunday supper on the table. The Freemans ate a big meal right after church, but Adele saved her best meal for later in the day. Brax often ate lightly at home after arriving home for church to save room for Adele's cooking.

This was the first time the group had played the sandlot game in at least a year. Moses had rounded up his friends at Braxton's urging.

"So, you gonna do it?" Brax asked. Moses knew exactly what he was asking about.

"I guess so. I start taking French lessons this week," Moses replied. "*French.* Why do I need to learn French?"

"I don't know," Brax said with a shrug. "Coach Halliday says all you transfers have to speak two languages."

"Yeah, right," Moses said. "I've already taken two years of Latin. But they say it don't count because Latin isn't taught at Takasaw High."

True, you could take French or Spanish at the school, but not Latin. Peggy Freeman had often complained about that. Latin, she said, was the key that unlocked all other languages (of course, she's majored in romance languages at Judson). Braxton had taken a year of Spanish, but was still struggling.

"Coach Halliday says we'll have a good team," Brax said. "With you at quarterback, he thinks we could go undefeated."

"We went undefeated at our school last season," Moses said. "Don't see why we couldn't do it at your school. Just a bunch of white boys, right?"

Brax laughed. "Yeah, except you'll be our ringer spook."

Moses laughed back.

This was the first time they'd really talked about the integration of the school. Brax knew Halliday had met with Moses the day before, but didn't know how it had gone, except what little Halliday had told him in the hurried phone call earlier in the day.

"Do you wanna do it?" Brax asked.

"Yeah, I guess so. Mama's not sold on it, yet." Adele was Moses' grandmother but she'd reared him, so Moses had always called her Mama. "She thinks it might start trouble. Me? I don't know. It might help me get a better scholarship somewhere if some redneck doesn't kill me."

Braxton had his heart set on an athletic scholarship. But his reason was simple: He wanted to play at the next level and he wanted someone to believe he was good enough. That belief would come in the form of a free ride – Alabama or Auburn, if he had a great season. If not, a smaller school. Harold and Peggy had long ago started setting aside money for college, but if he could get a free ride ... maybe they'd use the money they'd saved and help him buy a car.

Moses' situation was much different. Brax knew Moses had little chance of going to school without working a full-time job unless he got a scholarship. Then again, college coaches had already begun sending Moses Burks recruiting letters. The kind Brax had yet to hear about or see firsthand, but expected would soon be coming, according to what Halliday was telling him.

"Thing is, Brax, I don't know if changing schools makes sense if I still end up at a Negro college. Even if I go to your school, Coach Halliday doesn't think the white colleges are ready for a colored player unless I go up North or something. I don't want to do that. But we could play together. That would be something, wouldn't it? And maybe it'll help me get out of this town."

"Something else. We wouldn't need a playbook. You could just draw it up in the dirt," Brax said.

They were near Moses' house now. Brax could smell the fried chicken already.

"Mama wants you to have supper with us. You want to?" Moses asked.

Braxton replied with his goofiest grin.

Josiah sat in front of the black-and-white television, watching a rerun of *Gunsmoke*. Adele could be heard in the back of the house, finishing the cooking. Brax followed Moses through the maze of the house to find Adele standing over the stove frying.

A girl, about Braxton's age, stood next to Adele. Brax didn't recognize her, but he immediately noticed how pretty she looked. Straightened hair, pulled back by a white headband. She wore a red dress with white polka dots. She was average height and slim.

"B-Bear," Adele said sweetly. "Give Miss Adele a hug."

He saw her every day, yet he never got tired of the big bear hugs she gave him. He hugged her back. It was natural with Adele.

Moses dipped a finger into a steaming bowl and pulled a dab of mashed potatoes away. Adele slapped at him. "Moses, where'd you get those manners?"

He moved deftly away, hiding the evidence in his mouth. "Sorry, Mama. It's just so *good*."

Adele returned to the skillet, where the last of the chicken was cooking. The girl smiled at Braxton, then turned her attention to Adele, who was showing her the ropes.

"Just like *that*," Adele said, pulling a leg out of the skillet with tongs.

The girl nodded, moving a platter covered with a paper towel and already finished chicken to take the offering from Adele. The girl placed the chicken on the counter, then looked at Brax.

"Hi," she said. "I'm Natalie."

"Lordy, where are *my* manners?" Adele said. "Braxton Freeman, this is my niece, Natalie. Natalie Young. Natalie, this is the Braxton you've heard me talk about as long as you can remember."

"Yes, ma'am. Nice to meet you, Braxton Freeman."

Brax nodded and grinned back.

"Natalie's my niece Ester's only daughter," Adele said. "Her mama and daddy just moved back to Takasaw. He's a professor at the Institute."

"Oh," Brax said. He couldn't remember hearing about her before. But Adele had family everywhere. "What grade are you going to be in?"

"I'll be a junior at the high school this fall."

"Takasaw High?"

"No, the Institute High. For Negroes."

Soon, Takasaw High will have them too, Brax thought, *including Moses.*

Adele intruded, bearing the platter of chicken. She handed it to Natalie, who turned toward the dining room.

"C'mon, B-Bear," Adele said. "Let's eat."

* * * *

The bi-racial committee had gathered at the Presbyterian Church. Twelve members – six black, six white –all civic leaders were there. The list included the dean of students at Takasaw Institute, the famed black college in town, and the Rev. Alfonse Tompkins, the man who shepherded the largest colored church in the county.

Tompkins was popular among both races, although he'd become more outspoken, and a little more isolated from white businessmen, since his old seminary mate, Martin Luther King Jr., had begun raising a ruckus in Montgomery.

Harold Freeman was at the meeting. So was Scott Douglass, the county prosecutor who had been absent from the meeting of the other white members at the Freemans' July fourth barbecue.

"What are you going to do, Mr. Douglass, about the Klan?" asked Tompkins.

Douglass looked around the room, then settled on Tompkins. He pushed his horned rimmed glasses back up his nose before replying. "They could be a problem, reverend, but I'm not expecting them to react in big numbers as long as we keep the lid on the kettle."

"The Klan is always a problem, Mr. Prosecutor."

"Not if they don't know our plans."

"Scott, they'll know our plans," Harold Freeman interrupted. "Word's out. I don't know how, but it is."

Douglass took the glasses off and rubbed his brow. "Yeah, I guess it was too much to expect to keep it all a secret."

Tompkins maintained his gaze on Douglass. He wanted a concrete answer.

"If anybody in the Klan gets out of hand, we'll move, legally, to stop them," Douglass said. "Easier said than done. We can stop them out in the open. Otherwise, it's a lot harder."

Dean Ralston from the college patted Tompkins on the arm. "Brother Tompkins, we'll all do the best we can do. Nobody said it would be easy." Ralston nodded at Tompkins, who nodded back, still miffed, in agreement. Originally, Tompkins had been the biggest dissenter of the plan. The dean had reservations of his own before agreeing with the plan grudgingly. His point had been salient. If integration did become the rule across the South, it might soon make the long-standing black colleges across the region non-existent.

Yet, beginning with the Supreme Court's ruling nine years earlier and, more recently with Frank Jackson's orders in federal court up in Montgomery, integration was an eventuality, come Hell or high water.

To oppose it meant siding with Governor George Wallace, the

firebrand segregationist. None of the black leaders wanted to be perceived as aligned with Wallace. Nor did many of the white leaders. Unfortunately, many of the progressive white leaders in the state opted for silence.

"We do have some help, reverend," Douglass continued. "I believe you've met Rosenberg, the FBI agent. He's monitoring Klan activity in the county. If anything major is coming, he'll tip us off if he can't stop it. But … we need hard evidence for anything to stick. That won't be easy."

"Don't take this wrong, Mr. Prosecutor," Tompkins said, "but how is a Jew from the North going to know what the Klan is up to?"

"He's good," Douglass said in a matter-of-fact tone.

An explanation wasn't needed, thought Harold Freeman. The FBI most likely had placed someone in the local Klan, someone who would keep the committee up to date. The FBI had done it throughout the South, breaking open murder cases from Mississippi to South Carolina.

"Plus," Douglass began again, "we all know the local Klan leaders. Neither I nor any of you think they pose any serious threats. They're more or less a bunch of good ol' boys."

"Good ol' boys don't promote beating the hell out of colored folks," Tompkins said.

"No they don't," Douglass responded sternly. "I meant it as a description. No one here condones their activity." Douglass looked around the room, getting nods from the other white members of the committee. "No one wants them active here. But they won't be shut down overnight."

Tompkins began to say something again, but the dean quieted him with another reassuring pat before speaking up. "Son, we have no reservations whatsoever about your intentions. Your family's always stood by our side, even when it hurt. We agree with you: let's fight one battle at a time."

There was silence. Then Douglass pulled the glasses off, rubbed his eyes. He put the rims back on and looked squarely at Tompkins.

"Make no mistake. This will be a battle, Reverend Tompkins," Douglass said. "And we'd better be prepared to fight it together, or someone's going to get hurt."

CHAPTER 5 /
August 1963

"FREEMAN!" SHOUTED HALLIDAY. "Get in there."

Brax pulled the chin strap tight and left the semi-circle for the spot dead in the middle. Nearly thirty players surrounded him. Now, he was the "bull" in the ring.

It was one of Halliday's favorite drills, probably because it was one of the Bear's favorites at Alabama. The coach would yell a player's name, and that player would charge out of the circle and try to knock the Hell out of the one in the middle. The object for the guy in the middle was to beat the charging player to the punch, staying on his feet as long as he could, and take on the next challenger.

"Ready?" Halliday barked. Brax responded by churning his legs and running in place. "Swank!"

The little freshman – now Brax knew his last name – hesitated a moment then charged at Freeman. Brax pivoted to face the pint-sized kid, legs still churning. The kid lowered his head and lunged at Brax, who grabbed him by the pads and flung him to the ground.

"Boone!" A bigger kid, but slow as an ox, growled as he charged. Brax lowered his shoulders and knocked him on his butt.

"Anderson!" Kyle rolled his eyes. He firmly expected to be cut at the end of the day and returned to his role as manager. Baseball was his sport, not football. And it showed as he tried to clumsily knock Freeman down. Brax sidestepped Kyle and shoved him away.

Halliday sent another and another after Brax. None offered difficult challenges. Still, the legs were beginning to burn and his shoulders were stinging from the contact when he had no other choice.

"Lomar!" Halliday ordered after the first seven players had failed to stagger the boy in the middle. Brax began turning, while still churning, trying to find the biggest player on the team. Edgar Lomar was well over 6 feet and 250 pounds. Brax was about to get creamed.

Lomar lowered his head as he came in. Brax did the same and met him squarely with his shoulders, pushing off with his hands. The collision rocked Brax up on his feet for a moment, but not off of them. Lomar pushed him back a couple of yards before Brax could get his feet planted again. He stopped Lomar's momentum and they began grappling like sumo wrestlers.

Braxton's calves were on fire. They'd already practiced for three hours —and that after a three-hour session at daybreak. His hands were slick with sweat, and beads on his face were dripping into his eyes, blurring them while delivering the sting of a wasp.

Yet Brax wouldn't back off. He was surprised Lomar hadn't pushed him back into the circle or onto his butt, which would've ended the drill right there. That surprise gave him a boost of whatever adrenaline was left. It was enough to keep him stable as he tried to move the ox.

Halliday ended it with three shrieks of his whistle, making it official. Practice was over.

The circle broke, with most of the players cheering the end of the day. Brax let go of Lomar, finally, realizing the big linemen had already released him. Even then, Brax wasn't making any progress. He bent over at the waist, gulping in air. Lomar popped Brax on the back of his helmet, getting his attention. Brax looked up, and Lomar winked at him. "Good lick, Freeman."

Halliday signaled the team to take a knee. "Good work, team, good work," Halliday said, pacing in front of them. "It's early, but we've got the making of a real good team, here. I like what I'm seeing."

Hardass paused and looked over the group. He scanned the players, then seemed to stop as he looked at Brax.

"Yeah, I like what I see. Most of you have worked hard this summer, and it shows. Now ... now comes the hard part. We've got a week left before school starts. Less than two weeks before the first game. It's time to get serious. By the time you get out of the showers and get dressed, I'll have the cut list up."

In all, forty players had come out for the team – the largest number in the last three or four years. But the school only had uniforms for twenty-eight players. That meant a dozen would get cut. Another five would be selected as managers, given odd jobs during practice and games with the understanding that if anyone got hurt or left the team, one of the managers would rejoin the varsity.

"I wish we were a big enough school to have a junior varsity, but we ain't. Maybe someday ..."

With that, Halliday turned and headed back to the field house. Practice was over.

Brax was toweling his wet hair as Kyle returned from the chalkboard, where Halliday always posted the handwritten cut list on school stationary.

Anderson sat down next to Braxton, grinning.

"You made it?" Brax asked expectantly.

"Yep," Kyle said. "As a manager again." Anderson stood up and playfully grabbed the towel, scrunching Brax's head underneath it.

"Hey!" Brax yelled. He pulled the towel away and snapped it at his best friend. It hit Kyle limply, making Anderson's grin widen.

"Heck, B-Bear, baseball's my sport. I tried out and kept my Daddy happy. Now, when you guys are all beat up on Friday nights, I'll be fresh as a daisy chasing the babes."

"Right," Brax said. "Maybe some day you'll actually catch you one."

"In your dreams," Anderson said. "Who's been giving who advice, huh, B-Bear? I've been a regular Dr. Kinsey for you the last month with Katie Sullivan." Kyle laughed at the thought. "Speaking of that, how are things going?"

Reaching into his locker, Brax pulled out a white T-shirt and slipped it over his torso, tucking it into his jeans.

"It was going pretty good, but she left for home two weeks ago for some cheerleading camp."

"Is she coming back anytime soon?"

"Yeah, maybe. Her school's got a Thursday game in September. She said her mom was going to bring her down early the next day so they could see us play Tallassee."

"Sounds like love to ...," Kyle said, stopping in mid-sentence. Halliday was out of his office and into the locker room.

Halliday walked over to Brax. "Come into the office, Freeman. I need to talk to you."

Brax grabbed his sneakers from the bottom of the locker and picked up a pair of clean white socks, then turned to follow the coach.

"Coach?" It was Kyle. Halliday turned around, but didn't say anything. "How come there were 13 cuts instead of 12?"

"Got to save room for another player. We may have a transfer," Halliday said. He turned around, then turned back. "You think I should've kept you on the squad?"

"No sir," Kyle said. "Baseball is a better sport for me. Preserves my handsome looks."

Halliday glared, but almost let on that he liked Anderson's crack.

Sneakers in one hand, the socks in the other, Brax followed Halliday into the small, musty office. As usual, Halliday had the blinds covering the window looking out into the locker room closed.

"Sit down."

Brax sat across from Halliday on an old green couch.

"I'm naming captains tomorrow," Halliday said, leaning in to the desk with his elbows. "You're one, Lomar's the other. But don't say nothin' till I make the announcement in the morning."

Brax nodded and mumbled thanks.

"I'm not goin' to give you a speech about the responsibilities. You know most of them – leading the team on and off the field, leading practice, goin' out for the coin flip. You can handle all that. And, to be honest, you've impressed the hell out of me so far. You're the most improved player we've got, better than I expected you to be at this point. Course, I expect you to keep working the same way and get even better."

"I plan to, Coach."

"I know that, son. But I'm also naming you a captain for another reason."

Brax placed the shoes beside him on the couch and put his hands on his knees to let Halliday know he had his undivided attention.

Halliday continued, "Your friend, Burks, will join the team on the first day of school. No one knows that but you. I'm going to have him report a few minutes late, so he can dress by himself, and I'm going to hold him afterward a few minutes so things can clear out. I don't want any incidents. Know what I mean?"

Brax understood. Let the players see Moses before they judged him.

"Some aren't going to like this one bit," Halliday said. "But I think most of 'em won't complain much or care. I'm counting on you to diffuse any major problems. If it's something you can't handle, you come to me. Understand?"

"Yes, sir, I do."

"Good. I don't know Lomar's feelings or if he'll back you. But the other boys look up to you."

Halliday stood up and walked over to the chalkboard, the one on wheels he could roll out to the locker room for quick skull sessions. The punt return team was covering the majority of the board, but in the right-hand corner Halliday had written down the Takasaw schedule in his hard-to-read block lettering. His Xs and Os were legible, but the other letters were chicken scratch.

"We open with Shorter. That's winnable, even without Burks at quarterback."

Brax looked at him quizzically. If Moses were coming to play ball for Takasaw, why not at quarterback? Halliday seemed to understand the confusion.

"Freeman, he's showing up the first day of school. We've got three practices before the game. We can't make the move that quick. The new kid can handle Shorter. God damn. I could play quarterback and we'd still beat Shorter by three touchdowns."

Better put you at tackle.

"If we run up the score, we'll play him a little. Meanwhile, I'm moving the current backup to split end and safety. He can help us on defense."

Halliday went down the list, putting a W by seven of the 10 games listed. Beside Tallassee, Opelika and Lanier, he listed Ls.

"Without Burks, we're a 7-3 team. A good team," Halliday said. Then he went down the list, recording the Ws to the right of the first ones. Beside Union Springs, he put a W. Next to Tallassee and Opelika, he listed question marks.

"With him, we're 8-2 at worse. We're undefeated if he's half as good as I think he is."

Halliday dropped the chalk into the board's tray, then sat back down in his chair.

"He *is* that good. I watched your last Sunday pickup game. Sat in my car, about a block-and-a-half away. What an arm that boy has. And I've also worked him out once over at the Institute. He's the real thing."

Halliday leaned back in the chair, putting his hands behind his head. Uncharacteristically, he smirked.

"Now, let me tell you what I hadn't counted on."

Brax leaned forward again.

"The colored boy's smart as a whip. I don't know what I was expecting, but I didn't expect him to be so smart. I quizzed him on the playbook. He knows it better than either of the yahoos we've got working at quarterback now. Good enough that I think he can call his own plays."

It didn't seem like that much of a revelation to Brax. Why wouldn't Moses be smart? Damn, he'd taken Latin. And didn't Halliday always let his quarterbacks call the plays? Actually, Brax wasn't certain. Most of his playing time had been limited to backup duty. When he had been in, Halliday had called the plays with hand signals from the sideline.

"We're going undefeated, Freeman, undefeated," Halliday said, grinning wildly. "I've coached 30 years. I've had one undefeated team."

When? Not any time I can remember.

"I've got the two of you for a helluva season. By the time you leave here, son, you'll be ready for big-time ball. Trust me. The Bear will know everything about you. So will Coach Jordan and Auburn."

"I hope so, Coach," Brax said. *Brilliant response.*

Halliday sent Brax on his way. The locker room was clear. Even Kyle had left. Brax slipped on his socks and shoes and headed out the door for the half-mile walk home.

Away from the high school, he wanted to think about anything but football. Football consumed the day. It hadn't consumed the summer.

He had seen Katie often after the scare behind the high school. Only one other car date, when they went to see a movie in Auburn and parked afterward, this time in a dark spot on her street, where there were no light poles.

They'd kissed at the pool. She'd surprised him one day, just after he'd left the tower. He'd gone outside the pool, onto the golf course, to retrieve a golf club Halliday had left for him to take to the pro shop for repair. Next to the cinder-block wall that housed the maintenance building, she'd come up and spun him around, laying a wet kiss. Tongue and all.

Shocked for a moment, he'd responded. This was probably the closest he'd gotten to the bobcats. They pressed against him with only the thin fabric as a barrier as he held her. He could feel something against her chest and … it was heaven.

There'd been the picnic, where they'd met in a clearing near her house, spread a blanket and feasted on ham and cheese sandwiches and RC Colas. That had led to kissing, him on top of her. But like his earlier efforts, attempts to unleash the bobcats were gently rebuffed. He'd gotten a handful, outside the dress, that day, but it was fleeting.

Still, it was enough.

When they made out, it was heaven. The awkwardness was gone. The heat was obvious, but he could control himself, as a gentleman should.

When they were silent, things were still good. She had been a regular at his baseball games until the season ended. He didn't hit any more homers, but his play improved. His team had gone 8-1 down the stretch, winning the tri-county title.

When they talked, things weren't good. Invariably, the subject of integration was raised. The plan to bring the handful of black kids to Takasaw High was known by everyone. Few of Braxton's friends seemed to have any major objections. But Katie, who didn't even have to worry about it in her lily-white suburb of Birmingham, didn't like the idea.

That fact she made clear, again and again. When they talked, she wasn't as attractive, yet she wouldn't back down. Brax tried to change the subject, but she was wouldn't let it go. He'd given up arguing, to the point that he was agreeing with her to shut her up. It didn't work.

He didn't know how he felt about Katie Sullivan, though he was looking forward to her next visit, for the Tallassee game.

As long as she watched. As long as she kept her mouth shut.

Natalie Young was a different matter.

Adele's great-niece had become a regular at Sunday suppers, so much so that Brax had gone through the motions the rest of the day. She was on his mind throughout the sandlot game. She was on his mind a lot more than that.

She was on his mind so much, Brax was bothered. She was a Negro. She was off-limits. And he had something going with Katie. He still needed someone to talk to about the whole thing. But who? Certainly not Kyle. Not even Moses. They'd never talked about girls – well, not girls of other races. Moses had told Brax all about his girlfriends. Brax had told him most of what he'd felt with Katie Sullivan – skipping any mention of her objection to the integration plan.

But Natalie was Moses' blood relative. And Natalie, like Moses, was black. Had Brax known anyone who fell in love with someone outside his race? No. Had he ever known of anyone anywhere who'd done the same?

Hell no. Not that this was lust. It was … well, he didn't know.

The extent of his knowing Natalie Young was minimal: Sunday suppers every other week, a few stolen moments of conversation in the kitchen. That was it.

That's how it would remain. He saw no other choice.

* * * *

The work was easy. The work was boring as hell.

Eight hours a day, five days a week, Andy Laduke stood at the same station, checking the outgoing material for flaws. He'd pick up the piece of cotton, hold it to the intense spotlight, and scan it. Maybe one in thirty pieces had something wrong. When he spotted a flaw, he'd pull it off the conveyor belt and toss it into the basket.

He knew no one, not the way you're supposed to know your co-workers. But they all worked the same way, individually at a station, each worker given a specific responsibility. It all was beneath Andy. As for the solitude, it didn't matter. He had always been a loner.

It took him a half hour to get to work, a half hour to get home. That worked out well. The bastard was usually sleeping when he left and in a drunken stupor when he got home. He'd fix something to eat, then go to his small room and turn on the radio. Sometimes, he'd tune in KMOX out of St. Louis and listen to a Cardinals' baseball game. Andy didn't care much about baseball –or any sport for that matter. But he liked the idea of hearing something from far, far away.

It was a Friday, and he was ready for the weekend. Of course, he had no plans, except to sleep. That was, unless the bastard stayed at home. Then he'd drive somewhere.

He'd cut back on running numbers. Just once a week, on Sundays, he would make pick-ups and distribute the new cards, providing a little income. Between the numbers and his new job at the mill, he came close to what he made in a slow week running shine.

So why was he doing it? Because it was Keith Lockett's idea. Andy Laduke wanted to impress Keith Lockett.

Keith Lockett! Andy had forgotten about the meeting Keith had called for ten o'clock that night. He was too tired. But now he was in the Klan. He had a sworn duty.

He'd been daydreaming – an occupational hazard on the line – and allowed three pieces to slip by unnoticed. He reached for the last one and held it up, only to hear the bell that signaled the end of the work day.

The conveyor belts and sewing machines that ran constantly throughout the mill began shutting down. The noise from the last eight hours would leave a ringing in his ears Andy wouldn't shake for hours.

He grabbed his Thermos bottle from the lunchroom without saying anything to anyone, then headed down the corridor toward the back lot, where he and every other mundane mill worker parked.

"Laduke. Laduke!"

Andy turned around slowly. Someone had seen the three pieces he'd forgotten.

Shit. It was Carruthers, the foreman.

Carruthers was standing halfway out of his office, waving Andy back.

Shit.

Andy walked back down the long corridor, ready for a reaming. Instead, Carruthers extended his hand and shook Andy's.

"How are you liking it here, Laduke?" asked Carruthers, pulling Andy inside the office while closing the door behind him.

"Uh, fine. Just fine."

"Good. Mr. Lockett speaks highly of you. I can see why. You've got a future here."

Andy slumped against the closed door. He was too tired to chat.

"How'd you like to be an assistant foreman?"

Andy slid up the door, straightening out a little.

"Uh, I'd like that, Mr. Carruthers."

"We're expanding," Carruthers said. "We've got two new orders – big orders – so we're adding a third shift. That means midnight to eight in the morning. You'd be one of the supervisors."

Andy was thinking. When he was running 'shine, he stayed out late and slept later. But it meant he was around the bastard more, though the bastard usually left him alone if Andy was asleep in his own room and out of sight. He could handle midnight to morning, all right. If the bastard was around, he'd stay in bed and catch more sleep. Never could get enough sleep, anyway.

"It means a nice raise for you, too. I've got to get the owner to approve it, understand? But I bet I could get you another 15 cents an hour."

Andy did the quick math, to no avail. Ten hours a day would mean an extra buck-fifty a day. Except he worked in eight-hour shifts.

Damn. It ought to add up a little.

"That would be fine, Mr. Carruthers. Fine. I'd like that."

"Good, good," Carruthers said. He reached around Andy, grasped the knob and cracked the door open. "Let me get final approval and I'll give you something concrete later this week. You'd start next Tuesday. We're off for Labor Day."

* * * *

No one was home when Brax entered the house. He called for Peggy, but didn't get an answer. "Dad?" Again, nothing. He wasn't used to having an empty house. But an empty house usually meant he was on his own.

Brax pulled a bottle of Coke out of the fridge, popped the cap, and sprawled on the couch after turning on the television. Nothing worth watching, but he left it on the NBC station out of Montgomery anyway.

Thirty minutes, maybe more, had passed. He was used to late nights for his father, but Peggy Freeman was almost always home. Had she had some sort of meeting he'd forgotten about?

The phone rang and Brax let it ring twice, instinctively thinking someone would answer it. He got it on the third ring.

"Freeman residence."

"Braxton, honey? You're home," said Peggy on the other end. There was noise on the other end, noise he could hear but couldn't make out. She seemed out of breath.

"Where are you, Mom?"

"I'm at the hospital. Something's wrong with Adele."

"Adele? What's wrong? Is she gonna be alright?"

Peggy didn't answer. In the background he could hear her voice, muffled, talking to someone else.

"Braxton? You still there?"

"Yes, ma'am. She gonna be all right?"

"I think so, with time," Peggy said. "But she's gonna be here for awhile, I'm afraid. Luckily, Moses got her to the hospital in a hurry."

"What was it?" Brax asked. Over the phone, he heard a loud intercom, with a doctor being paged. And voices. Many voices.

"I'm going to stay with her for awhile, Brax. But I need you to do something," Peggy said. "Go down to Adele's house and sit with Josiah until Moses can get back. He's afraid of the dark."

Adele was protective of Josiah and rarely left him alone.

"Okay, Mom. I'll head over now."

He hadn't had supper. But he didn't feel like eating anyway.

* * * *

Andy was out on the porch, smoking a Marlboro and waiting for Lockett to pick him up. It wasn't quite 9:45 yet, the time Lockett had told him he'd swing by.

As usual, the bastard had been asleep when Andy had gotten home from the mill, so he'd been able to get something to eat and listen to a little radio in peace. But for the last few minutes, he'd heard the bastard moving inside the tiny house.

C'mon, Keith. Get your ass moving.

He could hear the front door opening, then the screen door swinging. Andy didn't turn around.

"What you doing out here at this hour, boy?" asked the bastard in the voice made raspy by booze and too many cigarettes for as long as Andy could remember.

"Waiting on a friend."

"Jesus," said the bastard, settling on the porch with a plop. "You ain't got no friends. Don't lie to me."

Andy didn't turn around. Why bother? "I got a couple."

"Right. Yeah, right."

Once upon a time, the bastard had been like a father. Really, the only father Andy had ever known. His real father, the one who'd made his mother pregnant, had been killed near the end of World War II. Andy had been his parting gift. They'd been married a few months, and he'd gotten her pregnant on his last leave before shipping overseas. Andy hadn't even been born when the telegram came, saying Andrew Lafayette Jones had been killed in a battle fighting for General Patton. He was 19 years old.

Andy had arrived two weeks later, three weeks premature.

For his first two years, Andy and his mother had lived with her mother and father, in a nice house on Gautier Street, as nice as the Freemans' home. He remembered the house, but not the time there. She'd always told him it had been comfortable, but not lasting. She had to get out on her own.

She'd met the bastard, Leonard Laduke, when Andy was still waddling around in diapers. She called him her white knight. He'd fought in WWII himself, and had come away from it with a withered right arm. But he had a decent job at a car lot in Opelika. And he wanted to have a family.

So he got one instantly. When Andy was five, Laduke had legally adopted him. Thus, Andrew Lafayette Jones Jr. became Andrew Lafayette Laduke.

It wasn't an idyllic life, but it was comfortable enough. They lived in the same house Andy and the bastard shared now, but it was well kept, then: Fresh paint and new shutters with a little garden out front. It was respectable.

Life was respectable enough that when the Freemans visited, or when they went to visit his cousin, he wasn't embarrassed. He was older than Brax, and they rarely did things together. But he at least felt he belonged.

It all changed when his mother was killed in a car wreck. A drunk driver had clipped her car one afternoon as she returned from the grocery store, running her into a telephone pole that cut the car in half and snuffed out her life on impact.

His grandparents died within the next two years. And the bastard, Leonard Laduke, slowly went to pieces.

He lost the job at the car lot. Then lost one selling carpet. Another, selling clothes. He'd always been a drinker, but the drinking increased to the point where Leonard Laduke was stumbling or in a stupor nearly every waking hour.

Andy had been forced to get menial jobs to help cover expenses. He'd liked the one as a bag boy, but it didn't last long enough. The bastard had come in one Friday afternoon and made a scene, calling Andy every name in the book – in his colorful, four-letter vocabulary – and created a scene. Andy wasn't quite certain why the bastard was ranting.

The manager didn't care. "Sorry, son," he'd said. "I can't put up with this. It's bad for business."

That led to his introduction to running moonshine. Leonard would come home with groceries every few weeks, always after somehow cutting the booze off long enough to disappear for a few hours. He'd begun running shine. When he became undependable, he turned the job over to Andy, who was almost 16 and could use the ratty old pickup for deliveries.

Andy quit school and the bastard didn't object a bit. "School's for dumbasses," he always said. Soon, Andy's part-time job had become full-time work. And he liked it, a hell of a lot more than he liked the job Lockett had arranged at the mill.

The bastard was still rambling about something. Andy didn't pay much heed to it, because it meant Leonard was still drunk and about to pass out again.

"Your mama," Leonard said before he was interrupted by a belch that bellowed from the depths. "Your mama ... she loved us both."

Leonard sprawled on the porch, one leg suspended off the ledge, the bottle still in his hands.

Andy enjoyed the silence again, but not for long. He recognized Lockett's truck coming down the road.

* * * *

Brax knocked on the door to no avail. Letting himself in, he found Josiah huddled in a fetal ball in the corner of the living room, sobbing and mumbling.

Brax kneeled down, not quite sure what to do, and patted Josiah on the head, the way he would have done a little child he found the same way. The fact that Josiah was nearly twice his age didn't matter.

Josiah looked up, blinking through red eyes and tears, and grabbed Brax out of fright. Recognizing him, Josiah released his grip and held on to the young white man with all his might.

"B-Bear," said Josiah. "Mama sick."

"I know," Brax said, fidgeting in Josiah's strong grasp. "I know. But it's gonna be okay."

Josiah released his grip for a moment and looked at Brax, the way a puppy would, then hugged him again. Brax could smell something. Ammonia? No, stronger. Then he realized his knee, against the hardwood floor, was wet. Brax craned his neck to look and saw the puddle. Josiah had peed on himself.

Brax had always been comfortable around Josiah for as long as he could remember. When he and Moses graduated from the crib and were allowed to rough house together, Adele brought Josiah over to play with them. He was already in his teens then, but he delighted in playing children's games – tag and hide-and-seek when Adele would send them to the back yard.

Josiah was more mobile then, able to keep pace with the two little boys. But in the last few years, Josiah had slowed down considerably. Most of the time, when Brax came over now, Josiah was perched on the couch watching TV – or staring elsewhere if it wasn't on.

Adele said his heart was giving out, but she didn't say so ruefully. "B-Bear, soon after Josiah was born I knew something was wrong with him. The first doctor I saw told me he was a Mongoloid, and he told me my baby wouldn't live to age three. So every day he's with us is a blessing."

The thought made Brax guilty now, with Josiah such a wreck. Adele never treated Josiah any differently than the other kids. She still read the Dr. Seuss books to him before bedtime. The last time Brax had seen that, he and Moses had gotten the giggles so bad that Adele had shooed them out of the house.

It seemed funny then. A grown man sitting in bed, head on his mama's breast, listening to *Green Eggs and Ham*. It didn't seem funny now.

That Adele would keep Josiah in the house, Peggy had often told Brax, was unusual. The Freemans had known a couple of other families who had children with Down Syndrome. Each family had institutionalized the child, seemingly to disappear without a mention.

Josiah, Peggy said, was no better off mentally or physically than any of the others at the same early age when the drastic steps to institutionalize were made. But he'd been blessed with an angel named Adele.

It was beginning to darken outside. Brax began to wonder if he would hear from Peggy or Moses anytime soon. Would he need to stay the night? What did he need to do? He couldn't hug Josiah all night.

An idea.

"Have you eaten, Josiah?"

"I be hungry, B-Bear. Real hungry."

"Let's get something to eat."

Brax pried Josiah's arms away and began to rise. Then he helped Josiah to his feet and led him to the kitchen. Raiding Adele's kitchen wasn't easy. The ice box was full of fresh meat, cheeses and the stuff

Adele used to cook. She always cooked from scratch. The idea of cooking from scratch himself wasn't going to work.

Two plates were covered with aluminum foil. Brax unwrapped the first one to find fried green tomatoes.

That might work. What else?

The other plate was fuller. He uncovered a portion to find fried chicken.

"Josiah, you want some chicken?"

"No. No chicken."

"What would you like to eat, then?"

Josiah paused a moment to reflect on the choices. "Peanut butter samwich."

That, I can handle.

Knowing his way around the kitchen like his own, Brax pulled out half a loaf of homemade bread and began rifling through the cabinets for peanut butter. There were condiments and enough cans to feed a family through the Apocalypse. But no peanut butter.

"I'm hungry, B-Bear," Josiah said, rubbing his big belly. "Samwich?"

"Yes. A sandwich. But we'll have to do it at my house, okay? Go change your britches and we'll go."

Josiah's eyes lit up. "B-Bear's house," he said smiling.

"Yes, my house. Come on."

Brax knew where the peanut butter was at home and he made Josiah the best peanut butter sandwich in history, letting him wash it down with bona fide Coca-Cola. Adele never had Cokes at the house. She always bought the cheap substitutes.

"B-Bear?" Josiah asked. Brax turned around. Josiah had stopped shy of the living room.

"Yes, Josiah?"

"Can we play hide and seek at B-Bear's house?"

"Yes," Brax said, grinning. "We'll play hide and seek at B-Bear's house."

* * * *

The meeting was held at an old farmhouse owned by one of the members of the Klan. Lockett and Andy were joined by four other men, none of whom he knew.

Keith Lockett was clearly in charge as it began.

"The rumors we've been hearing are all true. These nigger lovin' members of the bi-racial committee are integrating Takasaw High next week."

There were murmurs of protest. "Niggers at our school," said the host. "What's this world coming to?"

Andy nodded agreement. *It's going to Hell in a hand basket.*

"We've got to take a public stand on this," Lockett said. "I want every McMahon County member in his robe in front of the school by daybreak Tuesday morning. I don't want any stragglers."

"Are we goin' to bust some nigger heads?" asked the host.

"No," Lockett replied, cutting a sharp look at the farmer. "Remember, these are gonna be nigger kids. White ones, too. No violence. At least not there."

"Then what the hell are we doin'?" asked the farmer. He was a good 10, 15 years older than Lockett. Still, Andy was surprised he was challenging Lockett. No one else had the balls.

"We're taking a stand in public. I want to be understood, perfectly. We'll yell, we'll intimidate the hell out of 'em, but we don't break ranks."

Another man spoke up. Andy had never seen him before. "We do nothing in public. Do I take that to mean we do something away from the school?"

"Yes," said Lockett. "I'll get to that in a minute."

For the first time, Andy spoke up. "You said we had help."

"We do, boy, we do," Lockett replied. "First, the state's imperial wizard is aware of our situation. He'll be talking to me on the hour – Albert wants to stay out of this. But they're both serious when they say no public displays. We've got work to do, and it ain't goin' to get done if half of our Klan gets thrown in jail."

"You said 'first.' What's the other help?" asked the host.

"Y'all will like this," Lockett said. "The Governor is sending down state troopers to block the school from opening its doors."

"Guv'nah George C.," said the host. "Hot damn! I knew there was a reason I voted for the sumbitch."

"Governor Wallace is sympathetic to our problem here," Lockett said. "He'll stop it. Believe me, there won't be any mixing of the races at Takasaw High. There won't be any open violence, period. That's our job, to make sure everybody keeps his head on straight."

Andy recognized the man who owned the farmhouse. He'd seen him in town a few times. The other man who'd spoken up, like the farmer much older than Andy, was a mystery. So was the remaining man, the one who had yet to say a thing. He was somewhere between Lockett's and Andy's ages. Like Lockett, he had an air of something about him. Education? Hell, Lockett never made it past the 12th grade, but he sure came off smart. The other man, though, looked like one of the college frat boys he'd sometimes run moonshine to at the college in Auburn. Except this one was past college age.

"Keith, you said we wouldn't do anything in public, but private was a different matter," said the host.

"Yeah, I did," the leader said. "But don't you worry about that. Me and Laduke will take care of that."

The man nodded, satisfied.

"Everyone understand? We need everyone dressed at daybreak, lining the street facing the front of the high school. The orders are simple: We'll stand shoulder to shoulder and we'll scare the hell out of them. Yell whatever you want to yell, it's still a free country. But don't break ranks unless all hell breaks loose. If it does, follow my lead."

* * * *

Brax had enjoyed himself. He'd made Josiah the peanut butter sandwich, then made one to enjoy himself – his with grape jelly splattered on top, too. Then he'd poured them both a glass of soda. Josiah had talked all through dinner, mouth full, unable to make a clear sentence because of the sticky food. But Josiah was happy.

They cleared the table and played hide and seek in the house. Brax would count to 50, lowering his head on the kitchen table. Each time, Josiah hid in the same place, behind the easy chair in the living room. As soon as Brax said, "Ready or not, here I come," Josiah began giggling. Brax still pretended he couldn't find Josiah until the big man slowly rose and shuffled to the kitchen, which Brax had called home. Brax let Josiah win every time.

When it was Braxton's turn to hide, he went to the same place. Josiah counted to five, then headed right at him. Brax ran in place – so afraid he'd knock something over – until Josiah tagged him.

The game didn't last long because Josiah tired quickly. By eight-thirty, he was lying on the couch watching an old movie with Brax.

Within five minutes, he was snoring and kicking Brax off the other end.

Peggy and Harold arrived a while later. Their presence together explained to Brax how she'd gotten Adele to the hospital. Harold had left his office the minute Peggy called, which she'd done when Moses came running to the house with the news. Moses probably needed Harold's help to lift her into the car.

They saw Josiah sleeping when they walked in.

"We figured you two would be over here when we dropped Moses off at his house and y'all weren't around," Peggy said. "How'd it go?"

"It went fine. I fixed him a peanut butter sandwich, we played a little and he fell asleep. You want me to wake him up and walk him home?"

"No," Harold said. "Let him sleep here tonight."

"I'll get him a pillow and a blanket," Peggy said. "Then I'm going to bed."

"Me, too," Brax said. "I'm worn out."

"Two-a-days have been tough?" Harold asked.

"Yes sir," Brax said. "But worth it. Guess what?"

"What?"

"Coach Halliday's naming me a captain in the morning."

"Well I'll be danged," Harold said, clapping his hands. "Congratulations. We ought to celebrate."

"We ought to," Brax said. "But I'm as tired as y'all are. I think I'll hit the rack, too. But I think I'll do it in here. I'll get my sleeping bag out, in case Josiah wakes up in the middle of the night and gets scared."

"Good idea," Harold said. He walked over and gave his son a quick hug. "I'm proud of you."

"Thanks. Being named captain surprised me, to be honest."

"I guess so," Harold said. "But that's not what I meant. You've always been a good athlete. I mean I'm proud of you for looking after Josiah tonight."

Peggy returned and began spreading a thick Afghan over the slumbering Josiah. She lifted his heavy head and wedged a pillow behind him.

"Peggy, guess what?" Harold said.

Peggy looked up, but her normally bright eyes had nearly disappeared behind heavy lids.

"Braxton's been named captain of the football team."

"Well, one of two, Dad."

"Okay. One of two. Still ..."

"Oh, Brax, dear, I'm so proud of you," Peggy said as she reached up to give him a peck on the cheek.

Brax walked behind his parents, down the corridor toward his bedroom to retrieve the sleeping bag out of the closet. "Hey, you didn't tell me how Adele's doing."

"She suffered a stroke, son," Harold said. "She's going to need a long time to recover. But she's going to live. That's the key."

"Thank God for that," Brax said.

"Yes, thank God," Peggy echoed.

* * * *

Andy Laduke had been the only one Lockett had taken with him to the meeting. Now, they were back in his pickup truck, driving down a dirt road Andy didn't recognize. They reached another road, one that led to a house set back 50 feet, and Lockett stopped.

He honked his horn. In seconds, Laduke spotted a figure headed through the darkness toward the pickup.

Who the hell is it?

"Get out and let her in," Lockett ordered. Andy did as told. A girl wearing a mismatched skirt and a weathered plaid shirt slid past him, and hopped into the cab next to Lockett. It was Donna, the girl from high school -- and the one he'd been with after the Klan rally.

Lockett patted her on the knee. "Let's go for a ride. You remember my new boy, here, doncha?"

Donna smiled at Andy. "Sure, Sugar. What's your name again?"

"Andy. We went to high school ..."

"Yeah, I remember," she said, turning toward to Lockett. "Baby, you got anything to drink?"

Lockett reached under the seat and pulled out a fifth of Jack Daniels and handed it to her. Donna took a big swig, then wiped the excess off with the back of her hand.

"I think the boy here is sweet on you," Lockett said.

"How sweet?" Donna said. She leaned over and slid a tongue into Andy's ear. "Maybe I'm sweet on him, too."

"That's why you're here. Show him."

She took his earlobe into her mouth and bit it gently. Her left hand made a quick beeline for his lap. She took another swig from the bottle before pressing it against Andy's lips. And when he took a few gulps, she turned her attention to his zipper.

Afterwards, Lockett pulled over on to the shoulder of the road. "My turn, baby."

Donna hiked up her dress and moved to straddle him, but Lockett turned furious and backhanded her hard across the face, knocking her against Andy.

"Stupid bitch!" Lockett hissed. "You know I ain't going to cheat on my wife! What if you turned up pregnant?"

Andy stared as Lockett jumped out of the truck and grabbed her by the arm and yanked her out. He pulled her hard, sending her sprawling into the road.

"Walk home," he said. He climbed back in, gunned the engine and left her in the darkness.

CHAPTER 6

HALLIDAY MADE THE announcement at the start of practice, then let Braxton and Lomar lead the team in calisthenics before the real work began.

It went smoothly, despite Braxton's sluggishness due to the events of the night before – not to mention the six-thirty start. Halliday focused on the offense before moving to the kicking game. Braxton learned quickly he wouldn't get much rest. Halliday had him at right halfback on offense, safety on defense and on every special team except the field goal protection unit. After two years of being a scrub and one year lost to injury, Braxton wanted the extra work.

Halliday cut the workout short after two solid hours, surprising everyone by announcing there would be no afternoon practice.

"We ain't ready to play," Halliday said. "But I've got things to take care of this afternoon. If I wouldn't get every preacher in the county pissed at me, I'd have you back here in the morning. But you guys are moving like you've got cast irons on your legs. I'll give you 48 hours to get some rest. And I mean rest, no horseplay. I want everyone back here at six Monday morning."

The last command elicited scattered groans throughout the huddle. Monday was Labor Day, a holiday.

"We've got a game Friday," Halliday said in answer to the complaining groans. "We can't afford to take two days off. If you've got plans for the holiday, better bring them to an end by Sunday night. Dismissed."

Braxton was still on a knee when Kyle Anderson sidled up and pounded him hard on the shoulder pads.

"Captain, man, captain!" Anderson said. "Let's celebrate tonight. A movie?"

"No movie," Braxton said, struggling to his feet. The cast irons

103

Halliday had described, Braxton must have had two on each leg. "Adele, our housekeeper, had a stroke. I'm going to the hospital to visit her."

"Oh, Brax. Sorry," Kyle said. "But you ain't gonna be there all night, are you?"

"I don't know. Tell you what; I'll call you after supper. Let me see what's going on, okay?"

"That'll work," Kyle said. He picked out one of the freshman managers and yelled, telling the new arrival to cart in the water buckets while Kyle put the blocking sled back into the storage room.

Peggy was waiting on Braxton when he got home. Harold had left with the county prosecutor, Scott Douglass, before Braxton departed for practice, the two headed for another of the secretive bi-racial committee meetings. Braxton had taken two steps inside the door when Peggy tossed him the keys.

"Let's go to the hospital, Hon."

The drive to Takasaw General was quick. In a world of Jim Crow laws, the rules passed after the great chaos of Reconstruction to prohibit what blacks could and couldn't legally do, Takasaw General was a rare exception in the Deep South. A public hospital, it was open to both black and white patients. All the doctors were white, as were most of the nurses.

But the patients were predominantly black. Whites would go to Takasaw General in emergency situations or if they were indigent and had no other choice, but the great majority of whites elected to go to other hospitals, even if it meant a drive of an hour, where they would be surrounded by their own kind.

Takasaw General had changed little over the years. The original front wing of red brick construction had been erected during Roosevelt's WPA building boom. The two expansions on the sprawling, one-story infirmary were made of cinder block, painted white and peeling, that gave the entire edifice a dreary look. Inside wasn't much better. Dull green paint – vomit green was the term they used at Takasaw High where the walls were similar – with a nagging smell of antiseptic and formaldehyde permeating everything. Braxton hadn't been there in years, not since they brought Andy's mom to the hospital after the car wreck. She had been declared dead at the scene, but was transported to the hospital by an ambulance so the coroner could sign her death certificate and release her to a funeral home after arrangements were made.

It had been just Brax and Harold there. Peggy had refused to go. She had vowed never to come back after Candace.

Braxton remained in the front waiting room while Harold went back to the morgue to make the official identification. No one could reach Leonard Laduke, which was somewhat of a blessing. It meant Andy could be told about the accident later, under better circumstances than the hospital and by someone better than a sheriff's deputy -- or a drunken Leonard Laduke.

Braxton thankfully missed that, too. He sat out in the car while Harold went inside the Laduke's house and broke the news to Andy and Leonard.

A long time later, in a biology lab at school, Braxton finally identified the smell that had stayed with him so long while dissecting a frog.

The hospital hadn't changed much, except the vomit green paint looked a little fresher. The receptionist at the front desk was the same, only older, and Braxton remembered her from Candace's early visits.

She'd spent most of the summer before she entered first grade battling a cold or flu. She'd have a fever, throw up, and then chase the illness only to see it return shortly.

A couple of weeks after Candace started school, Brax came home to find Adele holding Peggy the way Peggy so often held Candace. He'd never seen his mother cry that hard or that long, as Adele cradled her on the couch, wrapping Peggy with both arms while brushing back the hair and the tears.

If only he'd understood. Instead, he ran into his own room, bursting into tears when the door was closed. What was so wrong?

It seemed like forever before Adele came into his room, leaving Peggy alone. The old black woman's eyes were red and weary as she sat down next to Brax and began explaining.

That morning, Brax's parents had taken Candace to a specialist in Montgomery recommended by the local doctor who wouldn't tell them the reason she couldn't shake the cold. She had to undergo tests over the next few days, but the nurses had urged Peggy to take Candace home for the night.

The tests that followed proved what the family doctor had feared, but wouldn't admit aloud. The specialist in Montgomery, more certain of the diagnosis, confirmed the fear.

Candace had advanced leukemia.

Brax woke up the next morning to find himself alone in the house with Adele, who was making pancakes. Where was everyone else? Gone to Montgomery, she'd said. Harold, Peggy and Candace had left at 6 o'clock for more tests.

Brax would see Candace once more, in the hospital, a few weeks later. She'd lost weight and glops of hair from treatments. But she smiled when she saw him, clutched the teddy bear, and said in a whisper, "My B-Bear."

Peggy stayed in Montgomery the entire time, sleeping on a cot the nurses brought in at night. Harold went back and forth, the commute wearing him down. Yet before bed, he'd answer Brax's endless questions patiently, always ending the same way.

"You'll see Candace again some day, son, somewhere."

He would see her again, a month later.

Dressed in her yellow Sunday dress, a white braid keeping the bangs out of her face, Candace lay eternally still in the tiny, walnut coffin. Her hands were clasped together at her waist, her lips pursed in a faint smile. The wig almost looked like her real hair.

For weeks, he wouldn't play with Moses. Adele never asked why. In truth, it just hurt too much. Because every time he saw Moses meant he might see one of Moses' cousins who often visited dressed in one of Candace's hand-me-downs.

It wasn't until Brax was 11 or 12 that he finally asked his father what he'd meant about seeing Candace somewhere later. He explained it simply, as he said he always believed.

"You live this life the best you can for a better life after," Harold Freeman began. "Treat people right, do good things and follow God's commands and you'll see Candace again. Not in this life, but the next."

It remained the most religious thing he ever heard his father say.

****

Braxton was a tagalong again, but this time he followed Peggy through the waiting room and down the corridor until they stopped in front of a room. Peggy knocked softly before prying the partly closed door open and urging Braxton to follow.

Adele lay in the bed, eyes closed, her heavy chest moving slowly up and down. Tubes were going into her nose and into her right arm, the latter pumping a clear liquid into her veins from a stand above.

A middle-aged black couple stood by the bed, the lady holding Adele's hands as Adele sat quietly in a chair beside the bed. Seeing the Freemans, the man circled the bed and extended a hand to Peggy.

"You must be Mrs. Freeman, nice to meet you. I'm Isaac Young. And this," he said, a hand sweeping toward the lady next to Adele, "is Ester."

"Good to finally meet you, Professor," Peggy said, shaking the man's hand softly. "We've heard a lot about you over the years."

"Same here," the bearded man said. "And we've heard a lot lately about your son. I'm assuming this is Braxton, the pride of Takasaw High."

Peggy smiled. "Indeed."

Braxton extended his hand and the professor shook it.

"How is she?" asked Peggy.

"In and out of consciousness," Young said. "She's having trouble talking, which the doctors expected. But she recognizes everyone. That's a positive sign."

Mrs. Young stood up and offered Peggy her seat but Peggy declined, instead sending Braxton outside to retrieve a couple of chairs that lined the hallway, which he lugged back in and placed next to where Mrs. Young was sitting. Peggy took the first one and, when the professor remained standing, updating Peggy on Adele's condition, Braxton took the second.

Isaac Young had folded his olive khaki jacket over the foot of Adele's bed, loosened his tie and rolled up the sleeves of his heavily starched dress shirt. Despite the heat, despite the casualness, he was immaculate. The armpits held only a hint of perspiration.

Ester Young wore a blue dress, with white and yellow flowers throughout. A white hat, with floral band matching the dress, lay on top of Isaac Young's jacket.

While the adults talked, Braxton stared at Adele. Her eyes had dark circles, as if she hadn't slept in days, and the arm with the IV had bruises. Adele was a solid, big woman, yet she'd never been sick in all the time Braxton had known her. Now she looked pitiful and helpless.

"I'm sorry, Mrs. Freeman, but it's going to be a long time before Aunt Adele does any work for you," Mrs. Young said. "I'll be glad to help you find someone new until she's back on her feet."

"No, no, no," Peggy said. "We'll get by. Let's not worry about anything but helping her get back on her feet."

Braxton had heard the late night conversations before, when Peggy and Harold huddled over the kitchen table or next to each other on the couch, watching TV, expecting him to be asleep. The boycott of white businesses the last year or so had severely affected Harold's income to the point where the Freemans had to make a number of changes. They'd sold the second car, which Harold had gotten Peggy a few years earlier. But one change they wouldn't make for a year was getting rid of Adele. Harold made the point and Peggy always agreed. Adele didn't cost that much, and though Peggy, with only one child – one in high school, at that – and she could do everything Adele did, Adele and the boys needed the income.

But the boycott had taken its toll to the point where Adele only worked three days a week instead of five until they relieved her altogether. The Freemans had tried to find her other work, but most of their friends were in the same financial shape.

Adele never complained. Moses never let on that things were any tougher.

Adele would have to remain in the hospital at least another three weeks, Mrs. Young explained, before she could be released to go home. Even then, she would need some supervision, as well as help running the house.

"We've looked into getting her a nurse," the professor said, "but to be perfectly honest ..."

"To be honest," chimed in Mrs. Young, "we can't afford that."

"No, we can't," the professor said. "It's a lot more expensive than we realized. Braxton's met our daughter, Natalie. She gets out of school at three every day. She's willing to go to Adele's house after school, cook dinner and get Josiah to bed every night."

"That would be good," Peggy said. "What about during the day?"

"I'm going to try to take some leave from work," Mrs. Young said. "I just started working in the admissions office. I don't have much leave time available. And we're not in a position for me to take off completely."

Braxton listened, not participating.

"I have an idea," Peggy said. The Youngs both looked at her. "I wake up pretty early. I can go over in the mornings, fix breakfast for Adele's family, then come back home and get my own brood off. Harold and Braxton are pretty self-sufficient at this stage anyway. Neither needs me a lot, any more."

She said it with a soft chuckle, and Mrs. Young responded with a smile.

"I can spend most of the mornings with her, if that's okay with y'all. The only conflict I would have is on Wednesdays, when I play bridge. I could quit, for awhile, I guess."

"Don't do that, Mrs. Freeman," Mrs. Young said. "I'll take a half-day off on Wednesdays, if you're sure it wouldn't be an imposition. It wouldn't, would it?"

"Heavens, no. As much as Adele has done for us over the years, it's the least I could do."

The Youngs thanked her before silence overwhelmed the room.

The professor was pacing. The image struck Braxton immediately. Harold always paced when he was nervous.

"Mrs. Freeman?" he said, interrupting the awkward silence. "I don't mean to be rude, but ..."

"Go ahead, ask."

"Natalie is rather adamant about helping out during the week. She can spend weekends with my aunt. But is it safe? I mean, she's a young, Negro girl. We haven't been back here very long, but I remember what it used to be like. I'm not sure I'm comfortable with her driving home by herself, at least the times we could let her use the automobile."

Peggy didn't reply immediately, which Braxton knew meant she was considering the question. Peggy rarely said something without considering the options.

"I'm sorry," Young offered apologetically. "I didn't mean to be so rude."

"No, Mr. Young. You weren't being rude. You were being realistic."

Peggy reached over and patted the top of Mrs. Young's hand, which was still holding Adele's loosely.

"No, unfortunately, things haven't changed much."

"We're told there's a bus route. Frankly, I'd rather her use the automobile when available."

"Well, the bus route would get her over there," Peggy said. "It only runs up and down Main, which would mean a five-block walk. But that wouldn't be a problem for Natalie in the afternoon. The problem is, bus service ends pretty early – usually by five or six."

Young considered Peggy's statement. "My last class ends at two-thirty. I have office hours after that and meetings scheduled. That might work. It's hard for me to take off."

Peggy nodded. Braxton continued to listen passively.

"I do most of my reading and grading at night. But I guess it wouldn't hurt for me to pick her up at night."

"That's an idea," Peggy said. "And I have another one."

Braxton could see Adele's slow, heavy breathing had changed. She was breathing more erratically now, and her eyes were beginning to flutter.

"Mama," Braxton said, pointing at Adele. Peggy and the Youngs looked as Adele's eyes opened wide, then rolled back.

"Aunt Adele?" Mrs. Young said, leaning over to look into Adele's eyes. Mr. Young left the room quickly, returning in moments with a nurse. The white woman assessed the situation quickly, pulling the clear fluid off the IV stand and replacing it. She then plugged the new liquid into the tube running into Adele's veins. Within seconds, Adele's eyes had closed again and the breathing became regular.

"She's still in a lot of pain," said the nurse while taking Adele's pulse. "Don't worry, though. She just ran out of pain killer."

Satisfied that everything was okay, the nurse left with a promise to check on Adele again in half an hour.

The silence returned. Braxton continued to stare at Adele, on the lookout for anything else unusual.

"Mrs. Freeman? You said you had an idea?"

"Oh, yes," Peggy replied. "What if Natalie takes the bus to Adele's and, when she gets ready to go home, either Harold or Braxton can give her a ride home? That would work for you, wouldn't it, Hon?"

She had directed the question to Brax, but he hadn't been paying attention.

"What? I'm sorry, Mama."

"Either you or Daddy could give Natalie a ride home at night, right?"

"Uh, yeah. Sure we could, most of the time. After I get home from practice …"

"Tell you what, Mr. Young," Peggy said, turning again to the professor. "We'll get her home. When we can't, she can spend the night at Adele's – or at our house, we have a spare bedroom. Then we'll get her home first thing in the morning. Would that work?"

"Like a Godsend," said Mr. Young.

* * * *

Andy Laduke had the list Keith Lockett had given him the night before resting on the table, where it had remained for the past half-hour. He wasn't comfortable with the assignment, but it was something he had to do.

Because Keith Lockett had told him so.

There were six names, and beside the names were phone numbers. Five white members of the bi-racial committee with one scratched out, that of Harold Freeman. Laduke had told Lockett he couldn't make the call to the Freeman house. Someone would recognize him, for certain. The remaining name was that of the Rev. Tompkins -- the only number Andy relished calling.

Below the names, typed neatly, were the instructions. He was to call each of the names, hanging up only if one of the men on the list answered. If a wife or a child answered he was to proceed with the script.

This wasn't why Andy had joined the Klan. He imagined himself fighting for the cause, and he clearly understood there would be violence -- necessary violence -- at times. But he had no desire to intimidate a woman or a child, especially a white woman or a child.

The orders were clear, however. And the calls had to be made by one o'clock, because Lockett said the bi-racial meeting would last at least until then.

He dialed the Tompkins house first, and the phone rang and rang with no answer. He hung up and redialed the number, letting it ring ten times before giving up. He wanted to deal with Tompkins first. Instead, he moved on.

The name at the top of the list was Scott Douglass. He'd known the family for years, even been to Douglass' youngest brother's birthday parties at Bradley Allen's big house on Gautier, down the street from the Freemans. But he'd always been a kid, and none of the adult Douglasses paid much attention to him.

The Douglasses wouldn't recognize him.

He dialed the number. Again it rang without a quick answer. But, on the fourth ring, a female answered with a hello. In the background, two little kids were crying.

Mrs. Douglass.

"Hello?" she said a second time.

Andy cleared his voice, swallowed hard, and picked up the script.

"We don't want niggers in our school," he said in a low rumble. "You tell ..."

"What?"

"You tell your husband that we don't want niggers in our school."

"Who ... who is this?"

He could hear the anxiety and fear in her voice.

"You heard me, Mrs. Douglass. You tell your husband: we don't want niggers in our school."

"Who are you? Why are you doing this?"

"You tell your husband, Mrs. Douglass. If he doesn't stop this now, someone will get hurt."

A glass shattered in the background, momentarily distracting the lady. "Junior," she said as she began to sob. "Why are you doing this? What have I done to you?"

"It's what your husband has done to us, all of us," said Andy, breaking from the script. "He's supposed to be one of us, but he's turned on us. Good white people don't like nigger lovers, Mrs. Douglass."

He could hear the phone drop. A few seconds later, the line clicked off.

The instructions were clear: don't let them off easy. Andy redialed the number. Mrs. Douglass picked up on the first ring, but didn't say anything.

"You heard me. Tell your nigger-loving husband to stop this now, or he'll be seriously hurt. And so will you and your little boys."

She hung up the phone again. When Andy called back, he got only a busy signal.

He'd dreaded the assignment when Lockett laid it all out the night before but now he felt something else, a sense of power. He wasn't threatening an innocent white person, he was threatening someone who was part of bringing ruin to his race. Their race, the white race.

He had intimidated the hell out of her, hadn't he? For the first time since joining the Klan, he had done something productive.

Time to call the next number.

* * * *

Moses could hear Josiah snoring from the comfort of the sleeping bag a few feet away as Moses hit the 4-foot mark. Tossing the next load of dirt aside, he leaned back against the pit to rest and tossed the shovel down.

A few nights a week, when there was a need for extra help and he felt restless, Moses showed up at the cemetery to dig graves in the middle of the night. Takasaw was a small town, but rarely a day went by without a death and a need for a new hole in the ground.

Grave digging was Rufus Dixon's job. The old family friend was pushing 60 now. He had a bad back and bad eyesight, but he needed the money. When Moses showed up, he let Moses do the work. But he still kept half the pay.

Moses never brought Josiah along, but with Adele in the hospital and not knowing how he'd buy groceries, Moses decided he had no choice. The sleeping bag was old Army surplus Braxton had given Moses when the two camped out in the backyard years ago and it didn't cover Josiah all the way. But Josiah was so tired, he'd fallen to sleep within minutes of arrival.

"Boy, why do you want to go to school with the white kids?" Rufus asked, taking a swig of the flask he always carried in the pocket of his overalls as he leaned against a grave marker.

"I don't know. They asked me to."

"Sheez, boy. Why you want to be a guinea pig?"

Moses put his arms over his head and looked into the sky. The stars were harder to find tonight as clouds were rolling in from the west.

"They asked me. Maybe I'll get a better education. Maybe I'll get a college scholarship."

Rufus replied with a harrumph. "College? Where's that going to get you?"

"Out of this town," Moses said, picking up the shovel and going back to the arduous task. *Two more feet to go.*

"Don't ever trust white people," Rufus continued, oblivious to Moses' efforts. "At least not down here. Maybe up North ..."

Moses tried to ignore the old man, but he knew Rufus was right. You couldn't trust whites. The Freemans were the exception. And Braxton was his oldest friend. But they couldn't get him a good job. They couldn't protect him if the Klan came around.

Why am I doing this? Why am I changing schools? Leaving my old friends behind? What, for football? For Brax and the coach?

Moses stopped for a second and looked Rufus in the eye.

"Why should I trust you, Rufus? I do the work and you take half the money."

Rufus laughed and slipped the flask back into his pocket.

"Because I'll never do you wrong, boy," he said with a twinkle. "I got you this job. But if you don't want me to take half … hell, keep it all."

Moses dug back in and started shoveling the dirt at a faster pace.

"Nah, it's alright, Rufus. You need it more than I do."

* * * *

The call hadn't bothered Braxton the day before. He and Peggy had stopped by the house on the way back from the hospital to change before going over to check in on Moses and the rest of Adele's family.

The voice was unfamiliar. "We don't want niggers in our school. Tell your daddy that, boy. We don't want no …"

"Up yours," Braxton had said uncharacteristically, then slammed the phone down. Luckily, Peggy was in the other room. He took the mouthpiece off the cradle, where it remained until they returned from fixing Adele's family dinner.

Too tired from football practice, too weary from Adele's health problems, he'd dismissed the call easily enough. It was Sunday afternoon. The Freemans had eaten a quick lunch after church and were sitting in the living room with the visitor before proceeding to the Douglass' house.

The visitor was a reporter from *Newsweek*, a magazine Braxton had heard about but couldn't remember ever reading. He was slightly younger than Harold, much shorter, with close-cropped red hair and an infectious smile. His name was Thomas Boudreaux, and he'd made introductions by telling the Freemans he went to school at Louisiana State University – LSU – something Braxton could relate to.

"Maybe it's none of my business, Mr. Boudreaux, but can you …"

"Please, Mr. Freeman, call me Tom."

"Tom, then. And call me Harold."

"Agreed."

"How does *Newsweek* know about our plans to integrate the high school? Frankly, why do y'all care?"

Boudreaux smiled at Harold, then shared the smile with Peggy and Braxton, wanting to put everyone at ease again.

"I've spent a lot of time in Alabama the last couple of years covering civil rights issues," Boudreaux said, "most recently in Tuscaloosa, when the University was integrated. I'm not at liberty to reveal my sources, but someone I've met tipped me off. And, from the looks of things today, tipped just about everyone else off, too."

Boudreaux laughed. Reporters from the *Washington Post* and *Time Magazine* were scheduled to meet with the bi-racial committee at the Douglass home.

"I understand that. But why is this of interest to you?" Harold said. "I don't mean to be difficult. I'm just wondering. We're not the first school system in America to integrate."

"No, you're not," Boudreaux replied. "But you are the first in Alabama. Whether you like it or not, you're the next battleground. I say that figuratively, not literally, though my source says Governor Wallace plans on stopping this with troops. That alone makes it a national issue."

Troops? Braxton had visions of the marines coming into town, taking over Takasaw by martial law. Harold, however, didn't seem surprised.

"Yeah, that's what we're told to expect," Harold said. "But we're not so sure ... Tom? Are we off the record?"

"At this point, yes we are."

"We've been told Wallace is sending in state troopers. But we expect it to be nothing more than a show, just like at the University. Maybe he'll show up like he did in Tuscaloosa and rile up the crowd."

"He may, then again ..." Boudreaux said. "Again, I can't reveal my source. But I think one of the reasons we've been tipped off is because Wallace wants to play politics again. By bringing in the press, he feels the situation won't get out of hand. He can make his point and improve his standing with the people. But I don't expect him to back down this time. He'd lose face."

That wasn't what Harold was expecting to hear. Braxton could see that in his father's reaction.

"Do you have anything solid to back you up?"

"To a degree. First, my source. Second, the federal government isn't getting involved this time. The same thing will be happening all across the South in a very short time. The President can't send Katzenbach every time a school integrates."

Harold rose from the couch, fishing his keys from the front pocket of his slacks.

"We'd better get moving," he said. "This is going to be hard enough as it is. From what you're telling me, harder than what we've anticipated."

Scott Douglass' small home was at the end of a new cull de sac and was next to impossible to navigate because cars lined each side. Harold pulled in behind a white Ford sedan three blocks away and led Peggy, Braxton and Boudreaux down the street.

The front door was open. Harold didn't bother knocking, instead opening the screen barrier and letting the new arrivals in. Douglass and the entire bi-racial committee, black and white, were situated around the cramped living room. Some in chairs, some standing. There were other men on hand that Braxton didn't recognize. Douglass shook Harold's hand and politely told Peggy and Braxton to join his wife and kids in the backyard.

Rev. Tompkins stood in the middle of the group, addressing the reporters. The list included Boudreaux, plus writers from *Time*, *The Washington Post* and *The Atlanta Constitution*. The latter had shown up unexpectedly, with the reporter from *The Post*. All four men were furiously scribbling notes as Tompkins spoke.

"All we want is for our Negro children to have the same opportunities as white children," Tompkins said. "Nothing less than what Thomas Jefferson demanded in the bill of rights."

"Reverend, are you the official spokesman for the bi-racial committee?" Boudreaux asked.

"No," Tompkins said curtly, as if he'd been rebuffed. "No, we've elected Mr. Douglass to be our official spokesman."

Tompkins sat down. Dean Ralston stood up.

"You've all met Mr. Douglass," Ralston said calmly. "He comes from one of the most respected families in our town, a family that's stood by Negroes and whites alike. That, plus the fact he's an elected official, made him the obvious choice."

Harold tried to contain a smirk. *Wasn't the mayor an elected official, too?* Of course, he was, but the politician had kept a very low profile from the beginning, afraid he'd lose too many votes. He'd been the strongest white dissenter of the plan in the committee, but had not dissented with any real passion. He was politicking, straddling the fence.

The reporters began firing questions at Douglass, who remained seated on the couch between Ralston and Tompkins.

"Is this plan really necessary?" asked the *Time* reporter. "My understanding is that the Negro high school at the Institute is outstanding."

"It is," Douglass replied. "It's probably the finest Negro school in the South. But there's another Negro high school in town, and it's a far cry from Institute High. Not only in terms of academics, but in terms of facilities, faculty, you name it. It gets a fraction of the money Takasaw High does. The same goes for the high school at the institute, but it's supplemented with funds from the college."

"I don't have the latest census figures. What's the ratio of Negroes and whites in Takasaw?" asked the reporter from Atlanta.

"Sixty-forty Negro," Douglass replied.

"Are you afraid that by integrating the school and by taking this stand, whites are giving up the power they seem to hold now?" the Atlanta reporter asked in a follow up.

Douglass shrugged his shoulders. He caught the glance of Rev. John Ed Mullens, the white Presbyterian minister, and deferred.

"It's not about power," said the minister. "It's about equal opportunity."

"Your name again, sir?" asked the *Post* reporter.

"Reverend John Ed Mullens."

"Gotcha."

Mullens came to the Presbyterian church, the one the Freemans attended, two years earlier, recommended for the post by Scott Douglass' twin brother, Bradley Alan Jr., a minister in Montgomery.

Harold Freeman liked Mullens from the beginning. He gave comforting sermons, getting the message across without all the fire and brimstone so common in small town religion. He was an educated man, a graduate of the University of Virginia, and came from affluence, which was evident in his carriage and demeanor. He had passed on an easier posting at a bigger church for Takasaw First Presbyterian, seeing it as a potential hot bed of civil rights. That alone was reason for respect.

Most of the white members of the bi-racial committee, Harold included, devised the integration plan because they believed the schools would be forced to merge eventually. Yet Mullens had a passion for the cause. Of all the members, black or white, Mullens seemed to hold the strongest belief that integration was, in strict moral terms, was the right path.

"What plans do you have to combat Governor Wallace when he sends in the troopers?" asked Boudreaux, who quickly scanned the room to judge reactions. Neither Freeman nor Douglass seemed surprised, but others did. Yet no one spoke up.

The question seemed to be directed to the minister, but he backed off, allowing Douglass to take the floor again.

"We have contingency plans for just such an event," Douglass said convincingly.

Except, Harold Freeman knew, Douglass was lying through his teeth. There were no plans – he and Douglass had learned about Wallace's plans earlier that morning. In all the planning, in all the long hours, the possibility of state intervention had never been discussed. Why would the governor of the state get involved in a small-town matter, especially with big cities like Huntsville and Mobile ordered by federal courts to integrate? That's why Douglass started contacting every member of the bi-racial committee at dawn, making certain everyone could attend an emergency meeting late that night.

This meeting was more for show, a show of solidarity, and an attempt to win the reporters over. Harold Freeman could see the reporters, if not swayed, were at least sympathetic. That would be important. No one in Takasaw wanted to become the next Bull Connor.

What an irony, Freeman mused. Connor had become infamous because he attacked Negro marchers in Birmingham with attack dogs and fire hoses, overseeing the carnage like a general in Nazi Germany. Their intentions here were polar opposites.

But the press, especially the national press, could make a villain out of anyone.

"Governor Wallace has no business sending state troopers to interfere in the everyday lives of the citizens of Takasaw," Douglass continued. "No business, whatsoever. For all his grand talk of an intrusive federal government, his sending state troopers here would prove both illegal and hypocritical."

"Amen, Brother, Amen," Tompkins said.

Boudreaux wasn't impressed with the answer. "But you *do* have contingency plans, right?"

"We do," Douglass replied. "But it wouldn't be prudent to discuss them now. I hope you understand that."

"Of course." Boudreaux paused momentarily before continuing to dig in. "Are you saying that your stance, the stance of the bi-racial committee, is the consensus of the people of Takasaw?"

Douglass looked around for help, realizing he had none. This was a difficult question.

"What we are proposing is what Takasaw's top leaders, Negro and white, have approved," Douglass said. "If ..."

Douglass stopped again, looking for help that wasn't coming.

"Gentlemen, can we go off the record for a moment?"

"Fine with me," Boudreaux said. The other reporters nodded agreement.

"If our plan went before a public vote, in a referendum, we wouldn't stand a chance in Hell of getting even a simple majority," Douglass said. "It wouldn't be approved by a majority of whites, nor would it be passed by the majority of Negroes. Most people would be against it because they object for moral reasons or because they believe there's nothing wrong with the status quo. Dean, Reverend," he said, looking to his left and right at Ralston and Tompkins. "Do you disagree?"

"No," said Ralston.

"Change is hard for many people," Tompkins piped in. "Sometimes, change has to come swiftly in the night. Prosecutor Douglass is right, unfortunately. Just as many Negroes would oppose this as whites. People here don't like change."

Satisfied that he wasn't speaking out of turn, Douglass tried to beat the reporters to the next question.

"So, why are we doing this? It's simple, really. First, it's the right thing to do. Second, it's coming, whether anyone likes it or not. The federal courts have spoken. We can either do it now on our own terms and at our own pace, or ..." Douglass trailed off, letting the thought remain unspoken.

The man from *The Post* held up his hand to stop Douglass from proceeding. "Is that last bit on the record?"

Douglass shrugged his shoulders. "Yeah, why not?"

All four reporters scribbled down the quote.

Harold Freeman was beginning to understand the rhythm of the reporters. Each was competing for better questions and better angles, a theory the *Time* reporter confirmed.

"Even if you've gotten city leaders to approve this plan, there has to have been some strong opposition to it," the reporter from Atlanta stated.

No one said anything. After an uncomfortable few moments, Harold spoke. "No, not really. There have been some comments, certainly, but they've been rather remote – a person here, a person there – although, at times, those comments have come from within our own extended families. But in terms of an organized opposition, no, there's not anything that we're aware of other than Governor Wallace's intentions."

"Let me reiterate," Douglass added quickly, "We will be prepared for anything, short of violence."

The reporters continued their sparring for another half hour before finally running out of gas. One by one, they bid the members of the committee farewell – Boudreaux spending a few minutes thanking Harold for his cooperation. Finally, they left, leaving the twelve Takasaw men alone.

"Did any of you receive threatening calls yesterday?" Douglass asked after the room had cleared.

Five of the men answered with hands raised or nods. Mullens, the minister, spoke first. "Yes, Scott. Someone said something to my eldest when he answered the phone, during our meeting. He was too young to comprehend much of it, but he could repeat one word: 'Nigger.'"

Alvin Blakeley, the president of the colored bank, said his wife had taken two calls, but had quickly hung up before finally taking the phone off the hook. "She's kind of used to bullshit like that."

"Well, my wife's not," said Douglass, who detailed Jan's call the day before and how it had genuinely frightened her. "I doubt this is a one-time deal. I expect more phone calls and we have to understand it may go beyond phone calls. Rosenberg from the FBI says he's working on it, but, truthfully, it's a wild-goose chase at this moment. I have one suggestion, and I hope you all take it. For the next week, I would suggest we all move within circles of two or three at all times, especially at night. Before we leave, we ought to draw up car pools for tonight's meeting."

Harold went out back to retrieve Braxton and Peggy. Peggy and Jan were in an animated discussion, laughing as Jan nursed her newborn from her breast. She saw Harold and quickly pulled the child from her nipple, blushing. Braxton was pitching a plastic ball to Douglass' 18-month-old, who was swinging from the heels and hadn't noticed.

Once in the car, headed back home, Harold decided it was time to ask.

"Did we receive any kind of unusual phone calls while I was at the meeting yesterday?"

Peggy didn't say anything.

"Yes, when Mama and I got back from the hospital," Braxton piped in after a quick pause.

"What did they say?"

"I don't remember the details. Basically, the guy calling said he didn't want niggers at our school."

"Did he make any threats?"

"No," Braxton replied, "but I didn't give him much of a chance. I cussed him, hung up and took the phone off the hook."

"What'd you say?" asked Peggy, surprised that Braxton hadn't mentioned any of it.

"I said, 'Up yours,'" Braxton beamed.

Peggy looked at him with astonishment. He'd never talked like that before in front of his mother. But it had been an unusual phone call, and it needed unusual language.

Brax's language stunned Peggy, but not Harold. He was smiling broadly.

" 'Screw you,' " he muttered. "I couldn't have said it better myself."

Peggy ignored the banter, and began relaying Jan Douglass' horror story from the day before, describing how upset the prosecutor's wife was even the next day, as Peggy and Braxton arrived in the backyard.

"Harold, do you think someone would actually try to hurt us?"

"Absolutely not," Harold said, lying the same way Scott Douglass had earlier. There was no point in scaring his wife and son, but the discussion at the end of the meeting had made it clear that the threats could escalate. "Just to be sure, Scott's asked his FBI friend to arrange some patrols by the local police tonight. We're holding an emergency meeting – we've got no choice if this is going to work. No one will bother you, okay? But a sheriff's car driving up and down the street every few minutes won't hurt a bit, will it?"

* * * *

The three men drove past Scott Douglass' house once again, looking for any evidence that the county prosecutor was home. Confident he'd joined the others, Keith Lockett drove around the block then headed in another direction. He drove for a few minutes before he pulled off onto a dirt entrance into woods, woods that backed up to the Douglass home.

"Put your robes on," Lockett commanded. Andy Laduke and the

other man, the one who hadn't spoken at the farmhouse meeting the other night, reached under the seat of the truck and pulled out the robes and began slipping them over their clothes. Satisfied, Andy looked up to see Lockett had his hood on, too. Andy quickly followed suit.

Lockett was thorough. He had two Klansmen providing surveillance of the meeting, and they were supposed to high tail it back to the Douglass house if the meeting adjourned early to warn the trio.

The Grand Dragon wanted to make a statement, and the Douglasses seemed to be the most vulnerable, at least from Laduke's recollection of the Saturday phone call. Targeting Scott Douglass' home made political sense, too, considering his position.

Andy had been relieved earlier that night when Lockett explained why they would not target the other members of the bi-racial committee, specifically his blood kin, the Freemans. Gautier Street wasn't busy at this hour, but too many people lived on it. The mission might be cut short by a stray passerby, or by one of the patrol cars they'd seen driving through town. There were at least three cars out on patrol. On any other typical night, there was no more than one. Obviously, the bi-racial committee was worried.

They'd give them something real to worry about, Lockett had said. Except they wouldn't be spotted.

There were other reasons to pick Douglass' house. It was on a quiet street, they could sneak up from behind, and they could get away before anyone reacted.

Lockett had done all the talking. Andy was too nervous to say anything, and the other guy hadn't talked at the farmhouse meeting and seemed to have nothing to say. This time, though, Andy thought he recognized him as one of the foremen on the second shift. Hadn't Andy seen him going into the mill on one of the days he was headed home?

Yet Lockett hadn't called him by name or introduced him. Lockett called the other man, who was closer to his age, "Brother." He continued calling Andy "Boy," as if he were a stupid kid.

Lockett led the trio through the woods without any light. He seemed to know the way already, through scrub pine trees and light brush. They walked just 50 feet until they reached the chain fence bordering a backyard. Lockett signaled Andy, and he understood quickly. He scaled the fence, gripping the kerosene can tightly, and crouched on the other side. Lockett followed, then helped the third man lower the heavy 8-foot cross he had lugged.

On the other side, Lockett signaled for them to stay put as he crept to the back of the house. He began looking in windows, one at a time, until he surveyed the entire back.

"All quiet," he whispered when he returned. "The kids are asleep in one room. The lights are off in the main bedroom, too."

He nodded to the third man, who lifted the cross with Lockett, then carried it to the middle of the yard. Lockett reached down and dug a quick hole with a small military shovel he pulled out from underneath the robe. Satisfied at the depth, he nodded again, then helped the quiet man lower the cross. It stood, with a slight lean. Lockett kicked dirt to stabilize it, and motioned to Andy.

He took the can and began dousing the cross as high up as he could reach.

"Get it all soaked," Lockett whispered, and Andy did as instructed, soaking the dry timbers. He then began making a trail back toward the back of the fence. Luckily, the ground was bone dry. It hadn't rained in a month, and that would make their job easy.

Lockett waited at the base of the fence for Andy and the third man to clear it, then followed. On the other side, he picked up two rocks, neither bigger than golf balls, then nodded again. The third man understood immediately. He pulled out a lighter, struck it, and held it to the end of the kerosene trail, igniting a fire that slowly engulfed the cross.

Lockett then reared back with one of the rocks in his right hand and threw it hard toward a middle window. It clanked against the brick siding.

"Shit!" he muttered. He shifted the other rock to his right hand and threw again. This time, it shattered a window.

Lights came on in the far left bedroom, and the drapes parted. The silhouette of a woman – Jan Douglass – appeared. She saw the cross and began screaming.

"We don't want niggers, bitch!" Lockett yelled. "Too bad your husband won't live to see his plan fall apart!"

He let out a rebel yell, then began running through the woods, back toward the truck. Andy watched the cross burn, watched Jan Douglass disappear from the window, and listened as the screaming grew louder. Then he turned and ran, trying to keep up with his leader.

* * * *

123

For the first time, Braxton Freeman had unleashed Katie Sullivan's bobcats from underneath her swimsuit. They stood there unprotected, ready for his hands and mouth.

"Braxton! Braxton!"

He opened an eye to see Peggy leaning over him, shaking him violently.

"Braxton Freeman! Wake up!"

Braxton shook his head and wiped a sliver of saliva from the corner of his mouth. He glanced at the clock by his bed.

Twelve-twenty-three. He'd been asleep for almost three hours.

"What's wrong, Mama?"

"Get dressed now."

"What's wrong?" he asked again, this time with urgency.

"We've got to go over to Scott Douglass' house now. Just put on some jeans and grab your sneakers. *Hurry!*"

Braxton waited for Peggy to leave the room, embarrassed by how the dream had affected him, then grabbed the blue jeans and yanked them on. He grabbed his tenny shoes from the closet, passing on socks, then headed into the living room, where Peggy was already dressed and waiting.

"What's wrong? Where's Daddy?"

"He's still at the meeting, with the others. We need to go over to the Douglasses house now. Here, take the keys. You drive."

Peggy explained what happened on the drive over. When they pulled into the same quiet cull de sac they'd left earlier in the day a police car was parked in the driveway and neighbors wearing robes and pajamas were milling around in the yard.

Peggy led them quickly through the maze. At the front door, a deputy stopped her.

"Mrs. Douglass is expecting us," she said.

The deputy moved aside and allowed them in. Jan Douglass was crying hysterically on the couch, holding the infant. The older boy, Brax's little baseball pal, was next to her, bawling as well.

Peggy went to Jan's side and hugged her. Braxton went to the toddler and picked him up. The toddler wouldn't stop crying, but he laid his head on Braxton's shoulder as he wailed.

Peggy continued to try to console the woman, stroking her cheek with a hand as she held on tight. Suddenly, she pulled away to look at the hand, and spotted traces of blood.

"Oh, my God! Jan? Are you okay?"

She replied without saying anything. Shaking her head, she pulled the newborn away. There was a small pool of blood on her blouse. Peggy saw the source of the blood: the nose and mouth of the baby.

"What happened, Jan? What happened?"

A second deputy, standing in the kitchen interjected. "Somebody threw stones through the baby's window and hit him in the face while in his crib," the man said with little emotion.

"Oh, God," Peggy said. "Have you called an ambulance?"

"Yes, ma'am. Should be here in a minute. But he's okay. It was just a glancing blow."

"He's a baby," Peggy said with a trace of anger Braxton wasn't used to. "I thought you were going to stop this from happening!"

"Ma'am, we were patrolling. We had 12 hours to patrol ..." the deputy said meekly.

Jan Douglass couldn't say anything. Peggy went to the kitchen, found a clean washcloth and saturated it with warm water, returning to the couch. She began wiping the drying blood off the baby's face.

The deputy motioned for Brax, then led him out back. Still holding the toddler, Braxton saw instantly what he was supposed to see: The dying embers of a cross in the middle of the backyard and scorched ground all around.

Braxton nodded to show he understood – was he supposed to say anything? The deputy nodded in return and led Braxton back inside.

The wailing of a siren could be heard. In minutes, two paramedics hustled through the door. They quickly grabbed the baby, trying to judge the extent of the injuries. One took a penlight and flashed it in the baby's eyes after prying them open. The baby awoke with a start and began wailing. Junior began wailing again, too. Braxton grabbed him tight, trying to keep Junior from tumbling to the floor.

"I think he's alright, Mrs. Douglass," said the paramedic. "Just as a precaution, let's take him to an emergency room."

The paramedics huddled to talk.

"Mrs. Douglass, you want to go to the hospital in Opelika?" asked the man.

"No," Peggy said firmly when Jan Douglass wouldn't say anything. "Take him to Takasaw General."

"Takasaw General, okay. Mrs. Douglass, you can ride with us and hold the baby. Miss," said the paramedic, turning to Peggy, "it wouldn't hurt if you rode with us."

"I'll do that," Peggy said, helping Jan Douglass to her feet. She spotted one of the deputies and got his attention. "Should my son and Junior Douglass stay here? Or do they need to go to the hospital?"

"Do you know when Mr. Douglass will return?" the deputy asked.

"No, I don't."

"Then why don't they follow in your car. He's old enough to drive, isn't he?"

"Yes," Peggy said indignantly.

As Peggy, Jan Douglass and the baby climbed into the back of the ambulance, Braxton carried Junior on his shoulder, easing him into the front seat of the Freeman's car. He slid in beside him, holding Junior's hand with his own, then started the car and followed the ambulance the two miles to the hospital.

There was but one doctor on duty in the emergency room. But it was a slow Sunday night. The Douglass baby was attended to immediately. Peggy followed Jan back into the examining room, then told Braxton to follow.

As the doctor examined the baby, Peggy continued to wrap an arm around Jan Douglass, who had quit crying. Now, she was shaking. It was 90 degrees, yet she shook as if it she were freezing.

"He's going to be fine, just fine," the doctor said reassuringly. "I need to stitch up the gash on his nose, that's all."

Peggy took the lead and nodded her approval.

"Just to be safe, let's keep both of them here overnight," the doctor said as a nurse brought in a suture kit. "Mrs. Douglass is suffering from shock, and she needs some supervision. Will that be okay?"

Peggy again gave him an approving nod.

The baby cried pitifully as a nurse held him down and the doctor began weaving the sutures into the fleshly ridge of the tiny nose. Braxton had to turn away. Luckily, Junior had fallen into a deep sleep on Brax's shoulder, forcing him to switch him every few minutes. Junior was getting heavy.

Finally, the nurse led them to a private room. "Mrs. Douglass, why don't you lie down and hold your baby," the nurse said. "I'll give you a sedative to rest your nerves if that's okay."

Braxton didn't need a sedative to fall asleep. It overcame him quickly.

Just as quickly he was awake.

"You said nothing would happen!"

Braxton woke again, nearly dropping Junior. Peggy was standing toe to toe with Harold Freeman, yelling at him.

Harold had his head lowered and was shaking it. "We didn't expect anything, honey. Honestly. I'm sorry. I'm so sorry."

"Where were you?" she asked, directing her fury at Scott Douglass who'd entered the room behind Harold.

Harold grabbed her by the hands, trying to calm her down. "We were at the meeting, you know that."

"You both should have been home protecting your families!" she shouted. "Why weren't you? Why?"

Harold tried to hug her into silence. Peggy broke away and began hitting him on the chest before breaking into a sob and collapsing against him.

"It's my fault," Scott Douglass said quietly. He stood stoically over his wife, a safe distance away. He didn't seem to know whether to touch her or back away. "It's all my fault."

The stoicism disappeared. Douglass began heaving. Pulling his glasses off, he tried to rub the tears away as he backed out of the room.

CHAPTER 7

BRAXTON RACED DOWN the slumbering street, over the cracked sidewalk, vaulting the front hedges at the Watson house to take the short cut through their backyard to Main Street.

He had awakened with regret after a few hours of fruitless sleep, realizing the instant he grabbed the alarm clock that he was in trouble. Football practice was already halfway over.

As he reached the high school, Braxton considered for a moment turning around and heading home. Not for the sleep, which he couldn't get back, but to avoid the ream-job that was sure to come from Hardass Halliday. Instead, the gait remained steady. He'd face the coach's wrath.

Halliday was already yelling – at Lomar, of all people – standing eyeball to eyeball with the other team captain. Halliday popped down into stance, and then began driving Lomar back until the behemoth flopped on his butt, showing how the block was supposed to be made.

The coach stood over Lomar, waiting for the lineman to hop to his feet, when he spotted Braxton making a stealthy dash for the locker room.

"FreeMAN!!!"

Braxton stopped in his tracks. Halliday stood with his arms crossed, the thick, biceps of a blacksmith looking more menacing than ever before. When Halliday was really pissed, he'd introduce the offending athlete to "Old Nellie," a foot-long wooden paddle he used to beat the living hell out of the guilty party's uncovered backside. Four holes were strategically drilled to make the paddling unforgettable.

Braxton had yet to face Old Nellie. Kyle Anderson had, and couldn't sit for a week afterward.

"Where the hell have you been, Freeman?" Halliday yelled. There was a slim possibility someone in Takasaw didn't hear him.

"Overslept," Braxton said.

"What? What did you say?" Halliday screamed again. "Louder!"

"I overslept, coach!" Braxton yelled back.

"No shee-it, Freeman." Halliday uncrossed the arms then waved Braxton over. He turned to Lomar. "Run toss sweep right again. This time, you'd better get those fat legs churning and lead the way!"

It wasn't eight in the morning, yet Braxton was soaked with sweat. He'd collapsed in bed with the clothes he'd worn to the hospital and had been too tired to switch the fan back for a little relief from the heat, an omission that left his cotton T-shirt soaked in the few hours he slept.

Yet he snoozed hard enough that he never heard the alarm clock's shrill warning. That forced him to run the distance barefooted, with only his gym shorts for cover, as the perspiration spread from brow to toe.

Braxton sidled up to Halliday, steeling himself for the impending royal ass-chewing. Instead, Halliday lowered his voice.

"Go home, Freeman," he said in a surprisingly soft tone. "Go home and get some sleep and be back here by three o'clock for the second practice."

Braxton looked at Halliday, unable to respond.

"Your Dad called me from the hospital late last night," Halliday said. "I know where you were."

The old coach then broke into an uncharacteristic grin, the kind Braxton only saw when he began talking about how good Takasaw might be when Moses Burks joined the team.

"You ain't in trouble. I just thought I'd put a little scare in ya."

He began laughing as he waved Braxton away and returned to practice.

* * * *

Across town, Andy Laduke hadn't slept any, either. He joined the Klan for many reasons. He hated niggers and wanted to keep them in their place. And he'd admired Keith Lockett for so long. Lockett was a leader, charismatic and always in command. Keith Lockett was everything Andy wanted to be.

But he hadn't joined the Klan to terrorize white people. Especially someone like Jan Douglass. The woman looked like an innocent doe in the woods last night, suddenly realizing she had no escape from the hunter who'd trained his sight on her. What kind of threat did she pose?

Sure, her husband had gone too far. Scott Douglass deserved the full wrath of the Klan – anything short of murder for the lawyer would've been deserved. The bi-racial committee wasn't the first time he or other members of his meddling family had stirred trouble with the races.

But to scare the living hell out of Jan Douglass and two baby boys? That wasn't right.

Andy had wrestled with the thoughts, the jumbled ideals, for most of the night. Not that he could think clearly. Leonard drank himself into a terrible depression and spent hours wailing for his deceased wife.

Sober, Leonard was tolerable. Drunk, he either turned into a pitiful bawler or a monster. There was no middle ground. Andy preferred the former. After a half hour, with the radio blaring, he could usually take his mind off the crying. But the violence still scared him. Until he'd quit school and learned to get out of the house more, Leonard slapped him around regularly in his drunken fury.

So why didn't he leave for good? Because it was his house as much as Leonard's. And because, despite all his faults – did he have any good points? – Leonard was the only father he'd known.

For that, Andy was loyal to Leonard, even if he despised the son of a bitch.

* * * *

Braxton beat the alarm clock the next morning by a good ten minutes. By six-thirty, he'd already showered, dressed and joined Peggy at the kitchen table for breakfast.

The first day of school fueled the same anticipation in Braxton that a big game did. Summers in a small town left you isolated. Even working at the country club, Braxton saw only a handful of classmates. Although a majority of the Takasaw High boys played football, the football field wasn't the place for reunions.

As the weeks approached the first day, Braxton had looked forward to walking to school with Moses Burks. But not until the week before had he even asked Moses his plans. Then, he'd been surprised to learn that Moses and the other handful of Negro students were meeting elsewhere and bussing to the school so they'd arrive together.

Moses was on his way, already, to the secretive meeting place. Harold Freeman and the other members of the bi-racial committee meeting had left before dawn, to make certain there would be no confrontations before the new transfers arrived at school.

There had been tension throughout the Freeman house. Peggy and Harold weren't speaking. Peggy's anger could still be felt every time Harold neared her.

There was a tension with Harold, too, though it wasn't directed at Peggy. Members of the committee addressed any and every conceivable problem during the late Sunday meeting. But that meeting had come before someone burned a cross in the Douglass' back yard, yelled threats at Jan and the children and hit the Douglass baby in the face with a rock through the window.

Harold's assumption was the one shared by most of the committee -- the Klan was responsible for the vandalism. But who, specifically, from the quasi-secret organization? Was it organized or merely a random act by a small group of good ol' boys?

Because of what had happened, the committee did not meet on Labor Day. Nerves were frayed and tensions within families were strayed. Harold and Peggy weren't the only ones having problems.

The doctors released both the baby and Jan early Monday morning, but not before sending her home with a sedative to help her relax. Scott Douglass didn't disclose what the doctors told him, but Peggy diagnosed Jan's nervous breakdown at the hospital. She'd picked up enough from the scattered whispering between the doctor and nurses to make the conclusion

Jan would need more than rest. She would need someone – someone clinical and professional – to help her talk things out. She would also need someone to stay with her and help her watch the kids for at least the next few days.

Peggy half-heartedly volunteered. She'd already committed to helping out at Adele's house. Fortunately, Scott Douglass decided to call his mother-in-law for help. She'd be arriving mid-Tuesday. Until then, Scott's sister-in-law could stay with Jan.

Anxious to get started, Braxton left for school a good forty-five minutes before the first bell, walking up Gautier Street alone. Most students rode to school in busses or in hot rods, both of which worked against his proximity.

The short cut through the Watson's backyard brought him out on Acorn Street, a block up from the high school. The street was already full.

The front walk to the school was blocked by dozens and dozens of Alabama state troopers, all dressed in the dark blue shirts and slate-gray pants with wide-brimmed hats and sunglasses. In all, there were dozens standing no more than a few yards apart, arms behind them and hands folded together.

Across the road stood the onlookers. Most were white men, dressed in the obligatory business-day outfits of short-sleeve shirts and khakis. But there were pockets of blacks and a few women in the crowd, staring as the troopers gazed dead ahead.

A handful of students stood on the far end of Acorn, the location for the minimal parking the school offered teen-agers. Among the group was Lomar, the other co-captain. That was invitation enough for Braxton. Lomar was sitting on the trunk of his old Chevy. Seeing him, Lomar patted a spot next to him.

"Some scene, ain't it?" Lomar said.

"Yeah," Braxton said. "A little crazy."

The two football captains watched quietly. Not so, the other early arrivals.

"You're telling me they're letting coloreds in our school?" asked a youngster Braxton didn't know.

Another boy shook his head. "That's why *they're* here," he said, pointing at the troopers with a sweep. "Governor Wallace wants them to stop it."

"Good for George C.," said the first youngster.

A redheaded girl Braxton knew to be a couple of years behind him in school stood alongside the two boys. He could place the face immediately, but not the name. He could also place the freckles. She'd been a regular visitor to the pool over the summer and, like Katie Sullivan, had seemingly blossomed overnight.

She had a nice body, though not as pretty in the face as Katie. But, like Kyle said all the time, "It sure would be fun to connect all of her dots."

"Why do you care if the coloreds go to our school?" she asked the first boy.

The boy looked at her, as if she'd asked the stupidest question in the world.

"Because."

That didn't satisfy her. "Because why?"

"Because it ain't right."

"Says who?"

"Says everybody. I ain't got nothing against them, but they've got their schools and we've got ours. Simple as that."

Braxton didn't want to get caught up in the argument, which bothered him. Had he not favored the integration from the first time he learned about it during the July fourth golf course tour with Halliday? Had he not helped Halliday pave the way for Moses Burks' transfer to Takasaw High?

He readily knew the answer. Still didn't make it anyone's business. Verbalizing it, taking a stand, was best left up to others. It wasn't a matter of fear. Braxton Freeman wasn't much for talking and wasting energy.

He wanted out, and he saw an opportunity. Halliday was standing in front of a couple of troopers shooting the breeze. Braxton saw him across the way and elbowed Lomar.

"There's Coach. Let's go see what he has to say."

The lineman rose slowly and lumbered behind Brax, who cut across the street in a jog. Halliday was still talking up a couple of troopers. One of the uniformed men acted as if he couldn't hear. The other one, a thick man almost as old as Halliday was laughing under his breath.

"Yeah, I played with the Bear and Don Hutson. Finest ballplayer I ever saw," Halliday said. "But he was a quiet guy. He did all his talking on the field. Now Bear, you know, was a leader from day one. He could talk a gallon of Jack Daniels out of Billy Sunday."

"Hey, Coach," Braxton said as Lomar arrived right behind him.

"Hey, Freeman, Lomar. Some spectacle, ain't it?"

Halliday said something in a deep rumble to the troopers then put his arms around the boys, and led them a few feet away. He took off his baseball cap and wiped the sweat from his brow with the brown-stained underneath of the bill.

"The way things look, boys, they ain't gonna let us practice today," Halliday said. "Jesus H. Christ! We've got a game on Friday. Doesn't the Governor know that?"

One of the state troopers left the ranks and walked to the head of the path, leading to the high school's front door. Pulling a bullhorn to his lips, he tried to get the milling crowd's attention.

"Ladies and gentlemen," he said flatly once, twice, until things quieted. "By the order of Governor George Wallace, I am directed to forbid the entrance into Takasaw High School by any student, teacher or administrator today or any day, until the matter of desegregation has been satisfactorily settled."

A buzz went through the crowd. From the beginning, Harold Freeman had promised there wouldn't be violence. But the troopers looked menacing in their uniforms, all wearing firearms on the side of their belts.

"We are merely here to ensure everyone's safety," the trooper barked over the battery-powered device. "Again, these are the Governor's orders, and it is our duty to keep order."

Halliday spit a dark stream of tobacco juice onto the sidewalk, hitting Lomar's white sneakers.

"Ain't my day, is it?" Halliday said looking at the new stain. "Or yours, Lomar."

He moved his right foot and tried to rub the juice off Lomar's sneaker with the sole of his weathered shoe. It only made the stain worse.

"I want you two to split up and find your teammates. Tell them to meet at 3 o'clock at the city park. Tell them to wear shorts, if possible, jeans if not. If they don't let us in the school, I don't believe they're going to let us on the practice field. Or to get our gear for a practice."

Halliday pointed toward his left and told Lomar to begin rounding up any players he could find and pass the word. Lomar moved slowly. Braxton turned to head in the other direction when Halliday stopped him.

"Hold it, Freeman," he said. He kneeled in a squat, ran some dry blades of grass through his hand absentmindedly. Braxton kneeled as well, in case Halliday had something to say. He did. "I hadn't counted on this. Guess your papa and the others hadn't either. Shee-it! Shee-it! Shee-it!"

Braxton did the same thing, grabbing blades of grass then throwing them in the air. There was no wind, not that he cared. The grass was still dewy.

"We gotta practice, just because," Halliday said. "But today's a waste of time, to be honest. I just don't see another choice."

135

If it's a waste of time, why not give us the day off?

Braxton kept his thought private. "Surely they'll let us in there tomorrow. Or at worse, the day after. Right, Coach?"

"I don't know, Freeman."

Halliday remained in the squat. Braxton rose, his thighs burning. When Halliday hung his head and remained silent, Braxton moved on, looking for members of the football team.

He was talking to one of the freshman players when he heard another buzz through the crowd, followed by murmurs and a quick turning of heads. Braxton had to push his way through a couple of adults to see what was causing the commotion.

From Main Street marched 20 or more men, dressed in the long white robes of the Ku Klux Klan. None of them wore hoods, but all wore big sunglasses that helped disguise their identities.

As they grew closer, Braxton could make out their chant.

"Niggers stay home! Leave our school alone!"

Four men walked out front. None were recognizable, except a boy close to Brax's edge on the right flank. Even with the large shades on, Braxton knew it was Andy Laduke.

You dumb ass, what the hell are you doing with those clowns?

The Klan members continued their uneven march until they'd spread across the street in front of the state troopers. The chanting continued until one of the men in front held his arms up to silence everyone. His robe was similar, but more elaborate, with gold piping on the shoulders and a red cross for a patch on the left breast.

"Braxton! Brax!"

Freeman wheeled to see Harold walking toward him. Braxton joined him quickly. He was about to say something when Harold put a finger to his lips, then pointed toward the Klan leader.

"Do we want niggers in our school?" the man yelled, not needing a bullhorn.

"Hell no!" replied the Klansmen in unison. A small echo of 'hell no's' emanated from the citizens in the crowd.

"Good white people of Takasaw, we are here to support our Governor and the rights of all white people! We are here to support him by stopping niggers from entering this school! Are you with us?"

"Yes!" came the reply. Braxton scanned the crowd quickly. The only ones replying were Klansmen.

"Stupid SOBs," Harold said, just loud enough for Braxton to hear.

"This will make our town look good, won't it?" He pointed toward the far end of the street. A horde of television cameramen had formed a line and were filming the episode. "That's exactly what we hoped to avoid."

Braxton hadn't seen any of the television cameras before, but as they materialized before him he realized he should have expected it after seeing the reporters at Scott Douglass' house a few days earlier. The reporter from *Newsweek* had explained how this would be a big story. Now Braxton was beginning to understand the magnitude.

He wished he'd stayed in bed and avoided it all.

"What a bunch of cowards," Harold said, again quietly enough so only Braxton heard. "It's against the law to wear their hoods, but they're still too chicken shit to show their faces."

Braxton looked down the line of Klansmen, and spotted Andy Laduke again.

"Dad? See that one?" he said, pointing toward where Andy stood 30 yards away. Just as soon as he pointed, he felt guilty, as if he'd tattled on his cousin.

"I'll be damned," Harold said. "I guess I should've expected it. But to be honest, I didn't. Andy? Good, God."

"What do you think will happen, Dad?"

Harold was looking off in the distance. After a pause, he turned back to Brax. "I don't know son, I don't know." He began to walk off in the direction he'd been staring, then stopped. "Come on with me, son. No school today."

They crossed Main Street, which ran perpendicular to the high school. Scott Douglass was talking heatedly to the FBI man Braxton had been introduced to at the barbecue, Rosenberg. Unlike Harold, both men had removed their jackets in the heat, slinging them over their shoulders. It was the only concession to calmness. As the Freemans reached the two, Braxton could see a large blood vein in Douglass' forehead protruding as he spoke angrily.

"I'll kill that sonuvabitch," Douglass said. "I'll kill him."

"Don't go there, Scott," Rosenberg said. "I told you because you have a right to know. But you let me handle it, okay? That's my job. Just give me some time. This is penny-ante stuff. I need something I can use to put him away for a long time. And I need something to shut the Klan down. This won't do it."

Braxton felt awkward. He'd felt awkward about Scott Douglass since seeing him unable to do anything at the hospital. He now felt more awkward, stumbling into the heated conversation.

"Time, Scott, time," Rosenberg said. "You owe that to me. We want to end this for good."

Douglass stewed for a moment. Harold put a firm grip on his shoulder.

"What's wrong?"

Rosenberg looked at Douglass sternly. Douglass began to say something, then stopped. "Nothing, Harold, nothing. Just getting a little worked up, is all."

Douglass began wringing his hands, then pounded a fist into an open palm.

"Harold, we need to get the others and meet as soon as possible," Douglass said. "Help me round them up, okay?"

Harold agreed.

Surprising himself, Braxton spoke up.

"Where are the Negro kids? Where's the bus?"

Douglass gave him a funny look, not so much a quizzical look but one like he was thinking of something else and had heard the words but not understood them.

"They're not coming," Harold said. "We thought it best. The troopers aren't going to let anyone in the school today."

Braxton returned his gaze to the line of state troopers. The head trooper was nose to nose with the leader of the Klan, gesturing wildly, while the Klansman was shaking his head sideways. Finally, the Klansman pulled away, signaled his followers. He began walking away from the school, the white-robed men behind him.

Someone called out Scott Douglass' name. From behind the row of cameramen, an arm was waving. The man pushed through a couple of photographers, waving again. It was the reporter from *Newsweek*.

Douglass saw him. "C'mon, Harold, let's put our best face on this."

Harold slipped his arm around Braxton's shoulder and led him over to the horde of reporters as Douglass led the way.

"Mr. Douglass?" asked the *Newsweek* reporter, Thomas Boudreaux. "Can we ask you a few questions?"

"Sure," Douglass said.

The cameramen formed a gauntlet, lining up in front and to the sides of Douglass. Harold led Braxton around and behind the cameras.

A man holding a microphone with the logo of one of the Montgomery television stations was trying to go the opposite way, fighting to get in front of the television cameras, and bumped into Braxton hard.

"Who is this?" he asked the Freemans after knocking Braxton half off his feet.

"Scott Douglass, the county prosecutor," Harold said. "He's speaking for the bi-racial committee."

The reporters began firing questions.

"Mr. Douglass, will this show of force stop your plans for integrating the high school?"

"I certainly hope not. We stand by our plan."

"Will you reply with force, if necessary?"

"No, no, no. There is no reason for violence"

"Do you resent what Governor Wallace has done today?"

Douglass' eyes bore into those of the reporter who asked the question. He straightened and cleared his throat before replying.

"The citizens of Takasaw resent this, yes," he said. "We resent that Governor George Wallace has to resort to the use of armed troopers to stop the citizens of Takasaw from doing what we feel is the right thing, and long overdue. Yes, we resent this intrusion on our sovereign rights very much.

"Governor Wallace speaks of the rights of the state, and lashes out against the federal government when it becomes involved in local matters. But he has shown his hand today, and it is the hand of a hypocrite."

* * * *

The crowds lingered for another two hours before thinning. None of the students tried to enter the school. The bus carrying the Negroes remained safely away. But the state troopers held fast, even as the sun began to rise directly overhead.

So did the gathering of television cameras and reporters scribbling every word of every question answered. They'd interviewed Scott Douglass, Rev. Tompkins, and then dispersed into the crowd, interviewing students and townsfolk alike.

Two men, one toting a heavy camera bearing the letters CBS, the other with a microphone that held the network's logo, approached a group of students, Kyle Anderson among them, Braxton had joined after leaving his dad.

"Can we talk to some of you about this?" asked the reporter.

"Talk to him," Kyle said, grabbing Braxton by the shirttail and pushing him forward. "He's the captain of the football team."

Braxton pushed back, trying to return to the crowd of students. The reporter with the microphone extended his hand.

"We won't bite, son. Let's hear what you have to say."

Kyle continued to push. Between his pushing and the reporter's handshake, Braxton had moved firmly out front.

The cameraman lifted the heavy equipment onto his shoulder and began framing the reporter and Brax, then nodded to his partner.

"What's your name, son?"

"Braxton Freeman," he said nervously.

"Braxton? B-R-A-X-T-O-N? You're the captain of the football team at Takasaw High School?"

"Yes sir."

"How do you feel about Negroes going to your school?"

"Uh," Braxton stammered for a moment. He knew damn well how he felt. But was it any one's business other than his own?

The reporter made a slashing movement across his throat. The cameraman lowered the heavy equipment to his waist.

"Don't be nervous, son," the reporter said kindly. "Just tell us what you're honestly feeling."

Honestly?

Braxton nodded.

"Braxton, how do you feel about Negroes going to your school?"

"I feel that there's nothing wrong with it, sir," Braxton said.

"Do most of your friends agree with you?"

"I don't know, sir. I've never asked them. That's just my opinion."

The other students murmured. Braxton didn't dare turn around. He was already very uncomfortable.

The reporter asked a few other questions. This time, Braxton kept his responses short – one or two words, nothing more.

Finally, the reporter relented. "Thanks, son. Anybody else want to say something?"

No one said anything. Some of the students began walking away. The reporter shook Braxton's hand and then moved on to find someone else to interview.

"B-Bear, you're going to be a TV star," Kyle said. Braxton turned around. Kyle was the only student left where ten or more had been standing minutes before.

"Yeah. I'm a regular Dobie Gillis."

* * * *

Braxton lingered in front of the school. He had no plans, nor anything to do until football practice in the afternoon. Most of the crowd had left – students, the few scattered teachers, even Halliday. He lingered because he was disappointed. Braxton wanted resolution quickly. He wanted the entire matter to blow over so that school could start.

And the season could begin.

Most of the reporters had left, too, but a few of the men Braxton recognized from Scott Douglass' house remained, talking to a few members of the bi-racial committee. With nothing better to do, Braxton ambled over.

Harold spotted him. "I'll give you a ride home before I go to the meeting. I parked at the office, okay?"

"Thanks, Dad," Braxton said half-heartedly. It was such a short walk home and really not worth the trouble to walk to the town square, where Harold's CPA office sat across from City Hall, but he wanted to talk.

But they wouldn't be able to talk alone. Scott Douglass joined them for the three blocks. The two men talked about the day, speculating on how the media coverage would go. The coverage, Douglass said, would have an impact on how their plans concluded.

"The national press is behind us," Douglass said. "At least I think so. Guess we'll find out tonight."

"We'll do fine, Scott," Harold said. "How do you think the state press will portray this?"

"I haven't a damn clue. I wish I'd paid more attention when Wallace blocked the schoolhouse door in Tuscaloosa, now."

They were a block from town square when Douglass stopped suddenly. His face reddened, and he began clenching and unclenching his fists until the knuckles looked to be sun-burned red.

"Hold up a minute," Douglass said. "I've got to take care of something."

He crossed the street without checking for traffic – luckily there wasn't a moving car in sight – and headed straight for the front door of Lockett Hardware and Feed.

Harold looked at Brax, shrugged his shoulders, and followed behind with Braxton in lockstep.

What was up?

Douglass swung the heavy glass door open forcefully, setting off the ringing of bells attached to the top of the frame. It slammed with a *swoosh* before Harold and Braxton could reach it. Harold pulled the door open a moment later and he and Braxton trailed Douglass inside.

A few customers were inside the store, a couple milling around, one standing in front of a counter while the only help inside labored to plop a heavy bag of chicken feed on the dusty top.

Douglass moved quickly, standing right next to the farmer. Before the employee could see him, Douglass began speaking.

"Where's your owner?"

The harshness of the question startled the young man. He looked blankly as Douglass repeated the question.

"He ain't here, sir," the man said meekly.

"Why don't you go in back and check," Douglass said. "I bet he just hung up his robe." The tone remained harsh. It wasn't a request, but a command.

The man backed away, his eyes wide and nervous, then spun around and headed through a swinging doors. Two voices could be heard in the back. In moments, the doors swung open again.

Keith Lockett, proprietor of Lockett Hardware and Feed ambled to the counter.

"Mr. Douglass, how are you?" Lockett said with an amiable grin. He extended his hand. It remained extended when Douglass refused to return the grasp.

"You sell rifles, don't you Mr. Lockett?" Douglass asked. He didn't respond with a smile of his own. His lips were pursed and his eyes were narrowed.

"Course we do, course we do. What are you interested in?"

"Show me what you've got, and I'll tell you."

Lockett pointed toward a corner of the store, then leaped over the counter and led Douglass. Harold and Braxton followed behind, not saying anything.

There was a counter of pistols and barrels full of ammo on the floor. Hung by nails to the wall were various hunting rifles and shotguns.

Lockett stood there, still smiling. Douglass brushed past him and pulled a shotgun off the wall. He opened it, checking the empty barrel, then held it against his shoulder and aimed at an imaginary target against the wooden wall.

"Think this one will do just fine," Douglass said. He kept the shotgun in his hands, running a finger up and down the trigger. "I'll need some ammo, too. It's a 12-gauge, right?"

"Uh, yeah, it tis," Lockett said. "The ammo is over there."

Douglass followed Lockett's pointing and reached into the wooden barrel containing shotgun shells. He filled one pocket of his suit pants with shells, then turned to fill the other.

"This'll do," he said.

"Good choice," Lockett said, still working on the sale with a grin. "I'll ring you up."

Lockett headed back, vaulting the counter, and began ringing up the transaction on the cash register. He checked a printed table for sales tax, added it and then blurted out the total.

Douglass pulled his wallet out and gave the man two large bills.

Lockett took the bills, opened the register and counted out the change. Handing it over, he said, "You're not going to catch a deer with that thing, Mr. Douglass."

"I don't give a shit about any deer," Douglass said.

The smile faded immediately from Lockett's face. "Whatever you say."

"No, I've got plans for this," Douglass said, lifting the shotgun to eye level and scanning the store visually through the sight. "Gonna saw off the end ..."

"That's illegal, Mr. Douglass," Lockett said, "you know that."

"Not if you're the county prosecutor," Douglass said coldly. "And I'm the God damned prosecutor. I can get away with anything."

Lockett crossed his arms, looking uncomfortable.

"Whatcha going to use it for Scott?" Harold prodded.

"I thought," Douglass said, bringing the shotgun back to his shoulder and eyeing another imaginary target just above Lockett's head, "I thought I'd teach my wife how to use it the next time some cowardly redneck son of a bitch wants to pay another midnight visit to our house."

Douglass feigned a blast, pulling the shotgun back as if he could feel the reverb.

"Boom!" he said, then smiled for the first time. "My Jan may be quiet, but she can be a bitch when someone messes with her children. Don't you think Harold?"

"Yeah, I do," Harold said. He now wore the grin that had faded from Lockett's face.

"And nothing makes her – or me – madder than some coward who doesn't have the balls to do anything better than scare a defenseless housewife and her babies."

Douglass lowered the gun, gripping it in his left hand and extended his right hand to the proprietor. As Lockett numbly shook the hand, Douglass broke into a big grin.

"Know what I mean you yellow-bellied son of a bitch?"

Douglass left without another word to Lockett, the Freemans or the other stunned men in the store.

"Guess we'd better go, too, son," Harold said, slipping his arm around Brax.

They walked quietly the rest of the way until reaching the car. Harold slid in the driver's side while Brax went around and climbed in the passenger's side.

Harold clicked on the ignition and pulled the car away from the curb.

"Daddy, did that man look familiar?"

"What man, Braxton?"

"Mr. Lockett, the owner."

"Yeah. Why? He's been around forever."

"He looked and sounded like the guy leading the KKK."

"You were paying a little more attention than I reckoned you would today," Harold said. "Yeah, it was him. And your cousin was right behind him. Andy's one screwed up kid. And the crowd he's hanging around is going to make him even worse to deal with. Keith Lockett is not a man to be dealt with lightly. I hope Scott didn't go too far today."

* * * *

Some wore T-shirts and jeans, other wore old football jerseys and shorts. Some had on sneakers, the rest were barefoot. But it was less than a full squad, half-full at best.

After an hour and a half of running through plays on offense and defense, without any opposition since there were no pads and helmets available, Halliday called the practice session to an abrupt end.

"Go home. This ain't worth a shee-it," Halliday said in disgust. The players began to slowly break out of the half huddle, but Halliday stopped them with a raised hand. "Let's hope the crap at the school gets worked out tomorrow morning. Otherwise, meet here again, same time tomorrow afternoon."

Halliday lowered the hand to release them, punctuating the command with one final, "Shee-it." Not once had he asked where the missing players were, which was uncharacteristic of the demanding football coach.

The park was a good two miles from home. But before anyone could offer him a ride, Braxton took off running toward the house. He didn't feel like talking to anyone.

So much had happened in such a short time, he needed to clear his thoughts. Running usually did the trick. It was always the same: He'd run hard, hard enough that his legs began burning and his chest began pounding. Then he'd hit the wall – that's what Halliday called it – and the running became effortless and the thinking crystallized.

Adele was in the hospital, unable to talk above a garbled whisper. That had created chaos at the Freeman house, as well as concern. Adele had always been his rock. When Candace died, Peggy and Harold weren't the same. It had taken a couple of years before his parents, especially his mama, had shown signs of normality again. But Adele he could always count on, for advice, for comfort, for a good meal.

There were twinges of guilt. Because with Adele in the hospital, he'd spent too much time thinking of the turmoil at the high school. True, there'd been no serious threats of violence that morning. But the entire experience had been surreal. It was as if a foreign army invaded Takasaw.

Past that, there was the growing possibility that they might have to forfeit the season opener. It was Tuesday, and the opener was just three days away. If the matter wasn't resolved quickly, could they play with nothing more than half-assed practices in street clothes at the park?

Even thinking about it – did it really matter with Adele's health still in question? – sent a shiver of remorse through Braxton.

* * * *

The Freemans sat around the kitchen table devouring the meatloaf Peggy had made, along with green beans and carrots. Moses and Josiah had joined them. Like Braxton, Moses wasted no time talking as he dug into the meal. But Josiah played with his food, showing little interest in eating.

"I want chicken," he kept saying.

"Eat what's in front of you, Josiah," Peggy replied again and again. With Moses and Josiah at dinner, Peggy tempered her anger.

Harold was also eating at a brisk pace, checking his watch every few minutes. Finally, he rose. "Good meal, Peggy. But it's time for the news. Leave the dishes on the table, and you can clean up afterward."

In the living room, which adjoined the kitchen through an open archway, Harold turned on the television, fiddled with the knobs and began moving the rabbit ear antennas until he was satisfied with the picture. He settled into the soft, green upholstered couch, patting a spot beside him without looking in Peggy's direction.

Moses shot a questioning glance at Brax, who merely shrugged. They both left the table at the same time, leaving Josiah, and sat Indian style in front of the couch.

A man with salt-and-pepper hair and a walrus mustache flashed on the screen. The anchorman introduced himself to the television audience. "I'm Walter Cronkite, and this is CBS News."

Braxton understood immediately. Harold wanted to see what, if anything, CBS had to report on the Takasaw situation.

"Turn off the air conditioner for a few minutes so we can hear," Harold directed.

Braxton headed to the side window where the house's only cooling unit was wedged and flicked the noisy apparatus off. The air conditioner had been a Godsend, but it rattled noisily throughout the summer. It was purchased as a luxury. But, given Takasaw's intense summers, it had become a necessity.

Cronkite quickly rattled off the lead stories, including one about President Kennedy's Peace Corps initiative. Cronkite returned after a brief film that showed post-college workers teaching English and building houses somewhere Braxton didn't recognize and the CBS anchor told of Kennedy's scheduled trip to Dallas in November to solidify Southern Democratic support before he officially announced plans to run for re-election.

Cronkite moved to the next story.

"At his inauguration as governor, Alabama's George Wallace vowed to defend state's rights," Cronkite said. "Promising `segregation now, segregation forever,' the firebrand populist has become a rising national political figure due to his defiance of the intervention of federal government. This morning, Wallace was defiant again. This time, the defiance came against a new target. Bob Cramer reports."

The screen flickered as a camera panned landmarks of Takasaw that Braxton recognized instantly. Town square, Takasaw Institute, stately homes and, finally, Takasaw High School. The last shot pulled back to show state troopers guarding the entrance to the school.

"The state troopers you see here are at the command of Governor Wallace," said the narrator. "They've been ordered to stop the planned desegregation of Takasaw High School, a plan city leaders, black and white, hammered out peacefully over the summer."

The television switched quickly to Capt. Mansfield of the state troopers, the man who had addressed the crowd with the bullhorn.

"We are here under the direction of the Governor. Our orders are clear: To prevent the integration of Negroes at this or any other school in the state of Alabama," said Mansfield from behind the reflective sun glasses in a close-up.

The reporter quickly summed up the day's events, accurately, Braxton noted, pointing out that there'd been no violence. He also showed a quick clip of the Klan's aborted stand. Then, the camera switched to a gray-haired woman standing amid the crowd. White type below her head showed her name. Beulah Land, it read, a name Braxton didn't recognize.

"Governor Wallace is standing up for the people of Takasaw," the lady said. "That's what we elected him to do."

The camera switched to a couple of students, neither of whom had much to say. Then, a face everyone in the room recognized.

In block white type, Braxton Freeman's name appeared below his face. On television, Braxton said nothing as he listened to the reporter. But the question couldn't be heard. Instead, the reporter was narrating.

"Not everyone in Takasaw supports the Governor's defiant stand. The captain of the school's football team, who is also the son of one of the bi-racial committee members that formulated the desegregation plan, is one of the dissenters.

"I guess I feel that there's nothing wrong with it, sir," Braxton said.

Another familiar face flickered on the screen. Scott Douglass.

"The citizens of Takasaw resent this, yes. We resent that Governor George Wallace has to resort to the use of armed troopers to stop the citizens of Takasaw from doing what they feel is just and right. Yes, sir, we resent this intrusion on our sovereign rights very much."

The picture switched to another panning shot of the state troopers blocking the entrance, then returned to Douglass.

"Governor Wallace speaks of the rights of the state, and lashes out against the federal government when it becomes involved in local matters. But he has shown his hand today, and it is the hand of a hypocrite."

The CBS reporter summed up the events, then threw Braxton a curveball.

"In a statement issued from the state capital, Governor Wallace reiterated that he will not back down on this issue. He plans to keep the state troopers in place until the matter is resolved. And he has offered white students the opportunity to transfer to any school in the state without repercussions.

"From Takasaw, Alabama, this is Bob Cramer reporting."

CBS cut back to Cronkite momentarily, before going to a commercial. Harold got off the couch and cut the television off.

"Looks to me like we've got a budding politician here," he said, grinning at Brax.

Moses nudged him. "I sure hope not," Braxton said.

Peggy stood up to return to the kitchen. "I'm proud of you for taking a stand, Braxton," she said. She turned to Harold. "I hope this doesn't lead to more incidents, though."

Braxton knew she was referring to the Sunday night cross burning and rock throwing at Jan Douglass' house.

"I don't think we have anything to worry about," Harold said, winking at Brax. "I think Scott took care of that today."

CHAPTER 8

THE BLOODLESS SIEGE of Takasaw High School continued the next morning, with the state troopers blocking the entrance as the students and citizens congregated across the street and the reporters took everything in with television cameras and notebooks. The Klan made another appearance, but this time remained on Main Street, chanting "Niggers go home!"

Except Andy Laduke wasn't with them this time. He'd worked his first overnight shift at the mill, returning home just before eight a.m. Within minutes, he was out. He heard the horn of Lockett's truck and responded by stuffing the pillow over his head to mute the rest of the world.

He didn't like the new hours and he hated the new job. At least on the line, he had something to do, however mundane. Now, for eight hours, he paced the floor making sure the line workers didn't screw up. It was a simple task, yet a responsibility. He'd had one assignment on the line. Now had to know if some idiot wasn't doing his job right.

Like everything else in his life, Laduke bluffed masterfully.

There had been one brief bright spot. During the lunch break – Andy thought it a stupid term since it was the middle of the night – he'd gone to the cafeteria for a cup of coffee. Sitting alone, he was startled when someone sat beside him. It was the Klansman he didn't know, the one he'd seen at the mill and joined on the cross burning at Scott Douglass' house.

"Bobby Joe McKenzie," the man said. And that was that. When Andy couldn't muster something to continue the conversation, McKenzie didn't bother to fill in the gaps.

Damn, it was too late to be chit-chatting anyway.

While Andy slept, little changed in the first hour at the school.

Again, the bus carrying the black students was a no show. Eventually, the reporters began fanning out to interview the people gathered around – most refused; a few even politely so. This time, Braxton made certain to stay clear.

But the tension remained palpable, though in different ways. Yesterday, Brax had worried that violence would erupt. Maybe the troopers would begin cutting down the onlookers. Or, better yet, beat the hell out of the Klan.

But the fear was gone, replaced by frustration. Brax felt it, the frustration of not being able to enter his school, of wasting another day.

Apparently he wasn't the only one.

It began with a small group of boys too young to be high school students, who began chanting along with the Klansmen, "Niggers go home! Niggers go home!"

Two middle-aged black men — one in overalls the other in a worn dress shirt and slacks — began shouting back, "Klan go home! Klan go home!" The white-robed men didn't seem to notice.

Eventually, the leader of the state troopers, the captain shown on the CBS broadcast the night before, pulled two troopers out of line. He sent one toward the Klan, another toward the boys yelling in support of the Klansmen.

The captain sauntered toward the black men. The one in the overalls shut up immediately, his eyes widening as the trooper approached. The other one continued to yell in the direction of the Klan.

Elbowing his way 25 yards, Braxton moved close enough to hear the exchange. Frustration replaced fear again.

"Mister, we'll have none of that," the captain said as he came face to face with the black man in the shirt and slacks.

"You're letting those KKK people say whatever they want," replied the man firmly. "Ain't this a free country? Can't I say my peace?"

The captain pointed in the direction of the Klan. As the trooper he sent over stood among them, the white-robed Klansmen began to disperse.

"We don't want any problems," the captain said.

"I ain't causin' no problems," the black man said. "They are." He paused a minute. "You people started it! You people, when the guvnah sent you here!"

Braxton eyed the captain for a reaction but saw none. Behind the fat, smoky sunglasses, he remained emotionless.

"Mister, we're here on the orders of Governor George C. Wallace," he said. "We're here to keep peace. Nothing more, nothing less."

The black man raised his hands, indicating he understood, and leaned his head sideways in a shrug. He backed away, and the man in overalls did so, too.

The crowd stilled and the silence prevailed, with only occasional murmurs throughout. Only after another half hour passed did Braxton realize that Harold Freeman and the other bi-racial committee members were nowhere to be found.

* * * *

Braxton found Harold at the office, shuffling papers at his desk. There was no secretary – Harold let her go six months earlier due to the consequences of the boycott –so Brax rushed through the waiting room and into the sparsely appointed office.

Ever frugal, Harold Freeman wasted little money on furnishings. The wooden desk, though spacious, had been retrieved from a junk pile years before. He now called it a classic antique. The chair had been purchased from the church for a dollar. For years, Peggy talked in vain of getting him a plush, leather chair, but Harold said the folding metal one did the same job.

The floor had no carpet covering, only dusty, creaky wood. At least when the secretary was employed, the floor got an occasional sweeping. Without her diligence, a small whirlwind of dust kicked up every time Harold moved about.

There was but one window, an ill-advised addition from the builder who had framed it years earlier. It looked out over an alley, providing a panoramic view of the overflowing trash cans that held the refuge from Miss Ellie's Home Cooking. Making the depressing view worse were the black metal bars over the outside of the window, which Harold had conceded to after a vandal climbed through the first-floor opening and pilfered an old Royal typewriter. That had also forced Harold to splurge, spending $7 on a used Smith-Corona.

The wood-paneled walls were covered with diplomas and certificates – the college degree, the MBA, the state CPA board – and family photos. In every hue of uniform, Brax Freeman looked down from the walls from this angle and that angle, from Little League to Takasaw High. Harold loved the sports portraits.

A single 8-by-10 family portrait on the desk provided the only recognition of Candace's life. It had taken Harold and Peggy so long to get over the tragedy. Now, it was as if Harold wanted to deny her existence.

Harold heard his son's arrival and waved him in with a hand, then, without looking up, signaled him to take a seat with a flick of the wrist. Brax did without complaint and sat idly for the next few minutes as Harold continued to scan a set of spreadsheets. Finally, he shuffled the papers and looked across at his son.

"Hey, son."

"Hey."

"How'd it go today?"

"About the same. A little yelling, a lot of standing around. Not much else." Nor, Braxton thought, had there been any progress. "Why weren't you out there?"

Harold rose and stared out the window into the drab alley. "We felt it was best to remain low-key. We let the reporters do their interviews at Scott's office."

Harold continued staring out the window, saying nothing. Brax didn't intrude, leaving him to his thoughts. Shortly, Harold wheeled and reached for the coat rack, grabbing his jacket and slipping it on.

"Let's go for a ride," Harold said, leading Brax out of the office.

* * * *

For Moses, the worst part of each day was the waiting.

So what if the troopers cordoned off the school and the Klan marched and onlookers gawked? Being in that mix was better than loading up in a hot school bus and sitting for hours on end, waiting for orders over a walkie-talkie on how to proceed.

Each day, they had to go to rendezvous points for delivery to the secret location. In Moses' case, it meant waiting in the bushes in front of the vacant Longshore house for the garbage truck to come by at 6 a.m. The truck pulled up, and without a word the passenger door opened and Moses climbed in the cab.

"Put this on," the driver said the first day, handing him a McMahon County Sanitation Department ball cap.

The cloak-and-dagger routine seemed over the top to Moses. Wouldn't the Klan eventually figure out that the garbage truck usually only ran on Fridays?

Still, there was one benefit. Five minutes later, when the garbage truck turned down Lemon, another student joined him for the daily ride. Tamika Long had arrived at Institute High midway through her junior year, after her father took a job with the college's administration, so he didn't know her well.

Like the others picked for the white high school, she was an egghead. Of course, Moses thought they were all eggheads, except for him. But while the others killed time reading, he'd catch her staring in his direction till he caught her, forcing her to blush and avert her eyes. At least for a few minutes.

They said nothing on the ride to the secret location, and little more once they got there. But he'd catch her looking. And at least once a day, when he did, he winked back at her, forcing her to smile.

The location was off a dirt road a few miles out of town. It was in a black section of the county, so there was less fear there would be interference from the Klan.

Now, their wait was getting shorter each day. After just a couple of hours, a voice crackled over the walkie-talkie and told the man from the school system who sat with them each day that the students could be released for the day.

There were private cars to get them back. Stay-at-home moms from Takasaw's small, black middle-class – mostly wives of college professors – arrived to ferry the students. Moses and Tamika got in the same car with Mrs. Daughtery, and when the car pulled up to Tamika's street, Moses got out, too.

"Thanks, ma'am, but I need the exercise today," Moses said.

He caught up to Tamika, who was walking without a concern about Moses' destination.

"You don't talk much," he said.

"Neither do you."

She didn't miss a beat, keeping her pace. She was now within two houses of her home. Moses wasn't used to being the pursuer. Since he'd turned 13, girls paid him a lot of attention. Now the one girl he was interested in was playing it coy.

She got to her house and turned. "Did you want to ask me something?"

Now, Moses played it coy.

"Maybe, just maybe."

She smiled again, but when he didn't say anything for a few seconds she turned and started up the walk to the front door. He moved quickly, grabbing her by the shoulder and turning her around.

"Dang, girl. You're not making this easy. I'd just like to spend some time with you, away from school, away from whatever it is we're doing now. Just you and me."

She looked down for a minute, as if she wasn't sure how to reply.

"I don't know, Moses. My father does not let me date."

She was one of the first to see the façade of Moses Burks' break. He always seemed confident and serious, but the look on his face bordered on despair.

She moved a little closer and he caught a fresh scent of something that reminded him of flowers. She pointed to the front, right window.

"See that? My bedroom's on the same side, in the back," she said. "My father doesn't let me date, but he's asleep by nine-thirty. Wait until ten and then come get me."

"How? How do I come get you?"

"Just come to the window. Make sure the lights are all off, first. If I don't see you, knock against the windowsill. I'll hear that."

The adrenaline coursed through him again while Moses watched her walk into the house. Suddenly, the cloak-and-dagger stuff suited him just fine.

* * * *

Not until they turned on to the road that led to Andy Laduke's house did Braxton realize where they were headed. Instantly, he felt pangs of regret for accompanying his father. He didn't want to see Andy, and he certainly didn't want to run into the old drunk, Leonard Laduke. Leonard was usually polite, but he was also usually stumbling drunk. He rambled incoherently, if you were lucky, or repeated the same questions over and over.

How could anybody live in this shithole?

Peggy had told Brax how it had once been a nice house with a pretty garden. It was hard to imagine. Shingles on the roof buckled while the wood boards of the house's exterior were spotted with chipping paint. The yard was a wreck. Three-foot tall weeds overrun what once was a small front yard. Beer cans, empty whiskey bottles and hundreds of cigarette stubs were scattered in clumps from the mailbox to the front porch.

Were they there to talk to Leonard? If so, why waste the time? Andy? Would he even be home? Brax knew the answer was likely yes. Andy couldn't hold a real job. The moon shining runs were all done, he'd always figured, under the cover of darkness.

Harold knocked three times before hearing muted noise from within. Finally, Andy cracked the door open. Seeing his uncle and cousin standing there, he opened the door completely. Andy stood there in ratty boxer shorts and nothing else. Behind him, sprawled on the couch, was Leonard Laduke. At first glance, he looked dead. His mouth was open and saliva was pooling on the sofa. The mouth was caved in because he'd left his dentures in the sink.

Andy reached into the back of his shorts and scratched as he moved aside and let the Freemans in. Seeing no place to sit – Leonard reserved the only possibility – they remained standing.

"What do you want?" Andy asked, ending the question with a yawn.

Geez, it's past noon, and you just woke up?

"We just want to talk to you, Andy," Harold said calmly. "Why don't you put some pants on, and we'll sit out on the porch."

Andy looked at Harold and Brax with indifference, swiveled around and moved to the cramped bedroom in search of a pair of jeans. With the door open, Brax could see the contrast. Though the front room, like the outside of the house, was an utter mess, Andy's room was reasonably neat.

Andy returned with the jeans on, but without shoes or a shirt. He walked past the Freemans, opened the screen door and pushed the thin front door aside and plopped down on the top set of the porch stairs.

"Andy, I want to know why you're getting mixed up with those people," Harold said gently as he sat next to Andy. Braxton moved into a catcher's crouch behind them.

Andy looked ahead, avoiding eye-to-eye contact. "What people?"

"You know good and well who I'm talking about. The Klan."

Andy's head pivoted. He faced Harold with anger. "What business is that of yours?"

Harold remained calm. "We're family, son, family. We're concerned about you."

Andy bent over, retrieving an almost empty whiskey bottle, grasping it in his hand, he reared back and heaved it across the street as he stood up.

"You're concerned? About me?" Andy turned to face Harold again. The anger remained visible. "It's a little late for that, ain't it?"

Harold remained sitting. "No, it's not. We've always cared."

Andy picked up another bottle and flung it across the road.

"We ain't much of a family then. All of the years that drunk bastard in there was beating the hell out of me, what'd you do about it?"

The question caught Harold off guard. It surprised Braxton, too. Leonard was a worthless drunk, but Andy's charge was coming as a surprise. Suddenly, Brax was full of unasked questions.

Harold rose and faced Andy at eye level. Immediately, Andy turned away, leaving Harold the view of the back of his head.

"Son, we didn't know anything about that," Harold said. "Honestly, we didn't. I guess ... I guess with what happened to Candace, we were too wrapped up ..."

Harold's voice trailed off.

Harold couldn't see Andy's facial reaction, but Brax could see from the profile that Andy's eyes were tearing.

"These people are my friends," Andy said, moving further away, his back still turned. "You got no business telling me who I can't see."

"These men aren't friends," Harold said, his voice rising. "They're low-life scum. Did you hear what they did to Scott Douglass' wife and kids? Did you?"

Andy shrugged, hiding his reaction from the uncle.

"They terrorized an innocent woman, burning a cross, yelling threats and throwing rocks through the baby's window. An inch here or there, and they could have killed the baby."

Andy shrugged again. "How do you know the Klan had anything to do with it?"

"We know, damnit, we know!" Harold said, finally giving in to the anger. Harold moved quickly toward Andy, reaching for him with both hands and spinning him around. "You know it, too. You'd better not be a part of that, Andy. So help me, you hear?"

Forcefully turned around, Andy's expression changed to one of innocence.

"No, Uncle Harold, no. I'd never do something like that."

"I didn't say you would. But I pray to God you'd never condone something like that."

"No sir, no sir! Never! I ain't got nothin' against white folks. I hate niggers, but I ain't out to harm white people!"

Harold let Andy go and slowly backed away.

"I don't understand that at all, why you hate Negroes. Not at all."

Neither do I, Brax thought, *especially after what we saw years ago.*

Harold moved his head in the direction of the car, summoning Braxton. "Andy, we need to go. But listen to what I have to say."

Andy stood firm while tugging at the waistband of his shorts.

"We haven't been there for you before, and that's my fault. You're a grown man now, and that means you have to make adult decisions. But if you want someplace else to stay, you're always welcome at our house. You understand?"

Andy nodded and began to say something. He opened his mouth and as quickly closed it without an utterance.

Harold and Brax headed for the car while Andy remained on the porch.

"Uncle Harold!" Andy shouted as Harold reached the car door. "I've got a good job, now. I'm assistant foreman at the mill in Tallassee."

Harold and Brax listened without responding.

"It's a good job. And I'll soon have enough money to get a place of my own."

"Good to hear, Andy," Harold said, opening the door. "The offer's still good, though. You're always welcome at our house. I should've known what's going on before. That's my fault. I ... um, we ... we'd like to make it up to you. But you have to meet us halfway."

Andy removed his hands from his pocket and stretched them skyward. Among the lumps of flab were hints of muscle. He'd never played ball of any sort, but Brax was impressed with the build that was starting to look more solid.

"Thank you, Uncle Harold," Andy said. "I'll keep that in mind."

* * * *

Halliday was mad as hell. He'd started calisthenics with only twelve players – a fraction of what he'd expected. The players on hand were led by only one of the captains. Braxton, as usual, was punctual. Lomar, however, had been a no-show.

Brax was leading his teammates in crunches when he saw a car pull up in the gravel lot and Lomar, wearing a blue blazer with a red-and-green rep tie, slowly get out. Halliday saw it, as well and muttered, "Oh, shit."

"Well, Captain Lomar," Halliday continued, keeping a tighter reign on the language until he could determine who had driven his ballplayer. "Hope you're ready to get your Sunday best a lil dirty with some hard work."

Lomar hung his head as he walked toward the coach. Halliday sensed something immediately and moved away from the team, so Brax moved on to hamstring stretches and watched as Halliday walked toward Lomar. Halliday was talking and Lomar was hanging his head. The player pointed back toward the car a couple of times, then led Halliday to the automobile.

"Neck bridges!" Brax said, moving into position but managing to twist around so he could continue to watch what was going on even if he had to do it upside down.

Lomar's father got out of the car from behind the driver's seat. He was the spitting image, only older. Then Lomar offered a hand and helped his mother out. Like Lomar, both were wearing church clothes.

Mr. Lomar shook Halliday's hand then began talking. Halliday nodded and nodded. The man pointed at his wife, then at Lomar, and Halliday nodded again. The man said something else.

"Jesus H. Christ!" Halliday's explosion could be heard all across the park. Like every one of his teammates, Brax rolled over and watched without any more pretenses. "Jesus H. Christ!" Halliday yelled again. Mr. Lomar looked unnerved. His wife looked mortified.

Now she knows what all of us are up against.

Halliday flung his hands in the air then shooed them toward the elder Lomars. He grabbed the football player by the arm and began dragging the team captain toward his teammates as the parents stood next to the car without saying a word.

"Jumping jacks!" Braxton yelled, trying to snap everyone to attention before Halliday arrived. So what if they'd already started the day with 15 reps?

Halliday blew his whistle three times as he approached, stopping the calisthenics, and leading Lomar into a hastily formed half circle.

"You tell them yourself, Lomar, *you* tell them," Halliday said.

Lomar kicked the ground with one of his shiny wing tips. "I'm transferring to another school."

"Raise your head and tell them again. Louder!"

Lomar lifted his head and searched his teammates. He settled on Braxton. His eyes were red-rimmed. "My parents want me to transfer to another school. We just got back from Montgomery. They enrolled me in the Academy."

It was Braxton's turn to aimlessly kick the ground and look away. Lomar's embarrassment was embarrassing him.

Why'd he have to look at me?

"OK, son, you can go," Halliday said with surprising normality. "When the school opens again, we'll work out something so you can come get your stuff out of the locker room."

Halliday lowered his head again and headed slowly back to his parents. As he lumbered, Brax could see the behemoth's shoulders sag, then begin shaking. Both hands shot to his face to cover the tears.

"This ain't worth a shit," Halliday said, more to himself than the team. He picked up the clipboard he'd dropped minutes earlier and looked at it. Then it was airborne, sailing off into the distance.

"We're through," he said. The dozen players remaining looked at each other, not understanding the meaning. No one moved.

Halliday turned around and watched as the Lomars drove off.

Kyle Anderson took two sideway steps so he could reach Braxton. When Kyle arrived for practice as student manager a half-hour earlier, Halliday told him to rejoin the team as a player. Kyle nudged Brax. When Brax didn't do anything, Kyle whispered, "Ask him what he means?"

"Coach?" Brax asked sheepishly. Halliday continued to stare now into the vacant distance. Kyle nudged him again. "Coach?"

"Yeah, yeah," Halliday said without looking.

"Same time tomorrow?"

Halliday wheeled around mad. "Hell no, Freeman. We're through. Period."

Like everyone else, Brax remained transfixed.

"We've got twelve players out here. How the hell are we goin' to play a game Friday night with twelve football players? Shee-it, do I have to spell it out?"

Brax shook his head no, though the question hadn't been directed at him.

"Go home, all of ya'll. If anything changes, I'll let you know tomorrow."

While the others began vacating the open field, Braxton remained. Halliday was staring again, this time out toward the outfield fence of the adjoining baseball field.

Brax walked closer, but not too close. He figured Halliday was going to say something, someday. It might as well be to him. Halliday seemed comfortable talking to him, after all.

Halliday stared for minutes, breaking the silence every now and then with a "Shee-it." When he decided he'd stared enough, he began scanning the field in search of something. His eyes settled on the clipboard he'd thrown discus-style earlier, then his feet followed.

"Coach?" Brax said.

Halliday wheeled around, startled.

"Shee-it, Freeman, what are you still doing here?"

"To talk, I guess."

"What the hell about?"

"I reckon I don't know."

"Shee-it. Go get my keys off the fence over there," he said, pointing. "I'll give you a ride home."

They'd driven a couple of blocks in Halliday's old Ford and were halfway down Gautier Street before the old coach ended the verbal embargo.

"I don't blame Lomar, really," Halliday began. "At least he had the balls to come tell me himself. No one else did."

Halliday began to explain. Of the missing players, he knew of at least fifteen who had already transferred or were in the process of doing so to another school, thanks to Wallace's offer the night before, allowing any white student at Takasaw High the right to move on to any other school, regardless of zones. He knew of eight players who were transferring because he'd received that many phone calls from parents or coaches at other schools who wanted to know if the kids were any good.

Lomar's parents had explained that they'd enrolled him in Montgomery Academy, a prestigious, and expensive, private school in the capital city. That's why Lomar had arrived at practice in a suit. He first had to pass an interview with the school's headmaster to gain admission. A spinster aunt who lived in Montgomery had the money and was willing to pay for tuition and let Lomar live with her through the school year.

"I told them," Halliday said, "that Montgomery Academy wouldn't do him a damn bit of good in football. It's a small school, with a crappy team. But they said it'll help him with his grades. He's more concerned about getting into Auburn and becoming an architect. A God damn architect. Jesus! With a body like that and the talent he's got, he could play in the God damn National Football League. And he wants to be an architect?!"

Halliday had driven past the Freeman's house, an error he didn't realize until Gautier came to an abrupt end a half-mile down the road.

"Shee-it," he said, banging the steering wheel in frustration before slamming the gears into reverse, and spinning back around.

Halliday yanked the car to a halting stop in front of Braxton's house. Brax got out and was surprised to hear the other door slam behind him. Halliday was coming around the car.

"I got to talk to your papa," Halliday said. "Burks lives down the street, right? Why don't you go get him. We'll talk this out together."

"He may be here already," Brax said. "He and his brother eat supper here while his mama's in the hospital."

Brax led Halliday into the house. He smelled fried chicken the moment he stepped inside, then saw Peggy preparing the dinner table.

"Hiya, Mama," he said.

She looked up and saw Halliday with him. "Hey, honey. Hi, Coach Halliday. Are you stopping by for supper?"

"No, ma'am," Halliday said. "I was just hoping to talk to Mr. Freeman and the boys."

Moses was out in the backyard, with Harold and Josiah. They were playing a gentle game of toss with Braxton's best football. Josiah was running in slow, uncoordinated steps for a pass that Harold threw gently. It hit him on the shoulder and bounced away, eliciting a laugh from Harold and a grin from Josiah.

For a moment, Brax felt jealousy. How long had it been since Harold had taken the time to throw the football – any ball – with him? Two, three years? Just as quickly, he released the thought when he saw the fun Josiah was having.

"Hey, Coach!" Harold said. He jogged over and gave Halliday a handshake. "Are you going to join us for dinner?"

"No, no. I was just hoping we all could talk."

"Absolutely," Harold said. "Want to do it out here?"

"Yeah, here would be fine."

Harold led him toward the picnic table, then went and picked up the football Josiah had left on the ground. He slipped an arm around Josiah's waist and helped lead him to the others.

"Coach Halliday, this is Moses' older brother, Josiah," Harold said.

Halliday offered an uncertain hand. Josiah, settling across the table from the coach looked at it, then slapped it. He grinned at the Coach.

Halliday pulled the hand back, staring at it in wonder.

"What do you want to talk about, Coach?" Harold asked. He sat next to Josiah. Moses and Brax flanked Hardass.

Halliday told him in a rush, about Lomar's defection, and how the team was down to twelve players.

"Truth is, Mr. Freeman, we ain't going to be able to field a football team, are we?"

Harold looked at Halliday, then back and forth at Moses and Brax. "No, it doesn't look like it," he said. "I wish I could tell you otherwise, but by allowing the white students to transfer wherever they want Governor Wallace has, uh, screwed us all."

The news hit Brax like a fist in the gut. Why hadn't his father told him this? Why was he learning something Halliday already seemed to know?

Brax looked across the coach at Moses, who seemed every bit as puzzled.

"As of late this afternoon, more than half of the white kids have already informed the school that they were transferring," Harold continued. "By the time we finally get the school open, you'll be lucky to have the twelve you've got now."

Halliday rose from the table. Lifting a foot to the bench, he dug a tin of chewing tobacco from his rolled up sock, pinched some of the shredded brown leaf between his thumb and index finger and moved it snugly against the cheek of his mouth.

He sat back down.

"What are you two goin' to do?" he asked, looking back and forth between Moses and Brax.

Moses shrugged his shoulders. When Halliday swiveled his head in Brax's direction, the youth did the same.

"Well, take my advice," Halliday said. "You two need to transfer. You both got the chance to get a scholarship, but you ain't goin' to get it here if we don't have a football team."

My senior year. And he wants me to transfer?

"That's out of the question," Harold said. "Moses has already enrolled. And Brax ... what will it look like if my son transfers to another school? Especially after I've been involved in pushing the desegregation plan?"

"I don't know how the hell it'll look, Mr. Freeman," Halliday said. "Does it really matter? Your boy's got a chance to play college ball, understand? That means tuition, books, room and board – everything – bought and paid for. And he's got the chance to go to Alabama or Auburn. But he ain't goin' to do it if he's twiddlin' his thumbs at our school."

Harold didn't respond. Neither did Braxton or Moses.

Halliday rose from the table again. "Think about what I'm saying, for their own good. Just think about it."

* * * *

Andy was finishing the last remnants of a ham sandwich on stale white bread when he heard the horn blare. He dropped the sandwich and raced outside, recognizing the sound of Keith Lockett's truck.

Lockett was leaning out the window. "Where the hell were you today, boy?"

Andy started to say something, then stopped. Lockett knew damn well that he'd worked all night. But the lack of response didn't satisfy Lockett. He angrily opened the door of the truck and scrambled out, slamming it noisily.

"I asked you a God damn question, boy!"

Lockett walked briskly until he was in Andy's face. Andy backed away in defense.

"I had ... I had to work all night, Keith," Andy said, his voice cracking due. "I thought you knew."

"You mean you're lazy?"

Lockett grabbed Andy by the neck of his T-shirt and twisted the cotton as he stretched it, pulling Laduke closer. He was a good three inches shorter than Andy, but solid. Andy didn't want to get into a fight with Lockett or anyone else. Lockett would beat him to a bloody pulp.

"I'm sorry, Keith. It was my first day. I ..."

"McKenzie was there. He worked the same shift. But he was there!"

Andy leaned back. The only thing holding him up was Lockett, with the firm grasp. The T-shirt ripped and gave way. Andy stumbled backward, and fell into the weedy front yard.

Lockett moved quickly and stood over Andy, balling a fist, preparing to hit him. Andy scooted back, on his hands and feet, trying to get out of the way.

Lockett reached down with the other hand and grabbed Andy by the throat. The grand dragon's eyes were bulging, the anger about to explode into full rage.

"You pussy! I bring you in, I get you a God damn job! You ain't nothin' but a pussy!"

The balled fist wasn't a threat. Lockett's right arm came down instantly, crushing into the side of Andy's face. He felt a terrible pain in the nose as the fist glanced off it, and felt blood begin pouring.

"Keith!" he cried. "I'm sorry!"

Lockett hit him again, doubling the pain that spread from the cheekbone to the destroyed nose. And again.

"*Blam! Blam!*"

Lockett stopped, his fist halfway toward another delivery, and looked for the source of the sounds. On the front porch of the house, Leonard Laduke stood shirtless, wearing only trousers, holding a shotgun. Fresh smoke drifted from the barrel.

Leonard lowered the barrel and pointed it directly at Lockett.

"Get away from my house," Leonard said firmly. "Now!"

"You better put that damn thing down now, old man!" Lockett yelled.

Leonard did, only long enough to load two more shells. In seconds, the shotgun was pointed at Lockett again.

"Do you know who I am?" Lockett demanded. He was standing straight now, both fists clenched. The anger was more apparent than when he had begun hammering Andy.

"I don't care who you are," Leonard said. "Get away from my boy now!"

Lockett looked down at Andy, who was shielding his face with his hands. Lockett spit at Andy before backing up.

"Old man, you're asking for big trouble!" Lockett said as he opened the door to the truck's cab.

"Get away," Leonard said, unfazed.

Lockett moved into the truck, firing the engine. He leaned out the truck again and looked at Andy. "You better be there in the morning," he said. Then, shouting at Leonard: "Old man, you're a dead son of a bitch!"

The truck sped off, spitting rocks that Andy felt as he continued to cover his bleeding face. He looked at his hands, saw the blood, and began crying.

"C'mon, son. Come into the house," Leonard said as if he'd done nothing more than break up a fight between two schoolyard bullies. "Let's get you washed up."

CHAPTER 9

"**A**RE YOU GOING to transfer?" Moses Burks asked. He and Brax were sitting on the bottom step leading to the Freeman's porch.

Brax shrugged. He hadn't given it much thought until Halliday brought it up before supper. "Are you?"

Moses looked away. "I'm screwed."

The screen door swung open. Peggy stood there with Josiah, who was eating a piece of pound cake with his hands.

"Moses, it's time for you and Josiah to go home," Peggy said.

Moses stood, and Josiah moved to join him. "Yes, ma'am. Thank you for supper."

"You're always welcome, Moses."

Moses grabbed Josiah by the hand and began leading his older brother slowly down the walkway.

"Mama, I'm gonna walk with them," Brax said, jumping to his feet to follow.

Josiah was struggling to walk. It was late in the day for him, and he'd eaten a big dinner. Moses patiently slowed his pace.

"What do you mean, 'screwed?' " Brax asked.

Moses didn't break his stride as he explained. When he had told the principal at Takasaw Institute High of his plans to transfer to the white high school, he'd been told clearly that there would not be an alternative if things didn't work out. The Institute's high school had a limited enrollment due to tight finances. If Moses' decision was final – and Moses, at the time, had assured it was – then the next student on the waiting list would be admitted.

Moses was stuck at Takasaw High, if it ever opened, without a football team, without a way to college. The only alternative was the county school for black students.

"What if they never let us in?" asked Brax. It had never crossed his mind that the school might not open.

"I don't know," Moses said. "I guess I could go to the other Negro school. But they don't have a football team, either. They dropped it a few years ago."

"Dang, Moses," Brax said sincerely. "I'm sorry."

Moses stopped. "What are you sorry for?"

"I guess I helped talk you into this," Brax said after considering his answer.

"Yeah, I guess you did," Moses said, cracking a smile. "Don't worry about it, Brax. Nobody knew what was going to happen. And you're screwed, too."

"Yeah," Brax said, wanting to agree. "Nobody knew."

The lights were on at Moses' house. The front door, like every one on Gautier Street, was unlocked. Moses twisted the fragile knob and opened the door. A sweet aroma immediately sifted through the opening. A black girl stood in the kitchen stirring a large pot on top of the stove.

Natalie Young saw the arrivals and flashed a smile.

"About time you got home," she said. "You've got company."

Natalie nodded toward the back of the house. Moses began running, with Josiah moving slowly in pursuit. "Mama?" he asked.

Brax could hear the voices, happy voices, as Moses and Josiah greeted Adele in the backroom. Brax stood awkwardly in the living room, until he spotted Natalie waving him into the kitchen.

"I'm making some chicken soup for Aunt Adele," she said, pulling a ladle out and holding it for sampling. "Try some."

As he'd done thousands of times with Adele, he did. It was more watery than the way Adele made it, but it was good. He relayed the positive review.

"Thank you," Natalie said. She dipped the ladle again and brought it up to her lips for a sample. "No one cooks as good as Aunt Adele, but, I have to admit, it's quite good."

Josiah's voice boomed through the thin walls. "Mama! I love you, Mama!"

Natalie grinned. "I know he's happy to have her home."

The hospital had released Adele a few hours earlier, in the care of Natalie's parents, saying there was nothing more they could do now that couldn't be done at home with some supervision.

"I'm spending the night," Natalie told Braxton. "Mother and Father told me I can stay home from school tomorrow and look after my aunt."

He liked the way she said "aunt," the emphasis on the blending of the letters "au." It sounded so regal. She seemed so regal, so much more polished than any Negro he knew. Or just about any white girl.

Except for Katie Sullivan.

"Want some?" Natalie asked as she began pouring a bowl full for Adele.

"Naw," Brax said, suddenly uncomfortable. "I best be goin' home."

* * * *

"Jesus! What happened to you?"

Andy was standing over a line worker, but not too close. His one goal was to stay out of the way and away from everyone. He was embarrassed by the way he looked. His left eye was swollen shut, the skin around both eyes covered in shades of deep purple and black. The nose remained swollen, with tiny tissue stuffed in the nostrils – a vain attempt to stop the trickle of blood that seemed endless. His left cheek had a small gash, flushed red with the bruising that, too, would soon turn darker.

His entire head ached, yet the embarrassment was more painful. Still, he had given only momentary consideration to calling in sick. He'd pissed off Keith Lockett once and paid the consequences.

Never again would he do anything to raise the ire of the grand dragon.

He tried to act if he didn't hear the question over the din of machinery.

"Jesus," someone said. That someone turned out to be Bobby Joe McKenzie.

The fellow Klansman grabbed Andy by the chin to study the battered face.

"Don't tell me. You ran headfirst into a Mack truck."

The attempt at humor only heightened Laduke's embarrassment.

Lowering his voice and pulling his hand away, McKenzie asked, "Who did this?"

"Keith … " Andy replied, trying to pull the word back as it left his lips, embarrassed that he'd admitted anything.

"Jesus! He catch you balling his wife?"

Andy shook his head emphatically without realizing McKenzie was joking. "No. I just messed up, that's all."

"You must've done something," continued McKenzie, not relenting.

Andy shrugged his shoulders. McKenzie sensed the discomfort. "Talk to me at the break, okay? I'll leave you alone for now."

The break came midway through the shift, marked by a stillness of the machinery that left an echoing hum through Andy's aching head. Instead of going to the cafeteria, he slumped down against the wall wanting to be left alone.

No luck. McKenzie came looking for him, taking a seat next to Andy on the hard floor.

"Tell me the truth, Andy," McKenzie said. "What happened?"

Andy cut him a glance just long enough to sense that maybe McKenzie was halfway sincere. So Andy unloaded, spilling everything – Lockett's arrival, his rage and how Leonard Laduke, of all people, had ended it.

"And that's all? He beat the hell out of you just because you didn't march this morning?"

"Yeah," Andy said. He buried his head in his hands and began rubbing the temples. The pain continued blaring its presence.

"Let me tell you something, just between us." McKenzie paused to see if Andy looked up, but Laduke didn't. "Keith Lockett is a bully. He feeds off his ability to intimidate other people."

Andy moved his hands to the side and looked at McKenzie.

No shit. He returned his hands and resumed the attempt to rub the pain away.

"Don't be intimidated. If you're not intimidated ..."

McKenzie didn't finish. Andy removed his hands again and saw that McKenzie was staring off in the distance.

What's with him? Why would he be so critical of Keith?

McKenzie seemed to snap out of the trance. "Why are you in the Klan?"

The question surprised Andy, it was so obvious.

"I hate niggers, why else?"

"Don't we all," McKenzie said, laughing. "Don't we all."

McKenzie braced himself with a hand, then rose unsteadily.

"Damn legs are asleep," he said, kicking his right foot to get the blood flowing again. "Hear what I say, Andy, but keep it between the two of us: Don't let Lockett bully you. Keep a safe distance whenever possible."

McKenzie was halfway toward the cafeteria when he turned around.

"One more thing. Don't you dare miss the march tomorrow."

* * * *

When he agreed to meet Tamika, he hadn't thought it out at all. He was supposed to meet Rufus at the graveyard for work and he had no alternate plan for watching Josiah. Yet things fell into place. Rufus called, saying they were caught up on graves. And, now, Adele was home and Natalie was spending the night and could take care of Josiah.

The next concern was where to take Tamika. It was a weeknight and it was late, so there wasn't any place public to go. He had no car, anyway.

But he had legs. And he knew his way around the cemetery. It was quiet, and it was only a mile from Tamika's house. She was impressed, if not a little leery, that he knew the shortcut through the woods behind her house that delivered them in about 15 minutes.

They sat on top of a squat tombstone, and drank the Pepsi bottles he'd brought along. He didn't quite know what to think of her after she'd told him to meet her late, after her father went to sleep.

All kind of ideas ran through his head the rest of the day. Now he was sure of one thing. She wasn't being forward, she just wanted to see him as much as he wanted to see her.

"We talked about it tonight. I was afraid he'd never go to bed," Tamika said. "I'm going back to Institute High if they don't let us in the school tomorrow."

"That's good," Moses said. "I may transfer, too. Do you want to go back to the Institute?"

"I don't know. My father said he'll have to pay some tuition for me to return, but he can afford it. Can you pay tuition?"

"Tuition? I don't know. I mean, why would I pay now?"

"There are just limited funds at the Institute, Moses. The class is already full."

Moses didn't know how to reply. He couldn't pay tuition. He wasn't sure if he could buy groceries and pay the gas bill when it came due.

Adele wasn't going to work anytime soon. The only income was the money Rufus paid him.

"Maybe things will work out at Takasaw."

It was past midnight when Tamika crawled back through the window. Moses headed home hoping now, more than ever that he'd be able to attend Takasaw High.

* * * *

Brax rose a little later than he had the two previous days, not quite ready to face another standoff with the state troopers. By the time he'd eaten, dressed and walked the short distance to Acorn Street, it was almost time for the first period bell.

Not that it would ring today.

But as he emerged on Acorn, he saw things had changed dramatically. Instead of dozens upon dozens of state troopers guarding the front of the school, there were only five. And they were outnumbered. A block away, stretched up and down Main, were the Klansmen. On the other end of Acorn, the horde of television cameras were poised for whatever happened. Their numbers had not decreased, either.

The onlookers who had ringed the perimeter the past two days were there in smaller numbers. Mostly blue hairs, with nothing better to do than gawk. Brax saw only a handful of students in the crowd, including one he recognized – the outspoken, freckle-faced, redhead from the first day.

"Where are all the other troopers?" Brax asked her, tapping her on the shoulder to get her attention.

"Oh, hey, Braxton," she said. Brax was surprised she knew his name.

"Where'd they go?" he repeated.

"I don't know," she said. "Someone said that the governor had sent most of them to other cities, to stop the same thing."

Brax began scanning the crowd, looking for his father or any of the other bi-racial committee members. He wasn't surprised when he didn't see anyone. Harold had said they'd stay away again.

"Thanks, uh," he said, trying to recall her name but drawing a blank. "Thanks."

She smiled at him as he turned away, then said loudly, "It's Elizabeth, Braxton. But everyone calls me Betty."

He'd walked only a short distance when he realized the thinned crowd was staring at something behind him. Brax wheeled, and saw the rickety yellow school bus was idling behind the gathering of newsmen, who were retreating to the sides of the street to allow it passage. The path cleared and the bus stuttered before moving again. The troopers also moved, this time forming a line across the street that formed a barrier.

But the barrier wasn't for the bus, which pulled to the front walkway of Takasaw High, stopping with a belch of black smoke out of the tailpipe. The line formed a barrier between the bus and the Klansmen, who seemed to be creeping ever closer to the school.

The bus door creaked open and, one by one, nine Negro students began filing out and walking silently down the path and into the front door of the high school.

"Damn, you, niggers!" shouted one of the Klansmen.

Glass shattered as a rock tossed by one of the Klansmen crashed through a bus window. The driver, the only one left in the bus, scurried out quickly.

One of the troopers, but not the captain who'd taken charge the day before, signaled to the others. In unison, they took five steps forward, closer to the Klan. The white robed men slowed as the one in the most ornate robe – the one Brax recognized from Lockett Hardware and Feed – stepped forward and waved them to a halt.

The reporters moved into position, too, with television cameras viewing the three-sided movements from varying angles. Shouts of "nigger" echoed from the angry, but immobilized, Klan.

When the last of the Negro students had disappeared inside the school, the lead trooper turned to face the crowd.

"Are there any other students out there who want to go in?"

The freckle-faced girl began to cross the street and another boy Brax didn't recognize, shorter than the little redhead, followed in step. She reached the sidewalk then turned, looking for someone.

She found him.

"Braxton Freeman? Aren't you coming?"

It caught him off-guard. The last two days had been a blur, so much that he had given up on the idea of starting classes any time soon. Halliday had blurred things further, with the suggestion that he and Moses transfer. Moses couldn't, he knew now – he'd been the second Negro off the bus – but Brax still could.

"Braxton?"

Harold had been adamant about not transferring and staying at Takasaw, hadn't he?

Brax Freeman stepped off the opposite sidewalk and jogged across the street, joining the freckle-faced girl for the final steps to the school.

"Nigger lover!" shouted someone from the mob of white robes. "You're a nigger lover, Freeman!"

Things were calm inside the school, serene by comparison. Three teachers stood inside the door – Mrs. Macon, his English teacher, was one – as Brax and the other two white students arrived. Mrs. Macon gave him a smile, then a wink, and pointed him toward the auditorium at the end of the long corridor.

The Negro students were filling up the front seats in the middle aisle. Brax, the redhead and the short boy took seats behind them. The irony made him smile for a second. He knew the routine. The first few minutes of the first day of school were spent in the auditorium. Principal Atchley made the introductions of the teachers and then the students headed to the stage, where their class schedules were waiting at stations. A-F there, G-L next to it, on down the line.

Atchley was a kindly, older man, a bit of oddball, Brax always thought. He had a shock of white hair and a goatee, the kind you'd see on old pictures of Mark Twain, and seemed an eccentric thanks to the bow tie he wore daily.

At least that had been Brax's opinion last spring, when school broke for summer vacation. Since then, he'd been told by both Harold and Hardass Halliday a lot of things, including how Atchley had been the first administrator to back the integration plan.

"He don't know nothin' 'bout football, but he leaves me alone," Halliday had said. "Gotta give him credit. He's got balls I didn't know he had."

Atchley let the students sit for a few minutes before striding to a lectern set in the middle of the stage. He tapped a microphone twice and heard the electronic scraping from the loudspeakers attached in the balcony. It was a fruitless gesture. Even with his Professor Henry Higgins way of talking – not an English accent, of course, but he danced and lingered with words in an aristocratic delivery – Atchley could have been easily heard by the small gathering without amplification.

"Welcome to Takasaw High School," Atchley said. "As you all are, we're anxiously looking forward to the upcoming school year. Before you confirm your class schedules, I'd like to first introduce you to the men and women who will serve as your teachers this year. Unfortunately, some are absent today because of the odd circumstances of this week."

Atchley made the introductions quickly, each of the all-white teachers waving, nodding or offering some form of recognition for the students. Atchley's remarks were stock. Brax had heard them four years running. As the principal reeled off the list in alphabetical order, Brax was relieved to see Halliday step forward at the mention of his name.

"Now, if you'll please file in orderly fashion at the proper table, we'll begin confirming class schedules."

Atchley stepped away, and the students began stirring. Before anyone left a seat, Atchley was back at the mic.

"Please remain seated for a moment, students," he said. Atchley's eyes moved leisurely up and down the two rows of students, all twelve. "Let me add something. Please understand, everyone here at Takasaw High School is committed to offering each and every one of you the finest education possible. That said, as each of you are aware, this is not your typical start to the school year."

The students remained seated. Unlike most first-day gatherings, Atchley had this group's undivided attention.

"I admire the courage every one of you, Negro and white, has shown today," Atchley continued. "It hasn't been an easy first step for anyone. I don't think all of the problems encountered this week will magically disappear, either. But if you'll stick with us, we'll solve this together."

Atchley stepped away again as the teachers broke ranks. Halliday moved into a chair behind the A-F table. Others moved to man the remaining tables. After a pause, the students left their seats and silently climbed the stairs on one side that led to the raised stage.

Moses was the first in line in the A-F table, with Brax behind him. Lines formed at the other tables, except the one at the far end, S-Z.

"Name?" Halliday asked Moses, then grinned when Moses looked dumbfounded. He reached into a file of index cards and thumbed through the thick file before pulling out a yellow three-by-five.

"Here's your class schedule, son," Halliday said. "Look it over and commit it to memory."

Moses looked at the list. Six periods. Classes from junior English to French to Algebra listed with a free period to close the day. All football players had a free sixth period for football practice – not that it would do any good now.

"Memorized it yet?" Halliday asked after a minute. Moses nodded. "Good, hand it back." Moses did and Halliday gave him another uncharacteristic grin as he ripped the card in two.

He handed Brax his class schedule with the same command. Brax already knew the schedule, having nailed it when he'd first seen it last spring. Halliday asked him if he'd memorized it, then, like before, ripped it in half, tossing it with Moses' into a nearby trash can.

What the hell?

"Both of you are here today," Halliday said more gravely. "But as long as those class schedules are torn up and unsigned, neither one or you is officially here. Understand?"

Moses nodded his head – *do you really understand, or are you just being agreeable, Moses?* – but Brax continued to stare at the coach.

"If you ain't registered, you ain't officially here," Halliday said. "I'm buying you both another day or two to consider transferring."

* * * *

The Klan disassembled without direction from Lockett, who was visibly frustrated but unusually silent. He was the first to leave, climbing into his pickup and driving in the direction of Auburn.

Andy Laduke left in a new model Chevy, the one he'd driven to the aborted march with McKenzie fresh off their shift. He didn't know why McKenzie had offered him the ride, nor did he know why he was accepted.

Except, although he didn't want to admit, he was scared to run into Keith Lockett by himself. Maybe McKenzie had sensed that, too. Yet on the half-hour ride over, he thankfully hadn't probed Andy with any more questions about the incident. He'd talked, but it had been inane chatter – family, history, education questions. Come to think of it, he'd gotten more out of Andy than anyone had in a long time.

"What say I just take you straight home, save you some time?" McKenzie asked as he also headed in the direction of Auburn. When Andy didn't answer, McKenzie continued. "It would save me some time, too. I live over near Opelika. What say I just pick you up on the way to work tonight, buddy? You can get your truck then."

"Yeah," Andy said. "That would save me a lot of time."

Again, McKenzie started asking questions. Again, they didn't challenge Andy much.

"Do you have a girlfriend, Andy?"

"Nah, not right now," Andy said, lying. *Not ever.* "You?"

"Something better. I've been married five years to my high school sweetheart. Got another baby on the way, too."

Andy nodded. It was easier when McKenzie carried the conversation.

"Did you graduate high school here in Takasaw?" McKenzie asked.

"No."

"Where, then?"

"Uh, nowhere. I never graduated. Dropped out in the 10th grade. When my mama died."

Again, he was lying. McKenzie probably knew it, too, but didn't let on that Andy's fibs were obvious.

"Well, you've got a good job now," McKenzie said. "You've got a chance to make a career out of it. They're good people at the mill."

"Yeah," Andy said.

McKenzie drew silent. Andy struggled to think of something to say. Finally ...

"You graduate from high school here? I mean, Opelika High?"

"No. I'm not from around here."

"Oh."

"Hey, I need directions," McKenzie said. "Where do I turn off?"

Immediately, Andy felt stupid. They were headed the opposite direction.

"About a mile back the other way," he said sheepishly.

McKenzie laughed, checked the rear-view mirror then made an unexpected u-turn in the middle of the road without slowing down. The car slid sideways as the rear tires went off the asphalt before the car righted itself in the correct direction.

"You dumb ass," McKenzie said, accentuating himself with a punch to Andy's right arm. But he was smiling. "It's been a long day for both of us. Guess I wasn't paying attention, either."

McKenzie dropped Andy off on the dirt road, then told him he'd be by again later that night to get to the mill.

"Get some sleep, buddy."

"Yeah, I will. You, too."

Andy stood in the road as McKenzie drove off, a dust cloud soon obscuring his car.

Why's he being so nice to me?

He turned to head inside the house. Another thought nagged him. If Leonard wasn't dead drunk, he'd want to know more about what had happened with Lockett the day before.

Leonard Laduke. Of all people, Leonard the son of a bitch had saved him from a worse ass beating … That was a Leonard he hadn't seen in years, not since mama died.

How'd he sober up long enough?

He wasn't up to facing Leonard. Luckily, he didn't have to. Leonard was passed out on the couch. And when Andy woke up hours later, after the sun had set, Leonard was gone from the house, looking to get drunk somewhere else.

* * * *

With nothing to do after school, Brax hurried home but detoured before arriving.

He wanted to see Adele. And, though he wasn't ready to admit it, Natalie Young.

The front door was left open to let any hint of breeze in to cool the house. Adele never bothered with a screen door. How much could it have cost? Apparently enough that she'd never needed it bad enough.

He'd walked home alone. Moses made that clear in sixth period, when they'd gone through the equipment room doing inventory as Halliday had told them to do – there was no practice, after all – and told him it wasn't a good idea.

"Why not? Shit, we live right down the street from each other."

"Just wouldn't be Brax, just wouldn't," Moses said without offering any more explanation. "Besides, Coach wants me to stay after for a few minutes for something or another."

At the front door, he could already smell something cooking in the kitchen.

"Adele? Josiah?" Brax asked. He didn't call for Natalie, though he knew she had to be the one in the kitchen. When he saw her, he wanted to act surprised as if he hadn't given her any thought.

He was surprised. An older voice called back from the kitchen. "Is that you, young Braxton Freeman?"

"Yes ma'am," Brax said, not knowing who it was.

Natalie's mother stepped out of the kitchen, darted through the front door and walked toward Brax. "Well, good afternoon, young man," she said warmly. "Come on in. Are you here to see Aunt Adele?"

Like Natalie, she said "aunt" so regally.

"Yes, yes ma'am, I am."

"Good," Mrs. Young said, taking Brax's arm in hers. "That'll make her day."

Mrs. Young led him back to Adele's room, though he knew the way better than she did. The room was dark and the single lamp on the bedside table was turned off. There were no windows allowing sunlight. Adele's house was like a catacomb. Additions over the years had enclosed her bedroom. It was large enough, but seemed enclosed like a closet. Her walls backed up to other walls in the house, but not to the outside.

Adele still looked ashen as she rested. Mrs. Young bent down and whispered in her ear, "Auntie, young Brax Freeman is here to see you," as she softly shook Adele's shoulder.

Adele's eyes fluttered. It took her a minute to focus, then her face warmed to the vision. She mouthed something without making a sound.

Mrs. Young pulled up a chair and motioned for Brax to sit beside Adele. He did and began talking. As Mrs. Young returned to the kitchen, Brax continued talking, telling Adele about the first day of school, how it started, how it went and how it ended as Adele seemed to listen and comprehend with a crooked grin.

He talked an uncharacteristic amount, wondering all the time why Natalie Young wasn't around.

* * * *

Brax headed home shortly after Moses arrived. Moses didn't say anything to him. He just moved to the other side of the bed, sat down on the edge, and started talking to Adele.

Brax left without a word.

An old station wagon was parked in front of the Freeman house, an automobile Brax didn't recognize. But as he entered the house, he recognized the elderly couple sitting on the couch talking to Harold and Peggy, who sat across from them.

Bradley Alan Douglass, the county prosecutor's father, was in his

60s. Dark hair turning gray, he was gaunt as a result of an illness he'd gotten on the boat sailing to fight the Kaiser in World War I.

Though old and getting frail, Douglass was well-known throughout Takasaw. Hated by many, respected by most, he was a distant man. He had a penchant for an occasional drink. Harold often recalled how one time, at a party the Douglass' held for the local Democrat party, Bradley Alan Douglass, spurred by a few shots of Jim Beam, had asked him what he thought about the new president, Jack Kennedy.

Harold had replied that he was impressed with the man's leadership abilities. Expecting a quick agreement or rebuttal, knowing the conservative mood in Alabama, Harold instead sparked a monologue. For the next three minutes, Douglass waxed on about Kennedy's leadership ability while the rest of the Democrats on the room looked on grimly.

Jack Kennedy was a Democrat, but not a Southern Democrat. Just four years earlier, every man in the room except Bradley Alan Douglass had supported the Dixiecrat ticket of Strom Thurmond and Alabama's own John Sparkman, the southern wing of the party's reply to the liberal and dull Adlai Stevenson.

"In three minutes, Bradley Alan had me believing Jack Kennedy was the second coming of George Washington, himself," Harold joked later. "I heard him talk more in those few minutes than I had in the last three years total."

Most folks in Takasaw would quickly tell you there was a reason Bradley Alan Douglass didn't talk a lot. He had little chance because of his wife.

Mrs. Douglass sat next to him on the Freeman's couch. Where Bradley Alan was thin, she was a robust woman, probably the size in width of Harold and Brax combined. Yet she carried herself with an air of importance. It was an importance she would remind you of, if needed. Miss Georgia Douglass was named after the state her father governed at the turn of the century.

They'd met at the university shortly after Bradley Alan returned from Europe and the first big war. She was a privileged graduate student pursuing a Master's degree. He was a second-year law student at UA, a poor farmer's kid from Takasaw. They married and settled in Takasaw, rearing a family and, over the years, a lot of controversy.

They were, Harold said often, the original "nigger lovers." Douglass' private law practice had deteriorated over the years, to the point where now he represented only blacks, most of them too poor to pay. Even in her late 50s, Miss Georgia had to go to work as his secretary – and chief bill collector – to keep a modest income viable.

She was Takasaw's original women's libber. She smoked cigarettes in public upon her arrival in Takasaw years before it became widely accepted for women. And though the Douglasses were mostly shunned by polite society, except when it came to political fund-raisers, where they could attract big wigs from elsewhere, she was a favorite of women's groups throughout the county because of her tales of her father's political career and her own grasp of the area's history.

Most of that history was unrecorded in books, but etched in Georgia Douglass' mind.

And she told those stories, those tales, that history in grandiose fashion. Among the women's circles, she was known for also adding bawdy sidebars – when only "the hens" were listening.

Harold saw Brax and rose to greet him.

"Mr. and Mrs. Douglass, you remember our son, Braxton, don't you?"

Bradley Allan nodded grimly – he always looked grim, due to ill-fitting dentures. Miss Georgia nodded as well, accompanying her recognition, "Why of course, Harold, dear, why of course."

Harold told Brax to grab a chair from the kitchen and join them.

"Braxton, honey," Peggy said when he straddled the kitchen chair he moved into the living room, "the Douglasses are here to talk about your future at the high school."

What do Bradley Alan and Miss Georgia care about my future at Takasaw?

"Actually, Braxton, they've got us rethinking some things," Harold said.

Brax looked at Harold, then back at Peggy wondering what the hell they were getting at.

"May I?" Miss Georgia asked and Brax gave her a half shrug. "Braxton Freeman, we've been talking to your parents about the possibility of you transferring to another school. What would you think of that?"

I don't know what I would think, but I don't know what business it is of yours …

He paused a minute, letting the thought pass before it slipped away.

"I don't know, ma'am. Coach mentioned it, but Dad pretty much said it was out of the question."

"Bradley Alan and I understand exactly what your father means," Miss Georgia continued. "But we both think," she paused, looking at her husband, who nodded his agreement, "it's something you should consider. Do you know our youngest son, Graham?"

Brax knew him vaguely. He was a good athlete, a seventh grader who could probably make the varsity if they'd let him try out. At thirteen, Graham Douglass was already three inches taller than Braxton.

"Well, dear, we're sending Graham off to a military school in Georgia, at least until things settle down here."

Settle down?

"Braxton," Harold interrupted. "As you're probably aware, Mr. and Mrs. Douglass have been aware and supportive of our plans to integrate the high school."

Brax nodded. If they weren't getting so old, the Douglasses would have led the movement themselves. Instead, son Scott Douglass was carrying the torch.

"But the Douglasses believe – and, frankly, they've made a good point – that you might be better off going to another school, where you're not the only white kid."

"I'm not the only white kid."

Braxton's response seemed to catch Harold off guard, momentarily.

"I know son. There are what, three white kids at the school?"

"Yes sir. Three."

"Dear," Miss Georgia said, "you've taken a stand, as has your father, as has my family, and we respect that. But for your future, you'd be better off at another school with other white kids."

"I thought … " Brax said, stopping to control a flare of anger. "I thought we were trying to integrate the school. Wasn't that the point?"

Miss Georgia looked at Brax stunned.

"Yes, Braxton, that was exactly the point," Harold said. "And we've done that, though not with the success we expected."

"But if I leave and the other white kids leave, then we're back to where we started. Except it's not all-white, but it's an all-Negro school."

"I know, son, I know."

No one spoke for a moment. Harold was gazing at the carpet. Peggy was looking back and forth, at Brax, at Miss Georgia, at Bradley Alan. Miss Georgia was stirring the cup of coffee in her right hand with a plastic straw.

"Boy," said Bradley Alan in a soft grumble. "No one's stood up more for the rights of Negroes in this county than my family. And, now, your family. We think you've got a good future ahead of you. Graham, too. Unfortunately, if you two stay and go to school here under the current circumstances ..."

A coughing jag stopped him for a moment. Clearing his throat, Douglass continued. "If you and Graham and the other white children stayed here in school, you're going to hear about it the rest of your lives. You're going to be called 'nigger lovers.' Your father and mother can live with that. They're older and established. God knows Georgia and I have lived with it. But there's no need you young 'uns have to sacrifice like we have. We've gone through a lot of hell over the years so your generation wouldn't have to sacrifice."

With that, Bradley Alan settled back into the couch with a sigh.

That's more than I've heard out of him my whole life.

"Your father says you're a pretty good football player, dear," Miss Georgia said.

"Yes ma'am, I think I am."

"He says you've got a chance to earn an athletic scholarship based on your abilities, too. Our understanding is that there aren't enough students to field a football team now. So if you go to another school, you'll still have that chance."

The conversation upset Braxton. Why? He didn't know, really. He had to play football, but how could he unless he transferred now. But since Harold had told Hard-Ass Halliday that he couldn't transfer under any circumstances, he'd considered the matter closed.

Now they were giving him a new option, and he felt like a human yo-yo.

Truth is, he had been uncomfortable most of the day. He'd been the only white kid in most of his classes. The redhead, a year behind, joined him for Calculus and French II. At the end of the day, he privately acknowledged the discomfort, and in return felt guilty for feeling that way.

He had been so keen on Moses coming to *his* school, not understanding how Moses would feel. Now it was more *Moses'* school, almost all black, and he didn't feel like he belonged. After all, nine of the 12 students were Negroes.

Damn. What about Moses?

"Ma'am," Brax said, looking Miss Georgia in the eye. "I'll do whatever my parents think is best for me. But ..."

His mind began whirring. He could find another school. More important, he could find a new team and play ball. Hadn't Halliday ripped up his schedule, ensuring that he wasn't yet officially enrolled? That meant he could transfer without penalty.

But if he left Takasaw, it would be as if he'd abandoned Moses. He had encouraged Moses to make the switch. Now he had the chance to play football. But Moses ...

Even without a scholarship, Brax could manage college somehow. Or, rather, Harold and Peggy could manage. Moses' one shot was a scholarship. A scholarship based on his ability to play football. And on an opportunity to play that was now gone.

"What is it, Brax?" Harold asked.

Brax ignored his father and looked Mrs. Douglass in the eye again.

"There's a Negro student at the school, Moses Burks, who lives down the street. He transferred at the urging of our football coach, Coach Halliday, and me because we thought he'd help our team. It just don't seem fair."

"It *doesn't* seem fair," Peggy corrected.

"Brax, you can't worry about ..." Harold began.

"We know who you're talking about," Bradley Alan said, leaning forward again. "Don't you worry about him, son."

"I'm sorry sir, but I can't help but worry about him. I'm kind of responsible. See, he can't transfer back to the Institute now, and without football he doesn't have a chance at an athletic scholarship."

"I said don't worry about it," Bradley Alan Douglass said impatiently. "It's already taken care of."

Brax turned to Harold. Without speaking, he tried to plead his case.

"Brax, what Bradley Alan is saying is that the Institute will take Moses back," Harold said.

"How? They've already told him ..."

"They've already told him they don't have any room at the school," Harold cut in. "They've got room, they just don't have the funds. Mr.

Douglass has already taken care of that. Moses can return to the Institute in the morning."

Brax gave his father the same look. Harold didn't understand either.

"Dear," Miss Georgia said. "Bradley Alan is on the college's board of trustees. He knows the people there and he has already made the arrangements. The Institute high school wasn't going to let Moses back due to financial constraints. We've already straightened that out. Bradley Alan and I will pay it. In fact, I expect they're all going back. We believe Takasaw High will suspend operations for the year because there aren't enough students."

It took a moment for Brax to comprehend what they were saying.

Takasaw High is shutting down? And you're going to pay Moses' way?

"I only asked them one thing," Bradley Alan Douglass said with a gruff laugh. "They have to come up with one good lawsuit so I can make my money back."

CHAPTER 10

HALLIDAY WAS POINTING, as if it did any good. From their vantage point, the top row of the swaying wooden stands, the play began to unfold.

"Look at that hole, Freeman, look at it."

Braxton saw the same thing: a wide hole, between the right tackle and guard, which held for a good two seconds before a linebacker recovered to close it. Plenty of time for a good halfback to find daylight.

But Natsuma High didn't have a good halfback. The guy taking the handoff was slow afoot and hesitant in reaching the opening. He cautiously committed to the opening only to be dropped behind the line of scrimmage when his indecisiveness proved fatal to the play.

"You'd have had 10, 20 yards easy, Freeman," Halliday said. "Easy. They've got a good enough line. All they need is one good runner."

Brax had accepted Halliday's unexpected invitation to watch the Natsuma opener earlier in the day after missing school. After meeting with the Douglasses, Harold and Peggy had both told him to skip Friday's classes, giving the entire family a weekend to think about the next step.

If Brax transferred, Natsuma seemed the best option. It was a smaller school than Takasaw and the team wasn't nearly as good. But they played a good schedule, and Halliday said Brax could help the team immediately.

When Brax —and, as it turned out, Moses – hadn't shown up for classes, Halliday was on the horn. First, calling Burks to see if the rumors that he could return to the Institute were true. Then he called the Freeman house and asked – actually ordered – Brax to go to the Natsuma opener with him.

Halliday had even paid for two plates at Piggy's Golden BBQ on the Natsuma Highway.

Who'da thunk it?

"Shee-it! What a crappy call," Halliday said.

Natsuma was lined up in punt formation. It was fourth down and maybe a yard to go with Natsuma at the opponent's 30-yard line.

"Don't kick the Goddamn ball. Go for it!" Halliday said loudly. Brax was relieved that no one turned around. Of course, there wasn't a soul within five rows of them. "Field position don't mean shee-it here. Those guys couldn't score with a nymphomaniac. Go for it, damnit!"

Halliday's back-row coaching did no good. The Natsuma punter lifted a high kick that flew out of the end zone for a touchback.

"They not only need a good halfback, they need a head coach with balls."

Luckily for Natsuma, the opposition was hapless. Natsuma managed a touchdown on an interception return and a safety for an ugly 8-0 victory.

As a small core of fans applauded the lackluster win politely, Halliday squeezed Brax on the shoulder. "C'mon, Freeman. Let me introduce you to your new coach."

Halliday led Brax down the rickety steps and out on the field. They crossed the field's beaten-down grass, following the Natsuma team to a door leading into the gym.

"Collins! Collins!" Halliday walked into the gym without hesitation and began yelling for someone. Standing in the side of a doorway, patting his players on the back as they made their way into the locker room stood the Natsuma coach. He was a tall man, tall enough to nearly scrape the top of the door frame. He looked much younger than Halliday, not much older than Brax. He had an athletic stature with the hint of the beginning of a beer belly.

"Coach Halliday!" Collins said as he spotted the bellowing Takasaw football coach. Collins left the door and met Halliday halfway, greeting him with an enthusiastic handshake. "What brings you here, Coach?"

"Ain't got nothin' better to do," Halliday said. "Ain't got a team to coach anymore."

"Yeah, yeah, I know. Sorry to have heard that," Collins said. "I've got eight of your former players, now. Four are already starting and a couple of more got the chance. Adding them has given us a chance at a winning season."

"Well, good," Halliday said. "I think you're about to meet your chance to win the region."

Collins looked at Halliday with surprise. Halliday had seen his team play. Unless he was shoveling something, he knew well that Natsuma was limited in talent.

Halliday looked to his left, then his right, then turned around.

"Damnit, Freeman, come here." Halliday grabbed Brax by the collar and yanked him forward.

"Meet Braxton Freeman, here, Coach," Halliday said proudly, as if he was introducing his son to the governor.

Collins extended his hand and accompanied it with an easy smile. "Nice to meet you Braxton. Name's Cecil Collins."

Brax shook the hand without saying a word.

"Brax was our captain at Takasaw," Halliday continued. "He's probably going to transfer here Monday. He was our best player, and he's going to get a scholarship to either Alabama or Auburn. All he needs is a chance to play."

"Transfer here? Well, hot damn," Collins said, his eyes widening at the thought. "You're the halfback, right?"

"Yes, sir," Brax replied.

"Some of your old teammates have talked about you, son. Glad to have you. You come out here for practice Monday afternoon, and we'll get a good look at you."

Halliday and Collins settled into a conversation about Xs and Os, and Collins began asking Halliday questions about his observations on the game. After a few minutes, Collins asked his coaching rival to join him in his office. Halliday agreed, and the two left Brax standing by himself.

He'd spotted a few of his old teammates from the back as the team headed toward the locker room. But they were showering and changing – he could hear the victory noise from his vantage point in the gym.

Not wanting to stand by himself like a dope, he headed back outside and began walking the length of the field. Like at Takasaw, the lack of rain for most of the summer had left the field worn and dry. Divots of grass were everywhere. Unlike Takasaw, there were also large barren spots where the dirt overwhelmed the dying grass.

At the 50-yard line, he got into his halfback stance, crouched with hands resting on his knees, and then listened to a silent snap count. On the second "Hut!" he exploded to his right, reached out for the imaginary lateral and gathered the ball at the same time he cut up field. Fifty yards later, he was crossing the goal line for an imaginary touchdown.

"Another Natsuma touchdown for Braxxxxxxxtonnnnnnnn Freeeeeeeeeeeman!"

"Braxton!"

The girl's voice startled him. Brax wheeled and saw the freckled redhead from Takasaw standing along the near fence with some adults.

Brax waved sheepishly. She took that as a sign to talk, said something to the adults, and joined him on the field.

"What are *you* doing here, Brax?" she asked.

"Coach Halliday and I came to watch them play."

What is her name?

"My older sister's a teacher here," the redhead said. "Since we don't have a team anymore, we thought we'd come here tonight. I helped her out in the concession stand. Did they win?"

Brax laughed at the dumb question. The scoreboard remained lit, with the rows of bulbs showing the obvious: Home 8, Visitor 0.

"Yeah, they did. Not much of a game, though. We would've beat Natsuma by two, three touchdowns, easy."

She smiled, as if waiting for him to say something else. As usual, Brax's lack of conversation skills created a silent siege.

"Guess I'd better go. Daddy doesn't like driving on the highway at night, anyway." The redhead took a few steps back toward her parents, then turned back. "Brax?"

"Yeah?"

"Why weren't you in school today?"

"Oh," he said, realizing he'd been caught playing hooky. "My parents told me I could skip. We're thinking about me transferring here."

The redhead's response was pained. "What? You're thinking about transferring. Now?"

"Yeah. I, uh ... my parents want me to play football so I can get a college scholarship. Can't do that at Takasaw."

Another half-truth. *Lying was becoming common place.*

"I can't believe you, Braxton Freeman," she said, spitting out the words. Her volume remained calm, but the tone was angry. "After everything that's gone on ... Your father was one of the leaders of the committee, and you're not going to see this through?"

It was Brax's turn to be stunned. Why'd she care?

"I've got a chance to go to college ..." he said defensively.

"Don't give me that. You can go to college. Your parents can sure afford it."

"Well, yeah ..."

The redhead spun around and began walking briskly toward her parents. A dozen steps later, she spun around again.

"I thought you were a better person than that, Brax Freeman. I thought you had a spine." she said. Her eyes were watering. Her bottom lip was quivering. "I thought you stood for something."

She left him and joined her parents for the walk to the parking lot. Brax stood and watched, a response stuck in his throat. His surprise quickly gave way to something else.

Frustration.

What business is it of hers? Besides, by Monday, Takasaw High will be shut down.

* * * *

Andy stopped at the red light. With the truck idling, he looked down at the paper that held the directions to McKenzie's house outside Opelika. McKenzie had written them down during lunch break of the shift the night before, in neat block letters, easy to read.

He took a right, then a left off Highway 280 just before reaching Opelika. Two miles later, he took one more right onto a gravel road. A few hundred yards down, the red mailbox with McKenzie's name stood as a can't-miss marker. Laduke turned into the dirt lane and followed it half-an-acre up to the freshly painted yellow farmhouse.

McKenzie hadn't said anything about the house, only that Andy was invited there for a small Saturday afternoon picnic with McKenzie's family and some friends. As he parked the truck off the side of the dirt path leading to the front door, he was surprised at the opulence of McKenzie's home.

The house wasn't new, but it was surprisingly big and well maintained. An island that the driveway created in front of the house had rows and rows of flowers surrounding a majestic weeping willow. A wrap-around porch stretching down both sides and meeting at the wide entrance to the front door offered a cozy welcoming. A young blonde child swayed in a swing anchored to the ceiling of the porch, with a soft cushion over the hardwood seat.

That he was there, at McKenzie's home, surprised Andy. He rarely did anything social. He had told McKenzie he would come, after much badgering, but didn't believe it when he said so. Yet here he was.

There wasn't much to do at home, anyway. He hadn't seen Leonard in a couple of days – nothing unusual for the old son of a bitch, who often disappeared for stretches – and had the house all to himself. Andy loved the rare solitude.

But after relaxing around the house for a few hours, he'd gotten restless.

The little girl said nothing, but pointed toward the front door, which was held open by a brick. A front foyer beckoned straight back to the yard, where Andy could already hear the party in progress.

The backyard was as surprising as the rest of the house. The grass was vibrant green and well kept, with a play set at the far end against a wooden fence. More surprising of all was an in-ground pool, shaped like an oval, full of young kids splashing about. One kid created a wave that lapped over the sides as he cannon balled off the diving board.

In all his life, Andy had seen one home with a swimming pool. His grandparents had one, with water turned a murky brown from the endless pecan shells that fell to the bottom and were only sporadically removed, when grandpa was nagged to the breaking point. His grandmother refused to cut down the pecan tree overhanging the pool. For the short time Andy and his mother lived there with his grandparents, it had been a welcome oasis. He had been allowed to frolic in the pool for hours, without supervision or interruption.

There were more people than Andy expected, mostly young couples he figured were about McKenzie's age – older than Laduke, but not by a lot of years. He didn't recognize a single person until McKenzie waved at him from his spot on the other side of the pool. That he didn't recognize anyone – particularly other members of the Klan – was an unexpected relief.

McKenzie was wearing a plaid, short-sleeved shirt with the tail hanging out over a swimsuit. He stood over two portable grills, flipping hamburgers with a spatula on one and squirting leaps of flames with a water bottle in the other hand.

"Hey, buddy!" McKenzie said, offering a hand and pulling it away just as quickly when he realized he still held the spatula. "Glad you found it okay."

"Yeah, I did. The directions was good."

"Good. Good to have you here. Hey, Julie! Julie!"

McKenzie waved someone else over. A tall woman left a couple at one of the patio tables and joined McKenzie and Andy. She was a few inches shorter than Andy, with brunette hair held back in pigtails. She wore no makeup, but got Andy's attention immediately with her skin, darkened by days at the pool, and round, green eyes. He also noticed that she wasn't so lean. Her stomach showed the advancement of an early pregnancy.

"Honey, this is Andy Laduke, the fellow I've been telling you about."

She shocked Andy by grabbing him by the shoulders and leaning forward to give a light brush of a kiss on his cheek.

"Welcome, Andy. We're delighted to have you here. Mac thinks a lot of you."

"Thank you, ma'am."

She stared for a moment at Andy's bruised face, then smiled and returned to her guests without comment. Andy blushed for a moment, realizing how beat up he looked.

"Did you bring your swim trunks?"

"Huh?"

"Did I forget to tell you?" McKenzie asked.

"Yeah. Guess ya did."

"You're about the size of Julie's dad. Tell you what, let me finish grilling, and I'll see if she has one of her dad's old swimsuits lying around. If you want to swim, I mean."

"Uh, yeah. That'd be fine."

"Good, good." McKenzie reached underneath the first grill and pulled out a platter. "Hold this," he said, handing the platter over to Andy. As Laduke held it, McKenzie began sliding the cooked burgers on the large plate.

"They look good."

"Yes, don't they? Hope you're hungry, buddy."

"Shore am."

"Good." McKenzie held the platter aloft, then announced to everyone, "Let's eat!"

The adults began moving toward a picnic table, where Julie was putting the last of the condiments next to paper plates and both hamburger and hot dog buns.

"Hey, buddy," McKenzie said in a lower tone as the migration continued. "Let's not talk about Klan business with any of our friends, okay? They're folks from our church."

"Yeah, course not."

"I don't mean just business, Andy. I mean, if anyone starts talking about the crap in Takasaw, shy away from it. Understand?"

"Yeah," Andy answered, though he didn't understand McKenzie at all.

* * * *

Without homework, without the job at the country club – the pool had closed down Labor Day weekend, just before classes had, in theory, resumed – Brax had little to do with his weekend. So he shuttled back and forth to Adele's house more than he could ever remember doing so, just to see how she was doing.

And to catch a glimpse of Natalie Young.

He caught a glimpse, but nothing more. She stayed away for most of the weekend, making an appearance for Sunday dinner. But her parents were with her then, so there was little chance for Brax to talk to her. It was a lost cause anyway. He had to join Harold and Peggy for Sunday supper, as well.

Nor was Moses around much. He'd made the decision to return to the Institute, but not without a price. Mr. Young explained it, how the coach was making Moses help him "gussy" up the playing field all weekend as punishment for his original defection.

He made a brief appearance as the family gathered for the post-church services meal, just long enough to show blisters breaking out on both hands from the endless manual labor.

At the Freeman home, it was a Sunday supper of fried chicken, garlic mashed potatoes and spinach that Harold finally brought up the possibility of transferring to Natsuma High again.

"Braxton, I guess it's up to you," he said. "I know how important playing ball is to you."

"Yes sir, it's important," Brax said. "Coach Halliday introduced me to their coach Friday. I think I could help their team."

"Then it's done. I'll drive you over there in the morning and fill out the paperwork."

Coach Collins greeted the Freemans the next morning. He'd heard the news from Halliday, whom Brax called after Sunday supper, and had the requisite papers ready and an assistant principal on hand to register Brax for classes. Brax picked the same schedule of classes he was supposed to have at Takasaw with the exception of Spanish. Natsuma offered French instead.

The first practice was like one of the Sunday sandlot games. He dominated. Natsuma ran out of the same T formation Halliday used, and Collins immediately put him at right halfback. The terminology was different, but the plays were the same. Collins called the play from the sideline, then held up a cardboard diagram. What had been "Power Sweep Left" at Takasaw was "Toss 37" at Natsuma. Same lead blocking by the fullback and left half, same pulling guard.

On his first carry, Brax burst through a slight hole and had only a linebacker in his way. He feinted right then spun as the linebacker dove for him, leaving the defender in a sprawl, and dashed unchallenged the remaining 35 yards.

It was too easy. The Natsuma defenders – the scrubs who couldn't make the first team – were slow, small and pathetic.

Only twice did the defense manage to stop him for anything less than a five-yard gain. The first time, when the pulling guard stumbled backward, tripping Brax as he tried to gather the pitch and cut up field. The second time came on a swing pass, thrown slightly behind him, when the same defensive back who had failed to react to the play the last three times it had been run – the three previous plays before this – got wise and hit Brax squarely between the numbers as he caught the pass.

Four touchdowns later, Collins called him over by sending the former right half into the huddle.

"Dang, Freeman. Halliday wasn't exaggerating."

"Thanks, Coach."

Defense came as easy. Collins lined Brax up at middle linebacker with just one command – chase the ball. He did it effortlessly. He was stronger than most of the scrubs who tried to block him. No one could match his speed. There were occasions he didn't make the play, but only because another Natsuma defender got there first. If the first-team offense versus the scrubs was a mismatch, the first-team defense made the practice a rout.

"What number'd you have at Takasaw?" Collins stood in the caged equipment room, sorting through a dozen unused jerseys.

"Twenty-four, sir."

"I've already given that one out," Collins said. "It would've been too small for you, anyway. How about this one?"

Collins tossed him one of the garnet jerseys. Already, Brax liked the colors better. Takasaw was an ordinary dark blue and white, but Natsuma had the reddish jerseys with yellow numerals and bright yellow pants, with two garnet stripes down the side. The helmets, unlike Takasaw's, were painted, as well. They also were garnet, though a slightly darker shade than the jerseys, with the school's mascot of an Indian chief on one side of the helmet.

The Natsuma Red Warriors. I like this.

"That was my number, Braxton, back when I was all-county here," Collins said.

Brax unfolded the jersey. The yellow numbers covered both sides: thirty-eight.

"See if it fits."

Brax struggled to get the practice jersey off. It took him a minute – the left sleeve got caught in a crevice of the shoulder pads. Once off, he slipped the new jersey on. It fit good, a little loose. Brax liked to have a little room.

"Fits good, Coach, real good."

"There's a little give in it," Collins said. "Normally, I don't like my backs to have loose fits – just more material for the defense to grab. With your speed, I get the feeling most of 'em will be grabbing at air, anyway. Let's play the first game and see how you do. If it's a problem ..."

"Nah, Coach. It won't be a problem," Brax said as he pulled the jersey back off. "Hey, Coach. Did you play college ball?"

"I did. At Florence Teachers College. Ever hear of it?"

"Yes sir. Up in the northern part of the state, ain't it?"

"Yep. I was pretty good, but I wasn't the best player on the team."

"Nope?"

"Nah. I played back. But our star was a guy named Harlon Hill. Heard of him?"

"Yessir. Plays for the Bears, right?"

"Yes, the Chicago Bears."

Brax nodded. Hill had gone straight from small-college stardom to the NFL, earning Rookie of the Year honors.

"Ever watch the *Andy Griffith Show?*"

"Yessir. Not a lot, but I've seen it."

"The guy who plays Goober Pyle on the show, George Lindsey, he was on the team, too. Funniest joker you ever met."

"No shit?"

"Er, no, Brax." Collins' amiable look changed quickly. "Son, I don't use that kind of language, and I don't allow my players to, either."

"I'm sorry, sir. Won't happen again."

"Better not, Brax, better not."

* * * *

To his credit, Coach Mitchell was a man of his word. When Moses returned to the Institute High team, he was no longer the starting quarterback. Bobby Mitchell understood Moses' decision to switch to Takasaw High, but he wasn't going to reward him for returning only because the desegregation plan went awry.

Besides, his sophomore quarterback had a lot of potential. Moses realized that as he watched the first game from the sidelines. Carver, the black school from Montgomery, had three times as many students and twice the number of players.

But the sophomore ran for two touchdowns and threw for another in a 21-7 victory.

Now, in his first practice back with his old team, Moses was playing receiver for the first time. He knew the playbook and he knew Mitchell would find a way for him to play a significant role. Moses knew he was still the best player on the team by a large margin.

There was another reason to feel comfortable. Up in the stands, taking it all in, was Tamika Long. She always stayed late, she explained, waiting for her dad to finish up work at the college. But this bought her a few minutes with Moses before and after practice.

"So, all is right with the world again?" she asked after he came out of the locker room, freshly showered.

"Yeah, I guess," he said, half-convincingly.

She seemed to read his mind. "You still wish you were back at Takasaw, don't you? I kind of wish I was, too."

She'd surprised him. Most of the nine students who'd been part of the experiment seemed relieved. After a week of tension, they could return to normalcy.

"I'm just like you, Moses," she continued. "I wanted to test myself against the white students. I wanted to prove I was just as smart and just as capable."

Moses saw her father walking briskly toward the field house. He was still three blocks away as he crossed over from the campus side, so Moses had to make his exit quick. He nodded in the man's direction, letting Tamika know he was coming.

"I know you're as smart as any of them already," Moses said. "Me, too. I just wanted to prove I belonged with them on the football field."

CHAPTER 11

NATSUMA WON THE coin toss, but Brax remained on the sidelines. Collins had made it clear: Sam Bolton, the starter at right halfback the week before would remain the starter. If the start was supposed to bolster the kid's confidence, the plan failed. On the second snap, Bolton dropped the lateral on a sweep and couldn't find the ball before a Bullock County defender recovered.

Bullock County did not squander the opportunity. It took just four plays until Bullock's powerful fullback crashed through the end zone from five yards out for the game's first score.

"Freeman, you go in on offense this series," Collins said. He had told Brax to stay close, and Brax hadn't allowed the coach to stray more than a few feet away.

Natsuma took over at its own 27-yard line after a wobbly kick and brief return. Brax snapped the chinstrap tight and raced out to midfield. He found Bolton in the huddle – Collins hadn't told him of the substitution. Brax tapped Bolton on the shoulder without a word and pointed his thumb toward the sideline. Bolton replied with a sourpuss look and sprinted for the bench.

"Forty-five power, on two," said the quarterback, repeating the call before the huddle broke with a clap of hands.

Brax lined up to the right of the other half and the fullback and got in his crouch. The hands settled on his knees momentarily until he began rubbing the building sweat off his hands on the knee pads of the new pants.

"Down ... set ... hut! Hut!"

The quarterback took the handoff and spun to his left, faking a quick pitch to the other halfback, who continued to carry out the deception. The quarterback continued to wheel, allowing the fullback to slide past him, then shuffled a couple of steps to his right and slipped the ball firmly into Brax's cradled arms.

He saw the hole open momentarily and burst forward. It closed upon arrival. Brax took a lateral step to his right, trying to work free outside but his own end blocked the path. Brax turned to his left and looked for an opening back in the center of the line.

Boom! A Bullock County linebacker hit him straight in the gut. Brax bobbled the ball, nearly losing it as he was flattened to the turf.

"Nice running, Freeman," said the Natsuma center sarcastically, extending a hand to help Brax back up.

"At least he didn't fumble the ball." It was Gus Gothard, the right tackle, one of Braxton's ex-teammates from Takasaw.

In the huddle, the quarterback stared at Collins, who signaled in the next play.

"Post-fly right, on one."

Brax knew the play, though his responsibility was different. In Halliday's offense, he lined up wide and ran a fly pattern, straight down the field, while the split end dug 10 yards downfield, then cut diagonally across the middle of the field.

When they'd practiced the play with Natsuma, however, it had been the left half who lined up in the slot. Braxton remained in the backfield, split behind the quarterback, next to the fullback, to pass block.

The quarterback again took the snap and dropped straight back. A stocky defensive lineman shot past the Natsuma center, arms raised in pursuit of the passer. Brax saw him and dropped down, cutting him out with a block to the knees.

He looked up in time, though his view was partially blocked, to see the split end past the defense. He didn't see the throw – the center, backpedaling, tripped and fell on top of Brax. But he heard the moan from the crowd as the horrific heave fluttered short of the intended receiver. A Bullock County defender waited on the pop fly and claimed the interception. He moved back upfield just a few yards before the split end threw him down from behind.

Needing to cover forty yards this time, Bullock began the assault. The Bullock line dominated, creating holes on both sides. It was only a matter of choosing the right one. The Bullock fullback made the decisions quickly, and bulled through for large gains. On the second play, Brax got to the hole in time, but the Bullock fullback lowered his head and ran over him. Unprepared for his strength, Brax could do no better than grab the brute's back shoe, which he wrenched off.

It made little difference. The fullback continued to barrel down the field until three Natsuma defenders combined to jump him inside the 10.

The Natsuma defense held for two downs – in part, because Bullock ran plays for its halfback. But on third down, the Bullock quarterback dropped back to pass and found his tight end wide open in the corner of an end zone for another touchdown.

The score remained 14-0 late in the second quarter. Natsuma did not have a first down – nor had Collins called another running play for Brax. Still, the Red Warriors defense managed to keep Bullock County out of the end zone. Bullock lost the ball once on downs, when Gothard stunted between blockers to trip the fullback behind the line of scrimmage, and again on a fumble, when the quarterback dropped the snap while backing away from center.

Unlike Halliday, who always seemed to have a solid plan ready, Brax thought Collins seemed to be feeling his way. He had called running plays for everyone in the backfield, including the quarterback on a naked bootleg, without any sustained success. After the ill-fated pass, he shied away from throwing the ball.

After the fumble, Natsuma inherited possession near midfield, its best start of the game. Collins still couldn't find a solution. A sweep to the right side gained only a yard, a half-hearted block by a frustrated Brax hadn't helped, and a dive up the middle by the fullback was rebuffed for no gain.

"Motion Lance, slip screen pass right, on three."

Collins was ready to give Brax another chance. The left halfback would go in motion to his side then sprint downfield, trying to lure defenders to chase him deep. Brax would slide to the left, as if to block, and then take a screen pass from the quarterback. If the left half's gambit worked, and if the fullback and end got over to make blocks, the play might work.

The blockers got in front of Brax, but having seen the Natsuma quarterback's weak arm the defense didn't buy the deep route. Thus, when the ball was thrown to Brax, he saw just a slight crease between the blockers.

Brax cradled the pass and turned upfield. The fullback missed his block, and a linebacker came charging at Braxton. Brax's head darted left, freezing the linebacker, then his legs instinctively cut right. The linebacker dived and missed.

Another defender hit him from the right, but it was a glancing blow. It knocked Brax sideways, but he maintained his balance with a quick assist from his left hand against the ground. The hit moved him toward the sideline, where he spotted a little daylight. Two defenders had an angle on him. Now, it was only a question of who was faster.

Brax had the first down when he realized the answer. The defenders weren't closing fast enough. At the thirty-five, one lunged in vain at him. Brax burst forward another step and left him sprawled on the turf. The other defender fell behind, puffing.

On the periphery, he saw the lumbering fullback, now playing middle linebacker. He was fast, but he had too far to go. All Brax had to do was keep his stride, and he'd have a touchdown.

No contest.

"Touchdown, Natsuma!" echoed the public address announcer over the two speakers.

Gothard was the first one to greet him in the end zone. He leaped into Brax's arms and knocked him down, then began pounding Brax on the helmet with his fists.

"Bullock County 14, Takasaw 6!" Gothard yelled before the others piled on.

Brax struggled to get out from underneath, before the referees penalized Natsuma. The bodies began unpiling only after one of the officials came over and issued a warning.

Brax joined his teammates in the huddle, and then broke again for the extra point. The snap was good and the hold was decent, but the kicker lined the ball straight off the backside of the center.

Running off the field for instructions before the kickoff, Brax scanned the stands. He spotted his parents in the mix of other moms and dads standing, applauding and grinning. He looked toward the upper reaches and saw a man standing alone.

Halliday gave him a thumbs-up, like Nero giving the last standing gladiator a reprieve.

The touchdown gave Natsuma the obvious lift in momentum. Brax could see it in most of his new teammates, teammates who no longer looked like they expected to be slaughtered. There was confidence, or at the very least the glimmer of hope he hadn't seen through most of the first half.

It got Collins' attention, as well. He began running plays specifically for Brax, and the Natsuma offense began rolling. But the same-old mistakes continued to stop the Red Warriors shy of the end zone. Penalties killed a drive midway through the third quarter and an intercepted pass – a nice play call on a second-and-short but another pitiful pass – squelched the next threat.

Yet Natsuma managed two points on a safety, another sign that it could play, defensively, with Bullock County. The visitors could move the ball liberally in the middle of the field but began misfiring as they neared the Natsuma goal line. Collins voided the advantage Bullock had in its strong fullback by assigning Brax and a safety to shadow him every play. The bullish back might run for five yards, but not for fifty against a double team.

Trailing 14-8 midway through the fourth quarter, Natsuma got another break. Gothard deflected a pass at the line of scrimmage and reacted quickly, snatching the interception before the ball could hit the ground.

Needing to cover seventy-seven yards, Natsuma got a good dozen on the opening play as Brax took the handoff and burst upfield for the quick gain. After another moderate gain, Brax took the handoff on a sweep. This time, Collins showed he had a good grasp for the game.

Instead of turning upfield, Brax slipped the ball into the hands of the split end, who was reversing the other way. As the Bullock defense bore down on Brax, the split end raced away. He was past midfield before the defense, after driving Brax five yards out of bounds, caught on and inside the Bullock thirty when he was dragged down.

With each gain, Brax could see the resignation in the faces of the Bullock defenders. There seemed to be little doubt whether Natsuma would score. The only question was if Natsuma would have to score again because of its own shaky kicking game.

The matter was made moot two plays later after Brax slipped past Gothard, who had created another huge hole, and bounded untouched eighteen yards into the end zone. On the sideline, Collins didn't hesitate on a decision. With the kicking problems obvious, he called for the same play on a two-point conversion.

Gothard created another hole and Brax again cruised across the goal line.

Natsuma 16, Bullock County 14.

It would remain that way until the final horn sounded. Most of the Natsuma players bounded across the field to shake hands with the opponents. Most of the coaching staff reacted with the same exuberance as Collins led them across the way, raising his fists in the air as he yelled across the field to someone in the stands.

Brax moved in a half trot after his teammates. Had Takasaw High remained together, the game with Bullock County would have been judged an automatic win. For Natsuma, the victory against the same team was cause for major celebration.

On the edge of the field, toward the locker room, stood Halliday. Knowing his parents would linger for awhile and meet him later after he showered and dressed; Brax left the other players to their midfield backslaps and resumed the trot in the curmudgeonly coach's direction.

He took the second hardest hit he'd absorbed all night – second to the Bullock fullback's bullish run over him – when Gothard chased him down and began pounding Brax's shoulder pads from behind.

"You'd think these dumbasses never won a game before, huh Brax?" Gothard laughed.

"You mean *we* dumbasses, don't you?"

"No. I mean *them*," Gothard said. "We play for them but we'll always be Takasaw boys. We both know we'd have drilled that team tonight if we still had our school."

Gothard celebrated with a loud "Wahoo!" and moved on. Brax could still see Halliday through the growing pedestrian traffic. The coach gave him a rare smile – it seemed forced, pained even – then gave him the thumb's up again.

Brax began running in the coach's direction but made it just a few yards when a familiar face blocked his path.

"Brax Freeman! Never knew you had it in you." The red-headed youth was a couple of inches shorter, his shoulders wider. Not stocky, but solidly built, much more so than the whippet he stood before. It was Gary Brokur, a former teammate at Takasaw, the running back Brax had backed up for two years. The one he was supposed to replace a year ago. The one he should've replaced this season.

"Good thing I graduated when I did," Brokur continued. "You're a helluva ballplayer. Course, this ain't the same as playing at Takasaw. But it's football."

Brax nodded and looked again for Halliday.

"What are you doing tomorrow?" Brokur asked.

Brax shrugged. What'd he ever do on a Saturday? Listen to a game. Eat supper ...

"I want you to come to my frat intramural game at Auburn and hang out, OK? Dress to play in the game and stick a change of clothes in a duffel bag. I'll pick you up at ten. Tell your parents we're going to a party afterward, OK?"

Brax shook his head.

"Ten sharp, OK?" Brokur grinned. "Gotta go. See you then."

Brokur left and Brax resumed his jog toward Halliday. By the time he reached the spot, Halliday was nowhere to be seen.

Collins was taking his turn greeting well-wishers, too. One grabbed him by the arm, leading him back to his office. Collins spun to see who had led him away.

"Keith Lockett, you old son'uva buck!" Collins said.

Lockett pulled him into the office, without returning the greeting.

* * * *

All week, Coach Mitchell told Moses he would still be a key contributor, but he was out of the lineup at halftime against DuBois Academy.

But only because the game was no longer competitive. Moses returned the opening kickoff for a touchdown and caught touchdown passes on two of the first three possessions. DuBois, a prep school for the numerous black colleges in Atlanta, was no match.

By halftime, the Institute led 28-0. Even without Moses, the scoreboard carnage continued until it was 42-0 and officials began running the clock without normal stoppage.

But the best part was the trip home. Because so many players had families in Atlanta and wanted to stay over, Mitchell told the team they could find alternate rides home. Moses opted to head back to town, but with the Longs.

Tamika introduced Moses as a classmate and a wiz at Calculus before the game. After seeing him play, Dr. Long quickly became enamored with his football ability.

"Son, you remind me of myself back at Hampton," Dr. Long said after the game. "If Coach Mitchell will let you, why don't you ride back home with us? I'm sure Tamika won't mind."

She didn't, holding his hand for the next two-and-half-hours. She sat on one side of the darkened backseat, with Moses in the middle. While Tamika caressed his hand, Tamika's grandmother slept, her head resting on Moses' shoulder.

So what if it cramped his style?

CHAPTER 12

PEGGY LET HIM sleep in late Saturday morning. By the time Braxton stirred, he had just enough time for a shower and a quick glance at the Saturday *Montgomery Advertiser.* The front page of the sports section was devoted to Sidney Lanier, the city school, and stories about the upcoming seasons for Alabama and Auburn. On page four he found a few paragraphs on Natsuma's big victory.

"NEWCOMER FREEMAN LEADS NATSUMA UPSET." There was no byline, just sentences recapping the game, the scoring and Braxton's stats. Without an accompanying photo, the blurb was buried near the bottom of the page.

He scanned some more and found an even smaller section committed to the black schools. Moses Burks and Institute High didn't even merit a headline, but Burks alone got two paragraphs.

> In his first game back, the superb Negro athlete caught two touchdown passes and returned a kickoff 83 yards for a third as The Institute routed DuBois Academy of Atlanta.

> Burks was Institute High's starting quarterback the past two seasons but lost his first-string position when he transferred to the white public school. He returned to the Institute this week after Takasaw High suspended operations.

A car horn honked. Braxton didn't stir.

"Braxton, someone's outside honking," Peggy Freeman said. "Will you go see what that's about?"

Braxton stood up, tucked his shirt inside his jeans. "It's for me, Mom."

He ran back to his room, grabbed his wallet off the bureau and bolted for the door.

"Brax, where are you going?" Peggy asked.

"To Auburn, Mom. With Gary Brokur. I'm going to watch his intramural game. Be back tonight."

He opened the door and vanished.

* * * *

He planned on watching the intramural game, but learned the Pikes planned on him playing for them. Gary Brokur handed him a garnet PiKA jersey, telling him, "You're name is Sam and you're a pledge. Pledges don't talk."

Brokur even provided something else – a date for the day. Vicki Cowart was a student at Georgia Tech visiting her best friend, who happened to be Brokur's girlfriend, Kelly. Braxton had never met either of the girls before and throughout the game wished he'd never met Vicki. The blonde was loud and cursed like a sailor every time the Sig Eps scored. That didn't happen often. The Pikes rolled to an easy flag football victory. The offense was simple. The Pike quarterback took turns throwing bombs to different receivers. Brokur settled under four for touchdowns.

"Sam the pledge" scored three.

Braxton took his football seriously, but this intramural game was less an athletic event disguised as a party. Kegs lined the side and came out for swigs of beer. Even after losing in lopsided fashion, the Sig Eps didn't seem to care as long as the beer was cold.

Brokur gulped his beer out of a plastic cup. The girls drank more slowly, but not slow enough. Vicki hugged Braxton every time he came off the field and offered him one beer after another, which he sipped to be polite. It smelled and tasted like piss.

If this was college life, Braxton wanted no part. There had to be a way to get out of the fraternity party that night and get home, even without transportation.

* * * *

Andy was in the middle of a deep sleep on the couch when he heard the knock on the front door. He was tired from the week's work, tired from having nothing to do. Since the school integrated, there was little Klan business, nor had Lockett bothered him. This wasn't sleep from exhaustion, however. It came from boredom.

The knock grew louder and Andy grudgingly stirred. He wouldn't have answered the door at all, except he knew it was Keith Lockett. And he'd learned he didn't want to piss him off again.

But it wasn't Lockett. As the door opened, Donna stood there in a plain brown dress. This wasn't the Donna as he remembered from his brief and unexpected encounters or the girl he remembered, from a distance, from school. She stood at the door silent, her hair disheveled, her face a mess and her left eye swollen. The beginnings of a bruise were evident. Both eyes were red from crying.

Andy looked at her and, not knowing what she wanted, didn't say a thing. Neither did she. Finally, he nudged his head in the direction of the couch, and she went inside quietly.

* * * *

The band at the Pike house was good, mixing Hank Williams with Elvis and Buddy Holly tunes. The frat boys and their dates danced in front of the bandstand. The booze continued to flow, this time with iced-down kegs on the patio of the huge fraternity house accompanied by bourbon poured by a black man behind a bar in the den.

Braxton had tolerated the beer during the day. Bourbon and Coke was a different matter. It had a better taste, and a bite. Harold had offered him a swig during a family barbecue once, but no more – and found the taste more than tolerable. So he drank to fit in.

Vicki Cowart drank to breathe. She'd switched from beer to whiskey and it seemed to have little impact. She'd been tipsy at the start of the day and stayed the same. She was lighthearted – and loud – and seemed to be having the time of her life. She'd even managed to drag Braxton onto the dance floor, so he'd awkwardly done his best to imitate the other frat boys. It wasn't that hard. He held one hand or two, and it didn't matter. She twisted around him and dipped now and then. Hell, it wasn't that hard. And as the drinks continued, shagging got downright easy.

Brokur's date was acting differently. Once the band began playing, she had been holding on to Brokur as if the world only existed for them. No matter the tempo, they danced slowly.

"C'mon Brax!" Brokur tapped him on the back as Freeman tried to fill another cup with the foamy keg brew. "Kelly wants to get out of here. And we can't go up there."

Brokur pointed to a window off the fraternity house. Shades were pulled down and a white sock hung from the half-opened window, attached to a hook.

"That's the sign, Freeman. Room's occupied, so we gotta find someplace else."

"Let's go." The response came from Vicki, not Brax, who grabbed her date by the hand and pulled him along as Brokur collected Kelly and headed out to the parking lot.

Brokur opened the front door for Kelly, allowing her in, and Braxton copied the move in the back.

"Crap," Brokur said. "Hold up."

Brokur disappeared into the dancing crowd and returned minutes later with two full glass milk bottles, filled to the top with beer. Handing them to Braxton he said, "These should last us awhile. Just don't spill any."

Braxton didn't know his way around Auburn, which wasn't much anyway except a college campus surrounded for a few blocks by homes and a small downtown. But he had no time to worry about the destination or Brokur's weaving driving. He was trying to keep the milk bottles from spilling, one in each hand, as Vicki snuggled against him and sang what sounded familiarly like the Georgia Tech fight song.

Brokur turned on a dirt road, drove up over a hill and pulled off into high grass next to an elm that branched out and obscured the moonlight. Brokur leaped out of the car, popped the trunk open and pulled out a blanket.

"You guys are on your own," Brokur said. Clutching the blanket in one hand, he wrapped his other arm around Kelly and grabbed one of the milk bottles. "Enjoy yourselves."

They disappeared behind the elm as they walked toward an unknown destination. Braxton stood with the other bottle and soon lost possession of it as Vicki snatched it away and took a long gulp. It was almost too dark to see anything. And it was quiet, save for the fading giggling of Kelly.

Vicki wiped foam off her upper lip, and smiled. "Is this your first frat party?"

Braxton nodded. It had to be pretty obvious.

"I love to come to Auburn. They know how to have a good time here. The guys are so stuffy at Georgia Tech."

Braxton felt like he did on the date with Katie Sullivan, not knowing what to say or do. Except then it had been mere nervousness. Now he was numb. And he thought he was beginning to sway, as if he stood on the bow of a small boat in a rough sea.

"Have you ever kissed a college girl, Braxton?" Vicki asked.

"Uh, yeah … sure."

Vicki smiled. Then she put the bottle on the roof of the car and moved closer. Putting her arms around Braxton she began kissing him. There was no pretense. Her tongue invaded immediately. Braxton kissed back. One hand clutched her neck, the other her back. And after a few minutes, he felt her hand pull his and place it on her right breast.

She was fleshy, chunkier than Katie Sullivan. But Katie Sullivan was a kid. This was a woman. And as his hands found out quickly, all woman. Her breasts were soft and supple as he squeezed them.

She broke the kiss. "Not so hard, baby. Soft, like this." She slipped her hand back over his and showed him how. Then she took his hand and moved it inside her blouse. Then, inside her bra.

He could feel her entire body against his, her warmth. The swaying was getting worse but she seemed to be holding him up. He leaned back against the side of the car to help with his balance. She stopped kissing him to unbutton her blouse, which she pulled off. She reached behind and undid her bra. And he stared.

She took over, unzipping his jeans. Suddenly, he wasn't so numb and her grasp sent an electric shock throughout his body.

"Do you have anything Braxton?"

He didn't understand. *Anything? Money? A ride home?*

"A rubber, baby, a rubber."

His usual response: He shook his head no.

"Then just keep your mouth shut, you hear? I don't want people talking about me."

She placed his hand back on her breast and started kissing him. Then she resumed her rhythmic movment. The next few moments were like nothing he'd ever experienced before. Heaven on earth, courtesy

211

of a blonde college girl. But the ecstasy was quickly overwhelmed by something else.

He began swaying dizzily, and the moves were accompanied with a gurgling in his stomach and a wave of sickness.

"Give me some warning, baby," she said, pausing for a moment, not knowing he was about to lose his lunch, which he did, lurching violently to the ground as he began vomiting.

* * * *

Andy held her throughout the night. Not the way you hold a lover, but the way you hold a child. She'd cried most of the night and for the first time he hadn't been encouraged to try a thing. They sat silently in the living room for what seemed hours until she left him for the adjoining kitchen, where, without asking him if he was hungry, she concocted a meal on the old gas stove from canned peas and corn. While they ate, she told him.

She was pregnant, with his child – after all, he was the only one she'd actually had sex with, she said – and her swelling belly had begun giving her away. Her mother was a devout Christian and knew the signs. And her father was a mean drunk and beat the hell out of her before kicking her out of the house. She had nowhere to go.

So she'd come here. She hadn't said whether she planned to stay or how long, but it didn't matter to him. Andy felt like he'd never had a family, not a real one. And after the initial shock, he liked the idea of having someone to care for.

He had a good job. Even if he hated it, it paid well. And when the old bastard, Leonard, finally returned, Andy would find some place else to live.

With Donna, whether the child was his or not. He would be a father, a *good* father, the kind he'd never had.

CHAPTER 13

ANDY WOKE THE way he'd never awakened before, to the smell of breakfast – a far cry from the stale cigarette smoke and bourbon mix Leonard usually left in his wake after a rough night. Donna somehow found bread and fresh eggs and made him French toast, serving him in bed. There was no syrup to drape the French toast, but he didn't care. The treat was a delicacy.

She looked different. The bruise on one eye had turned black and the eye was nearly shut. But the other eye was clear and as green as Lake Martin. She had no makeup, yet her face was fresher, younger looking than the day before. Her long hair was pulled back into a ponytail that gave her an innocent look.

He finished the last bite, and she took the plate away. Then she took off the clothes she'd worn to bed the night before, pulled the covers back and climbed in beside him.

* * * *

Braxton slept late again, so late that Peggy and Harold didn't bother him when they left for church without him. He vaguely remembered Peggy trying to shake him and, without success, exiting. Had his parents argued in the hallway, or had he dreamed an altercation?

He could not be sure how he got home the night before, how he wound up in his bed, in his underwear, with the messy clothes from the previous night nowhere to be found.

He couldn't remember missing a church service except the week Candace died. Peggy didn't go anywhere that week or the next, except to the funeral. Both Braxton and Harold knew better than to push her.

Now he wondered: Was he in trouble? How could he not be? No matter who cleaned him up or how well they'd done the job, Peggy had to smell the aftermath of beer, bourbon and vomit. Good God, he could still smell it, and that smell …

He cleaned up the aftermath on the rim of the toilet bowl with a hand towel, and then washed it out before depositing it in the hamper. Then he went to his parents' bathroom and searched the medicine cabinet. He needed aspirin, and he needed it now. His head pounded as if a marching band surrounded him. He cupped water from the faucet in his hand, choked down two tablets, and reached for the large bottle of Listerine Harold always kept on the sink. He gargled twice, replacing the sour bitterness with antiseptic fresh. It still didn't get all of the bad taste.

They'd left the Sunday paper on the kitchen table and, of course, Harold left the sports section on top. Braxton settled on the couch and absentmindedly thumbed through it without paying attention. More about Alabama's and Auburn's upcoming season openers, plus news on the NFL. He considered turning on the television for a distraction, but realized that would be a waste of time. None of the Montgomery television stations aired anything on Sundays until afternoon Westerns.

He realized he needed to shower and clean up before his parents returned and was headed for his bathroom when he heard a bellowing from outside.

"Miss Peggy! Braxton!" Heavy footsteps climbing the porch followed before the doorbell rang. "Mister Harold!"

He swung the door open in his underwear because he knew it was Josiah. Josiah was bawling.

"B-Bear," Josiah said in heaves. "Moses says someone's got to come to our house now!" He grabbed Braxton and began pulling him out the door. Braxton pulled back.

"Let me put some clothes on Josiah! Hold on."

"Hurry, Braxton, hurry!"

The radio blared in Adele's house when Braxton entered. She sat in a rocking chair, moving slowly back and forth. Moses sat in another chair, his head buried in his hands. The remains of breakfast remained on a cluttered table.

Josiah sat down on the floor. No one said a word. Gospel music filled the house from the old set.

"Terrible," Adele whispered with her now half-crooked mouth. "Just terrible."

It was the most he had heard her say in a while. But *what* was terrible?

The music ended abruptly and a baritone voice replaced it.

"There have now been four confirmed deaths from the explosion at the 16th Street Baptist Church in Birmingham. Once again, the blast occurred before the start of church services at the downtown sanctuary. At this point, local police have converged on the scene but are offering few answers."

The voice seemed to repeat itself, then closed with, "Let's all say a prayer for these people."

Then the music resumed, fittingly somber.

"That could have been us!" Moses yelled, standing now. "Any one of us!"

Braxton stood there, not grasping what Moses was upset about. An explosion at a Birmingham church, what did it have to do with us?

Moses stared at Braxton and understood he didn't know what to say.

"You don't get it Brax, do you? Do you? That's a Negro church. Some white man's blown up a Negro church!"

He'd never seen Moses this angry. And why was Moses jumping to conclusions? How'd he know it was a Negro church? Or that some white man had blown it up? Then it struck Brax, Moses should have known. The 16th Street Baptist Church had been a regular part of the news over the summer – the place where Martin Luther King Jr. addressed freedom riders, the location where civil rights protesters met before confronting Bull Connor's police dogs and fire hoses.

"Damnit, Brax! You just live in your own little world don't you?" Moses was standing in front of Braxton now. The heat of his anger seemed to burn. But why?

"Damn you, Brax! Damn you!" Moses raised his arms, then dropped them suddenly. He bolted for the door and began running down the street.

Adele just continued rocking. Josiah was now crying again, rocking as he sat on the floor. Braxton had never felt more uncomfortable – and certainly last night had been uncomfortable – but not to this degree. Last night, he didn't know what he was doing. Now he didn't know what to do.

Adele provided the answer. She raised her hand and he knelt beside her.

"Not your fault," she whispered. "Moses … is mad. Just … mad."

* * * *

She was asleep now, her head nestled against his shoulder and her legs intertwined with his. The bed sheet, splayed toward the foot of the bed, left her uncovered. With his head propped against the wall, Andy quietly surveyed it all – Donna's pale white buttocks, the soft shoulders and the seemingly flat stomach that she said had already begun to swell.

He couldn't see it. But he'd never seen anyone pregnant like this before.

She had told him he was the father and he hadn't asked any questions. Was it really his? Keith's? Someone else's? She hadn't volunteered, nor had she made accusations. She explained it matter of fact, then said it was the reason her father had thrown her out. He'd done so the night before after Mama had broken her promise not to say anything, at least for awhile.

Mama never kept her promises, though. And Daddy never could control his temper. No child of his was going to have a bastard child. She was no longer his, a point he emphasized with a blow to the face before grabbing her by the hair and pulling her out the door before she could recover from the initial assault.

"You go find the son of a bitch that did this and make HIM take care of you and the bastard!" he'd yelled before shutting the door. "Don't come back here!"

That she had come to Andy's house – how did she even know where he lived? Was he truly the father? Or was he merely refuge?

He didn't have the nerve to ask. And at this point, he didn't care. When was the last time he'd been needed for anything?

So she'd told him her story. And he'd told her, "You'll stay here, Donna."

His Sundays were usually lazy, wasted days, at least since he'd quit running 'Shine, but this one was blissful. He had the girl he hadn't had the nerve to approach in high school in his bed, naked.

There was nothing to do but sleep. And to interrupt the sleep as he'd done twice already, until time to go to work in the morning.

The honk of a truck horn distracted him. Leaping up, he scanned the floor for the jeans he'd worn before heading to sleep the night before and hurriedly slid the old, torn and faded denim on. The horn honked again, and he fell once trying to get the second leg into the pants. He didn't want Donna to stir.

He figured it might be the old bastard again, finally back home and too drunk to come into the door without help. It had been weeks since he'd even given him consideration. He certainly hadn't thought about him the last few hours. He'd promised Donna she could stay, but he hadn't seriously considered what might happen if the old man returned.

But it wasn't the old man. It was Keith. The window was rolled down and he had two Klansmen with him.

Andy stood outside the door and Keith cut him a glare that forced him to run toward the pickup.

"Hey, boy! You just sleepin' the Lord's Sabbath away?" Lockett asked. "Didn't see you at church today."

How often had he seen Andy? Joining the Klan was one thing, but if it meant going to church regularly …

"You hear about the nigger church in Birmingham?" Lockett asked as Andy sidled to the driver's side. It drew a shake of the head. "Somebody blew up the damn thing this morning. No telling how many niggers he killed."

"No matter how many, it wasn't enough," chimed in one of the Klansmen sitting next to Lockett.

"Yeah," Andy said.

"I want you dressed and ready to go at 8 tonight, and I'll pick you up here? Got it, boy?"

Dressed and ready meant in the white robe with hood on.

"Yeah," Andy said. "I got it."

"See you at eight," Lockett replied, pulling away without looking back.

* * * *

Braxton's stomach was upset again, but this time it was different. His insides were on a roller coaster ride and he was wondering how long he could hold it. Peggy and Harold sat on one side of him and the Longworths took up the rest of the pew. Rev. Mullens usually kept his

Sunday night sermons brief. Braxton needed him to do so one more time.

This could be attributed to nerves. He hadn't felt nauseous since the blow-up at Adele's house sobered him up. But now he felt his insides churning, maybe because Moses lashed out at him and, worse, Peggy and Harold hadn't said a thing.

Was Harold mad? He seemed to have things on his mind that had nothing to do with Braxton's problems the night before. Peggy, however, was. She hadn't talked to him since he'd returned from Adele's house and they'd returned from Sunday morning services. Nor had she talked on the way back to church that night.

He knew she was disappointed, although he didn't know how much of what had happened she'd put together. He'd never given her much to be disappointed about, so this hurt. He'd had fun the night before, hadn't he? But was it worth the price?

If only he could apologize. Except you don't apologize until you know exactly what you're apologizing for, right? He wanted to know exactly what she'd deduced before he served it up. So, she would have to bring it up first. There were few confrontations at the Freeman house and he had never been the instigator.

Moses was different. They'd fought all their lives over trivial things and forgotten what they'd fought about within moments. Never before had Moses gone crazy like that.

He wouldn't again, if Braxton had anything to do with it. He was staying away for good.

"The Bible sometimes provides us contradictory messages," said Rev. Mullens from the pulpit. "God tells us, 'An eye for an eye.' Then his son tells us to 'Turn the other cheek.' Different measures for different circumstances.

"You all know what happened in Birmingham today. They're saying now that the 16th Street Baptist Church was bombed, on purpose, by whites angry about the Negro marches there. You all know how I feel about civil rights – it hasn't made me very popular among some of you, and you've let me know that. But when anger spills over into bloodshed, it's unforgiveable.

"They're saying that four little Negro girls were killed there today. Four of God's innocent children. That's not an eye for an eye. That's murder. That's terrorism. I would pray that no matter how you feel about the race issue deep down, you will recognize this important difference.

And I hope you will pray with me now that justice is done and the perpetrators are found and punished quickly and fairly, and that this doesn't lead to more and more violence.

"Please bow your heads ..."

The entire church bowed. Even Alistar Lennox, the old Notasulga farmer who told nigger jokes in the fellowship hall every Sunday morning before going to Sunday school. Yet every Sunday afternoon, he returned to his farm and joined the colored sharecroppers who worked parts of his land for lunch. The people he mocked shared Sunday lunches, the food coming from his farm and their gardens, with his own family. That was the conundrum of Takasaw.

The line toward the front door of the sanctuary moved more quickly than normal. People were in a hurry to leave – or either they had nothing to say to Rev. Mullens as he shook hands and made small talk with the receiving line.

Braxton fell in line with Peggy and Harold.

"Touching sermon, John Ed," Harold said. "You may have reached some people you haven't been able to before."

The minister smiled, then released Harold's hand and grabbed Braxton's.

"There are times I wonder why God put me here," the minister said. He didn't shake Brax's hand. He merely held it in a vise grip. "There aren't many people here who don't know real right from wrong."

Braxton flinched. Did even *he* know what Braxton had done the night before?

"But knowing and acting on it are separate entities. If we sit quietly while an injustice is done are we any better than those who've done the injustice?"

"You're absolutely right, John Ed," Peggy said softly, the first words Braxton had heard from her all night. "Absolutely right."

Harold made small talk with a couple other members of the congregation before heading to the car. Peggy and Braxton quietly followed.

Back home, Peggy headed to the kitchen, pulled out a loaf of bread and some leftovers from the fridge.

"I'm going to bed, honey," she said to Harold. "You two can fix sandwiches for dinner."

"Yes, dear," Harold replied. He didn't seem to question the break from the norm.

"Braxton," Peggy said, stopping as she entered the hallway. Without turning around, she continued. "If you have homework, finish it. Otherwise, it's time for bed."

She didn't even look at him. It wasn't even eight o'clock. But he wasn't about to question her.

* * * *

Andy was dressed and ready, waiting on the porch, when Lockett pulled up. No one came down the dirt road unless they were coming to his house, so there was no reason to hide.

Even though it was dark, Lockett had to see him waiting. He still honked the horn loudly, twice. Andy trotted over and climbed into the passenger's side. Two other Klansmen were in the bed of the truck, dressed in their full regalia.

Lockett looked at the front window of the house and Andy's eyes followed. Donna was peering through the musty old drapes. You could only see her silhouette against the dark lamp in the room.

"Boy, you getting some poontang now?" Lockett asked with a grin. "Who is it, Laduke?"

"Ah, nobody."

Lockett turned. "Damn it, boy, I asked you a question. Who's the poontang?"

Andy mumbled the answer.

"Goddamn it, what are you so afraid of? Who the hell is it?"

He answered again. He didn't want Lockett to hear. He certainly didn't want the Klansmen in the back to hear.

"Jesus, Laduke. You getting Donna regularly now?"

Andy didn't say anything. Instead, he looked ahead.

"C'mon, let's go," he said softly to Lockett.

"Jesus, boy, Jesus. I've turned you into a sex machine," Lockett said, a sense of giddiness returning to his voice. "Just don't mess her up. That's one good piece of 'tang."

Andy said nothing.

In the same clearing where Andy had been initiated into the Klan three other pickups and an old sedan were parked and waiting when Lockett pulled up. Klansmen piled out and circled Lockett's truck.

"John Keith, you got the torches?" Lockett asked as he got out. The Klansman nodded. "Who brought the kerosene?" A hand was raised.

"Good, good," Lockett said. "Get back in your trucks and follow me. No lights."

Lockett led the caravan on dirt roads, occasionally flicking his lights long enough to find a turn. The moon was three-quarters full and the skies were clear, so there was enough light for the others to follow.

He pulled up about a quarter mile from an old church that even in the dimness obviously needed a paint job.

"These dumb niggers don't even treat God's temple right, do they?" Lockett asked as the group spilled out again. He pulled long matches from his truck, waited while one of the Klansman began pouring a liquid over the torches, then struck the match. The first torch flamed high.

When all were lit – thirteen, one passed to each man – Lockett put his hood on. The others followed suit.

"Wish we had dynamite like those good ol' boys in Birmingham," Lockett said. "We'll have to make do. Let's burn this nigger church. I want the man on the moon to be able to see it sizzle."

The group spread out in a horizontal line. Andy was the last one. He didn't know how they intended to do this, though he had a good notion. The others knew, of course. They'd done this before.

Andy stuck with Lockett as he began applying his torch to a wooden pillar that held up the front entrance. Andy copied him with the other pillar. The dry, chipped wood caught fire instantly. Within minutes, the entire church was ablaze.

"Ain't she beautiful, boys?" Lockett roared after the group retreated to the caravan of trucks. "Beautiful work, fellas, beautiful. Someday, when the rest of McMahon County comes to its senses and joins us, we'll do this right. We'll do this while the niggers are holding services!"

Twelve Klansmen cheered. Andy Laduke stood silently and watched as embers floated into the sky and the church began to disappear amid a mix of leaping flames and thick, black smoke.

* * * *

Moses couldn't shake the news of the bombing, even as he returned to the graveyard that night. Yet he had other things on his mind, including Tamika.

He liked her, although he was starting to feel uneasy. She was naïve and she'd never dated before. Plus, there was the specter of her father.

Moses respected Dr. Long and didn't want to get crossways with a man who held so much respect in the community. He had to be patient, something he'd never been before.

Rufus put into perspective. "Don't think with the wrong head, boy. Some girls are for fun, some are for the future. She's the future. Don't mess that up."

She sneaked out for a few minutes to bring him a sandwich at midnight, impressing Moses by traipsing through the woodsy shortcut alone.

He told Rufus to finish the work so he could walk her back. They talked about the bombing, and the frustration everyone felt.

"Do you think something like that could happen here?" she asked.

The question set off a bolt of anger. "Of course it could. It has ..." he offered before thinking it through.

"They've bombed people here?"

"Uh, well, no ... That's not what I mean."

He led her to the house without another word. When he got home, he reached under his bed and pulled out the scrapbook no one knew about, and carried it with him out on the back porch, using a candle for illumination.

All the information he'd collected over the years was there about Maurice Littlejohn. A student at Morehouse College in Atlanta, he'd gone missing in October, 1958 en route to see his family in Jackson, Miss., and discovered a week later, dead in a field outside Takasaw, the victim of multiple stab wounds.

He was savagely murdered, yet there was no motive, no suspects, and no arrests.

Moses had spent hours at the library copying articles from *The Atlanta Journal, The Montgomery Advertiser* and *The Jackson Clarion-Ledger.* The latter two used Associated Press reports, parroting the few paragraphs the Atlanta paper offered for a week before losing interest in the story.

Another dead black youth wasn't compelling enough news, apparently. Nor was it compelling enough for Moses to go forward and tell what he knew to authorities.

For five years, he'd put that lapse of courage to the side. Now he couldn't forget what he'd failed to do. Would anyone stand up for him one day?

CHAPTER 14

ANDY HAD WORKED the day in numb fashion, no different from any other day, really, except for once he was anxious to get home. He kept an eye on the clock, watching it drag toward quitting time, thinking this was the first time he had something to do or somewhere to go.

Quitting time finally did come and Laduke filed in line to punch out. He was returning the card to the slot when he felt a hand on his shoulder. Whirling, he saw Bobby Joe McKenzie.

"Hey Andy," McKenzie said warmly. "How are ya?"

"Fine, Mr. McKenzie, fine," Andy said.

"What's with the Mister stuff?" McKenzie said laughing. "I'm still plain, old Bobby Joe."

"Yes sir."

"C'mon outside with me, Andy. We need to go over some projection numbers for next month."

Andy followed McKenzie outside. McKenzie leaned against a wall, away from both the stragglers leaving and the next shift entering the plant. He went over a couple of charts, explaining the mill's projection goals for the month of October. But why? Laduke was a supervisor. McKenzie was the manager. It was his responsibility.

McKenzie put the pages back into his briefcase. "Hell, Andy, guess it doesn't mean much to you right now, does it?"

"No sir."

"Well, it will one day, if you keep up the good work."

Good work? Laduke did his job. Nothing more, nothing else. And he did it because Keith Lockett had told him to do so. He wasn't thinking career. He was thinking of keeping Lockett off his ass.

McKenzie looked around. Secure that the majority of workers had left he turned his attention back to Andy.

"Word is you had a good night last night," McKenzie said.

"Yeah, I guess so," Andy replied. Actually, he had figured McKenzie had there been, too. Sure, it had been dark and only Lockett had driven with his hood off. But McKenzie was always there when Lockett wanted something done.

"Sounds like you did a good job. Saw the church this morning on my way to work. Nothing left but ashes."

Andy shook his head.

"My wife has been sick," McKenzie said, volunteering an excuse for not being there. "Still, Lockett never said anything to me. Is something up?"

What the hell would be up?

"Not that I know of," Andy replied.

"Yeah, guess you're right. You know Keith. He likes to spread the jobs around."

They stood silently for a few moments.

"What'd you think about it?" McKenzie asked.

"About what?"

"The church? The fire?"

"Oh. It was fine, I guess. We did a good job."

"Yeah, I saw. We gotta put niggers in their place, right Andy?"

"Yeah," Andy said, struggling to find more words. "Especially … especially after what our guys did in Birmingham."

"Yeah, right," McKenzie said. "Now that took some balls."

McKenzie didn't say anything else. Eventually, he left, heading back into the mill. Relieved, Andy got into his truck and headed home.

He was looking forward to seeing Donna, yet he was apprehensive. Would she even be there? She'd made him breakfast that morning, but they'd eaten without saying much. What if she'd gone back home?

He wanted her to be there. But he didn't want anyone else. That's why, when he saw Lockett's truck parked outside, he scurried out of his truck and bounded toward the front steps.

"No Keith, no," he heard Donna cry out. The door was cracked.

He swung it open. Donna was sprawled on the couch, her blouse ripped. Lockett stood above her, his face red in anger.

"Don't fight me now!" Lockett screamed. "You ain't nothing without me."

"No, Keith ..."

She didn't finish. Her eyes widened as Andy crashed into Lockett from the side, sending him sprawling against the wall, where he slumped, but only momentarily.

"What's got into you, boy?" he screamed as he rose to his feet. "What the hell?"

Andy stood in front of Donna, balling his fist and readying for Lockett's assault.

Lockett's intense visage gave way to lightness. "Well I'll be God damned," he said, grinning. "You standing up for your girl, Laduke?"

Andy said nothing. He flexed his hand, regripping the fist, squeezing it into a ball.

"Well, now I've seen everything."

Lockett stood haughtily, arms akimbo. After a moment, he walked toward Andy, stopping within inches, face-to-face. Andy waited for a fist, a shove, violence.

"Boy, you'd better relax," Lockett said. "Relax."

Andy took a step back. Then he looked at Donna and gave her an order. "Go to the bedroom."

Donna looked at Andy, then back at Lockett before leaving without a word. Meanwhile, Andy's mind was flying – at least as fast as his could. Where had Leonard left the shotgun? If he could remember where it was, could he get to it?

"I said relax, boy, relax," Lockett said.

Andy ungripped his fist but remained poised to strike again.

"If you want your ass kicked, just say the word," Lockett said. No response. "You just better learn quickly which fight to pick."

Andy, teeth clenched, ready to pounce, glared.

Lockett's right hand shot out and he rocked Andy with a shove. Andy recoiled a couple of steps, but didn't lose his balance. His fist balled again.

Finally, Andy came up with the words. "I think you'd better leave." He said it in a low tone, but firmly.

"Jesus Christ," Lockett said, shaking his head. "Now I've seen everything."

The Klan leader got to the front door and stopped.

"She's Klan property, boy. Klan property. If I want a little fun – if anyone else wants her to spread, she does. You understand? DO YOU UNDERSTAND ME?"

"Leave," Andy replied.

Lockett's nose flared and the bitterness returned. He took a step forward, and Andy did likewise.

"You'd better not get stupid over a piece of ass, boy, 'specially that sloppy piece."

Andy took another step. Lockett wasn't threatened. He again approached Andy, getting close enough to spit in his face if he chose.

Lockett lowered his voice, but the venom remained.

"Boy, if you ever threaten me again ..." he paused before finally turning away. He headed out the door, then stopped one last time. "You mess with me again, Laduke, and you'll disappear for good. So will the slut."

Andy looked back toward the bedroom. The door was closed. He returned his stare toward the Grand Dragon.

"You hear me, boy?" Lockett said. "Your old man messed with me, and no one's seen him since, have they, boy? Don't you make that mistake!"

Lockett left. Andy collapsed to the floor, covered his eyes with his hands and began shaking.

* * * *

Collins wasn't organized, not the way Halliday was. On the first day of practice after a game, Halliday always had an updated depth chart posted on the locker room wall, reflecting any changes. He'd also meet with the team for 20 minutes, referring to a page or two on a legal pad as he recited the team's failures from the Friday night before.

That was Takasaw High. At Natsuma, the players filtered out on the practice field and stood idly until Collins and his two assistants joined them.

"First-team offense!" Collins yelled after signaling the group with a shriek of his whistle.

He placed the ball on the 30-yard line as players began separating – the first-teamers on his side, the scrubs on the other to play defense.

Braxton joined the offensive huddle only to realize the other players were staring at him. Why? Collins was screaming his name.

"Freeman! Freeman! What are you doing?" Collins yelled. Braxton looked over and gave him a quizzical look. "Get out of the first-team huddle and join the rest of the scout team!"

Shrugging his shoulders, Braxton obeyed. He spent the rest of the day working with the scrubs. And when Collins changed pace, and worked on the first-team defense, he again sent Freeman to the scrubs.

"What the hell is up with that?" Gothard asked in the locker room. Gothard had stripped off his jersey and shoulder pads and was about to head to the shower. Braxton was already slipping on his khakis with no intention of taking a shower. He just wanted to get out in a hurry.

"Hell if I know," Braxton replied.

He piled his football pants in the bottom of the locker, grabbed his T-shirt and slipped it over his shoulders. Then he grabbed his shirt in one hand and his shoes, socks stuffed inside, in the other and hurried out.

To his relief, Harold was already there, waiting, in the sedan. Braxton slipped in and the two listened silently to the radio half the way home, until Harold ended the stillness.

"Well, Son, how did school go today? Bet you were the talk of everyone."

"It was okay," Braxton said. He stared off, toward the road ahead, and Harold picked up on the glumness.

"What's wrong?"

"I don't know, it's …," Braxton had trouble getting the words out. Then he began tearing. Embarrassed that he was getting emotional, he tried to clear his throat of the building frustration and tried to wipe the moisture from his eyes with a backhand. The reaction surprised him. He was 17, for Christ sakes.

"C'mon, son, what's wrong."

"We started practice … " Braxton said, spitting the words out in scattered cadences. "We started practice, and Coach calls for the first-team offense. And when we huddle, he tells me to get the hell out and join the rest of the scrubs."

"Whatever for?" Harold asked, showing a tint of uncharacteristic anger.

"I don't know," Braxton said. Then he began sobbing.

Seventeen years old and he was crying like a baby.

Harold pulled off the road and wrapped Braxton in a hug – the best consolation he could manage from behind the steering wheel.

"Hey, son," he said gently. "Don't let this bother you. Okay? I'll go talk to Coach Collins tomorrow before practice."

"No, Dad, don't do that."

Embarrassed, Braxton began wiping the moisture with both hands, rubbing his eyes in the hope the friction would dry them quicker. Sensing his son's discomfort, Harold concluded the hug with a quick rub on the back of the neck, pulled away and steered the car back on the road.

It took Braxton a few minutes to regain his composure. When he did, the words still came slowly.

"Dad, it's not just being benched. It's ... it's just the whole thing. I mean ... this is supposed to be my senior year. And I'm supposed to be playing at *my* school. Instead ... instead I'm at a small school on a crap team playing for a coach who doesn't know his head from his ass."

Harold chuckled. "Know what? Halliday described him the same way."

"Well, he doesn't," Braxton said. "He doesn't know what the hell he's doing."

Harold pulled into the driveway and turned the car off. Looking at Braxton, he asked, "You ready to go in?"

Brax nodded.

"Tell you what, son. Let's just keep this between you and me, okay? Don't mention it to your mother."

Braxton nodded again. He hadn't said much of anything to Peggy since returning from Auburn Saturday night. He knew exactly what Harold meant – Peggy was still angry and now wasn't the time to face her.

CHAPTER 15

DONNA HAD TOLD him, over and over, things were alright and there wouldn't be any more problems. Still, Andy Laduke was uncomfortable around her the rest of the day. The image of Lockett and the tone of the man's words remained vivid. Andy continued to seethe, despite her promises that everything would be better.

He was seething even when he got off work; so much that he drove around for two hours waiting for the downtown businesses to open. When the umpteenth check of his watch showed it was nine a.m. he headed back to the old town square and parked in front of the hardware store.

He opened the heavy door with a heave, and left it open as he marched in and scanned the floor. A graying man stood behind a counter, smoking a cigarette.

"Where's Keith?" Andy asked harshly.

The man thumbed toward the back and Andy headed in that direction.

"Can't go back there," the man said.

Andy ignored him.

"Keith? Keith?" he yelled as he entered the darkened storeroom. Like the front, the back had high ceilings. Stairs led up to a loft that held crates and unloaded supplies.

"Yeah!" a voice yelled back. From behind a crate, Lockett's head emerged. "Hey, boy," he said, the tone softening. "What you want?"

"I want to talk to you!"

"Sure, boy, sure," Lockett said soothingly. "But tone it down, this is a business."

Lockett came down the steps, looked Andy up and down, then walked past him.

"Come on to my office, Laduke."

There was no real office, just a corner of the storeroom, where an old desk stood was cornered in front of a yellow, plastic-covered chair.

Lockett sat down, inviting Andy to do the same. Andy wheeled and saw there wasn't another chair, only a couple of boxes piled up to waist level.

"I'll stand up."

"Fine, Laduke, fine."

Lockett turned his attention to some papers on the desk and rifled through them with little interest in Andy. He continued to do so for a few minutes.

Andy continued to stand without complaint. That seemed to irritate Lockett.

"God damn it, Laduke," Lockett finally said, sending the papers to the desk with a loud slap. "If it's about that skanky whore again ..."

"Her name is Donna. Damn right it is," Andy said. "You ain't got no right to call anybody names."

Ire fueled his reason for wanting the confrontation. Now, standing in front of Lockett, the anger remained but the confidence began to wane.

Lockett stared him down, waiting for Andy to relax. He didn't. Lockett stood up.

"Everybody's had her, boy. Everybody. You want her? Fine with me. I've had better."

Andy stepped forward and raised his hand. Lockett grabbed him by the wrist and forced the hand down.

"Damnit it, Laduke," Lockett said harshly. "You're pressing your luck."

Andy tried to move his hand, but it remained immobile in Lockett's grasp. The frustration grew, but he didn't know what to do. Searching for a way to react, or for something to say ...

Finally.

"I saw you kill that nigger."

Lockett let go of the wrist. His eyes widened, then bore back in.

"What the fuck are you talking about?"

"Five years ago, near the Hobson farm. I was in the woods with two others. I saw you and the other guy with the nigger. I saw you cut his throat and kill him. I saw it all."

Now it was Lockett's turn to search for a response. Andy shifted in his stance, and began flexing his fist for the inevitable punch. Instead, Lockett turned around, opened a drawer of his desk and pulled out a set of keys.

"C'mon."

Lockett led him out the back, into his truck parked in the alley. He never turned around. Andy followed, too scared to run. He was too scared to do anything but slide in the passenger seat.

He regretted what he'd said, regretted that he hadn't thought before the words erupted, and felt now something bad would happen to him.

Lockett drove quickly out of town and into the countryside. Images flashed by – some recognizable, most hazy in his discomfort. He was distracted and scared.

He hadn't even realized they'd stopped until Lockett bounded out of the truck then walked to a headstone in an old country cemetery. Andy climbed out of the truck slowly, but proceeded no further.

"Come here, boy," Lockett said.

Lockett kneeled down over the grave and began tracing his finger over the engraving on the stone.

William Tolliver
Feb. 1938–Nov. 1958
"A good son."

"Know who this is?" Lockett asked in a low voice.

Andy shook his head.

"Tell me what you saw."

Andy shook his head again.

"God damnit, tell me what you saw!"

When Andy hesitated, Lockett reached up, grabbed him by the collar and yanked him down to his knees.

"Now tell me!"

Andy looked around for help. No one was around. The road leading to the cemetery was an old dirt road he didn't recognize. He didn't want to talk about it, yet he knew he'd said too much already.

"I saw you kill a nigger. That's all. You killed him. Another boy was with you."

Lockett tightened his grip and pushed Andy closer to the headstone.

"Ever hear this boy's name before? Billy Tolliver?"

Andy shrugged.

"He was the boy with me. It was supposed to be his initiation, but things went bad."

Andy tried to straighten up, but Lockett's grip was too tight. He stumbled, and butted his head on the headstone. The pain was quick and intense.

Lockett yanked at him again, this time bringing Andy to a sitting position.

"Billy had a habit of talking too much about that night," Lockett said, staring at the headstone. "One thing you can't do is talk. He talked too much and something had to be done. So I took care of it."

Lockett's explanation was vague, but Andy immediately understood the implication. What would Lockett do to him?

Lockett stood up as Andy cowered below.

"You said you weren't alone. Who else was with you?"

Andy began rubbing his head. The pain wasn't going away, and a welt had already developed.

"Who was with you?!"

"Just … just a couple of little kids."

"What kids? Goddamnit, I want to know!"

"My cousin, Brax, Braxton Freeman. And a little nigger kid in his neighborhood."

"Goddamnit!" Lockett shouted. He lashed out with his foot – not at Andy, but at the headstone, which toppled over.

"Who else knows, Laduke? Who else?"

"I … I …," Andy started crying.

"WHO ELSE?"

"I don't know," Andy said, sobbing now.

Lockett began pacing in circles, trampling a fresh set of flowers on a nearby grave.

"This ain't good, Laduke. Ain't good at all."

Andy stopped sobbing and tried to regain his composure. Suddenly, he was gasping for air as Lockett kicked him in the side. Andy crumpled as he tried to suck in a breath.

Lockett moved away. He paused momentarily, then moved to his truck. Laduke, his eyes blurred and his lungs aching, couldn't see Lockett retrieve a gun from a shotgun rack and return. But he felt the muzzle as Lockett pushed it hard against his cheek.

"How did you know it was me that killed that nigger?"

The gun pinned Andy tightly to the ground. He closed his eyes.

"Your voice. And your tattoo, Keith. I knew who you were 'cause of the tattoo. I could see it in the light."

Andy felt the pressure relent. Lockett withdrew the gun a few inches.

"What about Freeman and the nigger kid. Do they know?"

When Andy hesitated, Lockett pushed the muzzle back against his face.

"Do they KNOW?"

"No," Andy said. "No. I mean ... we never ever talked about it."

Lockett was yanking again, this time pulling Laduke back up. He pushed him all the way back to the truck and inside the cab. Andy slid the rest of the way just as Lockett slammed the door. He leaned as close to the door as he could.

Lockett went around and climbed in behind the steering wheel, resting the shotgun in his lap pointed at Laduke.

"I don't like people fucking with me, boy. That old drunk of a father of yours fucked with me once, and no one's seen him since. He won't fuck with anyone ever again."

The engine revved. The truck leaped forward, then back again, as Lockett turned back down the road and started driving.

"I better not hear about this again," Lockett said. "You understand?"

He raised the gun, stuck it in Andy's face.

"I ain't figured out what to do about this," Lockett said, his eyes on Andy. "Until I do, you just keep your damn mouth shut."

* * * *

"First-team offense," Collins yelled, and the players moved quickly to their positions. Despite the embarrassment of the day before, Brax Freeman moved with the others and settled in at halfback.

Collins looked on incredulously.

"What are you doing, Freeman?"

"I'm going to my position." Brax responded.

"Your position's with the scrubs," Collins said, waiting for Brax to retreat. Except he didn't.

Exasperated, Collins ran over to Brax, and began pushing him to the other side of the ball. But Brax stiffened, swung his shoulders to elude the man and Collins slid off and fell to the ground. Collins leaped up and got in the boy's face. All Brax noticed was the vein in Collins' forehead throbbing as if it would leap off his skull.

Collins bumped Braxton, but the player couldn't be moved. Collins then pushed the boy, but Brax held his ground. Collins moved closer. Brax responded by stepping forward.

"Why?" The other players stood frozen as Brax asked the question.

"What the hell?" Collins responded.

"Why?" Brax asked again.

"Because you're not worth a shit!" Collins screamed venomously. "You're not worth a shit and you're not a team player!"

Braxton's expression remained the same. Collins took a step back, blew his whistle and yelled to the others: "First-team offense, let's go!"

"Why?" came the question. Except it wasn't Braxton.

Gothard stepped out of position, and stood next to Freeman.

"I asked you a question, Coach," Gothard said.

Collins blew the whistle again, signaling the team to start. No one moved.

"Why?" Gothard repeated defiantly.

Collins slammed down his clipboard and approached Gothard.

"I told you why! Now, let's go!"

"You're full of shit!" Gothard said. Brax lowered his head for an instant to suppress a grin. "He's the best player out here and you know that!"

Collins looked at Gothard then pivoted to Brax. "I want you off the field now, Freeman! You're off the team!"

Brax stood still. "Why?" he asked.

"Why? Why!?" Collins yelled. The vein looked as if would erupt. "I'll tell you why! You're a nigger lover, boy. A NIGGER lover! And I don't want no part of that on my team!"

Collins caught Brax off guard. He knew Collins didn't like him, but he'd had no idea why until now. What made him a nigger lover? Moses Burks?

"He's not a nigger, sir," Brax said. "But you are a dumbass." He turned around and walked off the field.

The players watched him leave. Collins stood stewing, the vein thumping, thumping, thumping.

Brax was 20 yards away when he saw a helmet fly over his head. Brax turned to see if someone was throwing at him. No one was. Instead, he saw Gothard yanking off a shoe that quickly followed the helmet in flight.

"He's a nigger lover?" Gothard yelled at Collins before tugging the other shoe off and sending it airborne. "Brax is right! You're a dumb ass, Coach! A royal dumb ass!"

Brax raced back to the field house, trying to keep pace with Gothard. He'd never seen the big moose run faster.

CHAPTER 16

THE WEEK PASSED awkwardly and agonizingly slow for Braxton. Classes were hazy and the looks from classmates – at least his perception of the looks – left him uncomfortable. He'd never quit anything in his life.

Except for Gothard, few of the other football players even bothered talking to him. Save for Simpkins, the linemen who took Gothard's place in the lineup, who simply said one morning, "How you holding up, Freeman?"

He'd told Harold the entire story and been consoled. But Harold had cautioned him not to mention it to Peggy, who seemed to have a lot on her mind.

They'd planned to go out Friday night, like they would any other Friday before a football game, and find a way to kill time after convincing Peggy to stay and look after Adele.

"We'll tell your mom soon enough," Harold said. "Let me figure out when."

She surprised them both Thursday night at dinner. Typically, it was a late dinner to account for practice. Brax had spent the afternoon doing homework at Harold's office until they decided it was late enough to head home.

"Hon, Katie Sullivan's coming to town tomorrow just to go see your game," Peggy said. She looked radiant, the way she hadn't in recent weeks.

Brax looked to Harold for an answer. Harold merely winked at him in reply.

"Great, Peg, great," Harold said.

Harold handled all the arrangements. Peggy spent Friday night with Adele, who was speaking more clearly, though she remained bed bound.

Harold and Brax left earlier than they'd normally leave for a home game and went over to the Sullivan's. Katie was waiting for him on the front porch. She looked even older, wearing a pink sweater that accentuated her still golden tan. Her hair was pulled back in a more mature fashion.

She looked gorgeous. But she didn't look happy.

She gave Brax a nod as they arrived, and then followed him as Mr. Sullivan led them into the living room.

"We're sorry to hear about everything you've been through at Natsuma," Mrs. Sullivan said as they sat down.

"Thanks," Brax replied, glad that Harold apparently explained things ahead of time.

"What happened, Braxton?" implored Katie. "Did you quit or did you get kicked off the team?"

The question made Brax nervous. So did the attention. He could feel the scrutiny.

"I guess I got kicked off," he mumbled.

"Whatever did you do?" Katie asked.

"Katie …" interrupted Mrs. Sullivan. That would be enough for now.

They ate a dinner of country fried steak with the conversation meandering, but mercifully avoiding Natsuma High. It eventually turned to college plans and Katie dominated. She'd been accepted at Alabama, where she would major in education and become a Tri-Delt.

Brax listened, but offered nothing in return as he hoped he wouldn't be asked his plans. In the past week, whatever plans he'd had of receiving an athletic scholarship had been scrapped. Given the circumstances, college was an unknown.

"I didn't mean to embarrass you," Katie said out on the front porch. She sat in the swing, kicking back and forth with her legs. Brax stood next to the rail, glad the adults remained inside to listen to an old Frank Sinatra album while Mrs. Sullivan put the twins to bed.

"Still," she continued, "I'd like to know what happened."

Brax fidgeted at the inquisition. "I don't know, Katie. Coach only said I was a nigger lover."

"What does that mean?"

It seemed like a stupid question, especially considering the climate and what had happened. But it happened in Takasaw, Brax realized. It hadn't happened in Birmingham.

Yet so much else had happened in Birmingham: The church bombing, still unsolved; the civil rights marches; Bull Connor's attacks on the marchers with powerful water hoses – captured on film and broadcast to the world.

Conversation came in fits and starts, all carried by Katie, all seemingly meaningless and uneventful. Brax offered an occasional one word response as she carried on; looking into the living room through the front window in the hope that Harold would see his discomfort and rescue him.

Eventually, Harold did, bidding the Seavers good-bye.

"Thanks for dinner and thanks for understanding," Harold said, his comments directed toward Mrs. Seaver.

"Yeah, thanks," Brax offered. Turning his attention to Katie he said, "It was nice to see you again."

"Nice to see you, too, Brax," Katie said with a lack of emotion that told him everything he needed to know.

* * * *

Leaving the plant had been nerve-racking, day by day, just as the trip to Tallassee each morning had been. Andy constantly looked into the rear-view mirror for an image of Lockett's familiar truck, ready to high-tail it at the sight.

His worst fear never materialized. The week had been uneventful. He'd done his job with little interference, except for McKenzie, who'd try to get Andy to talk without success.

"You know, Andy, if something's bothering you, you can tell me," McKenzie said.

"Nothing's bothering me," Andy replied, walking away.

The nights were even more frightening. He kept the shotgun loaded and near the door. If Donna noticed, she wouldn't admit anything. She fell asleep in his arms, dozing as he stared for hours at the dark ceiling, and remained in a deep slumber long after he left for work.

Only toward the end of the week did it cross his mind to begin worrying about her safety while he was at work.

* * * *

Moses woke up early Saturday morning. With Adele and Josiah sleeping, he pulled the scrapbook from under the bed and began reading the articles about Maurice Littlejohn again and again. He had become obsessed with his failure to take a stand, to step forward, to do anything the last few months.

Who could he go to five years later? The sheriff? The FBI? The Freemans? Maybe if he and Braxton had just told Harold Freeman in the first place ...

The Freemans were the only white people he'd ever really trusted. But what could an accountant and a high school student do?

He was just 12 years old and terrified when it happened. He'd just seen a murder, a brutal murder, of a black man by two whites. A murder that he knew now, after reading all the articles, was random and without reason.

Littlejohn was a stellar student at Morehouse. He ran off the road and his car was abandoned somewhere on the highway to Atlanta, a mile or two short of Takasaw Road. Those were all the details the newspapers had until he turned up dead a week later near the farm of a man named Hobson.

He wasn't the first black murdered in McMahon County. There were unexplained deaths on a regular basis, many associated with but never pinned to the Klan. But he'd seen this one. Not that it would have mattered. Rarely did a case even go to trial.

Now the murder he'd witnessed was eating him alive. So, too, the guilt. The answer came quickly. He'd talk to Dr. Long when the college administrator returned to town from a conference that night. Finally, he had a solution. Dr. Long was a wise man and would know what to do.

* * * *

High noon on a football Saturday meant one thing at the Freeman household: Information overload. Harold had two radios tuned in, one to the Auburn pregame, the other to the Alabama broadcast of a game that would begin an hour later. In a couple of hours, when ABC had its college game of the week, the television would add to the chaos.

Harold was reared an Alabama fan. Peggy's family were diehard Auburn people. In a state where you chose alliances at birth, the mix of loyalty was a rarity. Thus, the compromise reached years ago. Braxton looked forward to the cacophony of football and, like Harold, had an innate ability to tune one broadcast out and focus on the other when something important happened.

"Another big night for Moses," Harold said, finishing off *The Advertiser* sports section. "Four touchdowns against the school from Columbus."

Braxton nodded. He should be happy for Moses, but he'd died a little more Friday night. Not playing was tough enough, facing Katie Sullivan had been even worse, leaving him depressed and sullen. Not even a football Saturday would lift him this day.

Auburn struggled early in a game it should have owned from the onset against the University of Houston. But the Tigers had their first serious drive going when Moses came bursting through the door.

"Mama can't breathe," he said in a rush. His eyes were wild and he looked desperate. "Hurry, Mr. Harold! We have to get her to the hospital!"

Braxton got there first, beating Moses and Harold. Adele was in the bed, gasping for air. Josiah was crying, holding her hand. Her color looked bad and her eyes kept rolling back in her head.

"Moses, you and Brax get a side. I'll get her feet," Harold said, and the three lifted her off the bed. They'd just gotten her up when Peggy arrived. She took charge quickly, bringing in the wheelchair Adele had come home in from the living room so the men could place her in and roll her to the car.

"Braxton, you stay here with Josiah," Peggy said. "We'll call you from the hospital."

* * * *

Donna had talked Andy into pulling weeds in the front "garden." The pile of overgrown weeds was three feet high and growing, and she seemed determined to turn the mess into something presentable. Andy wasn't about to argue.

She'd fixed breakfast again and taken him with her to the market, making sure he got to pick out something he liked for supper. She had coupons, clipped out from the weekly paper, and an organized list. She told him how to pick produce and made selecting fruit look like an art.

They were just about done with the left side of the yard when Lockett's truck came screeching down the road, braking to a stop in front. Andy's first thought was the shotgun, still in the house. His next was of Donna.

"Go inside," he said forcefully. "And lock the door."

She scrambled inside before Lockett got out and rushed to Andy. Laduke was ready for a brawl, but Lockett merely wanted to talk.

"I need you tonight. Klan business," Lockett said, as he laid out the plan. Andy needed to get Braxton and Moses at sunset and take them to Hobson's farm.

"No, Keith, no. They don't know nothin'," Andy countered.

"Boy, you get it done. That's an order."

"They ain't done nothin'. They ain't going to say nothin'."

"And I'm just going to make sure," Lockett said. "All I want to do is put a scare in them both."

Andy took a deep exhale. "What if I say no?"

Lockett sneered at the question. "Then you're all going to pay the price. And the first one that's going to pay is that slut of yours."

* * * *

Harold called a few hours later, explaining Adele's condition. Braxton still didn't quite understand, only that she'd had a respiratory attack, not another stroke.

He calmed Josiah down, heated some fried chicken and talked him into a nap back in his and Moses' bedroom. The first snore began when Brax started to get up off Moses' mattress.

He stepped on the edge of something, pushed under the bed. Curious, Brax squatted down to see a binder that he retrieved. It was a scrapbook of sorts, with yellowing articles and Xeroxed negatives of microfilm newspaper stories pasted throughout.

Maurice Littlejohn? Who is Maurice Littlejohn?

It didn't make sense initially. Why would anyone keep a scrapbook about a college student who went missing? What was the link?

The answer came on the third page, an Atlanta story about the discovery of the Morehouse student's body near a Takasaw farm with multiple stab wounds, brutally murdered.

Braxton never forgot the murder they witnessed five years ago, but he could go days, even weeks, without thinking about the incident. Obviously, Moses could not.

The scrapbook continued for page after page. Article after article, most saying the same thing: a senseless murder, no motive, no suspects, unsolved ...

"Anyone home?"

Brax recognized the voice. Moses said he'd call the Youngs and ask them to come look after Josiah. Now Natalie was at the front door. Brax hurriedly shoved the book back under the bed, deeper this time, and quickly weaved through the maze of the house till he found Natalie standing at the entrance.

"Good afternoon, Braxton," she said politely. "How is Josiah?"

"He's taking a nap. I think he's going to be out for awhile."

"Good. Come with me then."

She grabbed him by the hand and led him to the kitchen. He sat down as she began preparing lemonade. She pulled the lemons out of the ice box, found the bag of sugar, a pitcher and began mixing – talking all the while.

She explained how her parents dropped her off and headed straight to the hospital. They'd be back to pick her up after dark. Braxton was free to go back home, if he wanted, but she hoped he'd keep her company, at least until Josiah woke up.

When the concoction was ready, she poured two glasses and led him into the front sitting room, where the only place to sit was a small, weathered sofa. Braxton took the first sip, as she eyed him for a reaction.

"Wow. This is great. It's better than Adele's lemonade," he said truthfully.

She giggled. "Thanks."

They talked about school, about Adele and Josiah, about college plans for a half hour until the conversation stalled. Natalie got up, walked to the window and peaked out the curtains.

"It's going to get dark soon, Braxton. My parents will be coming to get me."

She sat back down and stared at Braxton. He initially felt discomfort. *Did I do something wrong?*

She looked away for a minute, then looked back at him. Now, she seemed more emboldened.

"Braxton, have you ever wondered what it would be like?" she asked.

"What ... what would it be like?"

"Braxton, don't make this hard," Natalie said. She leaned in, and he didn't need words to complete the sentence.

Her lips were fuller than Katie's were. Her tongue was more aggressive. He tasted the lemonade, the sweet and bitter danced with his mouth as he clutched her shoulder, pulling her in even more.

With Katie, the first kiss had been a prelude. The eventual target: The bobcats. With Natalie, he let the kiss linger and he luxuriated in the moment.

It wouldn't last long enough.

The front door slammed open.

"What the hell are you doing? That's my cousin!" Moses was bathed in a sweat from walking back from the hospital. Now he stood enraged a few feet away, until he began approaching.

He grabbed Brax by the collar and yanked him from the sofa. He didn't draw a fist back, but his words were harsh.

"That's my cousin! You got no right!"

Natalie tried to make peace, stepping between them, but Moses shoved her harshly aside. He looked at her, sprawled on the couch, and then pushed Braxton back a few feet.

"If I got caught kissing a white girl, they'd string me up and lynch me. But you … you can get away with anything."

"Moses, calm down," Natalie said. "He wasn't doing anything wrong. I was kissing him."

Moses looked at his cousin, at his old friend, and back again.

"I hate you Brax! I hate you!" Moses said, storming out of the house.

* * * *

Natalie told him not to worry, but Braxton couldn't get Moses' fury out of his head. He didn't want to kiss Natalie again, at least not now. Her parents would be there soon – yet another chance to get caught in the act. The mood was gone.

So he headed home with an apology, leaving her with a befuddled look. He let himself in the unlocked Freeman house and realized both radios were still blaring. The Auburn and Alabama games were long over – he didn't even know the scores –and music had replaced football. Top forty played on one station, country and western on the other.

He clicked both radios off and headed to the kitchen to scrounge for dinner.

He mentally checked off a half-dozen possibilities before he heard the knock on the door.

Andy stood there looking flustered as a truck he didn't recognize idled in the driveway.

"Moses was hit by a car," Andy said. "He needs help."

Common sense should have given Braxton pause, but his only thought was of his friend. If Moses was in trouble, he had to help. Just like that, he put Moses' fury behind him. He hopped in the truck with Andy and a man he didn't recognize.

He could think of nothing, except Moses.

* * * *

The other man headed out on the Shorter Highway, a route Braxton had taken many times on his own and with his parents. He thought nothing about it at first. Now, questions were coming to him with the speed of a machine gun.

"What's he doing out this far?" Braxton asked.

"How the hell do I know?" Andy said. "I just heard the call on the scanner. I thought you'd want to help."

"It's just that … I saw him at his house no more than an hour ago. He was on foot. How …."

The man took a right turn onto a dirt road violently, forcing Braxton nearly into Andy's lap next to him. Andy responded by pushing Brax back in the middle after the man righted the truck with a fishtail swerve.

In the next moment, Braxton felt a shiver, followed by a hard reality. He knew the place, and it wasn't a good memory.

This was the spot near Hobson's farm, where Braxton, Andy and Moses had seen Maurice Littlejohn murdered. Braxton looked at Andy, then at the other man. Both were fixed on the road in front. He swiveled to his left and spotted a shotgun on the rack. Braxton tried to reach for it, but Andy grabbed his right arm with a vise grip, yanking it down and away. He was much stronger than Braxton expected.

Just when Braxton broke free, the truck slammed to a stop. Not expecting the quick stop, Brax slammed headfirst into the daze, a sharp pain going from his nose to his skull. Before he recovered, the driver was out and dragging him from the vehicle. Andy took a foot to the chest from struggling his cousin before he got out and helped from the other side.

From the woods came a man with a flashlight, followed by another with a shotgun. Both wore white Klan robes. As Braxton struggled with Andy and the other man, the armed man fired the shotgun into the air.

The blast brought back fear Braxton hadn't known since he was a kid, since he was here in the same location.

Since he witnessed murder.

The shotgun pressed against Braxton's head.

"Tie him up," said the voice Brax recognized instantly. Keith Lockett pushed him with the barrel, forcing Brax back into the arms of the first stranger as Andy began tying his wrists with a rope and led him behind a hedge row into a clearing on the other side.

This is where Maurice Littlejohn died.

Someone was lying on the ground, moaning. His hands were tied, too, and a noose was around his neck. Keith Lockett went up to the figure and kicked him in the side.

Moses rolled over. His head was busted open and the right side of his face was covered with blood.

"The nigger put up a better fight than you did," Lockett said to Brax. "Any trouble, Laduke?"

"No sir."

As two new men grabbed Braxton from behind, a third slipped a noose around his neck and forced him to his knees, next to Moses. Braxton waited a second, then tried to get up quickly, but the noose tightened, cutting off his air. Someone from behind kicked him over.

"Keith ... Keith, this is enough." The voice belonged to Andy Laduke.

"Shut up," Lockett responded. He pulled his robe up and retrieved a long hunting knife from a sheath at his waist. The knife gleamed when it caught the beam of a flashlight.

"Keith, what are you going to do?"

Lockett laughed. "I'm not going to do anything. You are."

Lockett flipped the knife in the air, catching it by the handle. With the other hand he grabbed it by the blade and extended it toward Andy.

"They don't know anything Keith," Andy said, refusing to take the knife. "They won't say anything."

Moving quickly, more quickly than Andy could react, Lockett put the blade to Andy's throat and grabbed him by the head, not allowing him to move.

"It's you or them. They're going to die. It's up to you whether you do, too."

Andy could feel the tears start to flow. Moses was still prone. Braxton was looking at him, not with fear as much as contempt. Keith Lockett pressed the knife, and Andy could feel a slight cut that stung like ten wasp stings.

Lockett pulled the knife back, then extended it again. Knowing he had no choice, Andy took it.

"Pull the nigger to his feet," Lockett said. Two Klansmen followed orders. It took a moment to get Moses to his knees, then upright. Braxton saw that they'd gone a step further with Moses, binding his feet as well.

Moses was still half out of it. Whoever beat him up had beat him to the point of semi-consciousness. His eyes rolled around, then closed, unable to focus.

"You got two choices, boy. Gut him or cut his throat," Lockett said, standing side by side with Andy.

Andy's hands were noticeably shaking, so much he dropped the knife to the ground.

"PICK IT UP!"

Andy picked the knife up. But he couldn't move any closer.

"DO IT!"

Still shaking, Andy brought the knife closer to Moses. He didn't know what he would do or how he would do it. But he knew he had to do something.

Before he had a chance, Moses was knocked backwards. Braxton, though tied himself, was able to knock his friend off his feet. Now Braxton covered Moses with his body as the Klansmen worked to get them separated.

"Andy, you can't do this," Braxton said before he felt a boot to his side, knocking him over.

Moses was pulled back up. Now his eyes were wide and wild and his teeth were clinched. He seemed to know what was going on.

"Do it now, boy. Kill the damn nigger!" Lockett commanded.

Andy looked at Moses. Then at the knife.

"I … I can't. I got no problem with him. Keith, he ain't done nothing."

Andy took a half step back before Lockett seized his wrist and snatched the knife away.

"You fucking coward," Lockett hissed. With the knife in his hand he looked at the two boys, then at Andy Laduke. Lockett lurched forward, with the knife.

He sunk it deep in Andy Laduke's belly. When a surprised Andy reached down, thinking he could pull it out, Lockett wrenched it again, shoving it deeper.

With a gasp of air and a final cry, Andy Laduke tumbled over with a fatal wound.

A gunshot echoed through the East Alabama woods. Braxton watched as blood streamed out of a hole in Keith Lockett's hood. In his final act, Lockett started to pull the hood off, getting to the chin before he collapsed next to Laduke.

Holding a pistol, the man who had driven Braxton to the woods moved in front of the other Klansmen, the gun now pointed at his friends. The man bearing the shotgun dropped it. The others raised their arms.

"Get out of here now," Bobby Joe McKenzie barked to his Klansmen. "Just keep your mouths shut. I'll take care of this."

Two of the men bolted immediately. The other paused momentarily, then did his best to catch up as he hightailed it into the woods toward a waiting truck parked on a road a quarter-mile away.

Bobby Joe McKenzie pulled out a pocket knife and began cutting the rope that bound Braxton's wrists, freeing him. Then he handed the knife to Braxton.

"Cut your friend free, son," he said.

As Braxton did, McKenzie pulled out a handkerchief and carefully wrapped the dagger Lockett used to take Laduke's life, making sure he kept his fingerprints off.

"Don't touch the knife. We'll turn it over to the FBI," McKenzie said.

Braxton struggled to free Moses, who still seemed half-dazed. McKenzie laid the murder weapon down and helped Braxton finish the job.

"Come on, Freeman," McKenzie said. "We're going to have to help get him out in a hurry in case the others come back."

Braxton and the Klansman dragged Moses back to the cab of the pickup. As Braxton helped his friend in, McKenzie returned to the clearing to retrieve the knife while keeping the gun at his ready in case the Klan returned.

THE BUTTERFLIES, THE stomach-churning nervousness he hadn't known for years, were back. Just like before a football game.

It wasn't Braxton's idea. Allison made the arrangements – securing the babysitter, reserving the room and making sure there wouldn't be any last-minute problems at work – after making plans with Kyle Anderson surreptitiously for weeks.

The marquee outside the Governor's House hotel in Montgomery announced "Takasaw High Reunion." No specific class was given. Because the senior classes had been small, because the Takasaw High the grads all remembered had changed dramatically in the years since, the reunions were held every other year for all classes.

But Allison insisted this one was special, for it was the 20-year reunion for Brax's senior class. That's what didn't make sense to Braxton. The class didn't graduate together, everyone having scattered to other schools during those chaotic days of the failed desegregation, before Takasaw High suspended operations for the school year. The forced sabbatical proved to be temporary.

Takasaw High resumed classes the next fall, as Brax's class began college or sought fulltime jobs for the first time. The old school was never the same. Enrollment dropped drastically, and the once all-white school now had only scatterings of white students among the vast number of blacks. And those whites came from families who couldn't afford or bear the convenience of another school or, in rare cases, believed they were taking the high ground as the integration plans that failed the year before were finally being achieved.

The irony was that Brax's class at Natsuma held its 20th reunion the same weekend. Of course, he had never considered attending it and, to his unacknowledged relief, Allison never brought it up. She knew well enough, from hearing the stories from Brax and Harold, that his senior year at the school held few pleasant memories.

Had Allison not been so insistent and made all the plans, he wouldn't be standing outside the ballroom in an otherwise noisy registration line. She'd gotten her way, as she had for most of the last dozen years.

Brax met her his senior year of college, after taking off a year. She was a Tri-Delt he'd met at a pledge swap when she'd dumped her awkward freshman date and struck up a conversation with the older, quiet fraternity boy standing alone in a corner of the Kappa Alpha party room.

She dated him as he pursued his MBA and she left school, prior to her senior year, to marry him. That wasn't his idea – it was hers – but a year of wedding plans and setting up house hadn't slowed her. She finished at South Alabama, after they'd moved to Mobile, getting a degree in elementary education that she'd only put to use in the last few years as a substitute teacher.

Allison was the best thing to happen to him since leaving Takasaw, although he never told her often enough. While he was moody and still struggled to express himself as he approached his 40s, Allison was consistently upbeat.

They lived comfortably, on an old house on Government Street that constantly challenged his meager, but improving, handyman skills. The mortgage was within his range, but only because her parents provided a sizeable down payment as a wedding gift.

He had worked as an accountant for South Central Bell for six years before striking out on his own. Brax never considered himself successful, but they didn't want for anything. She managed the family income and managed it wisely. Luxuries were rare. They had two cars – his, the same Monte Carlo he'd owned since the late '70s, she the minivan he'd bought used from a friend two years earlier. Vacations meant a week in a small rental house on the beach of burgeoning Gulf Shores, an hour south of the city, or the occasional weeklong trip to a more exotic locale with the in-laws.

"B-Bear!"

In 20 years, only one person had called him by the old nickname, and then only on the rare occasions they saw each other. Allison was already smiling as Kyle Anderson sauntered over.

"Hey, buddy!" Kyle said, reaching out a hand but giving it up in lieu of the hug he initiated. He still had a youthful, wiry look. "I knew you'd get him here," he said, winking at Allison. "We're going to have a great time, B-Bear!"

"Yeah, Kyle, we will," Braxton replied. "We will. Thanks."

Kyle was small talking with Allison and others behind him in the line, others Brax didn't remember on sight, as the line moved. He found himself finally at the front of the registration line where two middle-aged women – weren't they all middle-aged now? – sat behind the table and a catalog of index cards.

"My name's Braxton Freeman, Class of '64, and I'm with my wife, Allison," Brax said.

"Brax Freeman!" One of the ladies said. "Who could forget Brax Freeman?"

Well, he didn't remember her. She wore a name tag pinned to the left breast of her blouse with the name in small type under an old class picture. But the light wasn't good and his eyesight couldn't compensate well enough even as he squinted to read.

"It's Betty Louder. Well, Betty Compton back then."

"Oh yeah," Brax said. But he didn't remember, and she knew.

"Oh, Braxton," she said with a smile and stood up. Unclipping her name tag, she handed it to him. It read: Betty Compton, Class of '66. And the picture? It was the little red-head, the one who'd given him grief for leaving Takasaw High that night after the Natsuma football game.

"I'm sorry, Betty," he said sheepishly. "Of course, I remember you."

"Don't worry about it," she said as she pulled his name tag from the index file. It had BRAX FREEMAN in narrow block letters under his junior class portrait – the last one he'd taken at Takasaw High. She then handed him a "My Name Is" tag after writing Allison's name in neat print.

"I'm on guard duty, unfortunately," Betty said. "But I'd love to catch up with you later. There's so much to talk about."

"Sure," Brax said, still embarrassed. "If I don't find you, you find me, OK?"

"C'mon, gang," Kyle said, grabbing Allison by the hand as she pulled Brax along. "Let's get a drink."

Kyle attended Auburn and took the usual route, graduating in five years with an accounting degree. But he'd been more ambitious than Brax and had successfully built a small savings and loan in Greenville, the halfway point on the Interstate trip between Montgomery and Mobile. He had a nice colonial-style house and sizeable acreage in a nearby community, Pine Apple. Brax and Allison had visited Kyle's family there twice, briefly rekindling old times with a barbecue, a lazy day of fishing on Kyle's stocked pond and a slow, no-keeping-score round of golf at the nearby club.

Kyle came to Mobile often on business, but the best they could manage was an occasional lunch downtown, near Brax's office. Once, the Andersons stayed a weekend during Mardi Gras, when Brax had relented and Allison had thrown a huge party at the house. They'd stayed in the den most of the evening, watching an Auburn basketball game on television with a few of the other men who had strayed away from the backyard gathering.

The reticence was all Braxton's. As close as they'd once been, he wasn't comfortable renewing the past with anyone any more. Brax's comfortable life meant work, family and occasional golf outings, the only social outlet he truly enjoyed, and little else. Was that any different than as a kid, when his entire life had been consumed by sandlot ballgames?

"Brax! Kyle! Come here you dogs!" This time, Brax could put the voice with the face. It was Gothard, his old football teammate at Takasaw, and until things went awry, at Natsuma.

Gothard was gathered with four other men and a couple of wives, none of whom he recognized immediately. Kyle greeted them warmly – he had no such problems – while Allison, as usual, made introductions. Brax remembered one of the men as another old teammate, a man a year of two older who'd played sparingly.

"Where are you now, Brax?" Gothard asked.

"Mobile. We've been there since we graduated from college," Brax said.

"Geez, I should've known that. I work as a claims adjustor and I knew your father had moved down there a few years ago to be near you."

The group was reliving old memories, mostly about the football team. Brax listened with passing interest until the subject changed.

"It's a shame they took the team away from Old Hard Ass," said the teammate Brax barely remembered. "He was a helluva football coach.

You can pin that one, and all that happened to him, on the blacks. Integration was the worst ..."

"The blacks didn't cost him the job," Gothard interrupted harshly. "The whites gave up on him after the school closed down."

"Well, it was his own fault for backing the blacks ..."

This time, the man stopped himself after catching Brax's glare.

"He was a helluva coach, no matter what happened," Kyle interjected. "And he wasn't that much of a hard ass, really. Brax and I got to know him during the summer, at the club."

Halliday never coached again. He found part-time jobs, the last one selling sporting goods to the same peers who could not find coaching jobs for him after the Takasaw fiasco. His lone highlight came in the spring, when Bear Bryant would invite him to Tuscaloosa to teach a seminar to the other high school coaches on the single-wing offense. It was a nice gesture, because most schools had abandoned the system. And Halliday hadn't coached the obsolete offense since before Brax arrived at Takasaw.

Brax kept in touch with the old coach as best he could. In fact, Halliday had arranged for a baseball scholarship at Alabama, which helped ease the burden for the Freemans immensely. Brax had moderate success, starting two years at third base on average teams, but realized quickly his athletic career would go no further.

Halliday had even bugged him into walking on in football, which Brax ignored until finally relenting for two-a-days before his sophomore year. It was a short and ill-advised folly. Walk-ons, with 100-plus players on scholarship, were treated with disdain by the coaches and players.

The closest Brax had come to Bryant was during a scrimmage. Playing defensive back on the scout team, he'd tried to stop the scrambling first-team quarterback in the open field and had been left with cleat marks as the only sign he'd provided an impediment.

"Damn good, Snake, damn good!" Bryant yelled over a megaphone from atop the coaching tower that scanned all during the practices.

Brax turned in his uniform later that afternoon. The equipment manager had to ask him his name three times before he got it right, to cross him off the list for good.

He'd seen Halliday one last time, meeting the old coach in Birmingham and then driving with him to Nashville to see Moses play. Brax's oldest friend earned a scholarship to Grambling, and they'd road-tripped to see the Tigers play a game at Tennessee State. The trip was regretful. The two watched the game from distant seats in the end zone, the only white people in the stadium. By the time they meandered to the field to say hi in person, the Grambling team was already back on the bus – in full gear – and en route to the airport for the trip home.

A few years later Halliday died alone in the apartment he'd rented in Montgomery from a self-inflicted shotgun blast. Brax heard the news weeks later from Harold and raced to the Mobile library to find the obit in a back issue of the *Montgomery Advertiser*. The obit addressed his coaching past and noted he had been cremated, but graciously avoided mentioning the conditions surrounding his death.

On the rare occasions the subject was raised in the years since, Brax noted to others that Halliday was facing a gruesome death from lung cancer. It wasn't true, but it made the death more tolerable. But the truth was, Halliday was heartbroken.

"I'll tell you this," Gothard was saying. "If Halliday had his way, we would've won the state title our senior year. That Moses Burks would've been the difference."

"Wouldn't have been worth it," said the other teammate.

"Hell," Gothard said. "Why not?"

"I mean, playing with niggers."

"Welcome to the 1980s, John Henry," Gothard said angrily. "All the schools in the state were integrated a few years later. We would've had a jump on everyone."

"Doesn't matter," the man replied. "I'm just glad it happened after I left."

John Henry looked around for confirmation, and got nothing. Again, he got a glare from Brax.

"Who knows," the man offered. "I mean if he was *that* good, who knows? I guess I never saw him play. Was he that good?"

"Jesus, boy," Kyle said. "He was the best player you ever saw. Faster even than ol' Brax. He ended up playing college football. Not many came out of Takasaw and did that."

"Yeah, at Grambling, right?" Gothard said.

"Well, good for him," John Henry said. "But that's a black school. I mean it ain't the same as an SEC school."

"He was a two-time All-American," Brax said softly. "Three of his teammates played in Super Bowls. I never played with anyone at Takasaw that could wear his jock strap."

"Well, whatever you say," John Henry replied.

It amazed Brax. To this day, football fans would cheer black players at Alabama and Auburn without regard to race. But put one at quarterback ... The one at Bama, Walter Lewis, had been hyped for the Heisman Trophy the previous autumn. Whether at work or at a social gathering, if talk started up about the state of the Crimson Tide football program, the first complaint would be about Lewis' performance. It had little to do with performance – Lewis owned a slew of school offensive records – but he had been hampered by a leaky defense and a coaching change.

There had been so many changes throughout the state. Most schools had long been integrated with few of the problems that plagued Takasaw. Birmingham now had a black mayor. And George Wallace, the man who stopped Takasaw's progressive plans to integrate the high school in its tracks, returned to prominence as governor of the state for another term. But this time, two years earlier, he'd ridden the votes of the black populace he had once so openly shunned.

Historians said the Wallace of the 1980s was the real Wallace, a return to the populist who first made political hay as a circuit judge in South Alabama defending the poor – black and white – that found their way into his courtroom. But he'd abandoned it all and taken the race-baiting strategy straight to Montgomery. It was the only way to get elected in those days.

It still was uncertain if Wallace had really changed politically, but he had certainly changed physically. A would-be assassin's bullet during a failed presidential run in 1972 left him paralyzed. He had divorced and remarried. He was a frail man, hard of hearing, who surrounded himself with old cronies and allowed minimal access to the media he'd once courted.

The irony of it all: The autumn before, he attended homecoming at the University of Alabama to crown the homecoming queen. It was a ceremonial task the state's governor always performed. Wallace did so on a sunny October day, crowning the queen as she bent over to receive the tiara from the old man in the wheelchair. Then, as he always had done, he gave the queen a polite kiss on the cheek.

Except this time, for the first time, the school's homecoming queen had been black. The new George Wallace assumed his duties without hesitation.

"Allison, can I borrow your Brax for a few minutes?" Betty Compton had one hand on the small of Allison's back while the other gripped Brax by the elbow.

"Of course you can," Allison said. "Just promise to bring him back."

Betty grinned and led Brax away from the crowd.

She recounted her life the past years – college, how she fell in love with her first husband but had been saddled with two kids when he bolted, falling in love again, this time for keeps, and how she'd finally found time and energy to pursue a graduate degree in history.

"You know, I gave you a hard time for leaving Takasaw," she said. "I guess you knew before the rest of us that the closing was inevitable. But it took me a long time to forgive you."

"Why?" He hadn't said anything throughout her spiel, but now he wanted to know why she still harbored a grudge after so much time had passed. He'd barely known her.

"Because you were one of the good people. You stood for something, but I felt you were abandoning it for football, of all things."

"Well, maybe I did."

She looked at him quizzically.

"It's hard to explain even now," Brax offered, "but at that age your life revolves around one or two things. And mine revolved around football. I didn't feel I was leaving a 'cause' or anything like that. Takasaw didn't have a football team and Coach Halliday wanted me to continue playing at Natsuma. That was a mistake – now I know it. To be honest ..."

He stopped, searching for what he wanted to say. She waited patiently.

"Honestly, I didn't stand for anything then. I don't stand for anything now. My father was part of the Bi-Racial Committee and was in the middle of things. That's all."

"No it's not," she said coldly. "I grew up three blocks from you. You probably never knew that because you didn't pay attention to me. But I'd walk down Gautier Street every Sunday afternoon after church and see you playing with all the black kids. Sometimes there were other white kids, but most of the time you were the only one.

"When the troopers stopped us from going to school, people were joking and saying cruel things. You never did. I never heard you use the N word, ever, when everybody else we knew used it like a common noun. People said cruel things behind your back. Yet you never saw race. You just saw friends."

Friends? He'd only had a few. Kyle, because Kyle made himself a friend. Moses, well, because he grew up with Moses.

"Maybe you're right. I never saw what the fuss was about."

"Me either," Betty continued. "I finished up at Takasaw. By the time I graduated, I was the only white in the class. In some ways, I felt isolated. But none of the other students treated me that differently. I just know if the roles were reversed, the people we grew up with wouldn't have treated the blacks with the same dignity."

Brax nodded. He'd thought the same thing over time. When he was playing with Moses and his friends, he was Brax Freeman. Not Brax, the white boy. But when Halliday first announced Moses would join the high school team there was loud opposition.

That's the way things were. And while racism was no longer easily tolerated, it still existed. You didn't hear "nigger" as much, but you still heard demeaning jokes. Friends who struggled in their careers did so not because of their own ability, but because "they want a minority." The fear remained, a fear of losing control. He had friends in Birmingham who had changed. They no longer lived in Birmingham – not the city with a black mayor – but lived in one of the Over The Mountain suburbs populated by the more affluent whites. It was an identity technicality that never seemed to matter in all the time before, when they'd lived in the same suburb.

But back then, you were from Birmingham. Now, you were from Vestavia. Or Homewood. Or Hoover.

"I'd better get back to Allison," Brax said, scanning for his wife.

Betty looked in the same direction. Allison was laughing as Kyle held court with a new group of people.

"I think she's doing just fine, Braxton," Betty said. "But I'll let you go. It's just ..."

He looked at her. This time she was searching.

"Braxton, I don't want to sound sappy, but I just wanted you to know that a lot of us looked up to you."

He stared at her. Twenty years later, she still didn't make sense.

"Thanks, Betty," he said. "Thanks."

* * * *

He'd taken Allison back to the room and told her he just needed some time alone. She knew him better than anyone, so she accepted his explanation without complaint.

The drive used to take an hour, before the interstate was completed. Now it took 45 minutes from the Governor's House, on the eastern edge of Montgomery. He'd returned to Takasaw before, to visit Peggy, but in the dark of the night, little seemed to have changed. He took the Takasaw/Franklin exit, where the houses that stood alongside the two-lane road during his youth still stood unaltered. The only difference? Franklin Highway, once full of potholes, was now smoothly paved and freshly lined.

Gautier Street hadn't changed much either, at least not at the south end as he made the turn. He parked in front of the familiar house and in the quiet just stared. It had a fresh coat of paint. But it looked so much smaller now. The front yard was now enclosed by a white picket fence, which seemed to diminish it even more, but framed it quaintly. Where his bike used to be propped up against the front steps, a toddler's plastic red-and-yellow Big Wheel now rested.

He wondered who lived in the Freeman house now. A family, obviously. Black? White? Did it matter? What did the father do for a living? Funny, when Harold said he was selling the house, he hadn't asked any of the questions nor had he cared for the answers. It had been a home, but by then was no longer his home.

He remained parked in front for only a few minutes, scared the strange car might alarm someone, then drove on down the road. The corner grocery still stood, small and dated from another era. But the windows were boarded and an Auction sign hung on the front door.

The old Douglass home, where the county prosecutor's parents lived, stood back from the road in the darkness. The dirt, horseshoe driveway was partially hidden by tall grass that served as an unkempt front yard.

The forever vacant lot they used for their weekend afternoon ballgames used to be next door. It had been replaced by a sprawling red-brick building. As he pulled alongside, he saw the sign: Takasaw Nursing Home.

Adele's house would be just past the sudden bend, to the left. But when he got there, it, too was gone. More red bricks, this time comprising units of small apartments.

The drive from Gautier Street took him through downtown, where you still circled the old statue on a one-way street that took you past

City Hall, past Harold's old office and storefronts. All the names of the businesses had changed.

First Presbyterian Church came up on the right. But the grand, two-story house a block down that he remembered had been replaced by a Burger King. He turned right a block later. Same old houses until the corner, where a county health center now stood.

The entrance to the cemetery, an arched, white, unlocked gate, gave him a sense of relief for it remained unchanged. He followed the narrow path, too big for more than one automobile, through twists and turns and past various plots until he found the marker. He reached into the backseat, unwrapped the green paper and pulled the roses out.

Kneeling at the gravestone, he laid the flowers at the base and then leaned to kiss Peggy's marker. She'd complained of fatigue for months, but hadn't seemed too concerned. And if there were signs of trouble, Harold hadn't picked up on them quick enough. Brax was off at college, and she'd made so little fuss to him when they talked.

Like Candace, the doctors hadn't offered false hope. When Peggy learned of the tumors, she hesitated. The only comfort came afterward, when the oncologist said that the cancer had been growing for years and the mastectomy she finally underwent after months of debate proved too little, too late.

He'd just come back to the fraternity house from a morning class, looking forward to the cook's chili to warm him on a surprisingly bitter October day, when the pledge ran up to him.

"Brax, you need to call home. Your dad's looking for you."

She died at home, as she insisted. He made it back, by a few hours, to spend some time with her. For only a second, the bright face he remembered seemed to light up at his arrival. But just as quickly, she lapsed back into the ashen-faced look he'd known the previous months.

Her final word still haunted him.

"Candace," she said, then took a wheezing last breath as her eyes rolled into her head.

Harold began crying. Brax left the room, not knowing what to say or do as he felt his own tears coming. When he'd cried it out in his bedroom, he returned to find Harold in bed with Peggy, cradling her as if she only had a cold.

The following days were blurry. The funeral plans – he helped

Harold make the arrangements, though Harold seemed to deal with the tragedy well enough – the wake, the funeral itself.

Only later, as he laid in his bedroom for hour upon hour at night unable to sleep, could he find clarity. In essence, Peggy had never been the same since Candace's death. She provided a bright and cheery façade, but only with the passing of years did he remember the times he'd come home unexpected and find her cradled in a ball, crying on the couch unable to forget the loss of a daughter.

Yet if Peggy couldn't escape, her death seemed to free Harold. Brax realized he, too, had been going through the motions, doing what was expected, trudging through life in routine manner.

After Brax returned to school, after dropping out for the semester, Harold closed his office and took a job with the IRS in Birmingham to be closer to his son. During Brax's senior season, Harold made every home game and even a few weekend road trips – to Auburn and Nashville.

And when Brax and Allison settled in Mobile, Harold followed without discussion, buying a small home in Daphne, just across the bay bridge, and relocating with the IRS. He was still working, on a part-time basis now, and spent most of his free time as a doting grandfather. He'd been a good father to Brax, but often absent.

Times were different. Peggy was there every day and Harold worked past sunset and often left for work before anyone else had risen. Now he was the primary babysitter. How many senior citizens would be comfortable keeping two preschoolers? Brax could picture Harold, laying on the couch, with two empty sleeping bags laid out in front of him while Harry and Burks sprawled on top of him in a deep sleep.

The fact they weren't blood relatives didn't seem to matter to Harold. At the reunion, everyone passed pictures of their kids around. Someone looked at the snapshots of the two boys and remarked, "You can tell these boys are Freeman."

Allison had beamed. They *were* Freemans. The adoption process had been arduous and frustrating. But they'd lucked out with two precious kids.

Brax took one of the roses he'd laid at Peggy's headstone and moved it to Candace's grave in the adjoining plot. He felt a sudden twinge of guilt. So many years had passed that his memories of Candace were limited to shaky snapshots – the "B-Bear" moment Kyle had inadvertently walked in on and never let him forget, the walk to the kindergarten and the farewell. Even then, the more vivid memory was before Candace's funeral, and Peggy's heaving collapse in Adele's arms after Candace died.

He stood up and scanned the cemetery, trying to find his bearings.

He still didn't understand the irony. Blacks and whites lived on the same street, at least on Gautier. And they shared the same neighborhood now, in the old cemetery. But for much of his life in Takasaw, that's all they were allowed to share.

He wandered in the direction he best remembered, checking headstones for a barometer. When he saw the Lightfoot plot, he knew he was near.

Adele's headstone was in the sign of a small cross. She'd never completely recovered from the first stroke, hanging on for a couple of years before another one felled her completely. But that she had held on was a blessing. Josiah would've been lost without her, but his own decline from the ravages of Down Syndrome took him away months before Adele finally succumbed.

His grave was next to hers. Though unmarked, he remembered that much. On the other side of Adele, withered flowers covered a rectangular stone.

Brax brushed the flowers away to read the inscription: Moses Ezekiel Burks, born Jan., 1946 – died Oct. 1966.

He'd read it as a blurb in the *Tuscaloosa News* on a Monday morning, killing time in the frat house after blowing off an English course.

"Negro grid star killed in crash."

Moses had scored twice in a football game, starring as a receiver for Grambling. That night, he'd celebrated with teammates. A party ran late, he later learned. Heading back to campus in a thick fog, the car Moses was in veered off a road and into a culvert, killing him instantly.

He'd been named small-school All-American the year before. He was honored again at the end of the 1966 season, posthumously.

He'd seen Moses after that dreadful night in the woods, at Adele's house, numerous times. He'd seen Moses, with Halliday, that afternoon in Nashville.

But they'd never really talked about what happened, not the murder, not the brush with death, thanks to Keith Lockett and the Klan.

Nor had he and Harold, in great detail. Harold knew what

happened even before the boys were brought home that night by Bobby Joe McKenzie. Brax had been surprised when Harold knew who Bobby Joe was, and only later did he understood why.

McKenzie was an FBI informant, infiltrating the Klan.

Harold knew. Scott Douglass knew. And the FBI agent, Rosenberg, knew. Now Brax and Moses knew. But that night, Harold told them both not to tell anyone what happened – not Adele, certainly not Peggy.

Neither had said a word. Brax scanned *The Montgomery Advertiser* and the local weekly at every chance, for some sort of news story. Certainly, two murders had to be reported.

But they weren't. And as that curiosity nagged at him, so did another. He'd taken a few trips to Montgomery, to the public library there, to look through microfilms of back copies of every conceivable paper for news of what had happened.

Nothing but a concocted story: Andy Laduke and Keith Lockett killed each other in a fight over an unnamed woman.

Years later, during a relaxed cookout in the backyard of the Government Street house as little Harry played in the sandbox, Harold brought up the subject out of the blue.

"They came in and put the revolver in Andy's hand after McKenzie brought y'all home," Harold said.

"Who did?"

"The sheriff and Rosenberg. There were four witnesses, right?"

Brax nodded.

"Scott Douglass and the FBI agent in charge, Rosenberg – remember him? – knew you and Moses would keep quiet. And they reckoned the two Klansmen who were there weren't about to go to the sheriff unless they wanted to face charges of attempted murder. So they concocted the story of a quarrel gone wrong. And they relocated McKenzie somewhere out of state to protect him.

"The way it was explained to me, there was no one to prosecute. McKenzie saved your lives while working for the FBI. Settling things in a courtroom could have proved messy. And without a trial, well that might have put the fear of God in the local Klan as much as taking them to court. They'd lost their real leader, by the hand of one of their own. If you'll recall, they never made much noise again. And for McKenzie's sake, it was best to relocate him somewhere safe. My only regret is Andy's memory. But, to those of us who actually cared, we knew the truth."

Harry came over, crying about something. Not understanding the blubbering gibberish, Brax picked him up and cradled him. Harry's crying ceased.

"Even now, I feel I let you down."

"Nah, Dad. Don't think that."

"I did, son, I did. I let down Andy – we just abandoned him after his mother died. And I let you and Moses down. I mean, Good God. What y'all witnessed as little kids, and I wasn't there for you."

"That wasn't the case, Dad," Brax said. "Moses was scared to say anything to anyone after we saw Keith Lockett kill that black man. Thing was, we didn't even know it was Keith Lockett then. We didn't know 'till the night he tried to kill us. And what if we had? What could you have done?"

Harold shrugged his shoulders. "I would've gone to the sheriff."

"Dad, what would they have done? I've looked back at old newspapers from those days. There was never any story about trying to find the killers. If we had gone to the law, no one was going to do anything based on the eyewitness testimony of three kids who had no idea who committed the murder. Not a white-on-black crime. Not in those days. And Moses would have been in danger. He made me swear on my life I wouldn't tell anyone."

Brax was finished.

Harold wasn't.

"That was a bad stretch, Braxton. I guess that's what I really mean. Candace had just died. If you'd come to me ... I wasn't in good shape. You probably didn't know that. Certainly your mom was still devastated. That would have meant more worries for her, more than she could have handled. Maybe you're right. Maybe I couldn't have done a thing ..."

Allison came out of the backdoor, carrying a sleeping Burks on one shoulder and a tray of uncooked hamburgers in her free hand. The conversation was over, never to be revisited.

But at least he'd had a moment with Harold.

He'd never had that chance with Moses. The day of the 16th Street Church Bombing, Moses had yelled at him and had run off. Brax and Moses had never had a meaningful conversation after that.

They'd never been close again.

A wave of emotions knocked him to the ground. Of all the people he'd known over all the years, had he been any closer to anyone than

Moses? The only difference in the two of them had been the color of skin that seemed to bother everyone else.

But not Brax Freeman. Not Moses Burks.

He cried hard. He cried so hard his chest heaved as if reaching for his final breath. He cried so hard his eyes turned to water, the salty tears stinging. He cried loudly, and for once, unashamed, as the night enveloped him.

He hadn't cried that hard when Candace died. Or when Peggy died, less than a month after Moses. But he hadn't cried at all when Moses died.

He'd stood on the perimeter of a large gathering of people surrounding the grave as they prepared to lower Moses into the ground. He'd stood dry eyed and stoic beside the only other whites among the sea of mourners, Harold and old Hard Ass Halliday.

He'd never mourned Moses.

He'd never mourned his best friend or, as Adele joked, his brother.

So he mourned now, years after the fact, in a flurry of choking, cleansing sobs. And when he was done, he stood up and realized he wasn't alone.

Another car was parked behind his. Two figures stood, propped against the doors, as he made his way back.

When he got there, he wiped the remnants of the tears away.

Allison hugged him quietly, but ferociously. Then little Kyle Anderson swallowed them both with his arms. Brax accepted the embrace for a minute, then pulled away and led the others to the car to head home, far away from the memories of Takasaw.

Printed in the United States
by Baker & Taylor Publisher Services